THE

WIGWAM AND THE CABIN.

THE WIGWAM and the CABIN.

THE

WIGWAM AND THE CABIN.

BY W. GILMORE SIMMS

" The ancient tales
Which first I learned
Will I relate."

EDDA OF SAEMUND.

New and Revised Edition.

AMS PRESS

NEW YORK

Reprinted from the edition of 1885, Chicago and New York
First AMS EDITION published 1970
Manufactured in the United States of America

SBN: 404-06038-2
Library of Congress Catalogue Card Number: 72-116014

AMS PRESS, INC.
NEW YORK, N.Y. 10003

CONTENTS.

NASH ROACH, ESQ.

OF SOUTH CAROLINA.

My Dear Sir:

WHEN, many years ago, the stories in this volume were first collected and brought together in one body, I then inscribed their contents to you, as in proof " of an affection which had steadily advanced with the progress of my acquaintance with your integrity and gentleness of character," as displayed during a long period of the most delicate and intimate relationship and intercourse. Time has since then greatly lengthened this term of our intercourse, and still I have no reason to alter this inscription; but, on the contrary, to deepen it rather, and to clothe its lines in warmer hues and colors, and, if possible, to fix the inscription in yet more imposing characters.

It may be permitted me, through you, to say to the general reader, that the tales in this collection have been the accumulation of many years, ranging backward to the dawn of my earliest manhood. It is more easy, I find, to acknowledge their faults, than to amend or to excuse them. But, to be apologetic where it is not possible to atone, is only a sort of humiliation which one need not gratuitously incur. Enough, that, if I could bring myself to the task, I might improve and amend my short-comings, and prune my excesses—I feel this—yet know not whether the value of the alteration would be sufficiently recognised to justify the labor. I find it much easier to invent a new story than to repair the defects of an old one.

These legends were mostly written for the annuals, in the period when annuals were supposed to be as essential to the Christmas and New Year holydays as the egg-noggin or the mince pie. But the expensive form of the annual kept it from the great body of readers; and, besides, the annuals have gone the way of all mortal publications! Gold and glitter could not save them!— the pomp of heraldry, or the gorgeous blazonry of art;—and the self-esteem of authorship denies that one's good things should be buried in the rust of that heraldric glare and glitter, by which they were smothered from the first. When originally published, these stories were held to give signs of much more vitality than the medium in which they were so gorgeously encradled. They were thought by certain "mouths of wisest censure," to be better of favor than many of their companions; and, though of elvish and gipsy complexion—with a wild stare of their own, and a peculiar visage—it was held, by some of the critics, that, for these very reasons—because of their answering truly for certain native characteristics, they merited a more permanent form of publication. The author finds it easy to persuade himself that all this is sober sense and just judgment, and he has resolved and done accordingly.

One word for the material of these legends. It is local, sectional—and to be *national* in literature, one must needs be *sectional*. No one mind can fully or fairly illustrate the characteristics of any great country; and he who shall depict *one section* faithfully, has made his proper and sufficient contribution to the great work of *national* illustration. I can answer for it, confidently, that these legends represent, in large degree, the border history of the south. I can speak with confidence of the general truthfulness of its treatment. I have seen the life—have *lived*

it — and much of my material is the result of a very early personal experience.   The life of the planter, the squatter, the Indian, and the negro — the bold and hardy pioneer, the vigorous
yeoman — these are the subjects.   In their delineation I have
mostly drawn from living portraits, and, in frequent instances,
from actual scenes and circumstances within the memories of men.
More need not be said.   I need not apologize for the endeavor
to cast over the actual that atmosphere from the realms of the
ideal, which, while it constitutes the very element of fiction, is
neither inconsistent with intellectual truthfulness, nor unfriendly
to the great policies of human society.

I must no longer trespass.   Enough has been said for the pur
poses of explanation, and more than enough, perhaps, by way of
apology.   You, my dear sir, will but too friendlily regard neither
apology nor explanation as at all necessary in the case ; but you
will not object that I should, through you, proffer both to the
general reader.   Very truly and affectionately

Your friend and servant,

W. Gilmore Simms

Woodlands, S. C.,
September 20, 1856.

THE WIGWAM AND THE CABIN.

GRAYLING; OR, "MURDER WILL OUT."

CHAPTER I.

THE world has become monstrous matter-of-fact in latter days. We can no longer get a ghost story, either for love or money. The materialists have it all their own way; and even the little urchin, eight years old, instead of deferring with decent reverence to the opinions of his grandmamma, now stands up stoutly for his own. He believes in every "ology" but pneumatology. "Faust" and the "Old Woman of Berkeley" move his derision only, and he would laugh incredulously, if he dared, at the Witch of Endor. The whole armoury of modern reasoning is on his side; and, however he may admit at seasons that belief can scarcely be counted a matter of will, he yet puts his veto on all sorts of credulity. That cold-blooded demon called Science has taken the place of all the other demons. He has certainly cast out innumerable devils, however he may still spare the principal. Whether we are the better for his intervention is another question. There is reason to apprehend that in disturbing our human faith in shadows, we have lost some of those wholesome moral restraints which might have kept many of us virtuous, where the laws could not.

The effect, however, is much the more seriously evil in all that concerns the romantic Our story-tellers are so resolute to deal in the real, the actual only, that they venture on no subjects the details of which are not equally vulgar and susceptible of proof. With this end in view, indeed, they too commonly choose their

2

subjects among convicted felons, in order that they may avail them selves of the evidence which led to their conviction; and, to prove more conclusively their devoted adherence to nature and the truth, they depict the former not only in her condition of nakedness, but long before she has found out the springs of running water. It is to be feared that some of the coarseness of modern taste arises from the too great lack of that veneration which belonged to, and elevated to dignity, even the errors of preceding ages. A love of the marvellous belongs, it appears to me, to all those who love and cultivate either of the fine arts. I very much doubt whether the poet, the painter, the sculptor, or the romancer, ever yet lived, who had not some strong bias—a leaning, at least,— to a belief in the wonders of the invisible world. Certainly, the higher orders of poets and painters, those who create and invent, must have a strong taint of the superstitious in their composition. But this is digressive, and leads us from our purpose.

It is so long since we have been suffered to see or hear of a ghost, that a visitation at this time may have the effect of novelty, and I propose to narrate a story which I heard more than once in my boyhood, from the lips of an aged relative, who succeeded, at the time, in making me believe every word of it; perhaps, for the simple reason that she convinced me she believed every word of it herself. My grandmother was an old lady who had been a res- ident of the seat of most frequent war in Carolina during the Rev- olution. She had fortunately survived the numberless atrocities which she was yet compelled to witness; and, a keen observer, with a strong memory, she had in store a thousand legends of that stirring period, which served to beguile me from sleep many and many a long winter night. The story which I propose to tell was one of these; and when I say that she not only devoutly believed it herself, but that it was believed by sundry of her contempora- ries, who were themselves privy to such of the circumstances as could be known to third parties, the gravity with which I repeat the legend will not be considered very astonishing.

The revolutionary war had but a little while been concluded. The British had left the country; but peace did not imply repose. The community was still in that state of ferment which was natu- ral enough to passions, not yet at rest, which had been brought

into exercise and action during the protracted seven years' struggle through which the nation had just passed. The state was
overrun by idlers, adventurers, profligates, and criminals. Dis-
banded soldiers, half-starved and reckless, occupied the highways,
—outlaws, emerging from their hiding-places, skulked about the
settlements with an equal sentiment of hate and fear in their
hearts ;—patriots were clamouring for justice upon the tories, and
sometimes anticipating its course by judgments of their own ;
while the tories, those against whom the proofs were too strong
for denial or evasion, buckled on their armour for a renewal of
the struggle. Such being the condition of the country, it may easily be supposed that life and property lacked many of their necessary securities. Men generally travelled with weapons which
were displayed on the smallest provocation : and few who could
provide themselves with an escort ventured to travel any distance
without one.

There was, about this time, said my grandmother, and while
such was the condition of the country, a family of the name of
Grayling, that lived somewhere upon the skirts of " Ninety-six "
district. Old Grayling, the head of the family, was dead. He
was killed in Buford's massacre. His wife was a fine woman,
not so very old, who had an only son named James, and a little
girl, only five years of age, named Lucy. James was but fourteen when his father was killed, and that event made a man of
him. He went out with his rifle in company with Joel Sparkman,
who was his mother's brother, and joined himself to Pickens's
Brigade. Here he made as good a soldier as the best. He had
no sort of fear. He was always the first to go forward ; and his
rifle was always good for his enemy's button at a long hundred
yards. He was in several fights both with the British and tories ;
and just before the war was ended he had a famous brush with
the Cherokees, when Pickens took their country from them. But
though he had no fear, and never knew when to stop killing while
the fight was going on, he was the most bashful of boys that I ever
knew ; and so kind-hearted that it was almost impossible to believe all we heard of his fierce doings when he was in battle.
But they were nevertheless quite true for all his bashfulness.

Well, when the war was over, Joel Sparkman, who lived with

his sister, Grayling, persuaded her that it would be better to move down into the low country. I don't know what reason he had for it, or what they proposed to do there. They had very little property, but Sparkman was a knowing man, who could turn his hand to a hundred things; and as he was a bachelor, and loved his sister and her children just as if they had been his own, it was natural that she should go with him wherever he wished. James, too, who was restless by nature—and the taste he had enjoyed of the wars had made him more so—he was full of it; and so, one sunny morning in April, their wagon started for the city. The wagon was only a small one, with two horses, scarcely larger than those that are employed to carry chickens and fruit to the market from the Wassamaws and thereabouts. It was driven by a negro fellow named Clytus, and carried Mrs. Grayling and Lucy. James and his uncle loved the saddle too well to shut themselves up in such a vehicle; and both of them were mounted on fine horses which they had won from the enemy. The saddle that James rode on,—and he was very proud of it,— was one that he had taken at the battle of Cowpens from one of Tarleton's own dragoons, after he had tumbled the owner. The roads at that season were excessively bad, for the rains of March had been frequent and heavy, the track was very much cut up, and the red clay gullies of the hills of " Ninety-six" were so washed that it required all shoulders, twenty times a day, to get the wagon-wheels out of the bog. This made them travel very slowly, —perhaps, not more than fifteen miles a day. Another cause for slow travelling was, the necessity of great caution, and a constant look-out for enemies both up and down the road. James and his uncle took it by turns to ride a-head, precisely as they did when scouting in war, but one of them always kept along with the wagon. They had gone on this way for two days, and saw nothing to trouble and alarm them. There were few persons on the high-road, and these seemed to the full as shy of them as they probably were of strangers. But just as they were about to camp, the evening of the second day, while they were splitting light-wood, and getting out the kettles and the frying-pan, a person rode up and joined them without much ceremony. He was a short thick-set man, somewhere between forty and fifty: had on very coarse and common garments, though he rode a fine black horse of remarkable strength and vigour. He was very civil of speech, though he had but little to say, and that little showed him to be a person without much education and with no refinement. He begged permission to make one of the encampment, and his manner was very respectful and even humble; but there was something dark and sullen in his face—his eyes, which were of a light gray colour, were very restless, and his nose turned up sharply, and was very red. His forehead was excessively broad, and his eyebrows thick and shaggy—white hairs being freely mingled with the dark, both in them and upon his head. Mrs. Grayling did not like this man's looks, and whispered her dislike to her son; but James, who felt himself equal to any man, said, promptly—

"What of that, mother! we can't turn the stranger off and say 'no;' and if he means any mischief, there's two of us, you know."

The man had no weapons—none, at least, which were then visible; and deported himself in so humble a manner, that the prejudice which the party had formed against him when he first appeared, if it was not dissipated while he remained, at least failed to gain any increase. He was very quiet, did not mention an unnecessary word, and seldom permitted his eyes to rest upon those of any of the party, the females not excepted. This, perhaps, was the only circumstance, that, in the mind of Mrs. Grayling, tended to confirm the nostile impression which his coming had originally occasioned. In a little while the temporary encampment was put in a state equally social and warlike. The wagon was wheeled a little way into the woods, and off the road; the horses fastened behind it in such a manner that any attempt to steal them would be difficult of success, even were the watch neglectful which was yet to be maintained upon them. Extra guns, concealed in the straw at the bottom of the wagon, were kept well loaded. In the foreground, and between the wagon and the highway, a fire was soon blazing with a wild but cheerful gleam; and the worthy dame, Mrs. Grayling, assisted by the little girl, Lucy, lost no time in setting on the frying-pan, and cutting into slices the haunch of bacon, which they had provided at leaving home. James Grayling patrolled the woods, meanwhile for a mile or two round the encampment, while his uncle, Joel Spark-man, foot to foot with the stranger, seemed—if the absence of all care constitutes the supreme of human felicity—to realize the most perfect conception of mortal happiness. But Joel was very far from being the careless person that he seemed. Like an old soldier, he simply hung out false colours, and concealed his real timidity by an extra show of confidence and courage. He did not relish the stranger from the first, any more than his sister; and having subjected him to a searching examination, such as was considered, in those days of peril and suspicion, by no means inconsistent with becoming courtesy, he came rapidly to the con-clusion that he was no better than he should be.

"You are a Scotchman, stranger," said Joel, suddenly draw-ing up his feet, and bending forward to the other with an eye like that of a hawk stooping over a covey of partridges. It was a wonder that he had not made the discovery before. The broad dialect of the stranger was not to be subdued; but Joel made slow stages and short progress in his mental journeyings. The answer was given with evident hesitation, but it was affirmative.

"Well, now, it's mighty strange that you should ha' fou't with us and not agin us," responded Joel Sparkman. "There was a precious few of the Scotch, and none that I knows on, saving yourself, perhaps,—that didn't go dead agin us, and for the tories, through thick and thin. That 'Cross Creek settlement' was a mighty ugly thorn in the sides of us whigs. It turned out a raal bad stock of varmints. I hope,—I reckon, stranger,—you aint from that part."

"No," said the other; "oh no! I'm from over the other quarter. I'm from the Duncan settlement above."

"I've hearn tell of that other settlement, but I never know'd as any of the men fou't with us. What gineral did you fight under? What Carolina gineral?"

"I was at Gum Swamp when General Gates was defeated;" was the still hesitating reply of the other.

"Well, I thank God, *I* warn't there, though I reckon things wouldn't ha' turned out quite so bad, if there had been a leetle sprinkling of Sumter's, or Pickens's, or Marion's men, among them two-legged critters that run that day. They did tell that some of

.he regiments went off without ever once emptying their rifles.
Now, stranger, I hope you warn't among them fellows."

" I was not," said the other with something more of promptness.

" I don't blame a chap for dodging a bullet if he can, or being
too quick for a bagnet, because, I'm thinking, a live man is always a better man than a dead one, or he can become so ; but to
run without taking a single crack at the inimy, is downright cowardice.   There's no two ways about it, stranger."

This opinion, delivered with considerable emphasis, met with
the ready assent of the Scotchman, but Joel Sparkman was not
to be diverted, even by his own eloquence, from the object of his
inquiry.

" But you ain't said," he continued, " who was your Carolina
gineral.   Gates was from Virginny, and he stayed a mighty short
time when he come.   You didn't run far at Camden, I reckon,
and you joined the army ag'in, and come in with Greene ?   Was
that the how ?"

To this the stranger assented, though with evident disinclination.

" Then, mou'tbe, we sometimes went into the same scratch together ?   I was at Cowpens and Ninety-Six, and seen sarvice at
other odds and eends, where there was more fighting than fun.
I reckon you must have been at ' Ninety-Six,'—perhaps at Cowpens, too, if you went with Morgan ?"

The unwillingness of the stranger to respond to tnese questions
appeared to increase.   He admitted, however, that he had been
at " Ninety-Six," though, as Sparkman afterwards remembered,
in this case, as in that of the defeat of Gates at Gum Swamp, he
had not said on which side he had fought.   Joel, as he discovered
the reluctance of his guest to answer his questions, and perceived
his growing doggedness, forbore to annoy him, but mentally resolved to keep a sharper look-out than ever upon his motions.
His examination concluded with an inquiry, which, in the plain-
dealing regions of the south and south-west, is not unfrequently
put first.

" And what mout be your name, stranger ?"

" Macnab," was the ready response, " Sandy Macnab."

" Well, Mr. Macnab I see that my sister's got supper ready

for us ; so we mou't as well fall to upon the hoecake and bacon.''

Sparkman rose while speaking, and led the way to the spot, neaı the wagon, where Mrs. Grayling had spread the feast.   " We'ıe pretty nigh on to the main road, here, but I reckon there's no great danger now. Besides, Jim Grayling keeps watch for us, and he's got two as good eyes in his head as any scout in the country, and a rifle that, after you once know how it shoots, 'twould do your heart good to hear its crack, if so be that twa'n't your heart that he drawed sight on. He's a perdigious fine shot, and as ready to shoot and fight as if he had a nateral calling that way."

" Shall we wait for him before we eat ?'' demanded Macnab, anxiously.

" By no sort o' reason, stranger,'' answered Sparkman. " He'll watch for us while we're eating, and after that I'll change shoes with him. So fall to, and don't mind what's a coming.''

Sparkman had just broken the hoecake, when a distant whistle was heard.

" Ha ! That's the lad now !'' he exclaimed, rising to his feet. " He's on trail.   He's got a sight of an inimy's fire, I reckon. 'Twon't be onreasonable, friend Macnab, to get our we'pons in readiness ;'' and, so speaking, Sparkman bid his sister get into the wagon, where the little Lucy had already placed herself, while he threw open the pan of his rifle, and turned the priming over with his finger. Macnab, meanwhile, had taken from his hol- sters, which he had before been sitting upon, a pair of horseman's pistols, richly mounted with figures in silver. These were large and long, and had evidently seen service. Unlike his companion, his proceedings occasioned no comment. What he did seemed a matter of habit, of which he himself was scarcely conscious. Having looked at his priming, he laid the instruments beside him without a word, and resumed the bit of hoecake which he had just before received from Sparkman. Meanwhile, the signal whistle, supposed to come from James Grayling, was repeated. Silence ensued then for a brief space, which Sparkman employed in perambulating the grounds immediately contiguous. At length, just as he had returned to the fire, the sound of a horse's feet was heard, and a sharp quick halloo from Grayling informed his

uncle that all was right. The youth made his appearance a
moment after accompanied by a stranger on horseback ; a tall,
fine-looking young man, with a keen flashing eye, and a voice
whose lively clear tones, as he was heard approaching, sounded
cheerily like those of a trumpet after victory. James Grayling
kept along on foot beside the new-comer ; and his hearty laugh,
and free, glib, garrulous tones, betrayed to his uncle, long ere he
drew nigh enough to declare the fact, that he had met unexpectedly with a friend, or, at least, an old acquaintance.

"Why, who have you got there, James ?" was the demand of
Sparkman, as he dropped the butt of his rifle upon the ground.

"Why, who do you think, uncle ? Who but Major Spencer—
our own major ?"

"You don't say so !—what !—well ! Li'nel Spencer, for sartin ! Lord bless you, major, who'd ha' thought to see you in
these parts ; and jest mounted too, for all natur, as if the war was
to be fou't over ag'in. Well, I'm raal glad to see you. I am,
.hat's sartin !"

"And I'm very glad to see you, Sparkman," said the other,
as he alighted from his steed, and yielded his hand to the cordial
grasp of the other.

"Well, I knows that, major, without you saying it. But
you've jest come in the right time. The bacon's frying, and
here's the bread ;—let's down upon our haunches, in right good
airnest, camp fashion, and make the most of what God gives us
in the way of blessings. I reckon you don't mean to ride any
further to-night, major ?"

"No," said the person addressed, "not if you'll let me lay my
heels at your fire. But who's in your wagon ? My old friend,
Mrs. Grayling, I suppose ?"

"That's a true word, major," said the lady herself, making her
way out of the vehicle with good-humoured agility, and coming
forward with extended hand.

"Really, Mrs. Grayling, I'm very glad to see you." And
the stranger, with the blandness of a gentleman and the hearty
warmth of an old neighbour, expressed his satisfaction at once
more finding himself in the company of an old acquaintance.
Their greetings once over, Major Spencer readily joined the

group about the fire, while James Grayling—though with some
eluctance—disappeared to resume his toils of the scout while the
supper proceeded.

"And who have you here?" demanded Spencer, as his eye
rested on the dark, hard features of the Scotchman. Sparkman
told him all that he himself had learned of the name and character of the stranger, in a brief whisper, and in a. moment after
formally introduced the parties in this fashion—

"Mr. Macnab, Major Spencer. Mr. Macnab says he's true
blue, major, and fou't at Camden, when General Gates run so
hard to 'bring the d—d militia back.' He also fou't at Ninety-
Six, and Cowpens—so I reckon we had as good as count him one
of us."

Major Spencer scrutinized the Scotchman keenly—a scrutiny
which the latter seemed very ill to relish. He put a few questions to him on the subject of the war, and some of the actions in
which he allowed himself to have been concerned; but his evident reluctance to unfold himself—a reluctance so unnatural to
the brave soldier who has gone through his toils honourably—had
the natural effect of discouraging the young officer, whose sense
of delicacy had not been materially impaired amid the rude jost-
lings of military life. But, though he forbore to propose any
other questions to Macnab, his eyes continued to survey the features of his sullen countenance with curiosity and a strangely
increasing interest. This he subsequently explained to Sparkman, when, at the close of supper, James Grayling came in, and
the former assumed the duties of the scout.

"I have seen that Scotchman's face somewhere, Sparkman,
and I'm convinced at some interesting moment; but where, when,
or how, I cannot call to mind. The sight of it is even associated
in my mind with something painful and unpleasant; where could
I have seen him?"

"I don't somehow like his looks myself," said Sparkman, "and
I mislists he's been rether more of a tory than a whig; but that's
nothing to the purpose now; and he's at our fire, and we've
broken hoecake together; so we cannot rake up the old ashes to
make a dust with."

"No, surely not," was the reply of Spencer. "Even though

we knew him to be a tory, that cause of former quarrel should occasion none now. But it should produce watchfulness and caution. I'm glad to see that you have not forgot your old business of scouting in the swamp."

"Kin I forget it, major?" demanded Sparkman, in tones which, though whispered, were full of emphasis, as he laid his ear to the earth to listen.

"James has finished supper, major—that's his whistle to tell me so; and I'll jest step back to make it cl'ar to him how we're to keep up the watch to-night."

"Count me in your arrangements, Sparkman, as I am one of you for the night," said the major.

"By no sort of means," was the reply. "The night must be shared between James and myself. Ef so be you wants to keep company with one or t'other of us, why, that's another thing, and, of course, you can do as you please."

"We'll have no quarrel on the subject, Joel," said the officer, good-naturedly, as they returned to the camp together.

CHAPTER II.

The arrangements of the party were soon made. Spencer renewed his offer at the fire to take his part in the watch; and the Scotchman, Macnab, volunteered his services also; but the offer of the latter was another reason why that of the former should be declined. Sparkman was resolute to have everything his own way; and while James Grayling went out upon his lonely rounds, he busied himself in cutting bushes and making a sort of tent for the use of his late commander. Mrs. Grayling and Lucy slept in a wagon. The Scotchman stretched himself with little effort before the fire; while Joel Sparkman, wrapping himself up in his cloak, crouched under the wagon body, with his back resting partly against one of the wheels. From time to time he rose and thrust additional brands into the fire, looked up at the night, and round upon the little encampment, then sunk back to his perch and stole a few moments, at intervals, of uneasy sleep. The first two hours of the watch were over, and James Grayling was relieved. The youth, however, felt in no mood for sleep, and taking his seat by the fire, he drew from his pocket a little volume of Easy Reading Lessons, and by the fitful flame of the resinous light-wood, he prepared, in this rude manner, to make up for the precious time which his youth had lost of its legitimate employments, in the stirring events of the preceding seven years consumed in war. He was surprised at this employment by his late commander, who, himself sleepless, now emerged from the bushes and joined Grayling at the fire. The youth had been rather a favourite with Spencer. They had both been reared in the same neighbourhood, and the first military achievements of James had taken place under the eye, and had met the approbation of his officer. The difference of their ages was just such as to permit of the warm attachment of the lad without diminishing any of the reverence which should be felt by the inferior. Grayling was not more than seventeen, and Spencer was perhaps thirty four—the very prime of manhood. They sat by the fire and talked of old times and told old stories with the hearty glee and good-nature of the young. Their mutual inquiries led to the revelation of their several objects in pursuing the present journey. Those of James Grayling were scarcely, indeed, to be considered his own. They were plans and purposes of his uncle, and it does not concern this narrative that we should know more of their nature than has already been revealed. But, whatever they were, they were as freely unfolded to his hearer as if the parties had been brothers, and Spencer was quite as frank in his revelations as his companion. He, too, was on his way to Charleston, from whence he was to take passage for England.

"I am rather in a hurry to reach town," he said, "as I learn that the Falmouth packet is preparing to sail for England in a few days, and I must go in her. '

"For England, major !" exclaimed the youth with unaffected astonishment.

"Yes, James, for England. But why—what astonishes you ?"

"Why, lord !" exclaimed the simple youth, "if they only knew there, as I do, what a cutting and slashing you did use to make among their red coats, I reckon they'd hang you to the first hickory."

"Oh, no ! scarcely," said the other, with a smile.

"But I reckon you'll change your name, major ?" continued the youth.

"No," responded Spencer, "if I did that, I should lose the object of my voyage. You must know, James, that an old relative has left me a good deal of money in England, and I can only get it by proving that I am Lionel Spencer ; so you see I must carry my own name, whatever may be the risk."

"Well, major, you know best; but I do think if they could only have a guess of what you did among their sodgers at Hobkirk's and Cowpens, and Eutaw, and a dozen other places, they'd find some means of hanging you up, peace or no peace. But I don't see what occasion you have to be going cl'ar away to England for money, when you've got a sight of your own already."

"Not so much as you think for," replied the major, giving an involuntary and uneasy glance at the Scotchman, who was seem

ingly sound asleep on the opposite side of the fire. "There is
you know, but little money in the country at any time, and I must
ge what I want for my expenses when I reach Charleston. I
have just enough to carry me there."

"Well, now, major, that's mighty strange. I always thought
that you was about the best off of any man in our parts; but if
you're strained so close, I'm thinking, major,—if so be you
wouldn't think me too presumptuous,—you'd better let me lend
you a guinea or so that I've got to spare, and you can pay me
back when you get the English money."

And the youth fumbled in his bosom for a little cotton wallet,
which, with its limited contents, was displayed in another instant
to the eyes of the officer.

"No, no, James," said the other, putting back the generous
tribute; "I have quite enough to carry me to Charleston, and
when there I can easily get a supply from the merchants. But I
thank you, my good fellow, for your offer. You *are* a good fellow, James, and I will remember you."

It is needless to pursue the conversation farther. The nigh
passed away without any alarms, and at dawn of the next da
the whole party was engaged in making preparation for a start
Mrs. Grayling was soon busy in getting breakfast in readiness.
Major Spencer consented to remain with them until it was over;
but the Scotchman, after returning thanks very civilly for his ac-
commodation of the night, at once resumed his journey. His
course seemed, like their own, to lie below; but he neither declared his route nor betrayed the least desire to know that of
Spencer. The latter had no disposition to renew those inquiries
from which the stranger seemed to shrink the night before, and
he accordingly suffered him to depart with a quiet farewell, and
the utterance of a good-natured wish, in which all the parties
joined, that he might have a pleasant journey. When he was
fairly out of sight, Spencer said to Sparkman,

"Had I liked that fellow's looks, nay, had I not positively dis-
liked them, I should have gone with him. As it is, I will remain
and share your breakfast."

The repast being over, all parties set forward; but Spencer,
after keeping along with them for a mile, took his leave also.

The slow wagon-pace at which the family travelled, did not suit
the high-spirited cavalier ; and it was necessary, as he assured
them, that he should reach the city in two nights more.   They
parted with many regrets, as truly felt as they were warmly expressed ; and James Grayling never felt the tedium of wagon
travelling to be so severe as throughout the whole of that day
when he separated from his favourite captain.   But he was too
stout-hearted a lad to make any complaint ; and his dissatisfaction only showed itself in his unwonted silence, and an over-anx-
iety, which his steed seemed to feel in common with himself, to
go rapidly ahead.   Thus the day passed, and the wayfarers at
its close had made a progress of some twenty miles from sun to
sun.   The same precautions marked their encampment this night
as the last, and they rose in better spirits with the next morning
the dawn of which was very bright and pleasant, and encouraging.   A similar journey of twenty miles brought them to the place
of bivouac as the sun went down ; and they prepared as usual
for their securities and supper.   They found themselves on the
edge of a very dense forest of pines and scrubby oaks, a portion
of which was swallowed up in a deep bay—so called in the dialect of the country—a swamp-bottom, the growth of which consisted of mingled cypresses and bay-trees, with tupola, gum, and
dense thickets of low stunted shrubbery, cane grass, and dwarf
willows, which filled up every interval between the trees, and to
the eye most effectually barred out every human intruder.   This
bay was chosen as the background for the camping party.   Their
wagon was wheeled into an area on a gently rising ground in
front, under a pleasant shade of oaks and hickories, with a lonely
pine rising loftily in occasional spots among them.   Here the
horses were taken out, and James Grayling prepared to kindle
up a fire ; but, looking for his axe, it was unaccountably missing,
and after a fruitless search of half an hour, the party came to
the conclusion that it had been left on the spot where they had
slept last night.   This was a disaster; and, while they meditated
in what manner to repair it, a negro boy appeared in sight, passing along the road at their feet, and driving before him a small
herd of cattle.   From him they learned that they were only a
mile or two from a farmstead where an axe might be borrowed ;

and James, leaping on his horse, rode forward in the hope to obtain one. He found no difficulty in his quest; and, having obtained it from the farmer, who was also a tavern-keeper, he casually asked if Major Spencer had not stayed with him the night before. He was somewhat surprised when told that he had not.

"There was one man stayed with me last night," said the farmer, "but he didn't call himself a major, and didn't much look like one."

"He rode a fine sorrel horse,—tall, bright colour, with white fore foot, didn't he?" asked James.

"No, that he didn't! He rode a powerful black, coal black, and not a bit of white about him."

"That was the Scotchman! But I wonder the major didn't stop with you. He must have rode on. Isn't there another house near you, below?"

"Not one. There's ne'er a house either above or below for a matter of fifteen miles. I'm the only man in all that distance that's living on this road; and I don't think your friend could have gone below, as I should have seen him pass. I've been all day out there in that field before your eyes, clearing up the brush."

CHAPTER III.

SOMEWHAT wondering that the major should have turned aside from the track, though without attaching to it any importance at that particular moment, James Grayling took up the borrowed axe and hurried back to the encampment, where the toil of cutting an extra supply of light-wood to meet the exigencies of the ensuing night, sufficiently exercised his mind as well as his body, to prevent him from meditating upon the seeming strangeness of the circumstance. But when he sat down to his supper over the fire that he had kindled, his fancies crowded thickly upon him, and he felt a confused doubt and suspicion that something was to happen, he knew not what. His conjectures and apprehensions were without form, though not altogether void ; and he felt a strange sickness and a sinking at the heart which was very unusual with him. He had, in short, that lowness of spirits, that cloudy apprehensiveness of soul which takes the form of presentiment, and makes us look out for danger even when the skies are without a cloud, and the breeze is laden, equally and only, with balm and music. His moodiness found no sympathy among his companions. Joel Sparkman was in the best of humours, and his mother was so cheery and happy, that when the thoughtful boy went off into the woods to watch, he could hear her at every moment breaking out into little catches of a country ditty, which the gloomy events of the late war had not yet obliterated from her memory.

"It's very strange !" soliloquized the youth, as he wandered along the edges of the dense bay or swamp-bottom, which we have passingly referred to,—"it's very strange what troubles me so ! I feel almost frightened, and yet I know I'm not to be frightened easily, and I don't see anything in the woods to frighten me. It's strange the major didn't come along this road ! Maybe he took another higher up that leads by a different settlement. I wish I had asked the man at the house if there's such another

3

road. I reckon there must be, however, for where could the major have gone ?"

The unphilosophical mind of James Grayling did not, in his farther meditations, carry him much beyond this starting point; and with its continual recurrence in soliloquy, he proceeded to traverse the margin of the bay, until he came to its junction with, and termination at, the high-road. The youth turned into this, and, involuntarily departing from it a moment after, soon found himself on the opposite side of the bay thicket. He wandered on and on, as he himself described it, without any power to restrain himself. He knew not how far he went; but, instead of maintaining his watch for two hours only, he was gone more than four; and, at length, a sense of weariness which overpowered him all of a sudden, caused him to seat himself at the foot of a tree, and snatch a few moments of rest. He denied that he slept in this time. He insisted to the last moment of his life that sleep never visited his eyelids that night,—that he was conscious of fatigue and exhaustion, but not drowsiness,—and that this fatigue was so numbing as to be painful, and effectually kept him from any sleep. While he sat thus beneath the tree, with a body weak and nerveless, but a mind excited, he knew not how or why, to the most acute degree of expectation and attention, he heard his name called by the well-known voice of his friend, Major Spencer. The voice called him three times,—" James Grayling !—James ! —James Grayling !" before he could muster strength enough to answer. It was not courage he wanted,—of that he was positive, for he felt sure, as he said, that something had gone wrong, and he was never more ready to fight in his life than at that moment, could he have commanded the physical capacity; but his throat seemed dry to suffocation,—his lips effectually sealed up as if with wax, and when he did answer, the sounds seemed as fine and soft as the whisper of some child just born.

" Oh ! major, is it you ?"

Such, he thinks, were the very words he made use of in reply; and the answer that he received was instantaneous, though the voice came from some little distance in the bay, and his own voice he did not hear. He only knows what he meant to say. The answer was to this effect.

"It is, James!—It is your own friend, Lionel Spencer, that speaks to you; do not be alarmed when you see me! I have been shockingly murdered!"

James asserts that he tried to tell him that he would not be frightened, but his own voice was still a whisper, which he him. self could scarcely hear. A moment after he had spoken, he heard something like a sudden breeze that rustled through the bay bushes at his feet, and his eyes were closed without his effort, and indeed in spite of himself. When he opened them, he saw Major Spencer standing at the edge of the bay, about twenty steps from him. Though he stood in the shade of a thicket, and there was no light in the heavens save that of the stars, he was yet enabled to distinguish perfectly, and with great ease, every lineament of his friend's face.

He looked very pale, and his garments were covered with blood; and James said that he strove very much to rise from the place where he sat and approach him;—" for, in truth," said the lad, " so far from feeling any fear, I felt nothing but fury in my heart; but I could not move a limb. My feet were fastened to the ground; my hands to my sides; and I could only bend forward and gasp. I felt as if I should have died with vexation that I could not rise; but a power which I could not resist, made me motionless, and almost speechless. I could only say, ' Murdered!'—and that one word I believe I must have repeated a dozen times.

" ' Yes, murdered!—murdered by the Scotchman who slept with us at your fire the night before last. James, I look to you to have the murderer brought to justice! James!—do you hear me, James?'

" These," said James, " I think were the very words, or near about the very words, that I heard; and I tried to ask the major o tell me how it was, and how I could do what he required; but I didn't hear myself speak, though it would appear that he did, for almost immediately after I had tried to speak what I wished to say, he answered me just as if I had said it. He told me that the Scotchman had waylaid, killed, and hidden him in that very bay; that his murderer had gone to Charleston; and that if I made haste to town, I would find him in the Falmouth packet,

which was then lying in the harbour and ready to sail for England. He farther said that everything depended on my making
haste,—that I must reach town by to-morrow night if I wanted to
be in season, and go right on board the vessel and charge the
criminal with the deed. 'Do not be afraid,' said he, when he
had finished; 'be afraid of nothing, James, for God will help and
strengthen you to the end.' When I heard all I burst into a flood
of tears, and then I felt strong. I felt that I could talk, or fight,
or do almost anything; and I jumped up to my feet, and was just
about to run down to where the major stood, but, with the firs'
step which I made forward, he was gone. I stopped and looked
all around me, but I could see nothing; and the bay was just as
black as midnight. But I went down to it, and tried to press in
where I thought the major had been standing; but I couldn't get
far, the brush and bay bushes were so close and thick. I was
now bold and strong enough, and I called out, loud enough to be
heard half a mile. I didn't exactly know what I called for, or
what I wanted to learn, or I have forgotten. But I heard nothing
more. Then I remembered the camp, and began to fear that
something might have happened to mother and uncle, for I now
felt, what I had not thought of before, that I had gone too far
round the bay to be of much assistance, or, indeed, to be in time for
any, had they been suddenly attacked. Besides, I could not think
how long I had been gone; but it now seemed very late. The
stars were shining their brightest, and the thin white clouds of
morning were beginning to rise and run towards the west. Well,
I bethought me of my course,—for I was a little bewildered and
doubtful where I was; but, after a little thinking, I took the back
track, and soon got a glimpse of the camp-fire, which was nearly
burnt down; and by this I reckoned I was gone considerably
longer than my two hours. When I got back into the camp, I
looked under the wagon, and found uncle in a sweet sleep, and
though my heart was full almost to bursting with what I had
heard, and the cruel sight I had seen, yet I wouldn't waken him;
and I beat about and mended the fire, and watched, and waited, until near daylight, when mother called to me out of the
wagon, and asked who it was. This wakened my uncle, and
then I up and told all that had happened, for if it had been to

save my life, I couldn't have kept it in much longer. But though mother said it was very strange, Uncle Sparkman considered that I had been only dreaming; but he couldn't persuade me of it; and when I told him I intended to be off at daylight, just as the major had told me to do, and ride my best all the way to Charleston, he laughed, and said I was a fool. But I felt that I was no fool, and I was solemn certain that I hadn't been dreaming; and though both mother and he tried their hardest to make me put off going, yet I made up my mind to it, and they had to give up. For, wouldn't I have been a pretty sort of a friend to the major, if, after what he told me, I could have stayed behind, and gone on only at a wagon-pace to look after the murderer! I dont think if I had done so that I should ever have been able to look a white man in the face again. Soon as the peep of day, I was on horseback. Mother was mighty sad, and begged me not to go, but Uncle Sparkman was mighty sulky, and kept calling me fool upon fool, until I was almost angry enough to forget that we were of blood kin. But all his talking did not stop me, and I reckon I was five miles on my way before he had his team in traces for a start. I rode as briskly as I could get on without hurting my nag. I had a smart ride of more than forty miles before me, and the road was very heavy. But it was a good two hours from sunset when I got into town, and the first question I asked of the people I met was, to show me where the ships were kept. When I got to the wharf they showed me the Falmouth packet, where she lay in the stream, ready to sail as soon as the wind should favour."

CHAPTER IV.

JAMES GRAYLING, with the same eager impatience which he has been suffered to describe in his own language, had already hired a boat to go on board the British packet, when he remembered that he had neglected all those means, legal and otherwise, by which alone his purpose might be properly effected. He did not know much about legal process, but he had common sense enough, the moment that he began to reflect on the subject, to know that some such process was necessary. This conviction produced another difficulty; he knew not in which quarter to turn for counsel and assistance; but here the boatman who saw his bewilderment, and knew by his dialect and dress that he was a back-countryman, came to his relief, and from him he got directions where to find the merchants with whom his uncle, Sparkman, had done business in former years. To them he went, and without circumlocution, told the whole story of his ghostly visitation. Even as a dream, which these gentlemen at once conjectured it to be, the story of James Grayling was equally clear and curious; and his intense warmth and the entire absorption, which the subject had effected, of his mind and soul, was such that they judged it not improper, at least to carry out the search of the vessel which he contemplated. It would certainly, they thought, be a curious coincidence—believing James to be a veracious youth—if the Scotchman should be found on board. But another test of his narrative was proposed by one of the firm. It so happened that the business agents of Major Spencer, who was well known in Charleston, kept their office but a few rods distant from their own; and to them all parties at once proceeded. But here the story of James was encountered by a circumstance that made somewhat against it. These gentlemen produced a letter from Major Spencer, intimating the utter impossibility of his coming to town for the space of a month, and expressing his regret that he should be unable to avail himself of the opportunity of the foreign vessel, of whose arrival in Charleston, and proposed time of departure, they had themselves advised him. They read the letter aloud to James and their brother merchants, and with difficulty suppressed their smiles at the gravity with which the former related and insisted upon the particulars of his vision.

"He has changed his mind," returned the impetuous youth · 'he was on his way down, I tell you,—a hundred miles on his way,—when he camped with us. I know him well, I tell you, and talked with him myself half the night."

"At least," remarked the gentlemen who had gone with James, "it can do no harm to look into the business. We can procure a warrant for searching the vessel after this man, Macnab; and should he be found on board the packet, it will be a sufficient cir- cumstance to justify the magistrates in detaining him, until we can ascertain where Major Spencer really is."

The measure was accordingly adopted, and it was nearly sun- set before the warrant was procured, and the proper officer in readiness. The impatience of a spirit so eager and so devoted as James Grayling, under these delays, may be imagined; and when in the boat, and on his way to the packet where the crimi- nal was to be sought, his blood became so excited that it was with much ado he could be kept in his seat. His quick, eager action continually disturbed the trim of the boat, and one of his mercan- tile friends, who had accompanied him, with that interest in the affair which curiosity alone inspired, was under constant appre- hension lest he would plunge overboard in his impatient desire to shorten the space which lay between. The same impatience en- abled the youth, though never on shipboard before, to grasp the rope which had been flung at their approach, and to mount her sides with catlike agility. Without waiting to declare himself or his purpose, he ran from one side of the deck to the other, greedily staring, to the surprise of officers, passengers, and seamen, in the faces of all of them, and surveying them with an almost offensive scrutiny. He turned away from the search with disappointment. There was no face like that of the suspected man among them. By this time, his friend, the merchant, with the sheriff's officer, had entered the vessel, and were in conference with the captain. Grayling drew nigh in time to hear the latter affirm that there was no man of the name of Macnab, as stated in the warrant among his passengers or crew.

"He is—he must be!" exclaimed the impetuous youth. "The major never lied in his life, and couldn't lie after he was dead Macnab is here—he is a Scotchman—"

The captain interrupted him—

"We have, young gentleman, several Scotchmen on board, and one of them is named Macleod—"

"Let me see him—which is he?" demanded the youth.

By this time, the passengers and a goodly portion of the crew were collected about the little party. The captain turned his eyes upon the group, and asked,

"Where is Mr. Macleod?"

"He is gone below—he's sick!" replied one of the passengers.

"That's he! That must be the man!" exclaimed the youth. "I'll lay my life that's no other than Macnab. He's only taken a false name."

It was now remembered by one of the passengers, and remarked, that Macleod had expressed himself as unwell, but a few moments before, and had gone below even while the boat was rapidly approaching the vessel. At this statement, the captain led the way into the cabin, closely followed by James Grayling and the rest.

"Mr. Macleod," he said with a voice somewhat elevated, as he approached the berth of that person, "you are wanted on deck for a few moments."

"I am really too unwell, captain," replied a feeble voice from behind the curtain of the berth.

"It will be necessary," was the reply of the captain. "There is a warrant from the authorities of the town, to look after a fugitive from justice."

Macleod had already begun a second speech declaring his feebleness, when the fearless youth, Grayling, bounded before the captain and tore away, with a single grasp of his hand, the curtain which concealed the suspected man from their sight.

"It is he!" was the instant exclamation of the youth, as he beheld him. "It is he—Macnab, the Scotchman—the man that murdered Major Spencer!"

Macnab,—for it was he,—was deadly pale. He trembled like

an aspen. His eyes were dilated with more than mortal apprehension, and his lips were perfectly livid. Still, he found strength
to speak, and to deny the accusation. He knew nothing of the
youth before him—nothing of Major Spencer—his name was
Macleod, and he had never called himself by any other. He denied, but with great incoherence, everything which was urged
against him.

"You must get up, Mr. Macleod," said the captain; "the circumstances are very much against you. You must go with the
officer!"

"Will you give me up to my enemies?" demanded the culprit.
"You are a countryman—a Briton. I have fought for the king,
our master, against these rebels, and for this they seek my life.
Do not deliver me into their bloody hands!"

"Liar!" exclaimed James Grayling—"Didn't you tell us at
our own camp-fire that you were with us? that you were at
Gates's defeat, and Ninety-Six?"

"But I didn't tell you," said the Scotchman, with a grin,
"which side I was on!"

"Ha! remember that!" said the sheriff's officer. "He denied,
just a moment ago, that he knew this young man at all; now, he
confesses that he did see and camp with him."

The Scotchman was aghast at the strong point which, in his
inadvertence, he had made against himself; and his efforts to excuse himself, stammering and contradictory, served only to involve him more deeply in the meshes of his difficulty. Still he
continued his urgent appeals to the captain of the vessel, and his
fellow-passengers, as citizens of the same country, subjects to the
same monarch, to protect him from those who equally hated and
would destroy them all. In order to move their national prejudices in his behalf, he boasted of the immense injury which he had
done, as a tory, to the rebel cause; and still insisted that the
murder was only a pretext of the youth before him, by which to
gain possession of his person, and wreak upon him the revenge
which his own fierce performances during the war had naturally
enough provoked. One or two of the passengers, indeed, joined
with him in entreating the captain to set the accusers adrift and
make sail at once; but the stout Englishman who was in com-

mand, rejected instantly the unworthy counsel. Besides, he was better aware of the dangers which would follow any such rash proceeding. Fort Moultrie, on Sullivan's Island, had been already refitted and prepared for an enemy ; and he was lying, at that moment, under the formidable range of grinning teeth, which would have opened upon him, at the first movement, from the jaws of Castle Pinckney.

" No, gentlemen," said he, " you mistake your man. God forbid that I should give shelter to a murderer, though he were from my own parish."

" But I am no murderer," said the Scotchman.

" You look cursedly like one, however," was the reply of the captain. " Sheriff, take your prisoner."

The base creature threw himself at the feet of the Englishman, and clung, with piteous entreaties, to his knees. The latter shook him off, and turned away in disgust.

" Steward," he cried, " bring up this man's luggage."

He was obeyed. The luggage was brought up from the cabin and delivered to the sheriff's officer, by whom it was examined in the presence of all, and an inventory made of its contents. It consisted of a small new trunk, which, it afterwards appeared, he had bought in Charleston, soon after his arrival. This contained a few changes of raiment, twenty-six guineas in money, a gold watch, not in repair, and the two pistols which he had shown while at Joel Sparkman's camp fire ; but, with this difference, that the stock of one was broken off short just above the grasp, and the butt was entirely gone. It was not found among his chattels. A careful examination of the articles in his trunk did not result in anything calculated to strengthen the charge of his criminality ; but there was not a single person present who did not feel as morally certain of his guilt as if the jury had already declared the fact. That night he slept—if he slept at all—in the common jail of the city.

CHAPTER V.

His accuser, the warm-hearted and resolute James Grayling,
did not sleep. The excitement, arising from mingling and contradictory emotions,—sorrow for his brave young commander's
fate, and the natural exultation of a generous spirit at the consciousness of having performed, with signal success, an arduous
and painful task combined to drive all pleasant slumbers from his
eyes ; and with the dawn he was again up and stirring, with his
mind still full of the awful business in which he had been engaged. We do not care to pursue his course in the ordinary walks
of the city, nor account for his employments during the few days
which ensued, until, in consequence of a legal examination into
the circumstances which anticipated the regular work of the ses-
sions, the extreme excitement of the young accuser had been renewed. Macnab or Macleod,—and it is possible that both names
were fictitious,—as soon as he recovered from his first terrors,
sought the aid of an attorney—one of those acute, small, chopping lawyers, to be found in almost every community, who are
willing to serve with equal zeal the sinner and the saint, provided that they can pay with equal liberality. The prisoner was
brought before the court under *habeas corpus,* and several grounds
submitted by his counsel with the view to obtaining his discharge.
It became necessary to ascertain, among the first duties of the
state, whether Major Spencer, the alleged victim, was really
dead. Until it could be established that a man should be imprisoned, tried, and punished for a crime, it was first necessary
to show that a crime had been committed, and the attorney made
himself exceedingly merry with the ghost story of young Grayling. In those days, however, the ancient Superstition was not
so feeble as she has subsequently become. The venerable judge
was one of those good men who had a decent respect for the faith
and opinions of his ancestors ; and though he certainly would not
have consented to the hanging of Macleod under the sort of testi-

mony which had been adduced, he yet saw enough, in all the cir
cumstances, to justify his present detention. In the meantime,
efforts were to be made, to ascertain the whereabouts of Major Spen
cer ; though, were he even missing,—so the counsel for Macleod
contended,—his death could be by no means assumed in consequence. To this the judge shook his head doubtfully. " 'Fore
God !" said he, " I would not have you to be too sure of that."
He was an Irishman, and proceeded after the fashion of his country. The reader will therefore *bear* with his *bull.* " A man may
properly be hung for murdering another, though the murdered
man be not dead ; ay, before God, even though he be actually
unhurt and uninjured, while the murderer is swinging by the
neck for the bloody deed !"

The judge,—who it must be understood was a real existence,
and who had no small reputation in his day in the south,—proceeded to establish the correctness of his opinions by authorities
and argument, with all of which, doubtlessly, the bar were ex
ceedingly delighted ; but, to provide them in this place would
only be to interfere with our own progress. James Grayling,
however, was not satisfied to wait the slow processes which were
suggested for coming at the truth. Even the wisdom of the judge
was lost upon him, possibly, for the simple reason that he did not
comprehend it. But the ridicule of the culprit's lawyer stung
him to the quick, and he muttered to himself, more than once,
a determination " to lick the life out of that impudent chap's
leather." But this was not his only resolve. There was one
which he proceeded to put into instant execution, and that was to
seek the body of his murdered friend in the spot where he fancied
it might be found—namely, the dark and dismal bay where the
spectre had made its appearance to his eyes.

The suggestion was approved—though he did not need this to
prompt his resolution—by his mother and uncle, Sparkman. The
latter determined to be his companion, and he was farther accompanied by the sheriff's officer who had arrested the suspected felon. Before daylight, on the morning after the examination before
the judge had taken place, and when Macleod had been remand-
ed to prison, James Grayling started on his journey. His fiery
zeal received additional force at every added moment of delay, and

his eager spurring brought him at an early hour after noon, to the neighbourhood of the spot through which his search was to be made. When his companions and himself drew nigh, they were all at a loss in which direction first to proceed. The bay was one of those massed forests, whose wall of thorns, vines, and close tenacious shrubs, seemed to defy invasion. To the eye of the townsman it was so forbidding that he pronounced it absolutely impenetrable. But James was not to be baffled. He led them round it, taking the very course which he had pursued the night when the revelation was made him; he showed them the very tree at whose foot he had sunk when the supernatural torpor—as he himself esteemed it—began to fall upon him; he then pointed out the spot, some twenty steps distant, at which the spectre made his appearance. To this spot they then proceeded in a body, and essayed an entrance, but were so discouraged by the difficulties at the outset that all, James not excepted, concluded that neither the murderer nor his victim could possibly have found entrance there.

But, lo! a marvel! Such it seemed, at the first blush, to all the party. While they stood confounded and indecisive, undetermined in which way to move, a sudden flight of wings was heard, even from the centre of the bay, at a little distance above the spot where they had striven for entrance. They looked up, and beheld about fifty buzzards—those notorious domestic vultures of the south—ascending from the interior of the bay, and perching along upon the branches of the loftier trees by which it was overhung. Even were the character of these birds less known, the particular business in which they had just then been engaged, was betrayed by huge gobbets of flesh which some of them had borne aloft in their flight, and still continued to rend with beak and bill, as they tottered upon the branches where they stood. A piercing scream issued from the lips of James Grayling as he beheld this sight, and strove to scare the offensive birds from their repast.

" The poor major! the poor major!" was the involuntary and agonized exclamation of the youth. " Did I ever think he would come to this!"

The search, thus guided and encouraged, was pressed with renewed diligence and spirit; and, at length, an opening was found through which it was evident that a body of considerable size had but recently gone. The branches were broken from the small shrub trees, and the undergrowth trodden into the earth. They followed this path, and, as is the case commonly with waste tracts of this description, the density of the growth diminished sensibly at every step they took, till they reached a little pond, which, though circumscribed in area, and full of cypresses, yet proved to be singularly deep. Indeed, it was an alligator-hole, where, in all probability, a numerous tribe of these reptiles had their dwelling. Here, on the edge of the pond, they discovered the object which had drawn the keen-sighted vultures to their feast, in the body of a horse, which James Grayling at once identified as that of Major Spencer. The carcass of the animal was already very much torn and lacerated. The eyes were plucked out, and the animal completely disembowelled. Yet, on examination, it was not difficult to discover the manner of his death. This had been effected by fire-arms. Two bullets had passed through his skull, just above the eyes, either of which must have been fatal. The murderer had led the horse to the spot, and committed the cruel deed where his body was found. The search was now continued for that of the owner, but for some time it proved ineffectual. At length, the keen eyes of James Grayling detected, amidst a heap of moss and green sedge that rested beside an overthrown tree, whose branches jutted into the pond, a whitish, but discoloured object, that did not seem native to the place. Bestriding the fallen tree, he was enabled to reach this object, which, with a burst of grief, he announced to the distant party was the hand and arm of his unfortunate friend, the wristband of the shirt being the conspicuous object which had first caught his eye. Grasping this, he drew the corse, which had been thrust beneath the branches of the tree, to the surface ; and, with the assistance of his uncle, it was finally brought to the dry land. Here it underwent a careful examination. The head was very much disfigured ; the skull was fractured in several places by repeated blows of some hard instrument, inflicted chiefly from behind. A closer inspection revealed a bullet-hole in the abdomen, the first wound, in all probability, which the unfortunate gentleman received, and by which he was, perhaps, tumbled from his horse. The blows on the head would seem to have been unnecessary, unless the murderer—whose proceedings appeared to have been singularly deliberate,—was resolved upon making "assurance doubly sure." But, as if the watchful Providence had meant that nothing should be left doubtful which might tend to the complete conviction of the criminal, the constable stumbled upon the butt of the broken pistol which had been found in Macleod's trunk. This he picked up on the edge of the pond in which the corse had been discovered, and while James Grayling and his uncle, Sparkman, were engaged in drawing it from the water. The place where the fragment was discovered at once denoted the pistol as the instrument by which the final blows were inflicted. " 'Fore God," said the judge to the criminal, as these proofs were submitted on the trial, " you may be a very innocent man after all, as, by my faith, I do think there have been many murderers before you; but you ought, nevertheless, to be hung as an example to all other persons who suffer such strong proofs of guilt to follow their innocent misdoings. Gentlemen of the jury, if this person, Macleod or Macnab, didn't murder Major Spencer, either you or I did; and you must now decide which of us it is! I say, gentlemen of the jury, either you, or I, or the prisoner at the bar, murdered this man; and if you have any doubts which of us it was, it is but justice and mercy that you should give the prisoner the benefit of your doubts; and so find your verdict. But, before God, should you find him not guilty, Mr. Attorney there can scarcely do anything wiser than to put us all upon trial for the deed."

The jury, it may be scarcely necessary to add, perhaps under certain becoming fears of an alternative such as his honour had suggested, brought in a verdict of " Guilty," without leaving the panel; and Macnab, *alias* Macleod, was hung at White Point, Charleston, somewhere about the year 178—.

" And here," said my grandmother, devoutly, " you behold a proof of God's watchfulness to see that murder should not be hidden, and that the murderer should not escape. You see that he sent the spirit of the murdered man—since, by no other mode could the truth have been revealed—to declare the crime, and to discover the criminal. But for that ghost, Macnab would have got off to Scotland, and probably have been living to this very

day on the money that he took from the person of the poor ma.
jor."

As the old lady finished the ghost story, which, by the way,
she had been tempted to relate for the fiftieth time in order to
combat my father's ridicule of such superstitions, the latter took
up the thread of the narrative.

"Now, my son," said he, "as you have heard all that your
grandmother has to say on this subject, I will proceed to show
you what you have to believe, and what not. It is true that
Macnab murdered Spencer in the manner related; that James
Grayling made the dicovery and prosecuted the pursuit; found
the body and brought the felon to justice; that Macnab suffered
death, and confessed the crime; alleging that he was moved to
do so, as well because of the money that he suspected Spencer to
have in his possession, as because of the hate which he felt for a
man who had been particularly bold and active in cutting up a
party of Scotch loyalists to which he belonged, on the borders of
North Carolina. But the appearance of the spectre was nothing
more than the work of a quick imagination, added to a shrewd
and correct judgment. James Grayling saw no ghost, in fact,
but such as was in his own mind; and, though the instance was
one of a most remarkable character, one of singular combination,
and well depending circumstances, still, I think it is to be accounted for by natural and very simple laws."

The old lady was indignant.

"And how could he see the ghost just on the edge of the same
bay where the murder had been conmitted, and where the body
of the murdered man even then was lying?"

My father did not directly answer the demand, but proceeded
thus :—

"James Grayling, as we know, mother, was a very ardent,
impetuous, sagacious man. He had the sanguine, the race-horse
temperament. He was generous, always prompt and ready, and
one who never went backward. What he did, he did quickly,
boldly, and thoroughly! He never shrank from trouble of any
kind: nay, he rejoiced in the constant encounter with difficulty
and trial; and his was the temper which commands and enthrals
mankind. He felt deeply and intensely whatever occupied his

mind, and when he parted from his friend he brooded over little
else than their past communion and the great distance by which
they were to be separated. The dull travelling wagon-gait at
which he himself was compelled to go, was a source of annoyance to him; and he became sullen, all the day, after the departure of his friend. When, on the evening of the next day, he
came to the house where it was natural to expect that Major
Spencer would have slept the night before, and he learned the fac.
that no one stopped there but the Scotchman, Macnab, we see
that he was struck with the circumstance. He mutters it over
to himself, "Strange, where the major could have gone!" His
mind then naturally reverts to the character of the Scotchman;
to the opinions and suspicions which had been already expressed
of him by his uncle, and felt by himself. They had all, previously, come to the full conviction that Macnab was, and had always
been, a tory, in spite of his protestations. His mind next, and
very naturally, reverted to the insecurity of the highways; the
general dangers of travelling at that period; the frequency of
crime, and the number of desperate men who were everywhere
to be met with. The very employment in which he was then
engaged, in scouting the woods for the protection of the camp,
was calculated to bring such reflections to his mind. If these
precautions were considered necessary for the safety of persons
so poor, so wanting in those possessions which might prompt cupidity to crime, how much more necessary were precautions in
the case of a wealthy gentleman like Major Spencer! He then
remembered the conversation with the major at the camp-fire,
when they fancied that the Scotchman was sleeping. How natural to think then that he was all the while awake; and, if
awake, he must have heard him speak of the wealth of his companion. True, the major, with more prudence than himself, denied that he had any money about him, more than would bear his
expenses to the city; but such an assurance was natural enough
to the lips of a traveller who knew the dangers of the country.
That the man, Macnab, was not a person to be trusted, was the
equal impression of Joel Sparkman and his nephew from the first.
The probabilities were strong that he would rob and perhaps
murder, if he might hope to do so with impunity; and as the

4

youth made the circuit of the bay in the darkness and solemn stillness of the night, its gloomy depths and mournful shadows, naturally gave rise to such reflections as would be equally active in the mind of a youth, and of one somewhat familiar with the arts and usages of strife. He would see that the spot was just the one in which a practised partisan would delight to set an ambush for an unwary foe. There ran the public road, with a little sweep, around two-thirds of the extent of its dense and impenetrable thickets. The ambush could lie concealed, and at ten steps command the bosom of its victim. Here, then, you perceive that the mind of James Grayling, stimulated by an active and sagacious judgment, had by gradual and reasonable stages come to these conclusions : that Major Spencer was an object to tempt a robber ; that the country was full of robbers ; that Macnab was one of them ; that this was the very spot in which a deed of blood could be most easily committed, and most easily concealed ; and, one important fact, that gave strength and coherence to the whole, that Major Spencer had not reached a well-known point of destination, while Macnab had.

" With these thoughts, thus closely linked together, the youth forgets the limits of his watch and his circuit. This fact, alone, proves how active his imagination had become. It leads him forward, brooding more and more on the subject, until, in the very exhaustion of his body, he sinks down beneath a tree. He sinks down and falls asleep; and in his sleep, what before was plausible conjecture, becomes fact, and the creative properties of his imagination give form and vitality to all his fancies. These forms are bold, broad, and deeply coloured, in due proportion with the degree of force which they receive from probability. Here, he sees the image of his friend ; but, you will remark—and this should almost conclusively satisfy any mind that all that he sees is the work of his imagination,—that, though Spencer tells him that he is murdered, and by Macnab, he does not tell him how, in what manner, or with what weapons. Though he sees him pale and ghostlike, he does not see, nor can he say, where his wounds are ! He sees his pale features distinctly, and his garments are bloody. Now, had he seen the spectre in the true appearances of death, as he was subsequently found, he would not

have been able to discern his features, which were battered, according to his own account, almost out of all shape of humanity,
and covered with mud; while his clothes would have streamed
with mud and water, rather than with blood."

"Ah!" exclaimed the old lady, my grandmother, "it's hard
to make you believe anything that you don't see; you are like
Saint Thomas in the Scriptures; but how do you propose to account for his knowing that the Scotchman was on board the Falmouth packet? Answer to that!"

"That is not a more difficult matter than any of the rest.
You forget that in the dialogue which took place between James
and Major Spencer at the camp, the latter told him that he was
about to take passage for Europe in the Falmouth packet, which
then lay in Charleston harbour, and was about to sail. Macnab
heard all that."

"True enough, and likely enough," returned the old lady;
"but, though you show that it was Major Spencer's intention to
go to Europe in the Falmouth packet, that will not show that it
was also the intention of the murderer."

"Yet what more probable, and how natural for James Grayling to imagine such a thing! In the first place he knew that
Macnab was a Briton; he felt convinced that he was a tory; and
the inference was immediate, that such a person would scarcely
have remained long in a country where such characters laboured
under so much odium, disfranchisement, and constant danger
from popular tumults. The fact that Macnab was compelled to
disguise his true sentiments, and affect those of the people against
whom he fought so vindictively, shows what was his sense of the
danger which he incurred. Now, it is not unlikely that Macnab
was quite as well aware that the Falmouth packet was in Charleston, and about to sail, as Major Spencer. No doubt he was pursuing the same journey, with the same object, and had he not
murdered Spencer, they would, very likely, have been fellow-
passengers together to Europe. But, whether he knew the fact
before or not, he probably heard it stated by Spencer while he
seemed to be sleeping; and, even supposing that he did not then
know, it was enough that he found this to be the fact on reaching
the city. It was an after-thought to fly to Europe with his ill

gotten spoils; and whatever may have appeared a politic course to the criminal, would be a probable conjecture in the mind of him by whom he was suspected. The whole story is one of strong probabilities which happened to be verified; and if proving anything, proves only that which we know—that James Grayling was a man of remarkably sagacious judgment, and quick, daring imagination. This quality of imagination, by the way, when possessed very strongly in connexion with shrewd common sense and well-balanced general faculties, makes that particular kind of intellect which, because of its promptness and powers of creation and combination, we call genius. It is genius only which can make ghosts, and James Grayling was a genius. He never, my son, saw any other ghosts than those of his own making!"

I heard my father with great patience to the end, though he seemed very tedious. He had taken a great deal of pains to destroy one of my greatest sources of pleasure. I need not add that I continued to believe in the ghost, and, with my grandmother, to reject the philosophy. It was more easy to believe the one than to comprehend the other.

THE TWO CAMPS.

A LEGEND OF THE OLD NORTH STATE

> " These, the forest born
> And forest nurtured—a bold, hardy race,
> Fearless and frank, unfettered, with big souls
> In hour of danger."

CHAPTER I.

It is frequently the case, in the experience of the professional novelist or tale-writer, that his neighbour comes in to his assistance when he least seeks, and, perhaps, least desires any succour. The worthy person, man or woman, however,—probably some excellent octogenarian whose claims to be heard are based chiefly upon the fact that he himself no longer possesses the faculty of hearing,—has some famous incident, some wonderful fact, of which he has been the eye-witness, or of which he has heard from his great-grandmother, which he fancies is the very thing to be woven into song or story. Such is the strong possession which the matter takes of his brain, that, if the novelist whom he seeks to benefit does not live within trumpet-distance, he gives him the narrative by means of post, some three sheets of stiff foolscap, for which the hapless tale-writer, whose works are selling in cheap editions at twelve or twenty cents, pays a sum of one dollar sixty-two postage. Now, it so happens, to increase the evil, that, in ninety-nine cases in the hundred, the fact thus laboriously stated is not worth a straw—consisting of some simple deed of violence, some mere murder, a downright blow with gun-butt or cudgel over the skull, or a hidden thrust, three inches deep, with dirk or bowie knife, into the abdomen, or at random among the lower ribs. The man

4

dies and the murderer gets off to Texas, or is prematurely caught and stops by the way—and still stops by the way ! The thing is fact, no doubt. The narrator saw it himself, or his brother saw it, or—more solemn, if not more certain testimony still—his grand-mother saw it, long before he had eyes to see at all. The cir-cumstance is attested by a cloud of witnesses—a truth solemnly sworn to—and yet, for the purposes of the tale-writer, of no man-ner of value. This assertion may somewhat conflict with the received opinions of many, who, accustomed to find deeds of vio-lence recorded in almost every work of fiction, from the time of Homer to the present day, have rushed to the conclusion that this is all, and overlook that labour of the artist, by which an ordi-nary event is made to assume the character of novelty ; in other words, to become an extraordinary event. The least difficult thing in the world, on the part of the writer of fiction, is to find the assassin and the bludgeon ; the art is to make them appear in the right place, strike at the right time, and so adapt one fact to another, as to create mystery, awaken curiosity, inspire doubt as to the result, and bring about the catastrophe, by processes which shall be equally natural and unexpected. All that class of sa-gacious persons, therefore, who fancy they have found a mare' nest, when, in fact, they are only gazing at a goose's, are respect-fully counselled that no fact—no tradition—is of any importance to the artist, unless it embodies certain peculiar characteristics of its own, or unless it illustrates some history about which curiosity has already been awakened. A mere brutality, in which John beats and bruises Ben, and Ben in turn shoots John, putting ele-ven slugs, or thereabouts, between his collar-bone and vertebræ—or, maybe, stabs him under his left pap, or any where you please, is just as easily conceived by the novelist, without the help of history. Nay, for that matter, he would perhaps rather not have any precise facts in his way, in such cases, as then he will be able to regard the picturesque in the choice of his weapon, and to put the wounds in such parts of the body, as will better bear the examination of all persons. I deem it right to throw out this hint, just at this moment, as well for the benefit of my order as for my own protection. The times are hard, and the post-office re-quires all its dues in hard money. Literary men are not pro-

verbially prepared at all seasons for any unnecessary outlay—
and to be required to make advances for commodities of which
they have on hand, at all times, the greatest abundance, is an injustice which, it is to be hoped, that this little intimation will
somewhat lessen. We take for granted, therefore, that our pro
fessional brethren will concur with us in saying to the public
that we are all sufficiently provided with " disastrous chances '
for some time to come—that our " moving accidents by flood and
field " are particularly numerous, and of " hair-breadth 'scapes"
we have enough to last a century. Murders, and such matters,
as they are among the most ordinary events of the day, are decidedly vulgar; and, for mere cudgelling and bruises, the taste
of the belles-lettres reader, rendered delicate by the monthly
magazines, has voted them equally gross and unnatural.

But, if the character of the materials usually tendered to the
novelist by the incident-mongers, is thus ordinarily worthless as
we describe it, we sometimes are fortunate in finding an individual, here and there, in the deep forests,—a sort of recluse, hale
and lusty, but white-headed,—who unfolds from his own budget
of experience a rare chronicle, on which we delight to linger.
Such an one breathes life into his deeds. We see them as we
listen to his words. In lieu of the dead body of the fact, we have
its living spirit—subtle, active, breathing and burning, and fresh
in all the provocations and associations of life. Of this sort
was the admirable characteristic narrative of Horse-Shoe Robin-
son, which we owe to Kennedy, and for which he was indebted
to the venerable hero of the story. When we say that the subject of the sketch which follows was drawn from not dissimilar
sources, we must beg our readers not to understand us as inviting
any reference to that able and national story—with which it
is by no means our policy or wish to invite or provoke compari.
son.

CHAPTER II.

THERE are probably some old persons still living upon the up
pei dividing line between North and South Carolina, who still re
member the form and features of the venerable Daniel Nelson
The old man was still living so late as 1817. At that period he
removed to Mississippi, where, we believe, he died in less than
three months after his change of residence. An old tree does not
bear transplanting easily, and does not long survive it. Daniel
Nelson came from Virginia when a youth. He was one of the
first who settled on the southern borders of North Carolina, or,
at least in that neighbourhood where he afterwards passed the
greatest portion of his days.

At that time the country was not only a forest, but one thickly
settled with Indians. It constituted the favourite hunting-grounds
for several of their tribes. But this circumstance did not discourage young Nelson. He was then a stalwart youth, broad-chested
tall, with a fiery eye, and an almost equally fiery soul—certainly
with a very fearless one. His companions, who were few in
number, were like himself. The spirit of old Daniel Boone was
a more common one than is supposed. Adventure gladdened and
excited their hearts,—danger only seemed to provoke their determination,—and mere hardship was something which their frames
appeared to covet. It was as refreshing to them as drink. Having seen the country, and struck down some of its game,—tasted
of its bear-meat and buffalo, its deer and turkey,—all, at tha
time, in the greatest abundance,—they returned for the one thing
most needful to a brave forester in a new country,—a good, brisk,
fearless wife, who, like the damsel in Scripture, would go whither-
soever went the husband to whom her affections were surrendered.
They had no fear, these bold young hunters, to make a home and
rear an infant family in regions so remote from the secure walks
of civilization. They had met and made an acquaintance and a
sort of friendship with the Indians, and, in the superior vigour of

their own frames, their great. courage, and better weapons, they perhaps had come to form a too contemptuous estimate of the savage. But they were not beguiled by him into too much confidence. Their log houses were so constructed as to be fortresses upon occasion, and they lived not so far removed from one another, but that the leaguer of one would be sure, in twenty-four hours, to bring the others to his assistance. Besides, with a stock of bear-meat and venison always on hand, sufficient for a winter, either of these fortresses might, upon common calculations, be maintained for several weeks against any single band of the Indians, in the small numbers in which they were wont to range together in those neighbourhoods. In this way these bold pioneers took possession of the soil, and paved the way for still mightier generations. Though wandering, and somewhat averse to the tedious labours of the farm, they were still not wholly unmindful of its duties; and their open lands grew larger every season, and increasing comforts annually spoke for the increasing civilization of the settlers. Corn was in plenty in proportion to the bear-meat, and the squatters almost grew indifferent to those first apprehensions, which had made them watch the approaches of the most friendly Indian as if he had been an enemy. At the end of five years, in which they had suffered no hurt and but little annoyance of any sort from their wild neighbours, it would seem as if this confidence in the security of their situation was not without sufficient justification.

But just then, circumstances seemed to threaten an interruption of this goodly state of things. The Indians were becoming discontented. Other tribes, more frequently in contact with the larger settlements of the whites,—wronged by them in trade, or demoralized by drink,—complained of their sufferings and injuries, or, as is more probable, were greedy to obtain their treasures, in bulk, which they were permitted to see, but denied to enjoy, or only in limited quantity. Their appetites and complaints were transmitted, by inevitable sympathies, to their brethren of the interior, and our worthy settlers upon the Haw, were rendered anxious at signs which warned them of a change in the peaceful relations which had hitherto existed in all the intercourse between the differing races. We need not dwell upon or describe these

signs, with which, from frequent narratives of like character, our
people are already sufficiently familiar. They were easily understood by our little colony, and by none more quickly than
Daniel Nelson. They rendered him anxious, it is true, but not
apprehensive ; and, like a good husband, while he strove not to
frighten his wife by what he said, he deemed it necessary to prepare her mind for the worst that might occur. This task over,
he felt somewhat relieved, though, when he took his little girl,
now five years old, upon his knee that evening, and looked upon
his infant boy in the lap of his mother, he felt his anxieties very
much increase ; and that very night he resumed a practice which
he had latterly abandoned, but which had been adopted as a
measure of strict precaution, from the very first establishment of
their little settlement. As soon as supper was over, he resumed
his rifle, thrust his *couteau de chasse* into his belt, and, taking his
horn about his neck, and calling up his trusty dog, Clinch, he
proceeded to scour the woods immediately around his habitation.
This task, performed with the stealthy caution of the hunter, occupied some time, and, as the night was clear, a bright starlight,
the weather moderate, and his own mood restless, he determined
to strike through the forest to the settlement of Jacob Ransom,
about four miles off, in order to prompt him, and, through him,
others of the neighbourhood, to the continued exercise of a caution
which he now thought necessary. The rest of this night's adventure we propose to let him tell in his own words, as he has been
heard to relate it a thousand times in his old age, at a period of
life when, with one foot in his grave, to suppose him guilty of
falsehood, or of telling that which he did not himself fervently believe, would be, among all those who knew him, to suppose the
most impossible and extravagant thing in the world.

CHAPTER III.

" WELL, my friends," said the veteran, then seventy, drawing nis figure up to its fullest height, and extending his right arm, while his left still grasped the muzzle of his ancient rifle, which he swayed from side to side, the butt resting on the floor—" Well, my friends, seeing that the night was cl'ar, and there was no wind, and feeling as how I didn't want for sleep, I called to Clinch and took the path for Jake Ransom's. I knew that Jake was a sleepy sort of chap, and if the redskins caught any body napping, he'd, most likely, be the man. But I confess, 'twarn't so much for his sake, as for the sake of all,—of my own as well as tne rest ;—for, when I thought how soon, if we warn't all together in the business, I might see, without being able to put in, the long yellow hair of Betsy and the babies twirling on the thumbs of some painted devil of the tribe,—I can't tell you how I felt, but it warn't like a human, though I shivered mightily like one,— 'twas wolfish, as if the hair was turned in and rubbing agin the very heart within me. I said my prayers, where I stood, looking up at the stars, and thinking that, after all, all was in the hands and the marcy of God. This sort o' thinking quieted me, and I went ahead pretty free, for I knew the track jest as well by night as by day, though I didn't go so quick, for I was all the time on the look-out for the enemy. Now, after we reached a place in the woods where there was a gully and a mighty bad crossing, there were two roads to get to Jake's—one by the hollows, and one jest across the hills. I don't know why, but I didn't give myself time to think, and struck right across the hill, though that was rather the longest way.

" Howsomedever, on I went. and Clinch pretty close behind me. The dog was a good dog, with a mighty keen nose to hunt, but jest then he didn't seem to have the notion for it. The hill was a sizeable one, a good stretch to foot, and I began to remember, after awhile, that I had been in the woods from blessed dawn ;

and that made me see how it was with poor Clinch, and why he
didn't go for'ad; but I was more than half way, and wasn't
guine to turn back till I had said my say to Jake. Well, when I
got to the top of the hill, I stopped, and rubbed my eyes. I had
cause to rub 'em, for what should I see at a distance but a great
fire. At first I was afeard lest it was Jake's house, but I considered, the next moment, that he lived to the left, and this fire was
cl'ar to the right, and it did seem to me as if 'twas more near to
my own. Here was something to scare a body. But I couldn't
stay there looking, and it warn't now a time to go to Jake's; so
I turned off, and, though Clinch was mighty onwilling, I bolted on
the road to the fire. I say road, but there was no road; but the
trees warn't over-thick, and the land was too poor for undergrowth;
so we got on pretty well, considering. But, what with the tire I
had had, and the scare I felt, it seemed as if I didn't get for'ad a
bit. There was the fire still burning as bright and almost as far
off as ever. When I saw this I stopt and looked at Clinch, and
he stopped and looked at me, but neither of us had any thing
to say. Well, after a moment's thinking, it seemed as if I
shouldn't be much of a man to give up when I had got so far, so
I pushed on. We crossed more than one little hill, then down
and through the hollow, and then up the hill again. At last we
got upon a small mountain the Indians called Nolleehatchie, and
then it seemed as if the fire had come to a stop, for it was now
burning bright, on a little hill below me, and not two hundred
yards in front. It was a regular camp fire, pretty big, and there
was more than a dozen Indians sitting round it. 'Well,' says I
to myself, 'it's come upon us mighty sudden, and what's to be
done? Not a soul in the settlement knows it but myself, and
nobody's on the watch. They'll be sculped, every human of
them, in their very beds, or, moutbe, waken up in the blaze, to be
shot with arrows as they run.' I was in a cold sweat to think of
it. I didn't know what to think and what to do. I looked round
to Clinch, and the strangest thing of all was to see him sitting
quiet on his haunches, looking at me, and at the stars, and not at
the fire jest before him. Now, Clinch was a famous fine hunting
dog, and jest as good on an Indian trail as any other. He know'd
my ways, and what I wanted, and would give tongue, or keep it

still, jest as I axed him. It was sensible enough, jest then, that
he shouldn't bark, but, dang it!—he didn't even seem to see.
Now, there warn't a dog in all the settlement so quick and keen
to show sense as Clinch, even when he didn't say a word ;—and
to see him looking as if he didn't know and didn't care what was
a-going on, with his eyes sot in his head and glazed over with
sleep, was, as I may say, very onnatural, jest at that time, in a
dog of any onderstanding. So I looked at him, half angry, and
when he saw me looking at him, he jest stretched himself off, put
his nose on his legs, and went to sleep in 'arnest. I had half a
mind to lay my knife-handle over his head, but I considered better of it, and though it did seem the strangest thing in the world
that he shouldn't even try to get to the fire, for warm sake, yet I
recollected that dog natur', like human natur', can't stand every
thing, and he hadn't such good reason as I had, to know that the
Indians were no longer friendly to us. Well, there I stood, a
pretty considerable chance, looking, and wondering, and onbe-
knowing what to do. I was mighty beflustered. But at last I felt
ashamed to be so oncertain, and theif again it was a needcessity
that we should know the worst one time or another, so I determined to push for'ad I was no slouch of a hunter, as you may suppose ; so, as I was nearing the camp, I begun sneaking ; and,
taking it sometimes on hands and knees, and sometimes flat to the
ground, where there was neither tree nor bush to cover me, I
went ahead, Clinch keeping close behind me, and not showing any
notion of what I was after. It was a slow business, because it
was a ticklish business ; but I was a leetle too anxious to be altogether so careful as a good sneak ought to be, and I went on
rather faster than I would advise any young man to go in a time
of war, when the inimy is in the neighbourhood. Well, as I went,
there was the fire, getting larger and larger every minute, and
there were the Indians round it, getting plainer and plainer.
There was so much smoke that there was no making out, at any
distance, any but their figures, and these, every now and then,
would be so wrapt in the smoke that not more than half of them
could be seen at the same moment. At last I stopped, jest at a
place where I thought I could make out all that I wanted. There
was a sizeable rock before me, and I leaned my elbows on it to look.

I reckon I warn't more than thirty yards from the fire. There were some bushes betwixt us, and what with the bushes and the smoke, it was several minutes before I could separate man from man, and see what they were all adoing, and when I did, it was only for a moment at a time, when a puff of smoke would wrap them all, and make it as difficult as ever. But when I did contrive to see clearly, the sight was one to worry me to the core, for, in the midst of the redskins, I could see a white one, and that white one a woman. There was no mistake. There were the Indians, some with their backs, and some with their faces to me ; and there, a little a-one side, but still among them, was a woman. When the smoke blowed off, I could see her white face, bright like any star, shining out of the clouds, and looking so pale and ghastly that my blood cruddled in my veins to think lest she might be dead from fright. But it couldn't be so, for she was sitting up and looking about her. But the Indians were motionless. They jest sat or lay as when I first saw them—doing nothing—saying nothing, but jest as motionless as the stone under my elbow. I couldn't stand looking where I was, so I began creeping again, getting nigher and nigher, until it seemed to me as if I ought to be able to read every face. But what with the paint and smoke, I couldn't make out a single Indian. Their figures seemed plain enough in their buffalo-skins and blankets, but their faces seemed always in the dark. But it wasn't so with the woman. I could make her out clearly. She was very young ; I reckon not more than fifteen, and it seemed to me as if I knew her looks very well. She was very handsome, and her hair was loosed upon her back. My heart felt strange to see her. I was weak as any child. It seemed as if I could die for the gal, and yet I hadn't strength enough to raise my rifle to my shoulder. The weakness kept on me the more I looked ; for every moment seemed to make the poor child more and more dear to me. But the strangest thing of all was to see how motionless was every Indian in the camp. Not a word was spoken—not a limb or finger stirred. There they sat, or lay, round about the fire, like so many effigies, looking at the gal, and she looking at them. I never was in such a fix of fear and weakness in my life. What was I to do ? I had got so nigh that I could have stuck my knife, with a jerk, into the heart of any one

of the party, yet I hadn't the soul to lift it; and before I knew
where I was, I cried like a child.   But my crying didn't make
'em look about 'em.   It only brought my poor dog Clinch leaping
upon me, and whining, as if he wanted to give me consolation.
Hardly knowing what I did, I tried to set him upon the camp,
but the poor fellow didn't seem to understand me; and in my
desperation, for it was a sort of madness growing out of my scare,
I jumped headlong for'ad, jest where I saw the party sitting, will
ing to lose my life rather than suffer from such a strange sort of
misery.

CHAPTER IV.

" WILL you believe me! there were no Indians, no young woman, no fire! I stood up in the very place where I had seen the
blaze and the smoke, and there was nothing! I looked for'ad
and about me—there was no sign of fire any where. Where I
stood was covered with dry leaves, the same as the rest of the
forest. I was stupefied. I was like a man roused out of sleep
by a strange dream, and seeing nothing. All was dark and silent.
The stars were overhead, but that was all the light I had. I was
more scared than ever, and, as it's a good rule when a man feels
that he can do nothing himself, to look to the great God who can
do every thing, I kneeled down and said my prayers—the second
time that night that I had done the same thing, and the second
time, I reckon, that I had ever done so in the woods. After that
I felt stronger. I felt sure that this sign hadn't been shown to me
for nothing ; and while I was turning about, looking and thinking
to turn on the back track for home, Clinch began to prick up his
ears and waken up. I clapped him on his back, and got my
knife ready. It might be a *painter* that stirred him, for he could
scent that beast a great distance. But, as he showed no fright,
only a sort of quickening, I knew there was nothing to fear. In
a moment he started off, and went boldly ahead. I followed him,
but hadn't gone twenty steps down the hill and into the hollow,
when I heard something like a groan. This quickened me, and
keeping up with the dog, he led me to the foot of the hollow,
where was a sort of pond. Clinch ran right for it, and another
groan set me in the same direction. When I got up to the dog,
he was on the butt-end of an old tree that had fallen, I reckon,
before my time, and was half buried in the water. I jumped on
it, and walked a few steps for'ad, when, what should I see but a
human, half across the log, with his legs hanging in the water,
and his head down. I called Clinch back out of my way, and
went to the spot. The groans were pretty constant. I stooped

down and laid my hands upon the person, and, as I felt the hair, I
knew it was an Indian. The head was clammy with blood, so
that my fingers stuck, and when I attempted to turn it, to look at
the face, the groan was deeper than ever; but 'twarn't a time
to suck one's fingers. I took him up, clapped my shoulders to it,
and, fixing my feet firmly on the old tree, which was rather slippe-
ry, I brought the poor fellow out without much trouble. Though
tall, he was not heavy, and was only a boy of fourteen or fifteen.
The wonder was how a lad like that should get into such a fix.
Well, I brought him out and laid him on the dry leaves. His
groans stopped, and I thought he was dead, but I felt his heart,
and it was still warm, and I thought, though I couldn't be sure,
there was a beat under my fingers. What to do was the next
question. It was now pretty late in the night. I had been all
day a-foot, and, though still willing to go, yet the thought of such
a weight on my shoulders made me stagger. But 'twouldn't do
to leave him where he was to perish. I thought, if so be I had a
son in such a fix, what would I think of the stranger who should
go home and wait till daylight to give him help! No, darn my
splinters, said I,—though I had just done my prayers,—if I leave
the lad—and, tightening my girth, I give my whole soul to it, and
hoisted him on my shoulders. My cabin, I reckoned, was good
three miles off. You can guess what trouble I had, and what a
tire under my load, before I got home and laid the poor fellow
down by the fire. I then called up Betsy, and we both set to
work to see if we could stir up the life that was in him. She cut
away his hair, and I washed the blood from his head, which was
chopped to the bone, either with a knife or hatchet. It was a God's
blessing it hadn't gone into his brain, for it was fairly enough
aimed for it, jest above the ear. When we come to open his
clothes, we found another wound in his side. This was done
with a knife, and, I suppose, was pretty deep. He had lost blood
enough, for all his clothes were stiff with it. We knew nothing
much of doctoring, but we had some rum in the cabin, and after
washing his wounds clean with it, and pouring some down his
throat, he began to groan more freely, and by that we knew he
was coming to a nateral feeling. We rubbed his body down with
warm cloths, and after a little while, seeing that he made some

5

signs, I give him water as much as he could drink.   This seemed
to do him good, and having done every thing that we thought could
help him, we wrapped him up warmly before the fire, and I
stretched myself off beside him.   'Twould be a long story to tell,
step by step, how he got on.   It's enough to say that he didn't
die that bout.   We got him on his legs in a short time, doing little or nothing for him more than we did at first.   The lad was a
good lad, though, at first, when he first came to his senses, he was
mighty shy, wouldn't look steadily in our faces, and, I do believe,
if he could have got out of the cabin, would have done so as soon
as he could stagger.   But he was too weak to try that, and, meanwhile, when he saw our kindness, he was softened.   By little and
little, he got to play with my little Lucy, who was not quite six
years old ; and, after a while, he seemed to be never better pleased than when they played together.   The child, too, after her
first fright, leaned to the. lad, and was jest as willing to play with
him as if he had been a cl'ar white like herself.   He could say
a few words of English from the beginning, and learnt quickly ·
but, though he talked tolerable free for an Indian, yet I could
never get him to tell me how he was wounded, or by whom.   His
brow blackened when I spoke of it, and his lips would be shut together, as if he was ready to fight sooner than to speak.   Well,
I didn't push him to know, for I was pretty sure the head of the
truth will be sure to come some time or other, if you once have
it by the tail provided you don't jerk it off by straining too hard
upon it.

CHAPTER V.

" I suppose the lad had been with us a matter of six weeks, getting better every day, but so slowly that he had not, at the end of that time, been able to leave the picket. Meanwhile, our troubles with the Indians were increasing. As yet, there had been no bloodshed in our quarter, but we heard of murders and sculpings on every side, and we took for granted that we must have our turn. We made our preparations, repaired the pickets, laid in ammunition, and took turns for scouting nightly. At length, the signs of Indians got to be thick in our parts, though we could see none. Jake Ransom had come upon one of their camps after they had left it ; and we had reason to apprehend every thing, inasmuch as the outlyers didn't show themselves, as they used to do, but prowled about the cabins and went from place to place, only by night, or by close skulking in the thickets. One evening after this, I went out as usual to go the rounds, taking Clinch with me, but I hadn't got far from the gate, when the dog stopped and gave a low bark ;—then I knew there was mischief, so I turned round quietly, without making any show of scare, and got back safely, though not a minute too soon. They trailed me to the gate the moment after I had got it fastened, and were pretty mad, I reckon, when they found their plan had failed for surprising me. But for the keen nose of poor Clinch, with all my skill in scouting,—and it was not small even in that early day,— they'd 'a had me, and all that was mine, before the sun could open his eyes to see what they were after. Finding they had failed in their ambush, they made the woods ring with the war-whoop, which was a sign that they were guine to give us a regular siege. At the sound of the whoop, we could see the eyes of the Indian boy brighten, and his ears prick up, jest like a hound's when he first gets scent of the deer, or hears the horn of the hunter. I looked closely at the lad, and was dub'ous what to do. He moutbe only an enemy in the camp, and while I was fighting in front, he might be cutting the throats of my wife and children within. I did not tell you that I had picked up his bow and arrows near the little lake where I had found him, and his hunting-knife was sticking in his belt when I brought him home. Whether to take these away from him, was the question. Suppose I did, a billet of wood would answer pretty near as well. I thought the matter over while I watched him. Thought runs mighty quick in time of danger! Well, after turning it over on every side, I concluded 'twas better to trust him jest as if he had been a sure friend. I couldn't think, after all we had done for him, that he'd be false, so I said to him—'Lenatewá !'—'twas so he called himself—'those are your people !' 'Yes !' he answered slowly, and lifting himself up as if he had been a lord—he was a stately-looking lad, and carried himself like the son of a Micco,* as he was—'Yes, they are the people of Lenatewá— must he go to them ?' and he made the motion of going out. But I stopped him. I was not willing to lose the security which I had from his being a sort of prisoner. 'No,' said I ; 'no, Lena- tewa, not to-night. To-morrow will do. To-morrow you can tell them I am a friend, not an enemy, and they should not come to burn my wigwam.' 'Brother—friend !' said the lad, advancing with a sort of freedom and taking my hand. He then went to my wife, and did the same thing,—not regarding she was a woman,—'Brother—friend !' I watched him closely, watched his eye and his motions, and I said to Betsy, 'The lad is true ; don't be afeard !' But we passed a weary night. Every now and then we could hear the whoop of the Indians. From the loop- holes we could see the light of three fires on different sides, by which we knew that they were prepared to cut off any help that might come to us from the rest of the settlement. But I didn't give in or despair. I worked at one thing or another all night, and though Lenatewá gave me no help, yet he sat quietly, or laid himself down before the fire, as if he had nothing in the world to do in the business. Next morning by daylight, I found him al- ready dressed in the same bloody clothes which he had on when I found him. He had thrown aside all that I gave him, and though

* A prince or chief.

the hunting-shirt and leggins which he now wore, were very much stained with blood and dirt, he had fixed them about him with a good deal of care and neatness, as if preparing to see company. I must tell you that an Indian of good family always has a nateral sort of grace and dignity which I never saw in a white man. He was busily engaged looking through one of the loop-holes, and though I could distinguish nothing, yet it was cl'ar that he saw something to interest him mightily. I soon found out that, in spite of all my watchfulness, he had contrived to have some sort of correspondence and communication with those outside. This was a wonder to me then, for I did not recollect his bow and arrows. It seems that he had shot an arrow through one of the loop-holes, to the end of which he had fastened a tuft of his own hair. The effect of this was considerable, and to this it was owing that, for a few hours afterwards, we saw not an Indian. The arrow was shot at the very peep of day. What they were about, in the meantime, I can only guess, and the guess was only easy, after I had known all that was to happen. That they were in council what to do was cl'ar enough. I was not to know that the council was like to end in cutting some of their own throats instead of ours. But when we did see the enemy fairly, they came out of the woods in two parties, not actually separated, but not moving together. It seemed as if there was some strife among them. Their whole number could not be less than forty, and some eight or ten of these walked apart under the lead of a chief, a stout, dark-looking fellow, one-half of whose face was painted black as midnight, with a red circle round both his eyes. The other party was headed by an old white-headed chief, who couldn't ha' been less than sixty years—a pretty fellow, you may be sure, at his time of life, to be looking after sculps of women and children. While I was kneeling at my loop-hole looking at them, Lenatewá came to me, and touching me on the arm, pointed to the old chief, saying—' Micco Lenatewá Glucco,' by which I guessed he was the father or grandfather of the lad. ' Well,' I said, seeing that the best plan was to get their confidence and friendship if possible,—' Well, lad, go to your father and tell him what Daniel Nelson has done for you, and let's have peace. We can fight, boy, as you see; we have plenty of arms and provis-

ions ; and with this rifle, though you may not believe it, I could
pick off your father, the king, and that other chief, who has so
devilled himself up with paint.' 'Shoot !' said the lad quickly,
pointing to the chief of whom I had last spoken. 'Ah ! he is
your enemy then ?' The lad nodded his head, and pointed to the
wound on his temple, and that in his side. I now began to see
the true state of the case. 'No,' said I ; 'no, Lenatewá, I will
shoot none. I am for peace. I would do good to the Indians,
and be their friend. Go to your father and tell him so. Go, and
make him be my friend.' The youth caught my hand, placed it on
the top of his head, and exclaimed, 'Good !' I then attended him.
down to the gate, but, before he left the cabin, he stopped and put
his hand on the head of little Lucy,—and I felt glad, for it seemed
to say, 'you shar't be hurt—not a hair of your head !' I let him
out, fastened up, and then hastened to the loop-hole.

CHAPTER VI.

"AND now came a sight to tarrify. As soon as the Indians saw the young prince, they set up a general cry. I couldn't tell whether it was of joy, or what. He went for'ad boldly, though he was still quite weak, and the king at the head of his party advanced to meet him. The other and smaller party, headed by the black chief, whom young Lenatewá had told me to shoot, came forward also, but very slowly, and it seemed as if they were doubtful whether to come or go. Their leader looked pretty much beflustered. But they hadn't time for much study, for, after the young prince had met his father, and a few words had passed between them, I saw the finger of Lenatewá point to the black chief. At this, he lifted up his clenched fists, and worked his body as if he was talking angrily. Then, sudden, the war-whoop sounded from the king's party, and the other troop of Indians began to run, the black chief at their head; but he had not got twenty steps when a dozen arrows went into him, and he tumbled for'a'ds, and grappled with the earth. It was all over with him. His party was scattered on all sides, but were not pursued. It seemed that all the arrows had been aimed at the one person, and when he sprawled, there was an end to it : the whole affair was over in five minutes.

CHAPTER VII.

" It was a fortunate affair for us. Lenatewá soon brought the old Micco to terms of peace. For that matter, he had only consented to take up the red stick because it was reported by the black chief—who was the uncle of the young Micco, and had good reasons for getting him out of the way—that he had been murdered by the whites. This driv' the old man to desperation, and brought him down upon us. When he knew the whole truth, and saw what friends we had been to his son, there was no end to his thanks and promises. He swore to be my friend while the sun shone, while the waters run, and while the mountains stood, and I believe, if the good old man had been spared so long, he would have been true to his oath. But, while he lived, he kepi it, and so did his son when he succeeded him as Micco Glucco. Year after year went by, and though there was frequent war between the Indians and the whites, yet Lenatewá kept it from our doors. He himself was at war several times with our people, but never with our settlement. He put his *totem* on our trees, and the Indians knew that they were sacred. But, after a space of eleven years, there was a change. The young prince seemed to have forgotten our friendship. We now never saw him among us, and, unfortunately, some of our young men—the young men of our own settlement—murdered three young warriors of the Ripparee tribe, who were found on horses stolen from us. I was very sorry when I heard it, and began to fear the consequences; and they came upon us when we least looked for it. I had every reason to think that Lenatewá would still keep the warfare from my little family, but I did not remember that he was the prince of a tribe only, and not of the nation. This was a national warfare, in which the whole Cherokee people were in arms. Many persons, living still, remember that terrible war, and how the Carolinians humbled them at last; but there's no telling how much blood was shed in that war, how many sculps taken, how much misery suffered by young and old, men, women, and children. Our settlement had become so large and scattered that we had to build a sizeable blockhouse, which we stored, and to which we could retreat whenever it was necessary. We took possession of it on hearing from our scouts that Indian trails had been seen, and there we put the women and children, under a strong guard. By day we tended our farms, and only went to our families at night. We had kept them in this fix for five weeks or thereabouts, and there was no attack. The Indian signs disappeared, and we all thought the storm had blown over, and began to hope and to believe that the old friendship of Lenatewá had saved us. With this thinking, we began to be less watchful. The men would stay all night at the farms, and sometimes, in the day, would carry with them the women, and sometimes some even the children. I cautioned them agin this, but they mocked me, and said I was gitting old and scary. I told them, ' Wait and see who'll scare first.' But, I confess, not seeing any Indians in all my scouting, I began to feel and think like the rest, and to grow careless. I let Betsy go now and then with me to the farm, though she kept it from me that she had gone there more than once with Lucy, without any man protector. Still, as it was only a short mile and a half from the block, and we could hear of no Indians, it did not seem so venturesome a thing. One day we heard of some very large b'ars among the thickets—a famous range for them, about four miles from the settlement ; and a party of us, Simon Lorris, Hugh Darling, Jake Ransom, William Harkless, and myself, taking our dogs, set off on the hunt. We started the b'ar with a rush, and I got the first shot at a mighty big she b'ar, the largest I had ever seen—lamed the critter slightly, and dashed into the thickets after her ! The others pushed, in another direction, after the rest, leaving me to finish my work as I could.

" I had two dogs with me, Clap and Claw, but they were young things, and couldn't be trusted much in a close brush with a b'ar. Old Clinch was dead, or he'd ha' made other guess-work with the varmint. But, hot after the b'ar, I didn't think of the quality of the dogs til I found myself in a fair wrestle with the brute. I don't brag, my friends, but that *was* a fight. I tell you my breath was clean gone, for the b'ar had me about the thin of my body, and I thought I was doubled up enough to be laid down without more handling. But my heart was strong when I thought of Betsy and the children, and I got my knife, with hard *jugging* —though I couldn't use my arm above my elbow—through the old critter's hide, and in among her ribs. That only seemed to make her hug closer, and I reckon I was clean gone, if it hadn't been that she blowed out before me. I had worked a pretty deep window in her waist, and then life run out plentiful. Her nose dropped agin my breast, and then her paws; and when the strain was gone, I fell down like a sick child, and she fell on top of me. But she warn't in a humour to do more mischief. She roughed me once or twice more with her paws, but that was only because she was at her last kick. There I lay a matter of half an hour, with the dead b'ar alongside o' me. I was almost as little able to move as she, and I vomited as if I had taken physic. When I come to myself and got up, there was no sound of the hunters. There I was with the two dogs and the b'ar, all alone, and the sun already long past the turn. My horse, which I had fastened outside of the thicket, had slipped his bridle, and, I reckoned, had either strayed off grazing, or had pushed back directly for the block. These things didn't make me feel much better. But, though my stomach didn't feel altogether right, and my ribs were as sore as if I had been sweating under a coating of hickory, I felt that there was no use and no time to stand there grunting. But I made out to skin and to cut up the b'ar, and a noble mountain of fat she made. I took the skin with me, and, covering the flesh with bark, I whistled off the dogs, after they had eat to fill, and pushed after my horse. I followed his track for some time, till I grew fairly tired. He had gone off in a scare and at a full gallop, and, instead of going home, had dashed down the lower side of the thicket, then gone aside, to round some of the hills, and thrown himself out of the track, it moutbe seven miles or more. When I found this, I saw there was no use to hunt him that day and afoot, and I had no more to do but turn about, and push as fast as I could for the block. But this was work enough. By this time the sun was pretty low, and there was now a good seven miles, work it how I could, before me. But I was getting ove my b'ar-sickness, and though my legs felt weary enough, my stomach was better, and my heart braver; and, as I was in no hurry, having the whole night before me, and knowing the way by night as well as by light, I began to feel cheerful enough, all things considering. I pushed on slowly, stopping every now and hen for rest, and recovering my strength this way. I had some parched meal and sugar in my pouch which I ate, and it helped me mightily. It was my only dinner that day. The evening got to be very still. I wondered I had seen and heard nothing of Jake Ransom and the rest, but I didn't feel at all oneasy about them, thinking that, like all other hunters, they would naterally follow the game to any distance. But, jest when I was thinking about them, I heard a gun, then another, and after that all got to be as quiet as ever. I looked to my own rifle and felt for my knife, and put forward a little more briskly. I suppose I had walked an hour after this, when it came on close dark, and I was still four good miles from the block. The night was cloudy there were no stars, and the feeling in the air was damp and on-comfortable. I began to wish I was safe home, and felt queerish, almost as bad as I did when the b'ar was 'bracing me; but it warn't so much the body-sickness as the heart-sickness. I felt as if something was going wrong. Jest as this feeling was most wor-risome, I stumbled over a human. My blood cruddled, when, feeling about, I put my hand on his head, and found the sculp was gone. Then I knew there was mischief. I couldn't make out who 'twas that was under me, but I reckoned 'twas one of the hunters. There was nothing to be done but to push for'ad. I didn't feel any more tire. I felt ready for fight, and when I thought of our wives and children in the block, and what might become of them, I got wolfish, though the Lord only knows what I was minded to do. I can't say I had any raal sensible thoughts of what was to be done in the business. I didn't trust myself to think whether the Indians had been to the block yet or no; though ugly notions came across me when I remembered how we let the women and children go about to the farms. I was in a complete fever and agy. I scorched one time and shivered another, but I pushed on, for there was now no more feeling of tire in my limbs than if they were made of steel. By this time I had reached

that long range of hills where I first saw that strange camp-
fire, now eleven years gone, that turned out to be a deception, and
it was nateral enough that the thing should come fresh into my
mind, jest at that moment. While I was thinking over the wonder,
and asking myself, as I had done over and often before, what it
possibly could mean, I reached the top of one of the hills, from
which I could see, in daylight, the whole country for a matter of
ten miles or more on every side. What was my surprise, do you
reckon, when there, jest on the very same hill opposite where I
had seen that apparition of a camp, I saw another, and this time
it was a raal one. There was a rousing blaze, and though the
woods and undergrowth were thicker on this than on the other
side, from which I had seen it before, yet I could make out that
there were several figures, and them Indians. It sort o' made
me easier to see the enemy before, and then I could better tell
what I had to do. I was to spy out the camp, see what the red-
devils were thinking to do, and what they had already done. I
was a little better scout and hunter this time than when I made
the same sort o' search before, and I reckoned that I could get
nigh enough to see all that was going on, without stirring up any
dust among 'em. But I had to keep the dogs back. I couldn't
tie 'em up, for they'd howl; so I stripped my hunting-shirt and
put it down for one to guard, and I gave my cap and horn
to another. I knew they'd never leave 'em, for I had l'arned
'em all that sort of business—to watch as well as to fetch and
carry. I then said a sort of short running prayer, and took the
trail. I had to work for'ad slowly. If I had gone on this time
as I did in that first camp transaction, I'd ha' lost my sculp to
a sartainty. Well, to shorten a long business, I tell you that I
got nigh enough, without scare or surprise, to see all that I cared
to see, and a great deal more than I wished to see; and now, for
the first time, I saw the meaning of that sight which I had, eleven
years before, of the camp that come to nothing. I saw that first
sight over again, the Indians round the fire, a young woman in
the middle, and that young woman my own daughter, my child
my poor, dear Lucy!

CHAPTER VIII.

" THAT was a sight for a father. I can't tell you—and I won't try—how I felt. But I lay there, resting upon my hands and knees, jest as if I had been turned into stone with looking. I lay so for a good half hour, I reckon, without stirring a limb; and you could only tell that life was in me, by seeing the big drops that squeezed out of my eyes now and then, and by a sort of shivering that shook me as you sometimes see the canebrake shaking with the gust of the pond inside. I tried to pray to God for help, but I couldn't pray, and as for thinking, that was jest as impossible. But I could do nothing by looking, and, for that matter, it was pretty cla'r to me, as I stood, with no help—by myself—one rifle only and knife—I couldn't do much by moving. I could have lifted the gun, and in a twinkle. tumbled the best fellow in the gang, but what good was that guine to do me? I was never fond of blood-spilling, and if I could have been made sure of my daughter, I'd ha' been willing that the red devils should have had leave to live for ever. What was I to do? Go to the block? Who know'd if it warn't taken, with every soul in it? And where else was I to look for help? Nowhere, nowhere but to God! I groaned—I groaned so loud that I was dreadful 'feared that they'd hear me; but they were too busy among themselves, eating supper, and poor Lucy in the midst, not eating, but so pale, and looking so miserable—jest as I had seen her, when she was only a child—in the same fix, though 'twas only an appearance —eleven years ago! Well, at last, I turned off. As I couldn't say what to do, I was too miserable to look, and I went down to the bottom of the hill and rolled about on the ground, pulling the hair out of my head and groaning, as if that was to do me any good. Before I knew where I was, there was a hand on my shoulder. I jumped up to my feet, and flung my rifle over my nead, meaning to bring the butt down upon the stranger—but his voice stopped me.

" ' Brother,' said he, ' me Lenatewá !'

" The way he talked, his soft tones, made me know that the young prince meant to be friendly, and I gave him my hand ; but the tears gushed out as I did so, and I cried out like a man struck in the very heart, while I pointed to the hill—' My child, my child !'

" ' Be man !' said he, ' come !' pulling me away.

" ' But, will you save her, Lenatewá ?'

" He did not answer instantly, but led me to the little lake, and pointed to the old tree over which I had borne his lifeless body so many years ago. By that I knew he meant to tell me, he had not forgotten what I had done for him ; and would do for me all he could. But this did not satisfy me. I must know how and when it was to be done, and what was his hope ; for I could see from his caution, and leading me away from the camp, that he did not command the party, and had no power over them. He then asked me, if I had not seen the paint of the warriors in the camp. But I had seen nothing but the fix of my child. He then described the paint to me, which was his way of showing me that the party on the hill were his deadly enemies. The paint about their eyes was that of the great chief, his uncle, who had tried to murder him years ago, and who had been shot, in my sight, by the party of his father. The young chief, now in command of the band on the hill was the son of his uncle, and sworn to revenge the death of his father upon him, Lenatewá. This he made me onderstand in a few minutes. And he gave me farther to onderstand, that there was no way of getting my child from them onless by cunning. He had but two followers with him, and they were even then busy in making preparations. But of these preparations he either would not or could not give me any account ; and I had to wait on him with all the patience I could muster ; and no easy trial it was, for an Indian is the most cool and slow-moving creature in the world, unless he's actually fighting, and then he's about the quickest. After awhile, Lenatewá led me round the hill. We fetched a pretty smart reach, and before I knew where I was, he led me into a hollow that I had never seen before. Here, to my surprise, there were no less than twelve or fourteen horses fastened, that these red devils had stolen from the settlement that very day, and mine was among them. I did not know it till the young prince told me.

"'Him soon move,' said he, pointing to one on the outside. which a close examination showed me to be my own—'Him soon move,'—and these words gave me a notion of his plan. But he did not allow me to have any hand in it—not jest then, at least. Bidding me keep a watch on the fire above, for the hollow in which we stood was at the foot of the very hill the Indians had made their camp on—though the stretch was a long one between—he pushed for'ad like a shadow, and so slily, so silently, that, though I thought myself a good deal of a scout before, I saw then that I warn't fit to hold a splinter to him. In a little time he had unhitched my horse, and quietly led him farther down the hollow, half round the hill, and then up the opposite hill. There was very little noise, the wind was from the camp, and, though they didn't show any alarm, I was never more scary in my life. I followed Lenatewá, and found where he had fastened my nag. He had placed him several hundred yards from the Indians, on his way to the block ; and, where we now stood, owing to the bend of the hollow, the camp of the Indians was between us and where they had hitched the stolen horses. When I saw this, I began to guess something of his plan. Meantime, one after the other, his two followers came up, and made a long report to him in their own language. This done, he told me that three of my hunting companions had been sculped, the other, who was Hugh Darling, had got off cl'ar, though fired upon twice, and had alarmed the block, and that my daughter had been made prisoner at the farm to which she had gone without any company. This made me a little easier, and Lenatewá then told me what he meant to do. In course, I had to do something myself towards it. Off he went with his two men, leaving me to myself. When I thought they had got pretty fairly round the hill, I started back for the camp, trying my best, you may be sure, to move as slily as Lenatewá. I got within twenty-five yards, I reckon, when I thought it better to lie by quietly and wait. I could see every head in the huddle, and my poor child among them, looking whiter than a sheet, beside their ugly painted skins. Well, I hadn't long to wait, when there was such an uproar among the stolen horses in the hollow on the opposite side of the hill—such a trampling, such a whinnying and whickering, you never heard the like. Now, you must know, that a stolen horse, to an Indian, is jest as precious as a sweet-heart to a white man ; and when the rumpus reached the camp, there was a rush of every man among them, for his critter. Every redskin, but one, went over the hill after the horses, and he jumped up with the rest, but didn't move off. He stood over poor Lucy with his tomahawk, shaking it above her head, as if guine to strike every minute. She, poor child—I could see her as plain as the fire-light, for she sat jest on one side of it—her hands were clasped together. She was praying, for she must have looked every minute to be knocked on the head. You may depend, I found it very hard to keep in. I was a'most biling over, the more when I saw the red devil making his flourishes, every now and then, close to the child's ears, with his bloody we'pon. But it was a needcessity to keep in till the sounds died off pretty much, so as not to give them any scare this side, till they had dashed ahead pretty far 'pon the other. I don't know that I waited quite as long as I ought to, but I waited as long as my feelings would let me, and then I dropped the sight of my rifle as close as I could fix it on the breast of the Indian that had the keeping of my child. I took aim, but I felt I was a little tremorsome, and I stopped. I know'd I had but one shoot, and if I didn't onbutton him in that one, it would be a bad shoot for poor Lucy. I didn't fear to hit *her*, and I was pretty sure I'd hit him. But it must be a dead shot to do good, for I know'd if I only hurt him, that he'd sink the tomahawk in her head with what strength he had left him. I brought myself to it again, and this time I felt strong. I could jest hear a little of the hubbub of men and horses afar off. I knew it was the time, and, resting the side of the muzzle against a tree, I give him the whole blessing of the bullet. I didn't stop to ask what luck, but run in, with a sort o' cry, to do the finishing with the knife. But the thing was done a'ready. The beast was on his back, and I only had to use the knife in cutting the vines that fastened the child to the sapling behind her. The brave gal didn't scream or faint. She could only say, ' Oh, my father !' and I could only say, ' Oh ! my child !' And what a precious hug followed ; but it was only for a minute. We had no time to waste in hugging. We pushed at once for the place where I had left the critter, and if the good old nag ever used his four shanks to any purpose, he did that night. I reckon it was a joyful surprise to poor Betsy when we broke into the block. She had given it out for sartin that she'd never see me or the child again, with a nateral sculp cn our heads.

6

CHAPTER IX.

" THERE's no need to tell you the whole story of this war be·
tween our people and the redskins. It's enough that I tell you
of what happened to us, and our share in it. Of the great affair,
and all the fights and burnings, you'll find enough in the printed
books and newspapers. What I tell you, though you can't find it
in any books, is jest as true, for all that. Of our share in it, the
worst has already been told you. The young chief, Oloschottee
—for that was his name—the cousin and the enemy of Lenatewá,
had command of the Indians that were to surprise our settlements;
and though he didn't altogether do what he expected and intended,
he worked us quite enough of mischief as it was. He soon put
fire to all our farms to draw us out of the block, but finding that
wouldn't do, he left us; for an Indian gets pretty soon tired of a
long siege where there is neither rum nor blood to git drunk on.
His force was too small to trouble us in the block, and so he
drawed off his warriors, and we saw no more of him until the
peace. That followed pretty soon after General Middleton gave
the nation that licking at Echotee,—a licking, I reckon, that they'll
remember long after my day. At that affair Lenatewá got an
ugly bullet in his throat, and if it hadn't been for one of his men,
he'd ha' got a bag'net in his breast. They made a narrow run
with him, head foremost down the hill, with a whole swad of the
mounted men from the low country at their heels. It was some
time after the peace before he got better of his hurt, though the
Indians are naterally more skilful in cures than white men. By
this time we had all gone home to our farms, and had planted and
rebuilt, and begun to forget our troubles, when who should pop
into our cabin one day, but Lenatewá. He had got quite well
of his hurts. He was a monstrous fine-looking fellow, tall and
handsome, and he was dressed in his very best. He wore pantaloons, like one of us, and his hunting shirt was a raally fine blue,
with a white fringe. He wore no paint, and was quite nice and

neat with his person. We all received him as an old friend, and he stayed with us three days. Then he went, and was gone for a matter of two weeks, when he came back and stayed with us another three days. And so, off and on, he came to visit us, until Betsy said to me one day, 'Daniel, that Indian, Lenatewa, comes here after Lucy. Leave a woman to guess these things.' After she told me, I recollected that the young prince was quite watchful of Lucy, and would follow her out into the garden, and leave us, to walk with her. But then, again, I thought—'What if he is favourable to my daughter? The fellow's a good fellow; and a raal, noble-hearted Indian, that's sober, is jest as good, to my thinking, as any white man in the land.' But Betsy wouldn't hear to it. 'Her daughter never should marry a savage, and a heathen, and a redskin, while her head was hot:'—and while her head was so hot, what was I to do? All I could say was this only, 'Don't kick, Betsy, till you're spurred. 'Twill be time enough to give the young Chief his answer when he asks the question; and it won't do for us to treat him rudely, when we consider how much we owe him.' But she was of the mind that the boot was on the other leg,—that it was he and not us that owed the debt; and all that I could do couldn't keep her from showing the lad a sour face of it whenever he came. But he didn't seem much to mind this, since I was civil and kind to him. Lucy too, though her mother warned her against him, always treated him civilly as I told her; though she naterally would do so, for she couldn't so easily forget that dreadful night when she was a prisoner in the camp of the enemy, not knowing what to expect, with an Indian tomahawk over her head, and saved, in great part, by the cunning and courage of this same Lenatewá. The girl treated him kindly, and I was not sorry she did so. She walked and talked with him jest as if they had been brother and sister, and he was jest as polite to her as if he had been a born Frenchman.

"You may be sure, it was no pleasant sight to my wife to see them two go out to walk. 'Daniel Nelson,' said she, 'do you see and keep an eye on those people. There's no knowing what may happen. I do believe that Lucy has a liking for that redskin, and should they run!'—'Psho!' said I,—but that wouldn't do for

her, and so she made me watch the young people sure e.10ugh.
'Twarn't a business that I was overfond of, you may reckon, but
I was a rough man and didn't know much of woman natur'. I left
the judgment of such things to my wife, and did pretty much what
she told me. Whenever they went out to walk, I followed them,
rifle in hand; but it was only to please Betsy, for if I had seen
the lad running off with the girl, I'm pretty sure, I'd never ha'
been the man to draw trigger upon him. As I said before, Lenatewá was jest as good a husband as she could have had. But,
poor fellow, the affair was never to come to that. One day, after he had been with us almost a week, he spoke softly to Lucy,
and she got up, got her bonnet and went out with him. I didn't
see them when they started, for I happened to be in the upper
story,—a place where we didn't so much live, but where we used
to go for shelter and defence whenever any Indians came about
us. 'Daniel,' said my wife, and I knew by the quickness and
sharpness of her voice what 'twas she had to tell me. But jest
then I was busy, and, moreover, I didn't altogether like the sort
of business upon which she wanted me to go. The sneaking afte
an enimy, in raal warfare, is an onpleasant sort of thing enough
but this sneaking after one that you think your friend is worse than
running in a fair fight, and always gave me a sheepish feeling
after it. Besides, I didn't fear Lenatewá, and I didn't fear my
daughter. It's true, the girl treated him kindly and sweetly, but
that was owing to the nateral sweetness of her temper, and because she felt how much sarvice he had been to her and all of
us. So. instead of going out after them, I thought I'd give them
a look through one of the loop-holes. Well, there they went,
walking among the trees, not far from the picket, and no time out
of sight. As I looked at them, I thought to myself, 'Would n't
they make a handsome couple!' Both of them were tall and well
made. As for Lucy, there wasn't, for figure, a finer set girl in
all the settlement, and her face was a match for her figure. And
then she was so easy in her motion, so graceful, and walked, or
sate, or danced,—jest, for all the world, as if she was born only
to do the particular thing she was doing. As for Lenatewá, he
was a lad among a thousand. Now, a young Indian warrior,
when he don't drink, is about the noblest-looking creature, as he

carries himself in he woods, that God ever did make. So straight.
so proud, so stately, always as if he was doing a great action—
as if he knew the whole world was looking at him. Lenatewa
was pretty much the handsomest and noblest Indian I had ever
seen ; and then, I know'd him to be raally so noble. As they
walked together, their heads a little bent downwards, and Lucy's
pretty low, the thought flashed across me that, jest then, he was
telling her all about his feelings ; and perhaps, said I to myself,
the girl thinks about it pretty much as I do. Moutbe now, she
likes him better than any body she has ever seen, and what more
naateral ? Then I thought, if there is any picture in this life more
sweet and beautiful than two young people jest beginning to feel
love for one another, and walking together in the innocence of
their hearts, under the shady trees,—I've never seen it ! I laid
the rifle on my lap, and sat down on the floor and watched 'em
through the loop until I felt the water in my eyes. They walked
backwards and for'ads, not a hundred yards off, and I could see
all their motions, though I couldn't hear their words. An Indian
don't use his hands much generally, but I could see that Lenatewá was using his,—not a great deal, but as if he felt every
word he was saying. Then I began to think, what was I to do,
if so be he was raally offering to marry Lucy, and she willing !
How was I to do ? what was I to say ?—how could I refuse him
when I was willing ? how could I say ' yes,' when Betsy said
' no !'

"Well, in the midst of this thinking, what should I hear but a
loud cry from the child, then a loud yell,—a regular war-whoop,
—sounded right in front, as if it came from Lenatewá himself.
I looked up quickly, for, in thinking, I had lost sight of them, and
was only looking at my rifle ; I looked out, and there, in the
twinkle of an eye, there was another sight. I saw my daughter
flat upon the ground, lying like one dead, and Lenatewá staggering back as if he was mortally hurt ; while, pressing fast upon
him, was an Indian warrior, with his tomahawk uplifted, and striking—once, twice, three times—hard and heavy, right upon the
face and forehead of the young prince. From the black paint on
his face, and the red ring about his eyes, and from his figure and
the eagle feathers in his head, I soon guessed it was Oloschottee,

and I then knew it was the old revenge for the killing of his father ; for an Indian never forgets that sort of obligation. Of
course, I didn't stand quiet to see an old friend, like Lenatewá,
tumbled in that way, without warning, like a bullock ; and there
was my own daughter lying flat, and I wasn't to know that he
hadn't struck her too. It was only one motion for me to draw
sight upon the savage, and another to pull trigger ; and I reckon
he dropped jest as soon as the young Chief. I gave one whoop
for all the world as if I was an Indian myself, and run out to the
spot ; but Lenatewá had got his discharge from further service.
He warn't exactly dead, but his sense was swimming. He
couldn't say much, and that warn't at all to the purpose. I
could hear him, now and then, making a sort of singing noise,
but that was soon swallowed up in a gurgle and a gasp, and it
was all over. My bullet was quicker in its working than Oloschottee's hatchet ; he was stone dead before I got to him. As for
poor Lucy, she was not hurt, either by bullet or hatchet ; but
she had a hurt in the heart, whether from the scare she had, or
because she had more feeling for the young prince than we reckoned, there's no telling. She warn't much given to smiling after
that. But, whether she loved Lenatewá, we couldn't know, and
I never was the man to ask her. It's sartain she never married,
and she had about as many chances, and good ones, too, as any
girl in our settlement. You've seen her—some among you—
and warn't she a beauty—though I say it myself—the very
flower of the forest !"

THE LAST WAGER,

OR THE GAMESTER OF THE MISSISSIPPI

———" I have set my life upon a cast,
And I will stand the hazard of the die."
SHAKSPEARE.

CHAPTER I.

OUR story will be found to illustrate one of the current commonplaces of the day. Ever since my Lord Byron, in that poem of excellently expressed commonplaces, Don Juan, declared that "truth was stranger than fiction," every newspaper witling rings the changes upon the theme, unfll there is no relief to its dull-toned dissonance. That truth should frequently be found to be much stranger than any fiction, is neither so strange nor out of the course of things ; but is just in accordance, if we bestow any thought upon the matter, with the deliberate convictions of every reasoning mind. For, what is fiction, but the nice adaptation, by an artist, of certain ordinary occurrences in life, to a natural and probable conclusion ? It is not the policy of a good artist to deal much in the merely extravagant. His real success, and the true secret of it, is to be found in the *naturalness* of his story, its general seemliness, and the close resemblance of its events to those which may or must take place in all instances of individuals subjected to like influences with those who figure in his narrative. The naturalness must be that of life as it is, or with life as it is shown in such picturesque situations as are probable—seemingly real—and such as harmonize equally with the laws of nature, and such as the artist has chosen for his guide. Except in stories of broad extravagance—ghost stories for example --in which the one purpose of the romancer—that of exciting wonder—is declared at the outset—except in such stories, or in others of the broad grin—such as are common and extravagant enough among the frontier *raconteurs* of the West, it were the very worst policy in the world for a writer of fiction to deal much in the marvellous. He would soon wear out the patience of the reader, who would turn away, with a dissatisfaction almost amounting to disgust, from any author who should be found too frequently to employ what is merely possible in human progress. We require as close reasoning, and deductions as logically drawn, in tale and novel, as in a case at law or in equity ; much more close, indeed, than is often found to be the case in a Congressional harangue, and a far more tenacious regard to the *interest* of the reader than is shown in the report of a modern secretary. Probability, unstrained, must be made apparent at every step ; and if the merely possible be used at all, it must be so used only, as, in looking like the probable, it is made to lose all its ambiguous characteristics. What we show must not only be the truth, but it must also seem like the truth ; for, as the skill of the artist can sometimes enable him to make what is false appear true, so it is equally the case that a want of skill may transmute the most unquestionable truth into something that nine persons in ten shall say, when they behold it, " it looks monstrous like a lie !"

That we are not at liberty to use too freely what is merely possible in the material brought before us, is a fact more particularly known to painters, who have often felt the danger of any attempt to paint the sky as it sometimes appears to them. They dread to offend the suspicious incredulity of the cold and unobserving citizen. They see, with equal amazement and delight—but without daring to delineate—those intenser hues and exquisite gradations of light and shadow, those elaborate and graceful shapes of cloud, born of the rainbow—carnation, green and purple, which the sun sometimes, in fantastic mood, and as if in equal mockery of human faith and art, makes upon the lovely background of the sky which he leaves at setting. The beautiful vision gone from sight, who would believe the poor artist, whatever his accuracy and felicity of touch and taste, who had endeavoured to transfer, before it faded, the vanishing glory to his canvass ? Who could suppose,

and how admit, that there had ever been such a panorama, of
such super-artistical splendour, displayed before his eyes, without
commanding his admiration and fixing his attention?　The very
attempt to impose such an exhibition upon him as natural, would
be something of a sarcasm, and a commentary upon the dull eye
and drowsy mind which had failed to discern it for themselves.
Nay, though the artist grappled the dull citizen by the arm at the
very instant, and compelled his gaze upon the glorious vision ere it
melted into the thin gray haze of evening, would he not be apt to
say, "How strange! how very unnatural!"　Certainly, it would
be a nature and a truth infinitely more strange than the most
audacious fiction that ever grew up at the touch of the most fantastic votary of art.

CHAPTER II.

THE sketch which I propose will scarcely justify this long digression; and its character will be still less likely to correspond with the somewhat poetic texture of the introduction. It is simply a strange narrative of frontier life; one of those narratives in which a fact will appear very doubtful, unless the artist shall exhibit such sufficient skill in his elaborations, as to keep its rude points from offending too greatly the suspicious judgment of the reader. This is the task before me. The circumstances were picked up, when, a lad of eighteen, I first wandered over the then dreary and dangerous wastes of the Mississippi border. Noble, indeed, though wild and savage, was the aspect of that green forest country, as yet only slightly smitten by the sharp edges of the ranger's axe I travelled along the great Yazoo wilderness, in frequent proximity with the Choctaw warriors. Most frequently I rode alone. Sometimes, a wayfarer from the East, solitary with myself, turned his horse's head, for a few days' space, on the same track with mine; but, in most cases, my only companion was some sullen Choctaw, or some still more sullen half-breed, who, emerging sud denly from some little foot-path, would leave me half in doubt whether his introduction would be made first with the tomahawk or the tongue. Very few white men were then settled in the country; still fewer were stationary. I rode forty and fifty miles without sign of human habitation, and found my bed and supper at night most generally in the cabin of the half-breed. But there was one, and that a remarkable exception to this universal necessity; and in this exception my story takes its rise. I had at length reached the borders of the nation, and the turbid waters of the Mississippi, at no great distance, flowed down towards the Gulf. The appearances of the white settler, some doubtful glimmerings of a more civilized region, were beginning to display themselves. Evening was at hand. The sun was fast waning along the mellow heights of heaven; and my heart was begin ning to sink with the natural sense of loneliness which such a setting is apt to inspire in the bosom of the youthful wanderer. It was also a question with me, where I should find my pillow for the night. My host of the night before, a low, dark-looking white squatter, either was, or professed to be, too ignorant to give me any information on this head, which would render the matter one of reasonable certainty. In this doubtful and somewhat desolate state of mind, I began to prick my steed forward at a more rapid pace, to cast my eyes up more frequently to the fading light among the tree-tops, and, occasionally, to send a furtive glance on either hand, not altogether assured that my road was as safe as it was lonely. The question "where shall I find my bed to-night?" was beginning to be one of serious uncertainty, when I suddenly caught a glimpse of an opening on my right, a sort of wagon-path, avenue like, and which reminded me of those dear, dim passages in my own Carolina, which always promised the traveller a hot supper and happy conclusion to his wanderings of the day. Warmed with the notion, and without a farther doubt or thought, I wheeled my sorrel into the passage, and pressed him forward with a keener spur. A cheery blast of the horn ahead, and the dull heavy stroke of an axe immediately after, were so many urgent entreaties to proceed ; and now the bellow of a cow, and next the smoke above the cottage roof-trees, assured me that my apprehensions were at an end. In a few seconds I stood before one of the snuggest little habitations which ever kindled hope and satisfied hunger.

This was one of those small log-cabins which are common to the country. Beyond its snug, trim and tidy appearance, there was nothing about it to distinguish it from its class. The clearing was small, just sufficient, perhaps, for a full supply of corn and provisions. But the area in front of the dwelling was cleanly swept, and the trees were trimmed, and those which had been left were evergreens, and so like favourite domestics, with such an air of grace, and good-nature, and venerableness about them, that one's heart warmed to see them, as at sight of one of " the old familiar faces." The aspect of the dwelling within consisted happily with that without. Every thing was so neat, and snug, and comfortable

The windows were sashed and glassed, and hung with the whitest curtains of cotton, with fringes fully a foot deep. The floors were neatly sanded, the hearth was freshly brightened with the red ochrous clay of the country, and chairs and tables, though made of the plainest stuffs, and by a very rude mechanic, were yet so clean, neat and well-arranged, that the eye involuntarily surveyed them again and again with a very pleased sensation. Nor was this all in the shape of unwonted comforts. Some other matters were considered in this cottage, which are scarcely even dreamed of in the great majority. In one corner of the hall stood a hat-stand; in another there were pins for cloaks; above the fire-place hung a formidable rifle, suspended upon tenter-hooks made of three monstrous antlers, probably those of gigantic bucks which had fallen beneath the weapon which they were now made to sustain. Directly under this instrument, and the only object beside which had been honoured with a place so conspicuous, *was a pack of ordinary playing cards*—not hung or suspended against the wall, *but nailed to it ;*—driven through and through with a tenpenny nail, and so fastened to the solid log, the black head of the nail showing with particular prominence in contrast with the red spot of the ace of hearts, through which it had been driven. Of this hereafter. On this pack of cards hangs my story. It is enough, in this place, to add, that it was only after supper was fairly over, that my eyes were drawn to this very unusual sort of chimney decoration.

At the door of the cottage sat a very venerable old man between seventy and eighty. His hair was all white, but still thick, betraying the strength of his constitution and the excellence of his health. His skin was florid, glowing through his white beard, which might have been three days old, and his face bore the burden of very few wrinkles. He had a lively, clear blue eye, and good-humour played about his mouth in every movement of his lips. He was evidently one of those fortunate men, whose winters, if frosty, had always proved kindly. A strong man in his youth, he was now but little bent with years; and when he stood up, I was quite ashamed to find he was rather more erect than myself, and quite as tall. This was the patriarch of the family, which consisted of three members besides himself. The first of these was his only son, a man thirty-eight or forty years of age, of whom it will be quite explicit enough to say, that the old man, in his youth, must very nearly have resembled him. Then, there was the wife of the son, and her son, a lad now ten years old, a smart-looking lad enough, but in no wise resembling his male parent. Instead of the lively, twinkling blue eye of his father, he had the dark, deep, oriental sad ones of the mother; and his cheeks were rather pale than rosy, rather thin than full; and his hair was long, black and silky, in all respects the counterpart of his mother's. A brief description of this lady may assist us in our effort to awaken the interest of the reader.

Conducted into the house by the son, and warmly welcomed by the old man as well as himself, I was about to advance with the bold dashing self-possession of a young cavalier, confident in his course, and accustomed to win " golden opinions of all sorts of people." But my bold carriage and sanguine temper were suddenly checked, not chilled, by the appearance of the lady in front of whom I suddenly stood. She sat beside the fireplace, and was so very different a looking person from any I had expected to see in such a region, that the usual audacity of my temperament was all at once abashed. In place of the good, cheerful, buxom, plain country housewife whom I looked to see, mending Jacky's breeches, or knitting the good-man's hose, I found myself confronted by a dame whose aristocratic, high-bred, highly composed, easy and placid demeanour, utterly confounded me. Her person was small, her complexion darkly oriental, her eye flashing with all the spiritual fires of that region; habitually bright and searching, even while the expression of her features would have made her seem utterly emotionless. Never did features, indeed, appear so thoroughly inflexible. Her beauty,—for she was all beauty,—was not, however, the result of any regularity of feature. Beauties of her order, brunette and piquant, are most usually wanting in preciseness, and mutual dependance and sympathy of outline. They are beautiful in spite of irregularity, and in consequence of the paramount exquisiteness of some particular feature. The charm of the face before me grew out of the piercing, deep-set, and singularly black eye, and the wonderful vitality about the lips. Never was mouth so small, or so admirably delineated. There was witchcraft enough in the web of it to make my own lips **water**. But I speak like the boy I was then, and am no longer.

Let me not be understood to mean that there was any levity, any lightness of character betrayed in the expression of those lips. Very far otherwise. While soft, sweet, beautiful, and full of life, they were the most sacred and sad-looking forms,—drooping blossoms of beauty, mourning, as it would seem, because beauty does not imply immortality; and this expression led me to observe more closely the character of the eye, the glance of which, at first, had only seemed to denote the brilliance of the diamond, shining through an atmosphere of jet. I now discerned that its intense blaze was not its only character. It was marked with the weight of tears, that, freezing as they had birth, maintained their place in defiance of the light to which they were constantly exposed. It was the brightness of the ice palace, in the Northern Saga, which, in reflecting the bright glances of Balder, the God of Day, still gives defiance to the fervour of his beams.

But a truce to these frigid comparisons, which suit any age but ours. Enough to say that the lady was of a rare and singular beauty, with a character of face and feature not common to our country, and with a deportment seldom found in the homely cabin of the woodman or the squatter. The deep and unequivocal sadness which marked her looks, intense as it was, did not affect or impair the heightened aristocratic dignity of her subdued and perfectly assured manner. To this manner did she seem to have been born; and, being habitual, it is easy to understand that she could not be divested of it, except in a very small degree, by the pressure of any form of affliction. You could see that there had been affliction, but its effect was simply to confirm that elevated social tone, familiar to all mental superiority, which seems, however it may feel, to regard the confession of its griefs as perhaps something too merely human to be altogether becoming in a confessedly superior caste. Whether the stream was only frozen over, or most effectually crystallized, it does not suit our purpose to inquire. It is, at all events, beyond my present ability to determine the doubt.

She was introduced to me, by the husband, as Mrs. Rayner. I afterwards discovered that her Christian name was Rachel a circumstance that tended to strengthen the impression in my mind that she might be of Jewish parents. That she was a Christian herself, I had reason to believe, from her joining freely and devoutly, and on bended knee, in the devotions of the night. She spoke seldom, yet looked intelligence throughout the conversation. which was carried on freely between the old man, the husband. and myself. When she spoke, her words and accents were marked by the most singular propriety. There was nothing in her utterance to lessen the conviction that she was familiar with the most select circles of city life ; and I could see that the husband listened to her with a marked deference, and, though himself, evidently, a rough honest backwoodsman, I detected him, in one or two instances, checking the rude phrase upon his lips, and substituting for it some other, more natural to the ear of civilization and society. There was a touching something in the meekness and quiet deportment of the boy who sat by his mother's knee in silence, her fingers turning in his hair, while he diligently pored over some little trophy of juvenile literature, looking up timidly at moments, and smiling sadly, when he met the deep earnest gaze of the mother's eyes, as she seemed to forget all around in the glance at the one object. I need not say that there was something in this family picture so entirely out of the common run of my woodland experience in the Southwest, at that early day, that I felt my curiosity equally excited with my pleasure. I felt assured that there was something of a story to be learned, which would amply recompense the listener. The old patriarch was himself a study—the husband a very noble specimen of the sturdy, frank, elastic frontier-man—a race too often confounded with the miserable runagates by whom the first explorations of the country are begun, but who seldom make the real axe-marks of the wilderness. You could see at a glance that he was just the man whom a friend could rely upon and a foe most fear—frank, ardent, firm, resolute in endurance, patient, perhaps, and slow to anger, as are all noble-minded persons who have a just confidence in their own strength ; but unyielding when the field is to be fought, and as cheerful in the moment of danger as he was good-humoured in that of peace. Every thing in his look, language and bearing, answered to this description ; and I sat down at the supper table beside him that night, as familiar and as much at my ease as if we had jumped together from the first moment of existence.

I pass over much of the conversation preceding, and at the evening repast ; for, though interesting enough at the time, particularly to me, it would only delay us still longer in the approach to our story. It was after the table had been withdrawn, when he family were all snugly huddled about the fireplace, and the dialogue, which had been rather brisk before, had begun to flag, that I casually looked up over the chimney-place, and discovered, for the first time, the singular ornament of which I have already spoken. Doubtful of what I saw, I rose to my feet, and grasped the object with my fingers. I fancied that some eccentric forest genius, choosing for his subject one of the great agents of popular pastime in the West, might have succeeded in a delineation sufficiently felicitous, as, at a short distance, to baffle any vision. But, palpable, the real—I had almost said, the living—things were there, unlike the dagger of Macbeth, as " sensible to feeling as to sight." A complete pack of cards, none of the cleanest, driven through with a tenpenny nail, the ace of hearts, as before said, being the top card, and very fairly covering the retinue of its own and the three rival houses. The corners of the cards were curled, and the ends smoked to partial blackness. They had evidently been in that situation for several years. I turned inquiringly to my hosts—

" You have a very singular ornament for your mantleplace, Mr. Rayner ;" was my natural remark, the expression of curiosity in my face being coupled with an apologetic sort of smile. But it met with no answering smiles from any of the family. On the contrary, every face was grave to sadness, and in a moment more Mrs. Rayner rose and left the room. As soon as she was gone, her husband remarked as follows:

" Why, yes, sir, it is uncommon; but there's a reason why it's there, which I'll explain to you after we've gone through prayers."

By this time the wife had returned, bringing with her the family Bible, which she now laid upon a stand beside the venerable elder. He, good old man, with an action that seemed to be perfectly habitual, drew forth the spectacles from the sacred pages, where they seemed to have been left from the previous evening, and commenced reading the third chapter of Ecclesiastes, begin- ning, "Hear me, your father, O children! and do thereafter, that ye may be safe." Then, this being read, we all sunk devoutly upon our knees, and the patriarch put up as sweet and fervent a prayer as I should ever wish to listen to. The conceited whip- ster of the school might have found his pronunciation vulgar, and his sentences sometimes deficient in grammatical nicety; but the *thought* was there, and the *heart*, and the ears of perfect wisdom might well be satisfied with the good sense and the true morality of all that was spoken. We rose refreshed, and, after a lapse of a very few moments which were passed in silence, the wife, lead- ing the little boy by the hand, with a kind nod and courtesy took her leave, and retired to her chamber. Sweetness and dignity were most happily blended in her parting movements; but I fancied, as I caught the glance of her eye, that there had been a fresh- ening and overflowing there of the deep and still gathering foun- tains. Her departure was followed by that of the old man, and the husband and myself were left alone. It was not long after this, before he, himself, without waiting for any suggestion of mine, brought up the subject of the cards, which had been so conspicu- ously elevated into a mantel ornament.

7

CHAPTER III.

"STRANGER," said he, "there is a sort of history in those cards which I am always happy to tell to any young man that's a beginner in the world like yourself. I consider them as a sort of Bible, for, when I look at them and remember all that I know concerning them, I feel as if I was listening to some prime sermon, or may be, hearing just such a chapter as the old man read to us out of the good book to-night. It's quite a long history, and I'll put on a fresh handful of lightwood before I begin."

The interruption was brief, and soon overcome, and the narrative of the husband ran as follows:

"It is now," said he, "going on to twelve years since the circumstances took place which belong to the story of those cards, and I will have to carry you back to that time before you can have a right knowledge of what I want to tell. I was then pretty much such a looking person as you now see me, for I haven't undergone much change. I was a little sprightlier, perhaps—always famous for light-headedness and laughing—fond of fun and frolic, but never doing any thing out of mischief and bad humour. The old man, my father, too, was pretty much the same. We lived here where you find us now, but not quite so snugly off—not so well settled—rather poor, I may say, though still with a plentiful supply to live on and keep warm and feel lively. There was only us two, and we had but two workers, a man and woman, and they had two children, who could do nothing for us and precious little for themselves. But we were snug, and worked steadily, and were comfortable. We didn't make much money, but we always spent less than we made. We didn't have very nice food, but we had no physic to take, and no doctor's bills to pay. We had a great deal to make us happy, and still more to be thankful for; and I trust in God we were thankful for all of his blessings. I think we were, for he gave us other blessings and for these, stranger, we are trying to be thankful also,

" Well, as I was saying, about twelve years ago, one hot day in August, I rode out a little piece towards the river bluff to see if any goods had been left for us at the landing. We had heard the steamboat gun the night before, or something like it, and that, you know, is the signal to tell us when to look after our *plunder*. When I got there I found a lot of things, some for us, and some for other people. There was a bag of coffee, a keg of sugar, hree sacks of salt, and a box of odds and ends for us. But the chaps on board the steamboat—which was gone—had thrown down the stuff any where, and some of the salt was half melted in a puddle of water. I turned in, and hauled it out of the water, and piled it up in a dry place. What was wet belonged chiefly to our neighbours, and the whole of it might have been lost if I had not got there in season. This kept me a good hour and as I had no help, and some of the sacks were large and heavy, I was pretty nigh tired out when the work was done. So took a rest of half an hour more in the shade. The heat was powerful, and I had pretty nigh been caught by sleep—I don' know but I did sleep, for in midsummer one's not always sure of himself in a drowsy moment—when I was suddenly roused up by a noise most like the halloo of a person in distress. I took the saddle on the spur, and went off in the quarter that the sound came from. It so happened that my route homeward lay the same way, and on the river road, the only public road in the settlement ; and I had only gone two hundred yards or thereabout, when, in turning an elbow of the path, I came plump upon a stranger, who happened to be the person whom I heard calling. He was most certainly in distress. His horse was flat upon his side, groaning powerfully, and the man was on his knees, rubbing the creature's legs with a pretty hard hand. A little way behind him lay a dead rattlesnake, one of the largest I ever did see, counting twenty-one rattles besides the button ; and the sight of the snake told me the whole story. I jumped down to see what I could do in the way of help, but I soon discovered that the nag had the spasms, and was swelled up to her loins. I however cut into her leg with my knife, just where she was bitten, and when I had dug out the poisoned flesh, as much as I thought was reasonable, I got on my horse and rode back to the salt bags at full speed, and brought away a double handful of the salt. I rubbed it into the animal's wound, I really believe, a few minutes after she had groaned her last and stiffened out, but I wasn't rubbing very long. She was about the soonest killed of any creature that I ever saw snakebit before.

It was only after I was done with the mare, that I got a fair look at her owner. He was a small and rather oldish man, with a great stoop of the shoulders, with a thin face, glossy black hair, and eyes black too, but shining as bright, I reckon, as those of the rattlesnake he had killed. They had a most strange and troublesome brightness, that made me look at them whether I would or not. His face was very pale, and the wrinkles were deep, like so many seams, and, as I have said, he was what I would call a rather oldish man ; but still he was very nicely dressed, and wore a span-new velvet vest, a real English broad-cloth coat, gold watch with gold seals ; and every now and then he pulled out a snuff-box made like a horn, with a curl at the end of it, which was also set with a gold rim, and had a cap of the same precious stuff upon it. He was taking snuff every moment while I was doctoring his mare, and when the creature went dead, he offered it to me ; but I had always thought it work enough to feed my mouth, and had no notion of making another mouth of my nose, so I refused him civilly.

" He didn't seem to be much worried by the death of his creature, and when I told him how sorry I was on his account, he answered quickly,

" ' Oh ! no matter ; you have a good horse ; you will let me have him ; you look like a good fellow.'

" I was a little surprised, you may reckon. I looked at the old man, and then at my creature. He *was* a good creature ; and as prime an animal as ever stepped in traces ; good at any thing, plough, wagon, or saddle ; as easy-going as a girl of sixteen, and not half so skittish. I had no notion of giving him up to a stranger, you may be sure, and didn't half like the cool, easy, impudent manner with which the old man spoke to me. I had no fears—I didn't think of his taking my nag from me by force— but, of a sudden, I almost begun to think he might be a wizard, as we read in Scripture, and hear of from the old people, or mou't be, the old devil himself, and then I did'nt well know what I had to expect. But he soon made the matter clear to me. Perhaps he saw that I was a little beflustered.

" ' Young man,' says he, ' your horse *is* a fine one. Will you sell him ? I am willing to pay you a fair price—give you his full value.'

" There was something to consider in that. When did you ever find a Western man unwilling for a horse-barter ? Besides, though the creature was a really first-rate nag, he was one more than I wanted. One for the plough, and one for the saddle—as the old man didn't ride often—was enough for us; and we had three. But Rainbow—that was his name—was so sleek an animal! He could a'most do any thing that you'd tell him. I did'nt want to sell him, but I didn't want to keep a mouth too many. You know a horse that you don't want begins by gnawing through your pockets, and ends by eating off his own head. That's the say, at least. But I raised Rainbow, fed him with my own hands, curried him night and morning myself, and looked upon him as a sort of younger brother. I hated powerful bad to part with him; but then there was no reason to keep him when he was of no use. 'Twas a satisfaction, to be sure, to have such a creature ; and 'twas a pleasure to cross him, and streak it away, at a brushing canter, of a bright morning, for a good five miles at a stretch ; but poor people can't afford such pleasures and satisfactions ; and when I thought of the new wagon that we wanted, and such a smart chance of other things about the farm, I looked at the old man and thought better of his offer. I said to him, though a little slowly,

" ' It's a famous fine horse this, stranger.

" ' I know it,' said he ; ' I never saw one that better pleased my eyes. I'll pay you a famous fine price for him.'

" ' What'll you give ?' said I.

" ' Pshaw !' said he, ' speak out like a man. I'm no baby and you are old enough to know better. What's your price ?'

" ' He's low,' said I, ' at one hundred and seventy dollars.'

" ' He is,' said he, ' he's worth more—will you take that ?'

" ' Yes.'

" ' You shall have it,' he answered, ' and I'll throw the dead
horse into the bargain; she was a famous fine animal too, in
her day, and her skin's worth stuffing as a keepsake. You can
stuff it and put it up in your stables, as an example to your other
horses.'

CHAPTER IV.

" ALL the time he was talking, he was counting out the money, which was almost all in gold. I was a little dub'ous that it wasn't good money; but I smelt it, and it had no smell of brass, and I was a leetle ashamed to let on that I didn't know good money from bad; besides, there was a something about the old gentleman so much like a gentleman, so easy, and so command-ing, that I couldn't find the heart to doubt or to dispute any thing he said. And then, every thing about him looked like a gentle-man : his clothes, his hat, the watch he wore, the very dead horse and her coverings, saddle, bridle, and so forth, all con-vinced me that there was nothing of make-believe.

" ' There,' said he, ' my good fellow,' putting the money in my hand, ' I reckon you never handled so much gold in your life be-fore.'

" ' No,' said I, ' to tell you the truth, though I've hearn a good deal of gold, and know it when I see it by what I've hearn, I never set eyes on a single piece till now.'

" ' May it do your eyes good now, then,' said he; ' you look like a good fellow. Your horse is sound ?'

" ' Yes,' said I, ' I can answer better for him than I can for your gold.'

" ' That's good.'

" ' Well !' said I, ' I'm not sure that I've dealt fairly with you, stranger. I've asked you a little more than I've been asking other people. My price on Rainbow has been only one hundred and fifty dollars, before.'

" ' And your conscience troubles you. You *are* an honest fel-low,' said he, ' but never mind, my lad, I'll show you a way to relieve it.'

" With these words he pulled out a buckskin roll from his pocket, and out of this he tumbled a pack of cards; the very cards which you see nailed above my fireplace.

" ' We'll play for that twenty dollars,' said he, throwing down two gold pieces on the body of the dead mare, and beginning to shuffle the cards immediately. Somehow, I did as he did. I put down two ten dollar pieces along with his. I couldn't help myself. He seemed to command me. I felt scared—I felt that I was doing wrong ; but he seemed to take every thing so much as a matter of course, that I hadn't the courage to say 'no' to any thing he did or said.

" ' What do you play ?' said he, and he named some twenty games of cards, some in French, I believe, and some in Spanish, but no one of which did I know any thing about. He seemed beflustered.

" ' Do you play any thing at all ?' he asked.

" ' Yes—a little of *old sledge*—that's all.'

" ' Oh ! that will do. A common game enough. I wonder I should have omitted it. Here ! you may shuffle them, and we'll cut for deal.'

" I didn't shuffle, but cut at once. He cut after me, and the deal fell to him. He took up and then put the cards down again —put his hand into his pocket, and drew out a little silver box, about the size of a small snuff-box,—that had in it a good many little pills of a dark gray gummy look. One of these he swallowed, then began to deal, his eye growing brighter every moment, and looking into mine till I felt quite dazzled and strange. Our table was the belly of the dead horse. He sat on one of the thighs. I knelt down upon the grass on the opposite side, and though it pained me, I couldn't take my eyes from him to save my life. He asked me a great many questions while he was throwing out the cards—how old I was—what was my name— what family I had—how far I lived—where I came from—every thing, indeed, about me, and my way of life, and what I had and what I knew :—and all this in no time—as fast as I tell it to you. Then he said, ' You are an honest fellow, take up your cards, and let us see if you are as lucky as you are honest.' It seemed as if I was, for I beat him. I played a pretty stiff game of *old sledge*, or as he called it, ' *all fours*,' for I used to play, as long as I could remember, with the old man, my father, every night. Old people like these plays, and it's good for them to play. It

A QUIET GAME OF OLD SLEDGE.

Page 88

keeps 'em lively, keeps them from sleeping too much, and from drinking. It's good for them, so long as it makes their own fire-side sweet to them. Well! I was lucky. I won the game, and it worried me mightily when I did so. I didn't touch the money.

"'I suppose,' said the stranger, 'that I must cover those pieces,' and before I could guess what he was about, he flung down four other gold pieces, making forty dollars, in the pile with mine, and began again shuffling the cards. If I was scared and unhappy before, I was twice as much so now. I could scarcely breathe, and why, I can't say exactly. It wasn't from any anxiety about the winning or the losing, for I preferred not to have the stranger's money: but it was his very indifference and unconcern that worried and distressed me. It seemed so unnatural, that I half the time thought that I was dealing with nothing human: and though I could shuffle, and cut, and play, yet it seemed to me as if I did it without altogether knowing why, or how. As luck would have it, I won the second time; and the third time he pulled out his purse and put down as many more pieces as lay there. I looked at the growing heap with a heart that seemed ready to burst. There was eighty dollars be-fore me, and I felt my face grow red when I caught his eye look-ing steadily at mine. I began to feel sort o' desperate, and flung about the cards like a person in liquor. The old man laughed, a low chuckle like, that made my blood crawl in my veins, half frozen, as it were. But, neither his skill and coolness, nor my fright, altered the luck at all. I again won, and trembled all over, to see the pile, and to see him take out his purse, and empty every thing upon it.

"'Stranger,' said I, 'don't think of it ; keep your money, and let me go home.'

"'Pshaw! said he, 'you're a good fellow, and as lucky as you are good. Why shouldn't you be my heir? I prefer that a good fellow should win my money if any body. It'll do your sight good.'

"'But not my heart, I'm afraid,' was my answer.

"'That's precisely as you use it,' said he; 'money's a good creature, like every other good creature that God gives us. It's a good thing to be rich, for a rich man's always able to *do* good,

when a poor man can only wish to do it.   Get money, my lad,
and be wise with it; wiser, I trust, than I have been.'

" With these words, he took out his silver box, swallowed another of the pills, and was busy dealing out the cards in another
moment. I, somehow, was better pleased with him for what he
said. The mention of God convinced me that he wasn't the
devil, and what he said seemed very sensible. But I didn't feel
any more right and happy than before. I only wanted the
strength to refuse him. I couldn't refuse him. I took up the
cards as he threw them, and it did seem to me that I scarcely
saw to make out the spots when I played them. I hardly knew
how the game was played; I didn't count; I couldn't tell what
I made. I only heard him say at the close of the second hand,

" ' The money's yours. You are a lucky fellow.'

" With these words he pushed the gold heap to me, and threw
me the empty purse.

" ' There's something to put it in.'

" ' No !' said I ; ' no, stranger—I can't take this money.'

" ' Why, pray ?'

" ' It's not right. It don't seem to me to be got honestly. I
haven't worked for it.'

" ' Worked, indeed ! If nobody used money but those who
worked for it, many a precious fellow would gnaw his finger ends
for a dinner. Put up your money !'

" I pushed it to him, all but the two eagles which I begun
with ; but he pushed it back. I got up without touching it.
' Stay,' said he, ' you *are* a good fellow ! Sit down again ; sit
down.' I sat down. ' I can't take that money,' said he, ' for it
is yours. According to my way of thinking, it is yours—it is
none of mine. There is only one way in which it may become
mine ; only one way in which I could take it or make use of it,
and that is by winning it back. That may be done. I will put
the horse against the gold.'

CHAPTER V.

My heart beat quicker than ever when he pointed to Rainbow. Not that I expected or wished to win him back, for I would only have taken him back by giving up all the money, or all except the hundred and fifty dollars; but it now seemed to me as if I looked on the old man with such feelings as would have made me consent to almost any thing he wished. I had a strange sort of pity for him. I considered him a sort of kind-hearted, rich old madman. I said, 'Very well;' and he took another pill out of his box, and begun again at the cards.

" 'You are a very fortunate fellow,' said he, 'and seem a very good one. I really see no reason why you should not be my heir. You say you are not married.'

" 'No.'

" 'But you have your sweetheart, I suppose. A lad of twenty-five, which I suppose is much about your age, is seldom without one.'

" 'It's not the case with me,' said I. 'In these parts we have mighty few folks and fewer women, and I don't know the girl among them that's ever seemed to me exactly the one that I should be willing to make my wife.'

" 'Why, you're not conceited, I hope? You don't think yourself too fine a fellow for a poor girl, do you?'

" 'No, by no means, stranger; but there's a sort of liking that one must have before he can think of a wife, and I haven't seen the woman yet to touch me in the right way.'

" 'You are hard to please, and properly. Marriage is easier found than lost. A man is too noble an animal to be kept in a mouse-trap. But there *are* women——'

" He stopped short. I waited for him to say something more, but by this time the cards had been distributed, and he was sorting his hand.

" 'There are women!' he said again, though as if he was

talking to himself. There he stopt for a minute, then looking up, and fixing his bright eyes upon mine, he continued:

" ' Come, Rayner,' said he, good-humouredly. ' The cards are in your hands, and remember to play your best, for that famous fine horse may become your own again. I warn you, I have a good hand. What do you do ?'

" ' Good or not,' said I, something more boldly, ' I will stand on mine.'

" I had a most excellent hand, being sure of high and low, with a strong leading hand for game.

" ' Play then !' he answered ; and at the word, I clapped down the ace of hearts, the very ace you see atop of the pack over the chimney now.

" ' You *are* a lucky fellow, Rayner,' said he, as he flung down the Jack upon it, the only heart he held in his hand. The game ended ; I was owner of horse and money. But I jumped to my feet instantly.

" ' Stranger,' said I, ' don't think I'm going to rob you of your horse or money. I don't exactly know why I played with you so long, unless it be because you insisted upon it, and I did'n wish to disoblige an old gentleman like yourself. Take your money, and give me my horse ; or, if you want the horse, leave me the hundred and fifty, which is a fair price for him; and put the rest in your own pocket. I wont't touch a copper more of it.'

" ' You *are* a good fellow, Rayner, but, with some persons, younger and rasher persons than myself, your words would be answered with a bullet. Nay, were I the boy I have been, it would be dangerous for you to speak, *even to me*, in such a manner. Among gentlemen, the obligation to pay up what is lost by cards is sacred. The loser *must* deliver, and the winner *must* receive. *There* is your money, and that is your horse again ; but I am not yet done with you. As I said before, you *are* a good fellow, and most certainly a lucky one. I like you, though your principles are scarcely fixed yet—not certain ! Still, I like you ; and there's some chance that you will be my heir yet. A few more trials at the cards must determine that. I suppose you are not unwilling to give me a chance to win back my losses ?'

" I caught at the suggestion.

" ' Surely not,' I replied.

" ' Very good,' says he. ' Don't suppose that, because you've emptied my purse, you've cleaned me out quite. I have a diamond ring and a diamond breastpin yet to stake. They are worth something more than your horse and your heap of money. We will place them against your eagles and horse.'

" ' No!' said I quickly. ' I'm willing to put down all the eagles, but not the horse; or I'll put down the horse and all the money, except the hundred and fifty.'

" ' As you please,' said he, ' but, my good fellow, you must take my word for the ring and breastpin. I do not carry them with me. I know it's rather awkward to talk of playing a promised stake against one that we see, but I give you the honour of a gentleman that the diamonds shall be forthcoming if I lose.'

" I began to think that what he said was only a sort of come-off—but I didn't want his money, and was quite willing that he should win it back. If he had said, ' I'll stake my toothpick against the money,' I'd have been just as willing, for all that I now aimed at was to secure my horse or the price of him. I felt very miserable at the thought of winning the man's money —such a heap of it! I had never played cards for money in all my life before, and there's something in the feeling of winning money, for the first time, that's almost like thieving. As I tell you, if he had said his toothpick, or any worthless thing, instead of his diamonds, I'd have been willing. I didn't say so, however, and I thought his offer to stake diamonds that he couldn't show, was pretty much like a come-off. But I was willing enough, for the money seemed to scald my eyes to look upon. He took out a pencil, the case of which I saw was gold also, and wrote on a slip of paper, ' Good for two brilliants, one a ring, the other a breastpin, the latter in form of a Maltese cross, both set in gold, with an inner rim of silver, valued at seven hundred dollars.' This was signed with two letters only, the initials of his name. I have the paper now. He bade me read it, and when I did so, I thought him madder than a March hare; but if I thought so then, I was more than ever convinced of it, when, a moment after, and when we were about to play, he spoke to this effect:

" ' There's one thing, Rayner. There's a little incumbrance on these jewels.'

" ' Well, sir,' I said.

" I didn't care a fig for the incumbrance, for I didn't believe a word of the jewels.

" ' If you win them, you win a woman along with them. You win a wife.'

" I laughed outright.

" ' Don't laugh,' said he; ' you don't see me laugh. I'm serious; never more so. You are unmarried, You need a wife. Don't you want one?'

" ' Yes! if I could get a good one—one to my liking.'

" ' You *are* a good fellow. You deserve a good wife, Rayner; and such is the very one I propose to give you.'

" ' Ay, ay,' said I; ' but will she be to my liking?'

" ' I hope so; I believe so. She has all the qualities which should command the liking of a sensible and worthy young man. She, too, is sensible; she is intelligent; she has knowledge; she has read books; she has accomplishments; she sings like an angel; plays on several instruments—piano and guitar!'

" ' Piano and guitar!' said I.

" I didn't know what they were. I felt sure that the old fellow was mad, just out of a hospital, perhaps; but then where did he get the money and the gold things? I began to think more suspiciously of him than ever.

" ' Yes, piano and guitar,' said he; ' she draws and paints too, the loveliest pictures—she can make these trees live on canvass; ah! can she not? Money has not been spared, Rayner, to make Rachel what she is.'

" ' Rachel—is that her name?' I asked.

" ' Yes, it is.'

" ' What's the other name?'

" ' You shall know, if you win the diamonds.'

" ' Yes—but how old is she? how does she look? is she young and handsome? I wouldn't want an ugly wife because she happened to be wise. I've heard that your wise women are generally too ugly for any thing else than wisdom.'

" ' You are a fool, Rayner, though a good fellow. But Rachel is beautiful and young—not more than seventeen—the proper age for you. You, I think you say, are twenty-eight. In this climate a man's wife should always be ten or twelve years younger than himself—provided he be a sober and healthy man, and if he be not, he has no business with a wife, nor a wife with him. You are both sober and healthy. You are a good fellow—I see that. I like you, Rayner, and for this reason I am willing to risk Rachel on the cards, playing against you. My loss will probably be her gain, and this makes me rather regardless how it ends. You shall be my heir yet.'

" ' Thank you, old gentleman,' said I, beginning to feel a little bold and saucy, for I now couldn't help thinking that the stranger was no better than a good-natured madman who had got away from his friends. 'Thank you,' said I. 'If Rachel's the girl you make her out to be, you can't bring her along a day too soon. But, may I ask, is she your daughter ?'

" ' My daughter !' he answered sharply, and with something of a frown on his face, ' do I look like a man to have children ?—to be favoured with such a blessing as a daughter ?—a daughter like Rachel ?'

" ' Now,' said I to myself, ' his fit's coming on,' and I began to look about me for a start.

" ' No, Rayner,' he continued, ' she is no daughter of mine, but she is the daughter of a good man and of honourable parents. You shall have sufficient proof of that. Have you any more questions ?'

" ' No, sir.'

" ' And you will take Rachel as your wife ? You have heard my description of her. If she comes up to it, I ask you, will you be willing to take her as your wife ?'

" I looked at him queerly enough, I reckon. He fixed his keen black eyes upon me, so that I couldn't look on him without shutting my own. I didn't know whether to laugh or to run. But, thinking that he was flighty in the upper story, I concluded it was best to make a short business of it, and to agree with any thing that he wished ; so I told him freely ' yes,' and he reached out his hand to mine, which he squeezed nervously for a minute, and then took out his box of pills, swallowed a couple of them, and began dealing out the cards. I had the strangest luck—the same sort of luck that had kept with me from the start. I won the diamonds and won Rachel!

" 'Well,' said he, 'I'm glad, Rayner, that you are the man-I've been long looking for an heir to my diamonds. They are yours—all is yours; and I shall have to be indebted to you for the loan of the horse, in order to go and bring you your wife.'

" 'Ay,' said I, 'stranger, the horse is at your service, and half of the money too. I never thought to take them from you at the first; I shouldn't have felt easy in my conscience to have used the money that I got in this way.'

" 'Pshaw!' said he, gathering up the cards, and wrapping them in the buckskin wallet from which he had taken them. 'Pshaw, you are a fool. I'll borrow your horse, and a few pieces to pay my way.'

" 'Help yourself to the rest,' said I, taking, as I spoke, fifteen of the eagles to myself, and leaving the rest on the dead body of the horse, where they had been growing from our first commencing to play.

" 'You are my heir,' he answered, 'and behave yourself as you should. Between persons so related there should be no paltry money scruples;' and, while he said these words, he stooped to take the money. I turned away that he shouldn't suppose I watched him, but I couldn't help laughing at the strange sort of cunning which he showed in his conceit. Says I to myself, 'You will take precious good care, old fellow, I see that, that I carry off no more than my own poor hundred and fifty.' But he was too quick in mounting and riding off to give me much time to think about it or to change in my disposition. It was only after he was off, out of sight, and in a full gallop, that, looking round upon the dead horse, I saw the eagles still there, nearly all of them, just as I had heaped them up. He had only taken two of them, just enough, as he said, to bear his necessary expenses.

"I was a little surprised, and was now more sure than ever that the stranger had lost his wits. I gathered up the money, and walked home, mighty slowly, thinking all the way of what had taken place. It seemed more like a strange dream than any thing else. Was there any man? Had I played *old sledge* with a stranger? I was almost inclined to doubt; but there was the dead horse. I went back to look at it, and when I thrust my hand .down into my breeches pocket, I brought it up full of the precious metal; but was it precious metal? I began to tremble at this thought. It might be nothing better than brass or copper, and my horse was gone—gone off at a smart canter. My heart grew chilled within me at this reflection. I felt wild—scareo half out of my wits, and instead of regarding the old man as a witless person escaped from his keepers, I now began to consider him a cunning sharper, who had found one more witless than I had fancied him.

8

CHAPTER VI.

But such reflections, even if well founded, came too late for remedy. The old man was gone beyond present reach, and when I reflected that he had taken two of the gold pieces for his own expenses, I began to feel a little reassured on the subject of their value. When I got home, I told my father of the sale of the horse, and the price, though I took precious good care to say nothing of the gambling. The old man, though he himself had taught me to play cards, was mighty strict against all play for money. I showed him only the fifteen pieces that I got for Rainbow, and the rest I put away quietly, meaning to spend them by degrees upon the farm, as chances offered, so as to prevent him from ever getting at the real truth. I felt myself pretty safe with regard to the strange gentleman. I never counted on his coming back to blow me, though, sometimes, when I wasn't thinking, an odd sort of fear would come over me, and I would feel myself trembling with the notion that, after all, he might return. I had heard of rich people having strange ways of throwing away their money, and taking a liking for poor people like myself; and then, there was a serious earnest about the strange gentleman, in spite of all his curiousnesses, that made me a little apprehensive, whenever the recollection of him came into my head.

"But regular work, day after day, is the best physic for mind and body; and, after three days had gone by, I almost ceased to bother myself with the affair. I passed the time so actively that I didn't think much about any thing. I took a trip down the river, some eighteen miles, to a wheelwright's, and bought a prime two-horse wagon, for ninety-five dollars, which made a considerable hole in the price of Rainbow; and, one thing with another, the week went by almost without giving me time to count if the right number of days was in it. Sunday followed, and then Monday. That Monday I was precious busy. I was always an industrious man—doing something or other—making this, or mending that. To be doing nothing was always the hardest work for me. But that Monday I out-worked myself, and I was really glad when I saw the sun sink suddenly down behind the woods. I threw down the broad-axe, for I had been hewing out some door-facings for a new corn-crib and fodder-house, and went towards the gallery (piazza) where the old man was sitting, and threw myself, at full-length, along the entrance, just at his feet. I was mighty tired. My jacket was off, my sleeves rolled up, my neck open, and the perspiration standing thick on my breast and forehead. At that very moment, while I was lying in this condition, who should I see ride into the opening, but the strange old gentleman. I knew him at a glance, and my heart jumped up into my mouth as if it was trying to get out of it. Behind him came another person riding upon a pretty little bay filly. Though it was darkening fast, I could make out that this other person was a woman, and I never felt so scared in all my life. I looked up at my father, and he at me. He saw that I was frightened, but he hadn't time to ask me a question, and I shouldn't have had the strength to answer if he had Up rode the strange old gentleman, and close behind him came the lady. Though I was mightily frightened, I looked curiously at her. I could make out that she was a small and delicate-framed person, but her face was covered with a thick veil. I could see that she carried herself well, sat her horse upright like a sort of queen, and when the old man offered to take her off, yielded herself to him with a slow but graceful stateliness, not unlike that of a young cedar bending to the wind.

"For my part, though I could see this, I was never more confounded in my life. I was completely horror-struck. To see the old gentleman again was a shocking surprise ; but that he should really bring the lady that I had won, and that she should catch me in that condition,—my coat off, my breast open, my face covered with dust and perspiration ! If the work made me sweat before, this surprise increased it. I got up, and made out to get a few steps towards the strangers. I said something by way of apology for being caught in that shabby fix ; but the old gentleman stopped me.

" 'Never mind, no apologies, Mr. Rayner. The proofs of

labour are always honourable, and if the heart can show that i
works as well as the body, then the labourer is a gentleman.
How are you, and—this is your father ?'

" I introduced him to the old man as the person who had bought
Rainbow, and we conducted them into the house.

" ' My ward, Mr. Rayner,' said the stranger, when we had
entered, ' this is the young friend of whom I spoke to you.'

" At these words the young lady threw up her veil. I stag-
gered back at the sight. I won't talk of her beauty, my friend,
for two reasons ; one of which is, that I haven't got words to
say what I thought and felt—what I think and feel now. The
other—but I needn't speak of the other reason. This one is
sufficient. The old gentleman looked at me inquiringly, and
then he looked at my father. I could see that there was a little
doubt and anxiety upon his face, but they soon passed away as he
examined the face of my father. There was something so good,
so meek, so benevolent about the looks of the old man, that
nobody could mistrust that all was right in the bottom of his heart.
As for my heart, the strange gentleman seemed to see into it quite
as quickly as into that of my father. He was not so blunt and
abrupt now in his manner of speaking to me as he had been when
we first met. His manner was more dignified and reserved.
There was something very lofty and noble about it, and in speaking to the lady his voice sunk almost into a whisper.

" ' Mr. Rayner,' said he, looking to my father, ' I trust that
you will give my ward a chamber for the night. I have heard
of you, sir, and have made bold to presume on your known benevolence of character in making this application.'

" ' Our home is a poor one, stranger,' said the old man ; ' but
such as it is, it is quite at the service of the young lady.'

" ' Good !' said the other ; ' you are the man after my own
heart. I am known,' he continued, ' where men speak of me at
all, as Mr. Eckhardt. My ward is the daughter of a very near
and dear friend. Her name is Herder—Rachel Herder. So
much is necessary for convenience in conversation ; and now, sir,
if you can tell Rachel where she is to find her chamber, so that
she may arrange her dress, and get rid of the dust of travel, she
will be very much obliged to you.'

" All this was soon arranged and attended to, and wnile the lady disappeared in our best chamber, Mr. Eckhardt proceeded to disburthen the horses, on both of which were saddle-bags that were stuffed almost to bursting. These were brought into the house, and sent to the chamber after the lady. Then the stranger sat down with my father, the two old men chatting quite briskly together, while I stripped the horses of their saddles, and took them to the stable. When I returned to the house I found them as free-spoken and good-humoured as if they had been intimate from the first day of clearing in that country.

CHAPTER VII.

" You may suppose what my confusion must have been, for I can't describe it to you. I can only say that I felt pretty much like a drunken man. Every thing swum around me. I was certain of nothing ; didn't know what to believe, and half the time really doubted whether I was asleep or awake. But there were the horses—there was Rainbow. I couldn't mistake him, and if I had, he didn't mistake me. When he heard my voice as I led him to the stable, he whinnied with a sort of joy, and pricked up his ears, and showed his feeling as plainly as if he had a human voice to speak it in words. And I reckon, too, it was a more true feeling than many of those that are spoken in words. I threw my arms round the good creature's neck, and if it hadn't been for thinking of Rachel Herder, I reckon I should have kissed him, too, it did me so much good to see him again. But I hadn't much time for this sort of fondness, and when I remembered the whole affair between the strange old gentleman, Mr. Eckhardt, and myself, I was too much worried to think any more of Rainbow. I couldn't bring myself to believe it true about the diamonds and the wife ; and when I remembered the sight that I had caught, though a glimpse only, and for a single moment, of the great beauty of the young lady, I couldn't help thinking that the stranger was only making merry with me—running his rigs upon a poor, rough, backwoodsman. But this notion roused up my pride and feeling. ' Not so rough,' says I to myself ; ' poor it may be, but not mean ; not more rough than honest labour makes a man. And poor as you please, and rough as you please, when the heart's right, and the head's no fool's head, the man's man enough for any woman, though she walks in satin !' With this I considered that I ought, at least, to make myself rather decent before I sat down to supper. My cheeks burned me when I looked at myself and remembered how she had caught me. I knew that good soft spring water, and my best suit, would turn me into quite another sort of looking man; but here **again was** difficulty. It was my chamber which my father had given up to the young lady, and all my clothes were in it. **My new coat** and blue pantaloons hung upon pegs behind the door; and all my shirts were in an old chest of drawers on which the looking-glass stood; and to get these things without her seeing was impossible. But it had to be done; so I called up the old negro woman servant we had, and told her what to do, and sent her for the clothes, while I waited for them at the back of the house. When she brought them, I hurried down to the branch (brooklet) and made a rapid and plentiful use of the waters. I then got in among the bushes, and made a thorough change in my dress, taking care to hide the old clothes in the hollow of a gum. I combed my hair smoothly over the branch, which answered me at the same time for a looking-glass, and had the effect of making me much more satisfied with my personal appearance. I needn't blush, my friend, at my time of life, to say that I thought myself then, and was, a tolerable comely fellow; and I couldn't help feeling a sneaking secret notion that the young lady would think so too. Well, I got in time enough for supper. Mr. Eckhardt looked at me, as I thought, with real satisfaction. He and my father had been keeping company all the time I was gone, and I could see, among other things, that they were mightily pleased with one another. By and by, supper was brought in, and Rachel Herder came out of her chamber. If I thought her beautiful before, I thought her now ten times more so. Once I caught her eyes fixed upon me, but she turned them away without any flurry or confusion, and I don't think that I saw her look at me in particular once again that night. This worried me, I confess. It seemed to show that she wasn't thinking of me; and, moreover, it seemed to show that Mr. Eckhardt hadn't said a word to her about the business; and this made me more ready to believe that he had only been running his rigs upon me. Yet there was something about his looks and in his words, whenever he spoke to me—something so real, serious, earnest, that I couldn't help believing, after all, that the affair wasn't altogether over. Nor was it, as you will see directly.

"Supper went forward. You know what a country supper is,

out here in Mississippi, so it don't need to tell you that cornbread, and a little eggs and bacon, and a smart bowl of milk, was pretty much the amount of it. The young lady ate precious little ; took a little milk, I believe, and a corn biscuit. As for me, I'm very sure I ate still less. My heart was too much in my mouth to suffer me to put in any thing more ; for, whichever way I thought of the matter, I was worried half to death. If the old gentleman was serious, it was still a mighty terrifying thing to have a wife so suddenly forced upon a body,—a wife that you never saw before and didn't know any thing about ; and if he wasn't serious, it was very hard to lose so lovely a creature, just too after your heart had been tantalized and tempted by the promise that she was all for yourself. As I tell you, my friend, whichever way I could think of it, I was still worried half to death.

"After supper, Mr. Eckhardt asked me to walk out with him ; so, leaving the young lady with my father,—who, by the way, had already grown mightily pleased with her,—off we went into the woods. We hadn't gone very far when the old gentleman spoke, pretty abruptly :

"'Well, Rayner, my lad, you've seen the lady whom I intend as your wife. Does she suit you ?'

"'Why, sir, you're rather quick. I can answer for her beauty : she's about the beautifullest creature I ever did see, but it's not beauty altogether that makes a good wife, and I ha'n't had time yet to judge whether she'll suit me.'

"'How much time do you want ?' said he shortly.

"'Well, I can't say.'

"'Will a week or ten days answer ?'

"'That's as it happens,' said I. 'Some men you can under-stand in an hour, just as if you had been with 'em all your life. I'm pretty much such a person myself,—but with some you can't get on so rapidly. You'll be with them a year, and know just as little of their hearts at the end of it, as you did at the beginning.'

"'Humph ! and whose fault will that be but your own ? There's an eye to see, Rayner, as well as a thing to be seen. It depends very much upon the seeker whether he shall ever find. But enough. There's no need in this case for much philosophy.

You are easily read, and so is Rachel. A week will answer to make you both acquainted, and I'll leave her with you for that time.'

" ' But are you serious ?' I asked.

" ' Serious ! But your question is natural. I am a man of few words, Rayner. You see something in my proceedings which is extraordinary. As the world goes, and acts, and thinks, perhaps it is ; but nothing was ever more deliberate or well advised, on my part, than this proceeding. Hear me, lad ! this lady is a ward of mine ; the daughter of a very dear friend, who gave her to my trust. I swore to do by her as a father. I am anxious to do so ; but I am an old man, not long for this world,—an erring man, not always sure of doing right while I am in it. I wish to find the child a protector,—a good man,—a kind man,—a man whom I can trust. This has been my desire for some time. I fancy I have found in you the very person I seek. I am a man to look keenly, judge quickly, and act in the same manner. As you yourself have remarked, you are a person easily understood. I understood you in a little time, and was pleased with what I saw of you. I have chosen you out as the husband of Rachel. She knows nothing yet of my purpose. You, I see, have kept your father in partial ignorance of our adventure. Perhaps you were right in this case, though, as a general rule, such secrecy between two persons placed as you are would have been an error. Well, Rachel shall stay with you a week. I know her so well that I fancy you will in that time become intimate and remain pleased with each other—sufficiently pleased to make the rest easy.'

" There was some more talk between us, as we went toward the house, but this was the substantial part of what was said. Once I made some remark on the strangeness of such a preference shown to me, when in the great cities he might have found so many young men better suited by education for a young lady whom he represented to be so accomplished ; but he had his answer for this also ; and so quickly uttered, and with such a commanding manner, that, even if I had not been satisfied, I should still have been silenced.

' ' Your remark is natural. Half the world, having such a child to dispose of, would have gone to the great city, and have preferred a fashionable husband. But I know her heart. It is her heart, and not her accomplishments, that I wish to provide for. I want a man, not a dandy,—a frank, noble-hearted citizen, however plain, not a selfish, sophisticated calculator, who looks for a wife through the stock market. Enough, my good fellow; no more words.'

CHAPTER VIII.

" THAT very night Mr. Eckhardt contrived, after the young lady had gone to bed, to let my father know that he would be pleased if his ward could be suffered to remain in his family for a few days, until he should cross the river, in order to look after a man on the west of the Misssisippi, who owed him money. He was unwilling to carry her with him into so very wild a region. He made every thing appear so natural to the old man, that he consented out of hand, just as if it had been the most reasonable arrangement in the world; and it was only after Mr. Eckhardt had set out,—which he did by daylight the next morning,—that my father said to me :

" ' It's very strange, William, now I come to think of it, that Mr. Eckhardt should leave the young lady in a family where there's none but men.'

" ' But she's just as safe here, father,' said I, ' as if she had fifty of her own sex about her.'

" ' That's true enough, William,' said the old man, ' and if the child feels herself at home, why there's nothing amiss. I'm thinking she's about the sweetest-looking creature I ever laid eyes on.'

" I thought so too, but I said nothing, and followed the old man into the house, with my feelings getting more and more strange and worrisome at every moment. I was in the greatest whirl of expectation—my cheeks a-burning,—my heart as cold as ice, and leaping up and down, just as scarily as a rabbit's when he's.finding his way through the paling into a garden patch. I felt as if the business now upon my hands was about the most serious and trying I had ever undertaken ; and it took all my thinking, I tell you, to bring my courage to the right pitch, so as to steady my eyes while I spoke to the young lady as she came out to the breakfast-table. My father had a message to her from Mr. Eckhardt, telling her of his absence ; and though she looked a little

anxious when she heard that he was already gone, she soon seemed to become quiet and at ease in her situation. Indeed, for that
matter, she was the most resigned and easy person I ever met in
my life. She seemed quite too gentle ever to complain, and I
may say now, with some certainty, that, whatever might be her
hurts of mind or body, she was the most patient to submit, and
the most easy to be pacified, of all human beings.

"Now, if you know any thing of a man of my description, if
you're any thing of a judge of human nature, you'll readily understand that, if I was scary and bashful at first, in meeting with
a young and beautiful creature like her, and knowing what I did
know of what was before me, it didn't take very long for the fright
to wear off. The man whose feelings are very quick, gets mightily confused at first, but give him time, don't hurry him, and he'll
come to his senses pretty soon, and they'll come to him, and they'll
be the sharper and the more steady, from the scare they had at first
—you can't scare them in the same manner a second time. Before that day was well out, I could sit down and talk with Rachel,
and hear her talk, without growing blind, dumb, and deaf in an
instant. Her mildness gave me encouragement, and when I got
used to the sound of my own voice, just after hers, I then found
out, not only that I had a good deal to say, but that she listened
very patiently, and I think was pleased to hear it. I found her
so mild, so kind, and encouraging, she seemed to take so much
interest in every thing she saw, that I was for showing her every
thing. Our cows, the little dairy, the new wagon, even to
the fields of corn, cotton, and potatoes, were all subjects of examination one after the other. Then, I could carry her along the
hill slopes, through as pretty a grove, too, as you would wish to
lay eyes on ; and down along just such another, even to the river
banks ; and we had odd things enough to show, here and there, to
keep up the spirits and have something to talk about. These
rambles we'd take either in the cool of the morning, or towards
sunset in the afternoon ; and, sometimes the old man would go
along with us—but, as he couldn't go very far at one time, we
had pretty much the whole chance to ourselves ; and what with
talking and walking with Rachel, and thinking about her when I
wasn't with her, I did precious little work that week. To short

en a long story, my friend, I now began to think that there was
nothing wrong in my gambling with Mr. Eckhardt, and to agree
in his notion that the loser was always bound to pay, and the winner to receive. Before he got back, which he did not until
ten days were fully over, I had pretty much concluded that I
should find it the most trying business in nature to have to give up
my winnings. I don't mean the diamonds ; for them I had not
seen, and hadn't cared to see ; but I mean the incumbrance that
came with them, which, by this time, was more than all the gold
or diamonds, in my sight, that the whole world could show.

CHAPTER IX.

" I was now as anxious to see Mr. Eckhardt as I had befor
been afraid of his coming. He overstayed his time a little, being
nearer two weeks gone than one. He was a keen-sighted man.
His first words, when we were again alone together, were, ' Well,
all's right on your part, Rayner. You are a good fellow—I see
that you will be my heir. You find that what I said of Rachel
is true ; and nothing now remains but to see what she will say.
Have you been much together ?'

" ' Pretty often. I reckon I've done little else than look after
her since you've been gone.'

" ' What ! you hav'n't neglected your business, Rayner ?'
said he, with a smile—' the cows, the horses ?'

" ' They've had a sort of liberty,' says I.

" ' Bad signs for farming, however good for loving. You mus⁺
change your habits when you are married.'

" ' Ah ! that's not yet,' said I, with a sigh. ' I'm dub'ous, Mr
Eckhardt, that Miss Rachel won't fancy me so soon as I do her !'

" He looked a little anxious, and didn't answer so quickly a⸴
usual, and my heart felt as heavy then as if it was borne down
by a thousand pounds of lead. It wasn't much lightened when
he answered, with a sort of doubting,—

" ' Rachel,' said he, ' has always heeded my counsel. She
knows my love for her—she has every confidence in my judgment. You, Rayner, have some of those advantages which
young women are apt to admire. You are well made, youthful,
manly, and with a masculine grace and beauty which you owe
to the hunter life. These are qualities to recommend the young
of one sex to the young of the other. You have something more.
You are a sensible youth, with a native delicacy of feeling which,
more than any thing beside, will be apt to strike Rachel. It
struck me. I will not presume to say that you have won either
her eye or her heart—the eye of a woman is easy won at all

times, the heart slowly. Perhaps it may be safe to say that hearts are not often won till after marriage. But, at all events, with your personal claims, which I think considerable, and the docility of Rachel, I have hopes that I can bring about an arrangement which, I confess to you, I regard as greatly important to my future purposes. We shall see.'

" At that moment I was quite too full of Rachel and my own hopes, to consider the force of the remark which he last made. I never troubled myself to ask what his purposes might be, beyond the single one which we both had in view. When Mr Eckhardt met with Rachel, and, indeed, while he spoke with me, I could observe that there was a gravity, like sadness, in his voice and manner, which was not usual with him, or at least had not shown itself in our previous meetings. He hesitated more frequently in what he had to say. His eye was less settled, though even brighter than before ; and I noted the fact that he took his pills three times as frequently as ever. Even when he spoke with a show of jesting or playfulness, I noted that there was a real sadness in what he looked, and even something of sadness in what he said, or in his manner of saying it. Nothing but this seriousness of look and manner kept me from thinking that he was playing upon my backwoods ignorance, when he was speaking my own good name and good qualities to my teeth. But when I doubted and began to suspicion that he was running rigs upon me, I had only to look into his face and see that he was talking in the way of downright, matter-of-fact business.

" When he came, Rachel went to him and put her hand in his, but she didn't speak. Nor did he at first. He only bent down and kissed her forehead ; and so he stood awhile, holding her hand in his, and talking to my father. It was a sight to see them two. I couldn't stand it. There was something in it, I can't tell you what, that looked so sadful. I went out and wiped the water from my eyes. It seemed to me then, as if the old gentleman was meditating something very distressing, and as if poor Rachel was half dub'ous of it herself. After a little while, my father came out and joined me, and we walked off together to the stable.

" 'William,' says the old man, 'these are strange people

They seem very sweet, good people; at least the girl seems very good, and is a very sweet girl; but there's something very strange and very sorrowful about them.'

" I couldn't say any thing, for my heart was very full, and the old man went forward.

" 'Now, what's more strange than for him to leave her here with us? though, to be sure, we wouldn't see her harmed even to the falling of a hair of her head—and I can answer for you, Bill, as I can for myself; but it's not every body that will say for us what we might feel for ourselves, and precious few fathers would leave an only daughter here, in strange woods, with such perfect strangers.'

" 'But she's not his daughter,' said I.

" 'It don't matter. It's very clear that he loves her as if she was his daughter, and I reckon she's never known any other father. Poor girl!—I'm sure I like her already so much that I wish he'd leave her here altogether.'

" These last words of my father seemed to untie my tongue, and I up and told him every syllable of what had taken place between me and Mr. Eckhardt, from my first meeting with him the day when I went to the river landing, up to the very moment when we were talking. I didn't hide any thing, but told the whole story of the cards, the gold, and the diamonds; and ended by letting him know that if he should be so sorry to lose Rachel, now that we both knew so much about her, it would go a mighty deal harder with me. I told him all that Mr. Eckhardt had said since his return, and what hopes I had that all would go as he wished it. But the old man shook his head. He didn't like what he heard about Mr. Eckhardt's gambling, and was very tight upon me for letting myself be tempted to deal with him in the same business. He didn't think the worse of Rachel, of course, but he looked upon it as a sort of misfortune to be in any way connected with a gambler.

" We hadn't much longer time for confabulating, for Mr. Eckhardt now came from the house and joined us. He was a man who always came jump to the business, whatever it was, that he had in hand. But he wasn't a rough man, though a quick one. He had a way of doing the bluntest things without rough-

ing the feelings. When he drew nigh, he took my father's arm
to lead him aside, speaking to me at the same time—'Rayner, go
to Rachel ;—I have prepared her to see you. I will explain
every thing to your father, if you have not already done it ; and
if you have, I still have something to say.'

"You may reckon I didn't stop to count the tracks after that.
I verily think that I made the door of the house in a hop-skip-and-
jump from the stable. Yet, when I got to the threshold, I stuck
—I stuck fast. I heard a low sweet sort of moaning from within,
and oh ! how my heart smote me when I heard it. I thought to
myself, it's so cruel to force this poor girl's inclination. What
can she see in me ? That was my question to myself, and it
made me mighty humble, I tell you, when I asked it. But that
very humbleness did me good, and gave me sort of strength. 'If
she don't see any thing in me to favour,' was my thought, 'at
least I'll show her that I'm not the mean-spirited creature to take
advantage of her necessity ;' and when I thought in this manner, I
went forward with a bound, and stood before her. I took her
hand in mine, and said,—but Lord bless me, it's no use to try
and tell you what I said, for I don't know myself. The words
poured from me free enough. My heart was very full. I meant
to speak kindly and humbly, and do the thing generously, and I
reckon that, when the heart means what is right, and has a
straight purpose before it, the tongue can't go very far out of the
way. Nor did mine, if I am to judge of the effects which followed it. It's enough for me to tell you, that, though the tears
wasn't altogether dried up in Rachel's eyes, her lips began to
smile ; she let her hand rest in mine, and she said something, but
what it was, I can't tell you. · It's enough to say that she let me
know that she thought that all that had been proposed by Mr.
Eckhardt was for her good and happiness, and she was willing to
consent to whatever he had said. He came in a little while after, and seemed quite satisfied. He talked, as if he himself was
particularly pleased, but there was a very great earnestness in
his looks that awed and overpowered me. His eyes seemed very
much sunk, even in the short time he had been gone, the wrinkles
seemed to have doubled in number on his face ; his form trembled
very much, and could perceive that he took his pills from the little

9

box of silver twice as often as ever   He didn't give himself
or me much time to think over what was to happen, for he hadn't
been ten minutes returned to the house, after the matter was understood all round, before he said to me in a whisper :

" ' Rayner, my lad, you are a good fellow ; suppose you ride
off at once for your parson. You have one, your father tells me,
within a few miles. A smart gallop will bring him back with
you before sunset, and I would see you married to-night. I shall
have to leave you in the morning.'

" Ah ! stranger, don't wonder if I made the dust fly after that
That night we were married.

CHAPTER X.

" The next morning, just as breakfast was over, Mr. Eckhardt rose and buttoned his coat.

" 'Rachel, my child,' said he, ' I shall now leave you. It will be perhaps some time before I see you again. For that matter, I may never see you again. But I have fulfilled my promise to your dear father. You are the wife of a good man—a gentle and kind-hearted man. He will make you a good husband, I believe and hope. You, I know, will make him a good wife. The seeds of goodness and happiness are here in this cottage—may they grow to fruits. Kiss me, my child! Kiss me! It may be for the last time!'

" ' No !' said she ; ' oh, no !' and she caught and she clung to him. It was a time to bring tears, stranger, not to talk. There was a good many words said by all of us, but not much talking. It was a cry and an exclamation like, with poor Rachel, and then she sunk off in the arms of Mr. Eckhardt. I was monstrous frightened ; but he carried her into the room and laid her on the bed. ' She will soon get over it,' said he, ' and in the mean time I'll steal away. When she recovers follow me. You will find me ——' He told me where to find him—at the place where we had played together on the dead horse—but the sentence he finished in a whisper. Then he stooped and kissed her, gave her one long look, and his lips moved as if he was speaking a blessing over her. After this he turned from me hurriedly, as if to conceal the tear in his eye. But I saw it. It couldn't be concealed. It was about the largest tear I ever did see in the eye of a man, but I reckon there was only that one. He was gone before Rachel come to herself. Till that happened I was about the most miserable creature on earth. When she opened her eyes and found that he was already gone, her troubles somewhat softened ; and when I found that, I set off to follow Mr. Eckhardt, as he had directed me   I found him at the place appointed, but he had no horse and no cloak, and didn't appear to have made any of the usual arrangements for travelling. I expressed my surprise. 'Where's your horse?' I demanded.—'I shall need none. Besides, I *have* none. You seem to forget, Rayner, that the horse is yours.'—'Mine!'—'Yes! you won him!'—'But you can't mean, sir——' I was beginning to expostulate, when he put his hand on my mouth. 'Say no more, Rayner. You are a good fellow. The horse *is* yours, whether you have him by your skill or my generosity. Did I not tell you that I intended to make you my heir?'

"I looked bewildered, and felt so, and said, 'Well, you don't intend to leave us then?'—'Yes I do.'—'How do you mean to go—by water?' Remember, the river was pretty near us, and though I didn't myself expect any steamboat, yet I thought it likely he might have heard of one. 'Very possible,' he answered, with something of a smile upon his countenance. He continued, after a short pause, 'It is difficult to say by what conveyance a man goes when he goes out of the world, Rayner. The journey I propose to take is no other. Life is an uncertain business, Rayner. Uncertain as it is, most people seem never to have enough of it. I am of a different thinking. I have had only too much. I am neither well in it, nor fit for it, and I shall leave it. I have made all my arrangements, settled my concerns, and, as I promised, you shall be my heir.' I began to speak and expostulate with him, but he stopped me. 'Rayner, you are a good fellow, but you shouldn't interrupt me. As I have but little time for talking, you should let me enjoy it all. You can say what you have to say when I am gone, and I promise you *I* shall never interrupt *you* then. You have heard me, you understand my words.'

"'I think I do,' was my answer; 'you mean to take your own life!'

"'True, Rayner! but you speak as if it was yours I were about to take!'

"I told him I felt almost as bad as if it was, and asked him why he should think of such a deed.

"'It's a long story, Rayner, and you would probably understand it as thoroughly in ten words as in ten thousand. Perhaps

I should say enough in telling you that I am sick of life, and that life sickens me. Every moment that I live humbles and degrades me. I have been the master of three princely fortunes; and now I have only the means to carry me on my last journey. I have had the reputation of talents, wit, and wisdom in high degree, but lack the strength to forbear the companionship of the basest, and the wit to keep from being the victim of the vilest. Had I been the only victim, Rayner! But that poor child, now your wife—the child of a dear relative and friend—entrusted to my guardianship in the confidence of love, which, at dying, demanded of me no pledge, but that which it fancied was speaking through my eyes—that child has been the victim also! Start not! The child is pure as any angel. It was the robbery of her fortune of which I speak. I squandered hers with my own. I did not bring her to beggary, Rayner. No! But I have lived in perpetual dread that I should do so! Now that she is yours, I have no such fears. I know that she is safe—that she will do well—that you will both do well. Do not fancy, my good fellow, when I tell you this, that I have been seeking in vain for a husband for the child. The thing is otherwise. Husbands have sought for her. Men of rank and substance, for whose attentions the mothers of most daughters would have worked their wits and fingers to the bone. But if I squandered Rachel's fortune—mark me—I was resolved that *she* should not be sacrificed. I resolved that I would do her justice, at least in that one respect—that she should never be yielded, if I could help it, to the shallow witling, the profligate, or the brute—let their social rank and worldly possessions be what they might. I knew her, and fancied I could tell what sort of person would suit her. I have found that person in you—so I believe—and my work is ended. The labourer knocks off when his work is done, and so will I. There is one thing, Rayner——'

" He took from his pocket the buckskin roll which contained his pack of cards.

" ' Do you see these ? I will not say that they have been my bane. I were a fool to say so. My own weakness was my bane. They were only the unconscious instruments in my hands, as innocent as the dirk or pistol in the hands of the as-

sassin. But they have their dangers, Rayner; and I would
protect you against them. Take them; I promised you should
be my heir. Take them, but not to play them. Keep them in
your eyes as an omen. Show them to your children as a warning.
Tell them what I have told you; and while you familiarize their
eyes with their forms, familiarize their hearts with their dangers.
There! do not lose sight of them. Leave me now. Farewell!
You see I am at the bottom of my box.'

"He thrust the cards into my hands, and as he spoke, he drew
out his little silver box, and took from it the only pill which remained. This he swallowed, and then handed me the box also.
I refused to take it. 'Pshaw!' said he, 'why not? your refusal
to take it can have no effect on my determination! Take it and
leave me!' But I still refused. He turned from me, saying:
'You're a foolish fellow, Rayner;' and walked down the road
leading to the river. I followed him closely. He turned half
round, once or twice, muttered and seemed discontented. I still
kept close with him, and began to expostulate. But he interrupted me fiercely; and I now perceived that his eyes began to
glisten and to glare very wildly. It had not escaped my observation, that the last pill which he had taken was greatly larger
than any he had used before; and I then remembered, that before the marriage ceremony was performed, on the previous
night, he had opened the box more than once, in my presence,
and I noted that it contained a good many. By this time we
reached the banks of the river. He turned full upon me.
'Rayner,' said he, 'you're a good fellow, but you must go home
to your wife.'—'It's impossible,' said I, 'to leave you.'—'We'll,
see to that,' said he, and he turned towards the river. I took it for
certain he was going to plunge in, and I jumped forward to seize
him, but, just as my arms were extended to embrace him, he
wheeled about and clapped a pistol to my head. I started back,
quickly enough, as you may suppose; and he exclaimed—'Ah!
Rayner, you are a good fellow, but you cannot prevent the
journey. Farewell!' With these words he flung me the pistol,
which I afterwards found was unloaded, and, before I could speak
or think, he sprang from the bluff into the stream. It appeared
to me as if I heard the splash before I saw the motion. I ran up

the bluff where he had stood, as soon as I could recover myself, and saw where the water-rings were spreading in great circles where he had gone down. I didn't give myself a moment after that. I could swim like a duck and dive like a serpent, and had no fear of the water for myself; so in I jumped, and fished about as long as I could stand it underneath; but I could find nothing of him. He had given himself up to the currents so entirely, that they whirled him out of sight in a minute. When I rose and got to the shore, I saw his hat floating among some bushes on the other shore. But as for poor Mr. Eckhardt, he was gone, sure enough, upon his last journey!

"You see our little family. The boy is very much like him in looks, and I reckon in understanding. He's very thoughtful and smart. We are happy, stranger, and I don't believe that Mr. Eckhardt was wrong in his notion that I would make Rachel happy. She tells me she is, and it makes me happy to believe her. It makes her sad to see the cards, and sad to hear of them, but she thinks it best for our boy that he should hear the story and learn it all by heart; and that makes her patient, and patience brings a sort of peace along with it that's pretty much like happiness. I could tell you more, my friend, but it's not needful, and your eyes look as if they had kept open long enough for one sitting. So come with me, and let me show you where you are to lie down!"

These words roused me! I half suspect that I was drowsing in my chair. I can hardly suppose, dear reader, that you could be capable of an act of like forgetfulness.

THE ARM-CHAIR OF TUSTENUGGEE.

A TRADITION OF THE CATAWBA.

CHAPTER I.

THE windy month had set in, the leaves were falling, and the light-footed hunters of Catawba, set forth upon the chase. Little groups went off in every direction, and before two weeks had elapsed from the beginning of the campaign, the whole nation was broken up into parties, each under the guidance of an individual warrior. The course of the several hunting bands was taken according to the tastes or habits of these leaders. Some of the Indians were famous for their skill in hunting the otter, could swim as long with head under water as himself, and be not far from his haunches, when he emerged to breathe. These followed the course of shallow waters and swamps, and thick, dense bays, in which it was known that he found his favourite haunts. The bear hunter pushed for the cane brakes and the bee trees; and woe to the black bear whom he encountered with his paws full of honeycomb, which he was unwilling to leave behind him. The active warrior took his way towards the hills, seeking for the brown wolf and the deer; and, if the truth were known, smiled with wholesale contempt at the more timorous who desired less adventurous triumphs. Many set forth in couples only, avoiding with care all the clamorous of the tribe; and some few, the more surly or successful—the inveterate bachelors of the nation—were content to make their forward progress alone. The old men prepared their traps and nets, the boys their blow guns, and followed with the squaws slowly, according to the division made by the hunters among themselves. They carried the blankets and bread stuffs, and camped nightly in noted places, to which, according to previous arrangement, the hunters might repair at evening and bring their game. In this way, some of the tribes followed the course of the Catawba, even to its source. Others darted off towards the Pacolet and Broad rivers, and there were some, the most daring and swift of foot, who made nothing of a journey to the Tiger river, and the rolling mountains of Spartanburg.

There were two warriors who pursued this course. One of tnem was named Conattee, and a braver man and more fortunate hunter never lived. But he had a wife who was a greater scold than Xantippe. She was the wonder and the terror of the tribe, and quite as ugly as the one-eyed squaw of Tustenuggee, the grey demon of Enoree. Her tongue was the signal for " slinking," among the bold hunters of Turkey-town ; and when they heard it, " now," said the young women, who sympathised, as all proper young women will do, with the handsome husband of an ugly wife, " now," said they, " we know that poor Conattee has come home." The return of the husband, particularly if he brought no game, was sure to be followed by a storm of that " dry thunder," so well known, which never failed to be heard at the farthest end of the village.

The companion of Conattee on the present expedition was named Selonee—one of the handsomest lads in the whole nation. He was tall and straight like a pine tree ; had proved his skill and courage in several expeditions against the Chowannee red sticks, and had found no young warriors of the Cherokee, though he had been on the war path against them and had stricken all their posts, who could circumvent him in stratagem or conquer him in actual blows. His renown as a hunter was not less great. He had put to shame the best wolf-takers of the tribe, and the lodge of his venerable father, Chifonti, was never without meat. There was no good reason why Conattee, the married man, should be so intimate with Selonee, the single—there was no particular sympathy between the two ; but, thrown together in sundry expeditions, they had formed an intimacy, which, strange to say, was neither denounced nor discouraged by the virago wife of the former. She who approved of but few of her husband's movements, and still fewer of his friends and fellowships, forbore all her reproaches when Selonee was his companion.   She was the meekest, gentlest, sweetest tempered of all wives whenever the young hunter came home with her husband; and he, poor man, was consequently, never so well satisfied as when he brought Selonee with him.   It was on such occasions, only, that the poor Conattee could persuade himself to regard Macourah as a tolerable personage.   How he came to marry such a creature—such a termagant, and so monstrous ugly—was a mystery which none of the damsels of Catawba could elucidate, though the subject was one on which, when mending the young hunter's mocasins, they expended no small quantity of conjecture.   Conattee, we may be permitted to say, was still quite popular among them, in spite of his bad taste. and manifest unavailableness; possibly, for the very reason that his wife was universally detested; and it will, perhaps, speak something for their charity, if we pry no deeper into their motives, to say that the wish was universal among them that the Opitchi Manneyto, or Black Devil of their belief, would take the virago to himself, and leave to the poor Conattee some reasonable hope of being made happy by a more indulgent spouse.

CHAPTER II.

WELL, Conattee and Selonee were out of sight of the smoke of "Turkey-town," and, conscious of his freedom as he no longer heard the accents of domestic authority, the henpecked husband gave a loose to his spirits, and made ample amends to himself, by the indulgence of joke and humour, for the sober constraints which fettered him at home. Selonee joined with him in his merriment, and the resolve was mutual that they should give the squaws the 'lip and not linger in their progress till they had thrown the Tiger river behind them. To trace their course till they came to the famous hunting ground which bordered upon the Pacolet, will scarcely be necessary, since, as they did not stop to hunt by the way, there were necessarily but few incidents to give interest to their movements. When they had reached the river, however, they made for a cove, well known to them on previous seasons, which lay between the parallel waters of the Pacolet, and a little stream called the Thicketty—a feeder of the Eswawpuddenah, in which they had confident hopes of finding the game which they desired. In former years the spot had been famous as a sheltering place for herds of wolves ; and, with something like the impatience of a warrior waiting for his foe, the hunters prepared their strongest shafts and sharpest flints, and set their keen eyes upon the closes' places of the thicket, into which they plunged fearlessly. They had not proceeded far, before a single boar-wolf, of amazing size, started up in their path ; and, being slightly wounded by the arrow of Selonee, which glanced first upon some twigs beneath which he lay, he darted off with a fearful howl in the direction of Conattee, whose unobstructed shaft, penetrating the side beneath the fore shoulders, inflicted a fearful, if not a fatal wound, upon the now thoroughly enraged beast. He rushed upon Conattee in his desperation, but the savage was too quick for him ; leaping behind a tree, he avoided the rashing stroke with which the white tusks threatened him, and by this time was enabled to fit a second arrow to his bow. His aim was true, and the stone blade of the shaft went quivering into the shaggy monster's heart; who, under the pang of the last convulsion, bounded into the muddy waters of the Thicketty Creek, to the edge of which the chase had now brought all the parties. Conattee beheld him plunge furiously forward —twice—thrice—then rest with his nostrils in the water, as the current bore him from sight around a little elbow of the creek. But it was not often that the Indian hunter of those days lost the game which he had stricken. Conattee stripped to it, threw his fringed hunting shirt of buckskin on the bank, with his bow and arrows, his mocasins and leggins beside it, and reserving only his knife, he called to Selonee, who was approaching him, to keep them in sight, and plunged into the water in pursuit of his victim. Selonee gave little heed to the movements of his companion, after the first two or three vigorous strokes which he beheld him make. Such a pursuit, as it promised no peril, called for little consideration from this hardy and fearless race, and Selonee amused himself by striking into a thick copse which they had not yet traversed, in search of other sport. There he started the she-wolf, and found sufficient employment on his own hands to call for all his attention to himself. When Selonee first came in sight of her, she was lying on a bed of rushes and leaves, which she had prepared under the roots of a gigantic Spanish oak. Her cubs, to the number of five, lay around her, keeping a perfect silence, which she had no doubt enforced upon them after her own fashion, and which was rigidly maintained until they saw him. It was then that the instincts of the fierce beasts could no longer be suppressed, and they joined at once in a short chopping bark, or cry, at the stranger, while their little eyes flashed fire, and their red jaws, thinly sprinkled with the first teeth, were gnashed together with a show of that ferocious hatred of man, which marks their nature, but which, fortunately for Selonee, was too feeble at that time to make his approach to them dangerous. But the dam demanded greater consideration. With one sweep of her fore-paw she drew all the young ones behind her, and showing every preparedness for flight, she began to move backward slowly beneath the overhanging limbs of the tree, still keeping her keen, fiery eye fixed upon the hunter. But Selonee was not disposed to suffer her to get off so easily. The success of Conattee had just given him sufficient provocation to make him silently resolve that the she-wolf—who is always more to be dreaded than the male, as, with nearly all his strength, she has twice his swiftness, and, with her young about her, more than twice his ferocity—should testify more completely to his prowess than the victory just obtained by his companion could possibly speak for his. His eye was fixed upon hers, and hers, never for a moment, taken from him. It was his object to divert it, since he well knew, that with his first movement, she would most probably spring upon him. Without lifting his bow, which he nevertheless had in readiness, he whistled shrilly as if to his dog; and answered himself by a correct imitation of the bark of the Indian cur, the known enemy of the wolf, and commonly his victim. The keen eye of the angry beast looked suddenly around as if fearing an assault upon her young ones from behind. In that moment, the arrow of Selonee was driven through her neck, and when she leaped forward to the place where he stood, he was no longer to be seen.

From a tree which he had thrown between them, he watched her movements and prepared a second shaft. Meanwhile she made her way back slowly to her young, and before she could again turn towards him a second arrow had given her another and severer wound. Still, as Selonee well knew the singular tenacity of life possessed by these fierce animals, he prudently changed his position with every shaft, and took especial care to place himself in the rear of some moderately sized tree, sufficiently large to shelter him from her claws, yet small enough to enable him to take free aim around it. Still he did not, at any time, withdraw more than twenty steps from his enemy. Divided in her energies by the necessity of keeping near her young, he was conscious of her inability to pursue him far. Carrying on the war in this manner he had buried no less than five arrows in her body, and it was not until his sixth had penetrated her eye, that he deemed himself safe in the nearer approach which he now meditated. She had left her cubs, on receiving his last shot, and was writhing and leaping, blinded, no less than maddened, by the wound, in a vain endeavour to approach her assailant. It was now that Selonee determined on a closer conflict. It was the great boast of the Catawba warriors to grapple with the wolf, and while he yet struggled, to tear the quick quivering heart from his bosom. He placed his bow and arrows behind the tree, and taking in his left hand a chunk or fragment of a bough, while he grasped his unsheathed knife in his right, he leapt in among the cubs, and struck one of them a severe blow upon the head with the chunk. Its scream, and the confusion among the rest, brought back the angry dam, and though she could see only imperfectly, yet, guided by their clamour, she rushed with open jaws upon the hunter. With keen, quick eyes, and steady resolute nerves, he waited for her approach, and when she turned her head aside, to strike him with her sharp teeth, he thrust the pine fragment which he carried in his left hand, into her extended jaws, and pressing fast upon her, bore back her haunches to the earth. All this while the young ones were impotently gnawing at the heels of the warrior, which had been fearlessly planted in the very midst of them. But these he did not heed. The larger and fiercer combatant called for all his attention, and her exertions, quickened by the spasms of her wounds, rendered necessary all his address and strength to preserve the advantage he had gained. The fierce beast had sunk her teeth by this into the wood, and, leaving it in her jaws, he seized her with the hand, now freed, by the throat, and, bearing her upward, so as to yield him a plain and easy stroke at her belly, he drove the deep knife into it, and drew the blade upwards, until resisted by the bone of the breast. It was then, while she lay writhing and rolling upon the ground in the agonies of death, that he tore the heart from the opening he had made, and hurled it down to the cubs, who seized on it with avidity. This done, he patted and caressed them, and while they struggled about him for the meat, he cut a fork in the ears of each, and putting the slips in his pouch, left the young ones without further hurt, for the future sport of the hunter. The dam he scalped, and with this trophy in possession, he pushed back to the place where he had left the accoutrements of Conattee, which he found undisturbed in the place where he had laid them.

CHAPTER III.

But where was Conattee himself during all this period ? Some hours had elapsed since he had taken the river after the tiger that he had slain, and it was something surprising to Selonee that he should have remained absent and without his clothes so long. The weather was cold and unpleasant, and it could scarce be a matter of choice with the hunter, however hardy, to suffer all its biting bleaknesses when his garments were within his reach. This reflection made Selonee apprehensive that some harm had happened to his companion. He shouted to him, but received no answer. Could he have been seized with the cramp while in the stream, and drowned before he could extricate himself. This was a danger to which the very best of swimmers is liable at certain seasons of the year, and in certain conditions of the body. Selonee reproached himself that he had not waited beside the stream until the result of Conattee's experiment was known. The mind of the young hunter was troubled with many fears and doubts. He went down the bank of the river, and called aloud with all his lungs, until the woods and waters re-echoed, again and again, the name of Conattee. He received no other response. With a mind filled with increasing fears, each more unpleasant than the last, Selonee plunged into the creek, and struck off for the opposite shore, at the very point at which the tiger had been about to turn, under the influence of the current, when Conattee went in after him. He was soon across, and soon found the tracks of the hunter in the gray sands upon its margin. He found, too, to his great delight, the traces made by the carcass of the tiger—the track was distinct enough from the blood which dropped from the reeking skin of the beast, and Selonee rejoiced in the certainty that the traces which he followed would soon lead him to his friend. But not so. He had scarcely gone fifty yards into the wood when his tracks failed him at the foot of a crooked, fallen tree, one of the most gnarled and complicated of all the crooked trees of the forest ; here all signs disappeared. Conattee was not only not there, but had left no sort of clue by which to follow him further. This was the strangest thing of all. The footprints were distinct enough till he came to the spot where lay the crooked tree, but there he lost them. He searched the forest around him, in every direction. Not a copse escaped his search —not a bay—not a thicket—not an island—and he came back to the spot where the tiger had been skinned, faint and weary, and more sorrowful than can well be spoken. At one time he fancied his friend was drowned, at another, that he was taken prisoner by the Cherokees. But there were his tracks from the river, and there were no other tracks than his own. Besides, so far as the latter supposition was concerned, it was scarcely possible that so brave and cunning a warrior would suffer himself to be so completely entrapped and carried off by an enemy, without so much as being able to give the alarm ; and, even had that been the case, would it be likely that the enemy would have suffered him to pass without notice. " But," here the suggestion naturally arose in the mind of Selonee, " may they not even now be on the track !" With the suggestion the gallant youth bounded to his feet. " It is no fat turkey that they seek !" he exclaimed, drawing out an arrow from the leash that hung upon his shoulders, and fitting it to his bow, while his busy, glancing eye watched every shadow in the wood, and his keen, quick ear noted every sound. But there were no signs of an enemy, and a singular and mournful stillness hung over the woods. Never was creature more miserable than Selonee. He called aloud, until his voice grew hoarse, and his throat sore, upon the name of Conattee. There was no answer, but the gibing echoes of his own hoarse accents. Once more he went back to the river, once more he plunged into its bosom, and with lusty sinews struck out for a thick green island that lay some quarter of a mile below, to which he thought it not improbable that the hunter might have wandered in pursuit of other game. It was a thickly wooded but small island, which he traversed in an hour. Finding nothing, he made his weary way back to the spot from which his friend had started on leaving him. Here he found his clothes where he had hidden them. The neighbourhood of this region he traversed in like manner with the opposite—going over ground, and into places, which it was scarcely in the verge of physical possibility that his friend's person could have gone.

The day waned and night came on, and still the persevering hunter gave not up his search. The midnight found him at the foot of the tree, where they had parted, exhausted but sleepless, and suffering bitterly in mind from those apprehensions which every moment of hopeless search had necessarily helped to accumulate and strengthen. Day dawned, and his labour was renewed. The unhappy warrior went resolutely over all the ground which he had traversed the night before. Once more he crossed the river, and followed, step by step, the still legible foot tracks of Conattee. These, he again noted, were all in the opposite direction to the stream, to which it was evident he had not returned. But, after reaching the place where lay the fallen tree, all signs failed. Selonee looked round the crooked tree, crawled under its sprawling and twisted limbs, broke into the hollow which was left by its uptorn roots, and again shouted, until all the echoes gave back his voice, the name of Conattee, imploring him for an answer if he could hear him and reply. But the echoes died away, leaving him in a silence that spoke more loudly to his heart than before, that his quest was hopeless. Yet he gave it not up until the day had again failed him. That night, as before, he slept upon the ground. With the dawn, he again went over it, and with equally bad success. This done, he determined to return to the camp. He no longer had any spirit to pursue the sports for which alone he had set forth. His heart was full of sorrow, his limbs were weary, and he felt none of that vigorous elasticity which had given him such great renown as a brave and a hunter, among his own and the neighbouring nations. He tied the clothes of Conattee upon his shoulders, took his bow and arrows, now sacred in his sight, along with him, and turned his eyes homeward. The next day, at noon, he reached the encampment.

10

CHAPTER IV.

THE hunters were all in the woods, and none but the squaws and the papooses left in the encampment. Selonee came within sight of their back settlements, and seated himself upon a log at the edge of the forest with his back carefully turned towards the smoke of the camp. Nobody ventured to approach him while in this situation; but, at night, when the hunters came dropping in, one by one, Selonee drew nigh to them. He called them apart from the women, and then told them his story.

" This is a strange tale which the wolf-chief tells us," said one of the old men, with a smile of incredulity.

" It is a true tale, father," was the reply.

" Conattee was a brave chief!"

" Very brave, father," said Selonee.

" Had he not eyes to see ?"

" The great bird, that rises to the sun, had not better," was the reply.

" What painted jay was it that said Conattee was a fool ?"

" The painted bird lied, that said so, my father," was the response of Selonee.

" And comes Selonee, the wolf-chief, to us, with a tale that Conattee was blind, and could not see ; a coward that could not strike the she-wolf ; a fool that knew not where to set down his foot ; and shall we not say Selonee lies upon his brother, even as the painted bird that makes a noise in my ears. Selonee has slain Conattee with his knife. See, it is the blood of Conattee upon the war-shirt of Selonee."

" It is the blood of the she-wolf," cried the young warrior, with a natural indignation.

" Let Selonee go to the woods behind the lodges, till the chiefs say what shall be done to Selonee, because of Conattee, whom he slew."

" Selonee will go, as Emathla the wise chief, has commanded,"

replied the young warrior. "He will wait behind the lodges, till
the chiefs have said what is good to be done to him, and if they
say that he must die because of Conattee, it is well. Selonee
laughs at death. But the blood of Conattee is not upon the war-
shirt of Selonee. He has said it is the blood of the wolf's mother."
With these words the young chief drew forth the skin of the wolf
which he had slain, together with the tips of the ears taken from
the cubs, and leaving them in the place where he had sat, withdrew, without further speech, from the assembly which was about
to sit in judgment upon his life.

13

CHAPTER V.

THE consultation that followed was close and earnest. There was scarcely any doubt in the minds of the chiefs that Conattee was slain by his companion. He had brought back with him the arms and all the clothes of the hunter. He was covered with his blood, as they thought; and the grief which filled his heart and depressed his countenance, looked, in their eyes, rather like the expression of guilt than suffering. For a long while did they consult together. Selonee had friends who were disposed to save him; but he had enemies also, as merit must have always, and these were glad of the chance afforded them to put out of their reach, a rival of whom they were jealous, and a warrior whom they feared. Unfortunately for Selonee, the laws of the nation but too well helped the malice of his foes. These laws, as peremptory as those of the Medes and Persians, held him liable in his own life for that of the missing hunter; and the only indulgence that could be accorded to Selonee, and which was obtained for him, was, that he might be allowed a single moon in which to find Conattee, and bring him home to his people.

"Will Selonee go seek Conattee—the windy moon is for Selonee—let him bring Conattee home to his people." Thus said the chiefs, when the young warrior was again brought before them.

"Selonee would die to find Conattee," was the reply.

"He will die if he finds him not!" answered the chief Emathla.

"It is well!" calmly spoke the young warrior. "Is Selonee free to go?"

"The windy moon is for Selonee. Will he return to the lodges if he finds not Conattee?" was the inquiry of Emathla.

"Is Selonee a dog, to fly!" indignantly demanded the warrior. "Let Emathla send a young warrior on the right and on the left of Selonee, if he trusts not what is spoken by Selonee."

"Selonee will go alone, and bring back Conattee."

CHAPTER VI.

THE confidence thus reposed in one generally esteemed a murderer, and actually under sentence as such, is customary among
the Indians; nor is it often abused.   The loss of caste which
would follow their flight from justice, is much more terrible
among them than any fear of death—which an Indian may avoid,
but not through fear.   Their loss of caste among themselves,
apart from the outlawry which follows it, is, in fact, a loss of the
soul.   The heaven of the great Manneyto is denied to one under
outlawry of the nation, and such a person is then the known and
chosen slave of the demon, Opitchi-Manneyto.   It was held an unnecessary insult on the part of Emathla, to ask Selonee if he
would return to meet his fate.   But Emathla was supposed to favour the enemies of Selonee.

With such a gloomy alternative before him in the event of his
proving unsuccessful, the young hunter retraced his steps to the
fatal waters where Conattee had disappeared.   With a spirit no
less warmly devoted to his friend, than anxious to avoid the dis-
graceful doom to which he was destined, the youth spared no pains,
withheld no exertion, overlooked no single spot, and omitted no
art known to the hunter, to trace out the mystery which covered
the fate of Conattee.   But days passed of fruitless labour, and the
last faint slender outlines of the moon which had been allotted
him for the search, gleamed forth a sorrowful light upon his path,
as he wearily traced it onward to the temporary lodges of the
tribe.

Once more he resumed his seat before the council and listened
to the doom which was in reserve for him.   When the sentence
was pronounced, he untied his arrows, loosened the belt at his
waist, put a fillet around his head, made of the green bark of a
little sapling which he cut in the neighbouring woods, then rising
to his feet, he spoke thus, in language, and with a spirit, becoming
so great a warrior.

"It is well. The chiefs have spoken, and the wolf-chief does not tremble. He loves the chase, but he does not weep like a woman, because it is forbidden that he go after the deer—he loves to fright the young hares of the Cherokee, but he laments not that ye say ye can conquer the Cherokee without his help. Fathers, I have slain the deer and the wolf—my lodge is full of their ears. I have slain the Cherokee, till the scalps are about my knees when I walk in the cabin. I go not to the dark valley without glory—I have had the victories of grey hairs, but there is no grey hair in my own. I have no more to say—there is a deed for every arrow that is here. Bid the young men get their bows ready, let them put a broad stone upon their arrows that may go soon into the life—I will show my people how to die."

They led him forth as he commanded, to the place of execution—a little space behind the encampment, where a hole had been already dug for his burial. While he went, he recited his victories to the youths who attended him. To each he gave an arrow which he was required to keep, and with this arrow, he related some incident in which he had proved his valour, either in conflict with some other warrior, or with the wild beasts of the woods. These deeds, each of them was required to remember and relate, and show the arrow which was given with the narrative on occasion of this great state solemnity. In this way, their traditions are preserved. When he reached the grave, he took his station before it, the executioners, with their arrows, being already placed in readiness. The whole tribe had assembled to witness the execution, the warriors and boys in the foreground, the squaws behind them. A solemn silence prevailed over the scene, and a few moments only remained to the victim; when the wife of Conattee darted forward from the crowd bearing in her hands a peeled wand, with which, with every appearance of anger, she struck Selonee over the shoulders, exclaiming as she did so:

"Come, thou dog, thou shalt not die—thou shalt lie in the doorway of Conattee, and bring venison for his wife. Shall there be no one to bring meat to my lodge? Thou shalt do this, Selonee—thou shalt not die."

A murmur arose from the crowd at these words.

"She hath claimed Selonee for her husband, in place of Conattee—well, she hath the right."

The enemies of Selonee could not object. The widow had, in fact, exercised a privilege which is recognized by the Indian laws almost universally ; and the policy by which she was governed in the present instance, was sufficiently apparent to all the village. It was evident, now that Conattee was gone, that nobody could provide for the woman who had no sons, and no male relations, and who was too execrably ugly, and too notorious as a scold, to leave it possible that she could ever procure another husband so inexperienced or so flexible as the one she had lost. Smartly striking Selonee on his shoulders, she repeated her command that he should rise and follow her.

"Thou wilt take this dog to thy lodge, that he may hunt thee venison ?" demanded the old chief, Emathla.

"Have I not said ?" shouted the scold—"hear you not ? The dog is mine—I bid him follow me."

"Is there no friendly arrow to seek my heart ?" murmured the young warrior, as, rising slowly from the grave into which he had previously descended, he prepared to obey the laws of his nation, in the commands of the woman who claimed him to replace the husband who was supposed to have died by his hands. Even the foes of Selonee looked on him with lessened hostility, and the pity of his friends was greater now than when he stood on the precipice of death. The young women of the tribe wept bitterly as they beheld so monstrous a sacrifice. Meanwhile, the exulting hag, as if conscious of her complete control over the victim, goaded him forward with repeated strokes of her wand. She knew that she was hated by all the young women, and she was delighted to show them a conquest which would have been a subject of pride to any among them. With this view she led the captive through their ranks. As they parted mournfully, on either hand, to suffer the two to pass, Selonee stopped short and motioned one of the young women who stood at the greatest distance behind the rest, looking on with eyes which, if they had no tears, yet gave forth an expression of desolateness more woful than any tears could have done. With clasped hands, and trembling as she came, the gentle maiden drew nigh.

" Was it a dream," said Selonee sorrowfully, " that told me of the love of a singing bird, and a green cabin by the trickling waters ? Did I hear a voice that said to me sweetly, wait but a little, till the green corn breaks the hill, and Medoree will come to thy cabin and lie by thy side ? Tell me, is this thing true, Medoree ?"

" Thou sayest, Selonee—the thing is true," was the reply of the maiden, uttered in broken accents that denoted a breaking heart.

" But they will make Selonee go to the lodge of another woman —they will put Macourah into the arms of Selonee."

" Alas ! Alas !"

" Wilt thou see this thing, Medoree ? Can'st thou look upon it, then turn away, and going back to thy own lodge, can'st thou sing a gay song of forgetfulness as thou goest ?"

" Forgetfulness !—Ah, Selonee."

" Thou art the beloved of Selonee, Medoree—thou shalt not lose him. It would vex thy heart that another should take him to her lodge !"—

The tears of the damsel flowed freely down her cheeks, and she sobbed bitterly, but said nothing.

" Take the knife from my belt, Medoree, and put its sharp tooth into my heart, ere thou sufferest this thing ! Wilt thou not ?"

The girl shrunk back with an expression of undisguised horror in her face.

" I will bless thee, Medoree," was the continued speech of the warrior. She turned from him, covering her face with her hands.

" I cannot do this thing, Selonee—I cannot strike thy heart with the knife. Go—let the woman have thee. Medoree cannot kill thee—she will herself die."

" It is well," cried the youth, in a voice of mournful self-abandonment, as he resumed his progress towards the lodge of Macourah.

CHAPTER VI.

It is now time to return to Conattee, and trace his progress from the moment when, plunging into the waters, he left the side of Selonee in pursuit of the wolf, whose dying struggles in the stream he had beheld. We are already acquainted with his success in extricating the animal from the water, and possessing himself of its hide. He had not well done this when he heard a rushing noise in the woods above him, and fancying that there was a prospect of other game at hand, and inflated with the hope of adding to his trophies, though without any weapon but his knife, Conattee hastened to the spot. When he reached it, however, he beheld nothing. A gigantic and singularly deformed pine tree, crooked and most irregular in shape, lay prostrate along the ground, and formed such an intricate covering above it, that Conattee deemed it possible that some beast of prey might have made its den among the recesses of its roots. With this thought, he crawled under the spreading limbs, and searched all their intricacies. Emerging from the search, which had been fruitless, he took a seat upon the trunk of the tree, and spreading out the wolf's hide before him, proceeded to pare away the particles of flesh which, in the haste with which he had performed the task of flaying him, had been suffered to adhere to the skin. But he had scarcely commenced the operation, when two gigantic limbs of the fallen tree upon which he sat, curled over his thighs and bound him to the spot. Other limbs, to his great horror, while he strove to move, clasped his arms and covered his shoulders. He strove to cry aloud, but his jaws were grasped before he could well open them, by other branches; and, with his eyes, which were suffered to peer through little openings in the bark, he could see his legs encrusted by like coverings with his other members. Still seeing, his own person yet escaped his sight. Not a part of it now remained visible to himself. A bed of green velvet-like moss rested on his lap. His knees shot out a thorny excrescence;

and his hands, flattened to his thighs, were enveloped in as complete a casing of bark as covered the remainder of the tree around him. Even his knife and wolf skin, to his great surprise, suffered in like manner, the bark having contracted them into one of those huge bulging knobs that so numerously deformed the tree. With all his thoughts and consciousness remaining, Conattee had yet lost every faculty of action. When he tried to scream aloud, his jaws felt the contraction of a pressure upon them, which resisted all their efforts, while an oppressive thorn growing upon a wild vine that hung before his face, was brought by every movement of himself or of the tree into his very mouth. The poor hunter immediately conceived his situation—he was in the power of Tustenuggee, the Grey Demon of Enoree. The tree upon which he sat was one of those magic trees which the tradition of his people entitled the "Arm-chair of Tustenuggee." In these traps for the unwary the wicked demon caught his victim, and exulted in his miseries. Here he sometimes remained until death released him; for it was not often that the power into whose clutches he had fallen, suffered his prey to escape through a sudden feeling of lenity and good humour. The only hope of Conattee was that Selonee might suspect his condition; in which event his rescue was simple and easy enough. It was only to hew off the limbs, or pare away the bark, and the victim was uncovered in his primitive integrity. But how improbable that this discovery should be made. He had no voice to declare his bondage. He had no capacity for movement by which he might reveal the truth to his comrade's eyes; and unless some divine instinct should counsel his friend to an experiment which he would scarcely think upon, of himself, the poor prisoner felt that he must die in the miserable bondage into which he had fallen. While these painful convictions were passing through his mind, he heard the distant shoutings of Selonee. In a little while he beheld the youth anxiously seeking him in every quarter, following his trail at length to the very tree in which he was bound, crawling like himself beneath its branches, but not sitting like himself to be caught upon its trunk. Vainly did the poor fellow strive to utter but a few words, however faintly, apprising the youth of his condition. The effort died away in the most imperfect breathing

sounding in his own ears like the faint sigh of some budding
flower.   With equal ill success did he aim to struggle with his
limbs.   He was too tightly grasped, in every part, to stir in the
slightest degree a single member.   He saw the fond search, meanwhile, which his comrade maintained, and his heart yearned the
more in fondness for the youth.   But it was with consummate
horror that he saw him depart as night came on.   Miserable, indeed, were his feelings that night.   The voice of the Grey Demon
alone kept him company, and he and his one-eyed wife made
merry with his condition, goading him the livelong night with
speeches of cruel gibe and mischievous reflection, such as the
following :

" There is no hope for you, Conattee, till some one takes your
place.   Some one must sit in your lap, whom you are willing to
leave behind you, before you can get out of mine," was the speech
of the Grey Demon, who, perched upon Conattee's shoulders, bent
his huge knotty head over him, while his red eyes looked into the
half-hidden ones of the environed hunter, and glared upon him
with the exultation of the tyrant at last secure of his prey.   Night
passed away at length, and, with the dawn, how was the hopeless
heart of Conattee refreshed as he again saw Selonee appear.   He
then remembered the words of Tustenuggee, which told him that
he could not escape until some one sat in his lap whom he was
willing to leave behind him.   The fancy rose in his mind that
Selonee would do this ; but could it be that he would consent to
leave his friend behind him.   Life was sweet, and great was the
temptation.   At one moment he almost wished that Selonee would
draw nigh and seat himself after his fatigue.   As if the young
hunter knew his wish, he drew nigh at that instant ; but the better feelings in Conattee's heart grew strong as he approached, and,
striving to twist and writhe in his bondage, and labouring at the
same time to call out in warning to his friend, he manifested the
noble resolution not to avail himself of his friend's position to relieve his own ; and, as if the warning of Conattee had really
reached the understanding of Selonee, the youth retraced his
steps, and once more hurried away from the place of danger.
With his final departure the fond hopes of the prisoner sunk within
him ; and when hour after hour had gone by without the appear

ance of any of his people, and without any sort of change in his condition, he gave himself up utterly for lost. The mocks and jeers of the Grey Demon and his one-eyed squaw filled his ears all night, and the morning brought him nothing but flat despair. He resigned himself to his fate with the resolution of one who, however unwilling he might be to perish in such a manner, had yet faced death too frequently not to yield him a ready defiance now.

CHAPTER VII.

But hope had not utterly departed from the bosom of Selonee. Perhaps the destiny which had befallen himself had made him resolve the more earnestly to seek farther into the mystery of that which hung above the fate of his friend. The day which saw him enter the cabin of Macourah saw him the most miserable man alive. The hateful hag, hateful enough as the wife of his friend, whose ill treatment was notorious, was now doubly hateful to him as his own wife; and now, when, alone together, she threw aside the harsh and termagant features which had before distinguished her deportment, and, assuming others of a more amorous complexion, threw her arms about the neck of the youth and solicited his endearments, a loathing sensation of disgust was coupled with the hate which had previously possessed his mind. Flinging away from her embrace, he rushed out of the lodge with feelings of the most unspeakable bitterness and grief, and bending his way towards the forest, soon lost sight of the encampment of his people. Selonee was resolved on making another effort for the recovery of his friend. His resolve went even farther than this. He was bent never to return to the doom which had been fastened upon him, and to pursue his way into more distant and unknown forests —a self-doomed exile—unless he could restore Conattee to the nation. Steeled against all those ties of love or of country, which at one time had prevailed in his bosom over all, he now surrendered himself to friendship or despair. In Catawba, unless he restored Conattee, he could have no hope; and without Catawba he had neither hope nor love. On either hand he saw nothing but misery; but the worst form of misery lay behind him in the lodge of Macourah. But Macourah was not the person to submit to such a determination. She was too well satisfied with the exchange with which fortune had provided her, to suffer its gift to be lost so easily; and when Selonee darted from the cabin in such fearful haste, she readily conjectured his determination

She hurried after him with all possible speed, little doubting that those thunders—could she overtake him—with which she had so frequently overawed the pliant Conattee, would possess an effect not less influential upon his more youthful successor.   Macourah was gaunt as a greyhound, and scarcely less fleet of foot.   Besides, she was as tough as a grey-squirrel in his thirteenth year. She did not despair of overtaking Selonee, provided she suffered him not to know that she was upon his trail.   Her first movements therefore were marked with caution.   Having watched his first direction, she divined his aim to return to the hunting grounds where he had lost or slain his companion; and these hunting grounds were almost as well known to herself as to him.   With a rapidity of movement, and a tenacity of purpose, which could only be accounted for by a reference to that wild passion which Selonee had unconsciously inspired in her bosom for himself, she followed his departing footsteps; and when, the next day, he heard her shouts behind him, he was absolutely confounded.   But it was with a feeling of surprise and not of dissatisfaction that he heard her voice.   He—good youth—regarding Conattee as one of the very worthiest of the Catawba warriors, seemed to have been impressed with an idea that such also was the opinion of his wife.   He little dreamed that she had any real design upon himself; and believed that, to show her the evidences which were to be seen, which led to the fate of her husband, might serve to convince her that not only he was not the murderer, but that Conattee might not, indeed, be murdered at all.   He coolly waited her approach, therefore, and proceeded to renew his statements, accompanying his narrative with the expression of the hope which he entertained of again restoring her husband to herself and the nation.   But she answered his speech only with upbraidings and entreaties; and when she failed, she proceeded to thump him lustily with the wand by which she had compelled him to follow her to the lodge the day before.   But Selonee was in no humour to obey the laws of the nation now.   The feeling of degradation which had followed in his mind, from the moment when he left the spot where he had stood up for death, having neither fear nor shame, was too fresh in his consciousness to suffer him to yield a like acknowledgment to it now; and though sorely tempted to

pummel the Jezabel in return for the lusty thwacks which she
had already inflicted upon his shoulders, he forbore, in consideration of his friend, and contented himself with simply setting forward on his progress, determined to elude her pursuit by an exercise of all his vigour and elasticity. Selonee was hardy as the
grisly bear, and fleeter than the wild turkey; and Macourah,
virago as she was, soon discovered the difference in the chase
when Selonee put forth his strength and spirit. She followed
with all her pertinacity, quickened as it was by an increase of
fury at that presumption which had ventured to disobey her commands; but Selonee fled faster than she pursued, and every additional moment served to increase the space botween them. The
hunter lost her from his heels at length, and deemed himself fortunate that she was no longer in sight and hearing, when he again
approached the spot where his friend had so mysteriously disappeared. Here he renewed his search with a painful care and
minuteness, which the imprisoned Conattee all the while beheld.
Once more Selonee crawled beneath those sprawling limbs and
spreading arms that wrapped up in their solid and coarse rinds the
person of the warrior. Once more he emerged from the spot
disappointed and hopeless. This he had hardly done when, to
the great horror of the captive, and the annoyance of Selonee, the
shrill shrieks and screams of the too well-known voice of Macourah rang through the forests. Selonee dashed forward as he
heard the sounds, and when Macourah reached the spot, which
she did unerringly in following his trail, the youth was already
out of sight.

"I can go no further," cried the woman—"a curse on him and
a curse on Conattee, since in losing one I have lost both. I am
too faint to follow. As for Selonee, may the one-eyed witch of
Tustenuggee take him for her dog."

With this delicate imprecation, the virago seated herself in a
state of exhaustion upon the inviting bed of moss which formed
the lap of Conattee. This she had no sooner done, than the
branches relaxed their hold upon the limbs of her husband. The
moment was too precious for delay, and sliding from under her
with an adroitness and strength which were beyond her powers
of preventior, and indeed, quite too sudden for any effort at re-

sistance, she had the consternation to behold her husband starting up in full life before her, and, with the instinct of his former condition, preparing to take to flight. She cried to him, but he fled the faster—she strove to follow him, but the branches which had relaxed their hold upon her husband had resumed their contracted grasp upon her limbs. The brown bark was already forming above her on every hand, and her tongue, allotted a brief term of liberty, was alone free to assail him. But she had spoken but few words when the bark encased her jaws, and the ugly thorn of the vine which had so distressed Conattee, had taken its place at their portals.

CHAPTER VIII.

THE husband looked back but once, when the voice ceasec —
then, with a shivering sort of joy that his own doom had undergone a termination, which he now felt to be doubly fortunate—
ne made a wide circuit that he might avoid the fatal neighbourhood, and pushed on in pursuit of his friend, whom his eyes, even
when he was surrounded in the tree, had followed in his flight.
It was no easy task, however, to overtake Selonee, flying, as he
did, from the supposed pursuit of the termagant. Great however
was the joy of the young warriors when they did encounter, and
long and fervent was their mutual embrace. Conattee described
his misfortunes, and related the manner in which he was taken ;
showed how the bark had encased his limbs, and how the intricate
magic had even engrossed his knife and the wolf skin which haa
been the trophy of his victory. But Conattee said not a word o.
his wife and her entrapment, and Selonee was left in the conviction that his companion owed his escape from the toils to some
hidden change in the tyrannical mood of Tustenuggee, or the
one-eyed woman, his wife.

" But the skin and the knife, Conattee, let us not leave them,"
said Selonee, " let us go back and extricate them from the tree."
Conattee showed some reluctance. He soon said, in the wo ds
of Macbeth, which he did not use however as a quotation, " I'll
go no more. ' But Selonee, who ascribed this reluctance to very
natural apprehensions of the demon from whose clutches he had
just made his escape, declared his readiness to undertake the adventure if Conattee would only point out to his eyes the particular excrescence in which the articles were enclosed. When the
husband perceived that his friend was resolute, he made a merit
of necessity.

" If the thing is to be done," said he, " why should you have
the risk, I myself will do it. It would be a woman-fear were I
to shrink from the danger. Let us go."

11

The process of reasoning by which Conattee came to this de-termination was a very sudden one, and one, too, that will not be hard to comprehend by every husband in his situation.   It was his fear that if Selonee undertook the business, an unlucky or misdirected stroke of his knife might sever a limb, or remove some portions of the bark which did not merit or need removal.   Co-nattee trembled at the very idea of the revelations which might follow such an unhappy result.   Strengthening himself, there-fore, with all his energies, he went forward with Selonee to the spot and while the latter looked on and witnessed the operation, he proceeded with a nicety and care which amused and sur-prised Selonee, to the excision of the swollen scab upon the tree in which he had seen his wolf skin encompassed.   While he per-formed the operation, which he did as cautiously as if it had been the extraction of a mote from the eye of a virgin ; the beldam in the tree, conscious of all his movements, and at first flattered with the hope that he was working for her extrication, maintained the most ceaseless efforts of her tongue and limbs, but without avail. Her slight breathing, which Conattee knew where to look for, more like the sighs of an infant zephyr than the efforts of a hu-man bosom, denoted to his ears an overpowering but fortunately suppressed volcano within ; and his heart leaped with a new joy, which had been unknown to it for many years before, when he thought that he was now safe, and, he trusted, for ever, from any of the tortures which he had been fain to endure patiently so long. When he had finished the operation by which he had re-obtained his treasures, he ventured upon an impertinence which spoke surprisingly for his sudden acquisition of confidence ; and looking up through the little aperture in the bark, from whence he had seen every thing while in the same situation, and from whence he concluded she was also suffered to see, he took a peep—a quick, quizzical and taunting peep, at those eyes which he had not so dared to offend before.   He drew back suddenly from the contact—so suddenly, indeed, that Selonee, who saw the proceed-ing, but had no idea of the truth, thought he had been stung by some insect, and questioned him accordingly.

" Let us be off, Selonee," was the hurried answer, " we have nothing to wait for now."

" Yes," replied Selonee, " and I had forgotten to say to you that your wife, Macourah, is on her way in search of you. I left her but a little ways behind, and thought to find her here. I suppose she is tired, however, and is resting by the way."

" Let her rest," said Conattee, " which is an indulgence much greater than any she ever accorded me. She will find me out soon enough, without making it needful that I should go in search of her. Come."

Selonee kindly suppressed the history of the transactions which had taken place in the village during the time when the hunter was supposed to be dead ; but Conattee heard the facts from other quarters, and loved Selonee the better for the sympathy he had shown, not only in coming again to seek for him, but in not loving his wife better than he did himself. They returned to the village, and every body was rejoiced to behold the return of the hunters. As for the termagant Macourah, nobody but Conattee knew her fate ; and he, like a wise man, kept his secret until there was no danger of its being made use of to rescue her from her predicament. Years had passed, and Conattee had found among the young squaws one that pleased him much better than the old. He had several children by her, and years and honours had alike fallen numerously upon his head, when, one day, one of his own sons, while hunting in the same woods, knocked off one of the limbs of the Chair of Tustenuggee, and to his great horror discovered the human arm which they enveloped. This led him to search farther, and limb after limb became detached under the unscrupulous action of his hatchet, until the entire but unconnected members of the old squaw became visible. The lad knocked about the fragments with little scruple, never dreaming how near was his relation to the form which he treated with so little veneration. When he came home to the lodge and told his story, Selonee looked at Conattee, but said nothing. The whole truth was at once apparent to his mind. Conattee, though he still kept his secret, was seized with a sudden fit of piety, and taking his sons with him, he proceeded to the spot which he well remembered, and, gathering up the bleached remains, had them carefully buried in the trenches of the tribe.

It may properly end this story, to say that Selonee wedded the sweet girl who, though willing to die herself to prevent him from marrying Macourah, yet positively refused to take his life to defeat the same event. It may be well to state, in addition, that the only reason Conattee ever had for believing that Selonee had not kept his secret from every body, was that Medoree, the young wife of the latter, looked on him with a very decided coolness. " But, we will see," muttered Conattee as he felt this conviction. " Selonee will repent of this confidence, since now it will never be possible for him to persuade her to take a seat in the Arm-chair of Tustenuggee. Had he been a wise man he would have kept his secret, and then there would have been no difficulty in **getting rid of a wicked wife** "

THE SNAKE OF THE CABIN.

CHAPTER I.

"They talk," said the stranger somewhat abruptly "They talk of the crimes of wealthy people, and in high life. No doubt there are very great and many wrong doers among the rich. People in possession of much wealth, and seeing how greatly it is worshipped, will very naturally presume upon and abuse its powers;—but it is not among the rich only, and in the great city, that these things happen. The same snake, or one very much like it, winds his way into the wigwam and the cabin—and the poor silly country girl is as frequently the victim, as the dashing lady of the city and city fashions. For that matter she is the more easily liable to imposition, as are all persons who occupy insulated positions, and see little of the great struggles of busy life. The planter and the farmer who dwell in the remote interior find the face of the visitor too interesting, to scrutinize it very closely. A pleasant deportment, a specious outside, a gentle and attractive manner, will win their way in our forest world, without rendering necessary those formal assurances, that rigid introduction, and those guaranties of well known persons, which the citizen requires before you partake of his bread and salt. With us, on the contrary, we confide readily; and the cunning stranger, whom other communities have expelled with loathing, rendered cautious and conciliatory by previous defeat, adopts the subtlety of the snake, and winds his way as artfully as that reptile, when he comes among us. We have too many sad stories of this sort. Yours is one of them. This poor girl, Ellen Ramsay, was abused thus, as I have shown you, by this scoundrel, Stanton. But finish your narrative. She had a short time of it, and a sad one, I do not doubt, with a creature so heartless and so vile."

"But a poor eleven months; and the change was too rapid," said young Atkins, "not to let us see that she was any thing but happy. To-day, the gayest of all God's creatures, as much like a merry bird in spring-time, singing over its young;—to-morrow as gloomy and miserable as if there was neither song nor sunshine in God's whole earth."

"Poor thing!" exclaimed Walter.

"It was the shortest life," said the other, "to begin so well, that I ever saw, and the story which you have ·heard is pretty much the truth."

"But the funeral?" said Walter.

"Ah! that was not exactly as you heard it," was the reply of Atkins. "I was at the funeral of Ellen Ramsay, as indeed was very nearly all the village, and I could refer you to twenty who will tell you the matter just as it occurred. In the first place, it is not true that any body expected Robert Anderson to be present. He sent no message of any kind to Stanton. It was very well known that he was sick—actually in bed, and had been so for more than a week before the death of Ellen. People almost thought they might go off together. There was a sort of sympathy between them, though I don't think, from the hour of her unlucky marriage, that the eyes of the two ever met, till they met in the world of spirits—unless it were, indeed, in their dreams. But they seemed to pine away, both of them, about the same time, and though he stood it longest, he did not outlast her much. When she died, as I tell you, he was very feeble and in bed. Nobody ever expected him to leave it alive, and least of all that he should leave it then, to stand among the people at her grave. The circumstances of her marriage with Stanton, were too notorious, and too much calculated to embitter his feelings and his peace, to make it likely that he would be present at such a scene. She had cast him off, slightingly, to give a preference to the more showy stranger, and she had spoken to him in a manner not soon to be forgiven by a man of sensibility. But he did forgive—that I know—and his love for Ellen was unimpaired to the last. She did not doubt this, when she married Stanton, though she expressed herself so. That was only to find some excuses to him, if not to her own conscience for her conduct. I'm sure she bitterly re-

pented of all before very long. She was just the girl to do wrong
in a hurry, and be sorry for it the next minute."

"But the funeral ?" said Walter.

"Ah! true—the funeral. Well, as I was telling you, when
the coffin was brought round to the burial place—you know the
spot, among a thick grove of stunted oaks, and the undergrowth
is always kept down by old Ramsay—who should come out from
behind one of the largest old trees, but Robert Anderson. He
was pale as a ghost, and his limbs trembled and tottered as he
walked, but he came forward as resolutely as if he felt no pain
or weakness. Stanton started when he saw him. He never expected his presence, I assure you. Every eye saw his agitation
as Robert came forward ; and I tell you, there was not a person
present who did not see, as well as myself, that the husband of
the poor girl looked much paler at that moment than her sick
lover. Robert did not seem to see Stanton, or to mind him as he
came forward ; indeed, he did not seem to see any body. His
eyes were fixed only on the coffin, which was carried by me,
Ralph Mason, Dick Rawlins, and I think Hiram Barker. He
did not shed a tear, which we all wondered at, for all of us expected to see him crying like any child, because we knew how
soft-hearted he always was, and how fond he had been of Ellen.
At first, we thought his not crying was because of his anger at
being so ill-treated, which was natural enough ; but what he said
afterwards soon did away with that notion. He came close to my
side, and put his hand on the lid of the coffin near the name, and
though he said not a single word to us, we seemed to understand
that he meant we should stop till he read it. We did stop, and
he then read the plate aloud, something in this manner—' Ellen '
—and then he stopped a little as he came to the word ' Stanton'—
and you could see a deep red flush grow out upon his cheek and
forehead, and then he grew pale as death—and held upon the
coffin as if to keep himself from falling—then he seemed to muster up strength, and he read on, in very deliberate and full accents, as if he had thrown all his resolution into the effort—' Ellen Stanton !'   These words he repeated twice, and then he passed
on to the rest—' WIFE OF GEORGE STANTON, BORN APRIL 7, 1817.
DIED,'—Here he stopped again, poor fellow ! as if to catch his

breath. He only gasped when he tried to go on with the reading. He could only say—'Died. Died!' and there he stopped like a man choking. By this time, Stanton came up close to him and looked at us, as if to say 'Why don't you go forward—why do you suffer him to stop you'—but he said nothing. Robert did not seem to mind or to notice him, but, with another effort, recovering his strength and voice, he read on to the end—'DIED MARCH 27, 1836—AGED EIGHTEEN YEARS, ELEVEN MONTHS AND NINETEEN DAYS.' Old John Ramsay by this time came up, and stood between him and Stanton. He looked up from the coffin, first at one and then at the other—and said quietly—without any appearance of anger or passion:"—

"This, Mr. Ramsay, is your daughter, Ellen—she was to have been my wife—she was engaged to me by her own promise, and you gave your consent to our marriage. Is not this true, Mr. Ramsay?"

"True," said the old man very mildly, but with a deep sigh that seemed to come from the bottom of his soul ;—"but you know, Robert, ——"

Then it was that Robert seemed to lose himself for a moment. His eye brightened with indignation and his speech came quick.

"I know that she is *here!*" he exclaimed—"here, in her coffin, dead to you, your daughter—dead to me, my wife—your Ellen! my Ellen!—My Ellen—my poor Ellen!" And then he sobbed bitterly upon the coffin. I believe that most of the persons present —and all had crowded round us—sobbed too. But I could not see them, for my own heart was overflowing. The interruption did not continue long. Robert was the first to recover himself. He had always a right idea of what was proper ; and no doubt, just then, he felt, that, according to the world's way of thinking, he was doing wrong in stopping the dead in its last progress to the place of rest. He raised up his head from the coffin plate, and said to us, speaking very slowly, for his breath seemed only to come in sobs, and then after great efforts—

"Do not think, my friends, when I speak of the pledges Ellen Ramsay made to me, that I am come here to utter any reproaches of the dead, or to breathe a single syllable of complaint against the blessed creature, who was always a sweet angel, now looking up in heaven. God forbid that I should speak, or that you should hear, any harm of a woman that I have always looked upon as the purest and truest-hearted creature under the sun. No! in telling you of this pledge, I come here only to acquit her of any wrong, or evil thought, or action, when she ceased to think it binding upon her. It is to say to you at her grave, for you all knew that we were to be married, that, as I never gave her any reason for believing me to be false, or more unworthy of her heart than when she promised it to me, so, also, I believe that nothing but some such persuasion could have made her deprive me of it. While I acquit her, therefore, of having done me any intentional injustice, I tell you, in the presence of her heavenly spirit, which knows the truth of what I declare, that she has been abused by some false slanderer, to do me wrong, and herself wrong, and to—"

By this time Stanton put in, and stopped whatever more Robert had to say. He had been getting more and more angry as Robert went on, and when he came to that solemn part about the slanderer, and lifted his hands to heaven and looked upward with the tears just beginning to come into his eyes, as if he did really see the spirit of Ellen at the moment above him, then Stanton got quite furious. Those words clinched him in the sore part of his soul ; and he made round the coffin towards where Robert stood, and doubled his fists, and spoke hoarsely, as if he was about to choke.

" And who do you mean slandered you to her ?" he cried to Robert, " who ! who !"

His face was as black as night, and his features, usually so soft and pleasing to the eyes of the young women, now looked rather like those of a devil than of a mortal man. We thought he would have torn the poor young man to pieces, but Robert did not seem at all daunted. I suppose if we had not been there, and had not interfered so quickly, there would have been violence ; and violence upon a frail, dying creature like Robert, would have been the most shocking cruelty. But Maxcy jumped in between them, and John Ramsay, Ellen's youngest brother, stepped forward also, and we all cried " shame," and this drove Stanton back, but he still looked furious and threatening, and seemed to wish for nothing more than to take Robert by the throat. Nobody seemed to mind him less than the poor fellow who had most reason to fear. Robert had a bold and fearless spirit, and there was a time, before he grew sickly and religious, when he would have grappled with him for death and life before the altar itself. But he was now subdued. He did not seem to mind his enemy, or indeed, any thing, but the coffin on which he hung. He did not, I really think, hear Stanton speaking at all, though, for a few moments, the fellow bullied pretty loud, and not a syllable that he said escaped any body else. His soul seemed to be in the coffin. His eyes seemed to try to pierce the heavy lid of pine, and the dark crape, and the shroud ; and one would think, from the eager and satisfied gaze, that he had succeeded in doing so. No doubt his mind deluded him, and he thought so—for you could hear him whispering—" Ellen ! dear Ellen !" Then he gave way to us, and reading the plate, he said—" But eighteen—but eighteen. But—it is all well now ! all well !" He suffered us then to go forward, and followed close, and made no objection, and said no more words. While we let the coffin down, he stood so nigh, tha the earth shelved with him, and he would have gone in with it, for he made no resistance, if we had not caught him in our arms and dragged him from the brink. But we could not soon get him from the spot. When all was done, he did not seem to mind that the rest were going, but stood looking down as earnestly as if he could still read the writing through six feet of earth. Stanton, too, did not seem willing to go, but we very well knew it was for no love he had for the poor girl that he wished to remain ; and Maxcy whispered to me that he would bring him off before he left the ground, for fear he might do some harm to Robert, who was no fighter, and was too feeble to stand one so strong. This he did, and after he was gone I tried to get Robert away also. It was some time before I did so, and then it seemed he went with me only to get rid of my presence, for he was back at the grave as soon as night set in, and there he might be found every evening at the same hour, just about sunset, for several months afterwards—for he lingered strangely—until they brought him to sleep beside her. Though sick, and pining away fast, the poor fellow never let an evening go by, whatever weather it might be, with but paying the grave a visit; and, one day, perhaps two weeks after the funeral, old Mrs. Anderson called me into her cottage as I was riding by, and said she would show me something. She took me up into her son's room, a little chamber in the loft, and what should it be but a head-board, that the dying lad had sawed out with his own hands, from a thick plank, and had smoothed, and planed, and painted, all in secret, so that he could print on it an inscription for the poor girl's grave; and you would be surprised to see how neatly he had worked it all. The poor old woman cried bitterly all the time, but you could still see how proud she was of her son. She showed me his books—he had more than a hundred—and she sighed from the bottom of her heart when she told me it was the books that has made him sickly.

"But he will read," she said, "say all I can; though he knows it's a-doing him no good. 'Ah, mother,' he says, when I tell him about it, 'though it may shorten my life to read, it will shorten my happiness not to read, and I have too little happiness now left me to be willing to lose any of it.' And when he speaks so," said the old woman, "I can't blame him, for I know it's all true. But I blame myself, Mr. Atkins, for you see it was all of my doing that he got so many books, and is so fond of them. loved to see him learning, and made him read to me so constantly of an evening, and it did my heart so much good to think that one day my Robert might be a great lawyer, or a parson, for I could see how much smarter he was than all the other boys of the village—and so I never looked at his pale cheeks, and had no guess how poorly he was getting, till, all of a sudden, he was laid up, on my hands, and pining away every hour, as you now see him. Things looked better for a while when he got fond of Ellen Ramsay, and she of him. But that Stanton, ever since he came among us, Robert has gone backward, and I shan't wonder if it's not very long before he wants his own tombstone!"

Poor old woman! I saw in a corner, half hidden behind an old trunk in the youth's chamber, what it was evident she had not seen, a head board, the very fellow to that which he had been making for Ellen!—but I said nothing to her at the time. When they were found after his death—for he said nothing of them while he lived—they were both neatly finished, with a simple but

proper inscription.   On his own was but one line above his name
It was this—

> " Mine *was* wo, but mine *is* hope.
>
> *Robert Anderson.*"

" You tell me of a remarkable young man," said Walter—
" and he was but twenty when he died ?"

" No more !"

" We will go and look upon his grave."

" You will see the head board there, but that for Ellen was
never put up—Stanton would not allow it."

" Ah ! but we shall mend that. I will pluck that scoundrel's
comb.   Is the head-board preserved ?"

" It is : his mother keeps it in his chamber, standing up beside
his little book-case ; but see, yonder is Stanton now. He is on
his way to Ramsay's house. They do not live together. He
boards at a little farm-yard about a mile from the village. They
say that there has been a quarrel between him and his brother-
in-law, young John Ramsay, something about his sister's property.   There are eleven negroes which were owned by young
John and herself, in their own right, from the grand-mother's gift,
which they have suffered the old man to work until now. Stanton wants a division, and young John tried to persuade him not
to touch them till his death, which must happen before long, he
sharing as before from the crop. But Stanton persists, and the
young fellow did not stop to tell him that he thought him a cruelly
base fellow.   This is the report. It is very certain that they are
separate now, and there is a difference between them."

" Very likely on the score of the negroes.   But we will save
them to the old man, and drive him from a spot which he had
made wretched."

" Can you do this ?   Are your proofs sufficient ?"

" Ample."

" You are yourself a lawyer ?"

" Yes ! But I shall have the assistance, if necessary, of Col.
Dawson, whom probably you know."

" A first rate gentleman, and one of our best lawyers."

" I bring letters to him—have already seen him on the subject,

and he concurs with me as to the conclusiveness of my proofs.
Would I had been with you a year ago. Could I have traced
him, this poor girl had not been his victim. I should at least
have driven the snake from this one cabin."

"Yes, if you had come a year ago, poor Ellen would have
been saved. But nothing could have saved the poor young man.
The rot was in the heart of the tree."

"Yet!" said the other, putting his hand upon the arm of Atkins
—"though the tree perished, it might have been kept green to
the last. Some hurts might have been spared it. The man
who died in hope, might not have found it necessary to declare, at
the last moment, that he had utterly lived in wo. Yes—a little
year ago, we might have done much for both parties."

"You will do great good by your coming now. The poor old
man loves his negroes as he does his children. They say he
looks upon the giving up the eleven to be sold, like a breaking up
of the establishment. His son says it will hurry him to the grave.
This was what he said to Stanton, which led to the quarrel.
Stanton sneered at the young man, and he, being pretty passion-
ate, blazed out at him in a way that pretty soon silenced the fellow."

"This class of reptiles are all, more or less, cowards. We must
not burn daylight, as, if they consent to a division, the scoundrel
may make off with his share. Let us go forward," continued
the speaker, with a show of feeling for which Atkins could not
well account—"I long to tread upon the viper—to bruise his
head, and above all to tear the fangs from his jaws. You
will, if Stanton be there, draw the old man aside and introduce me to him, with some quiet hint of what I may be able
to do."

"You say you have the papers with you?"

"Ay, ay,—here,"—striking his bosom—"I have here that
which shall confound him! Fear not! I do not deceive you. At
least I cannot deceive myself. I too have wrongs that need
avenging—I and mine! I and mine! Remember, I am Mr.
Jones from Tennessee—I must surprise and confound the fellow,
and would see how the land lies before I declare myself."

CHAPTER II.

Young John Ramsay was in the front piazza as they entered the little farm-yard. He was alone, and pacing the floor in evident agitation. His brow was dark and discontented, and he met the salutations of his visitors with the manner of a person who is ill pleased with any witnesses of his disquiet. But he was civil, and when Atkins asked after his father, he led the way into the house, and there they discovered the old man and George Stanton in close and earnest conversation. Several papers were before them, and Stanton held the pen in his hand. The tears stood in old Ramsay's eyes. His thin white hairs, which fell, glossy and long, upon his shoulders, gave a benign and patriarchal expression to a face that was otherwise marked with the characters of benevolence and sensibility. He rose at the appearance of the visitors. Stanton did not, but looked up with the air of one vexed at interruption in the most interesting moment. Young Ramsay, to whom the stranger had been introduced by Atkins, introduced him in turn to his father, but to his father only. He gave no look to the spot where Stanton was seated. Atkins took the old man into another room, leaving the three remaining in the apartment. Stanton appeared to busy himself over his papers. Young Ramsay requested the stranger to be seated, and drew a chair for himself beside him. There was no conversation. The youth looked down upon the floor, in abstract contemplation, while the stranger, unobserved by either, employed himself in a most intense watch of the guilty man. The latter looked up and met this survey seemingly with indifference. He too was thinking of matters which led him somewhat from the present company. He resumed his study of the papers before him, and scarcely noticed the return of old Ramsay to the room. His appearance was the signal to the son to go out, and resume his solitary promenade in the piazza. The old man promptly approached the stranger, whose hand he took with a cordial pres sure that proved how well Atkins had conveyed his suggestion. There was a bright hopefulness in his old eyes, which, had it been seen by Stanton, might have surprised him, particularly as, just before, they had been overflowing with tears and clouded with despondency.   He was, however, still too busy in his calculations, and possibly, in his own hopes, to note any peculiar change in the aspect or manner of his father-in-law.   But when some minutes had passed, consumed by the old man and the stranger, in the most common-place conversation—when he heard the former institute long inquiries into the condition of crops in Tennessee—the value of grain, the modes of cultivation, the price of lands and negroes ;—the impatient son-in-law began to show his restiveness.   He took up and threw down his papers, turned from them to the company, from the company to the papers again, renewed his calculations, again dismissed them, and still without prompting the visitor to bring to a close a visit seemingly totally deficient in object and interest, but which, to his great annoyance, all parties besides himself seemed desirous to prolong.   At length, as with a desperate determination, he turned to the old man and said—

" Sir—Mr. Ramsay, you are aware of my desire to bring this business to a close at once."

The words reached the ears of young Ramsay, who now appeared at the door.

" Father, pray let it be as this person desires.   Give him all which the law will allow—give him more, if need be, and let him depart.   Make any arrangement about the negroes that you please, without considering me—only let him leave us in our homes at peace !"

" I am sorry to disturb the peace of any home," said Stanton, " but am yet to know that to claim my rights is doing so.   I ask nothing but what is fair and proper.   My wife, if I understand it, had an equal right with Mr. John Ramsay, the younger, to certain negroes, eleven in number, namely, Zekiel, Abram, Ben, Bess, Maria, Susannah, Bob, Harry, Milly, Bainbridge and Nell, with their increase.   This increase makes the number seventeen. But you have never denied the facts, and I repeat to you the proposition which I have already made to you, to divide the property into two equal parts, thus :"—

Here he read from the strips of paper before him, enumerating the negroes in two lots—this done, he proceeded :

"I am willing that your son should have the first choice of these lots. I will take the other. I am prepared to listen to any other arrangement for a division, rather than be subject to any delay by a reference to the law. I have no wish to compel the sale of the property, as that might distress you."

"Distress !" exclaimed the young man—"spare your sympathy if you please. I consent to your first arrangement. Nay, sir, you shall choose, first, of the lots as divided by yourself. My simple wish now, sir, is to leave you wholly without complaint."

"But, my son"—began the old man.

"Pray, my father, let it be as I have said. We shall never have an end of it otherwise. The division is a tolerably equal one, and if there be any loss it is mine."

The old man folded his hands upon his lap and looked to the stranger. He, meanwhile, maintained a keen and eager watch upon the features of Stanton. It could be seen that his lip quivered and there was in his eye an expression of exultation and scorn which, perhaps, none perceived but young Atkins. Stanton, meanwhile, was again busy with his papers.

"It is admitted also," the latter continued, "that I have a right to one half of a tract of uncleared land, lying on the Tombeckbe, containing six hundred and thirty acres, more or less; to one half of a small dwelling house in Linden, and to certain household stuff, crockery, plate and kitchen ware. Upon these I am prepared to place a low estimate, so that the family may still retain them, and the value may be given me in negro property. I value the land, which I am told is quite as good as any in the country, at $5 an acre—the house and lot at $500—and the plate, crockery, kitchen ware, etc., at $250 more. I make the total of my share, at these estimates, to be $2075—we will say $2000— and I am willing to take in payment of this amount, the four fellows, Zekiel, Bob, Henry and Ben—named in one lot, or the two fellows, Abram and Bainbridge, and the two women, Milly and Maria, with their three children, named in the other parcel."

"You are extremely accommodating," said young Ramsay bitterly, "but I prefer that we should sell the land on the Tombeckbe, the lot in Linden, and the crockery, plate and kitchen stuff—unless you prefer that these last should be divided. This arrangement will occasion you some delay in getting your money, but it will save me much less loss than I should suffer by your estimates. Permit me to say that of the negroes in the lot which you may leave me, you shall not have a hair, and I would to God it were in my power to keep the rest, by any sacrifice, from your possession."

"No doubt you do, sir—but your wishes are not the law. I demand nothing from you but what is justice, and justice I will have. My rights are clear and ample. You do not, I trust, propose to go to law to keep me out of my wife's property."

"To law!" exclaimed the young man with indignation. He then strode fiercely across the floor and confronted Stanton, who had now risen. The strife in his soul was showing itself in storm upon his countenance, when the stranger from Tennessee rose, and placed himself between them.

"Stay, my friend—let me speak a moment. I have a question to ask of Mr. Stanton."

"You, sir"—said Stanton—"by what right do you interfere?"

"By the right which every honest man possesses to see that there is no wrong done to his neighbour, if he can prevent it. You are making a demand upon Mr. Ramsay, for certain property which you claim in right of your wife. Now, sir, let me ask which of your wives it is, on whose account you claim."

The person thus addressed recoiled as if he had been struck by an adder. A deep flush passed over his face, succeeded by an ashen paleness. He tried to speak, stammered, and sunk paralyzed back into his chair.

"What, sir, can you say nothing? Your rights by your wives ought to be numerous. You should have some in every State in the Union."

"You are a liar and a slanderer," exclaimed the criminal, rising from his seat, and, with a desperate effort, confronting his accuser—Shaking his fist at him, he cried—"You shall prove what you say! You shall prove what you say!"

12

The other coldly replied, while a smile of scorn passed over his lips—" I am here for that very purpose."

" You!—and who are you?" demanded the accused, once again stammering and showing trepidation.

" A man! one who has his hand upon your throat, and will stifle you in the very first struggle that you propose to make. Sit down, sir—sit down all—this business is opened before us, and we will go to it as to a matter of business. You, sir"—to Stanton, " will please school your moods and temper, lest it be worse for you. It is only by behaving with proper modesty under a proper sense of your position and danger, that you can hope to escape from the sharpest clutches of the law."

" You shall not bully me—I am not the man to submit ——"

" You are; ' said the other, sternly interrupting him—" I tell you, William Ragin, *alias* Richard Weston, *alias* Thomas Stukely, *alias* Edward Stanton—you are the man to submit to all that I shall say to you, to all that I shall exact from you, in virtue of what I know of you, and in virtue of what you are."

The sweat poured in thick streams from the brow of the criminal. The other proceeded.

" I am not a bully. It is not by swagger that I hope to put you down, or to punish you. On the contrary, I come here prepared to prove all that I assert, satisfactorily before a court of justice. It is for you to determine whether, by your insolence and madness, you will incur the danger of a trial, or whether you will submit quietly to what we ask, and leave the country. I take for granted that you are no fool, though, in a moral point of view, your career would show you to be an enormous one, since vice like yours is almost conclusive against all human policy, and might reasonably be set down by a liberal judgment, as in some degree a wretched insanity. If I prove to you that I can prove to others what I now assert, will you be ready, without more ado, to yield your claims here, and every where, and fly the country?"

" You can prove nothing: you know nothing. I defy you."

" Beware! I am no trifler, and, by the God of heaven, I tell you, that, were I to trust my own feelings, you should swing upon the gallows, or be shut in from life, by a worse death, in the penitentiary, all your days. I can bring you to either, if I will it, but there are considerations, due to the feelings of others, which prompt me to the gentler course I have indicated. It is enough for me that you have been connected by the most solemn ties with Maria Lacy. Her wishes and her memory are sacred in my sight, and these move me to spare the villain whom my own personal wrongs would prompt me to drag to the gallows. You see how the matter stands! Speak!"

"You then—you are ——"

"Henry Lamar, of Georgia, the cousin, and once the betrothed of Maria Lacy."

There was a slight tremour in the speaker's voice, as he made this answer;—but his soul was very firm. He continued: "I complain not of your wrong to me. It is enough that I am prepared to avenge it, and I frankly tell you, I am half indifferent whether you accede to my proposition or not. Your audacity here has aroused a feeling in me, which leaves it scarcely within my power to offer you the chances of escape. I renew the offer, while I am yet firm to do it. Leave the country—leave all the bounds, all the territories of the United States—and keep aloof from them; for, as surely as I have power to pursue, and hear of your presence in any of them, so surely shall I hunt you out with shot and halter, as I would the reptile that lurks beside the pathway, or the savage beast that harbours in the thicket."

The speaker paused, resumed his seat, and, by a strong effort of will, maintained a calm silence, looking sternly upon the criminal. Violent passions were contending in the breast of the latter. His fears were evidently aroused, but his cupidity was active. It was clear that he apprehended the danger—it was equally clear that he was loth to forego his grasp upon the property of his last victim. He was bewildered, and, more in his confusion than because of any thought or courage—he once more desperately denied the charges made against him.

"You are a bold man," said he to the stranger, affecting coolness—"considering you deal in slander. You may impose upon these, but it is only because they would believe any thing agains* me now. But you have no proofs. I defy you to produce any thing to substantiate one of your charges."

'Fool!" said the other coolly, "I have but to call in the slaves

—to have you stripped to the buff, and to discover and display to the world the marks upon your body, to which your wife swore in open court in New York State, on the trial of Reuben Moore, confounded in identity with yourself as William Ragin. Here is the report of the trial. Moore was only saved, so close was the general resemblance between you, as the scar of the scythe was not apparent upon his leg—to which all parties swore as certainly on yours. Are you willing that we should now examine your left leg and foot ?"

"My foot is as free from scar as yours; but I will not suffer myself to be examined."

"Did it need, we should not ask you. But it does not need. We have the affidavit of Samuel Fisher, to show that he detected the scar of the scythe upon your leg, while bathing with you at Crookstone's mill pond, that he asked you how you got such a dreadful cut, and that you were confused, but said that it was a scythe cut. This he alleged of you under your present name of Stanton. Here, sir, is a copy of the affidavit. Here also is the testimony of James Greene, of Liberty county, Geo., who knew you there as the husband of Maria Lacy. He slept with you one night at Berry's house on the way to the county court house. You played *poker* with a party of five consisting of the said Greene, of Jennings, Folker and Stillman—their signatures are all here. You got drunk, quarrelled with Folker and Stillman, whom you accused of cheating you, were beaten by them severely, and so bruised that it was necessary you should be put to bed, and bathed with spirits. When stripped for this purpose, while you lay unconscious, the scythe cut on your leg, and a large scar from a burn upon your right arm, to both of which your wife, Elizabeth Ragin, swore in New York, with great particularity—as appears in that reported case—were discovered, and attracted the attention of all present."

"Man or devil !" exclaimed the criminal in desparation,—" By what means have you contrived to gather these damnable proofs !"

"You admit them then ?"

"I admit nothing. I defy them, and you, and the devil. Let me go. I will hear nothing more—see nothing farther. As for you, John Ramsay, let me ask, am I to have any of my wife's

property ? Let me have it, and I leave the cursed country forever."

John Ramsay, the younger, was about to reply, when the
stranger silenced him.

"Stay! You leave not this spot, unless with my consent, or
in the hands of the sheriff. He is here in readiness. Are you
willing that I should call him in ? I am serious ! There must
be no trifling. Here are proofs of your identity with William
Ragin, who married Elizabeth Simpson, of Minden, Connecticut ;
—with Richard Weston, who married Sarah Gooch, of Raleigh.
N. C. ;—with Thomas Stukely, who married with Maria Lacy,
of Liberty county, Geo. ;—with Edward Stanton, now before us,
who married with Ellen Ramsay, of Montgomery county, Ala-
bama. Of these wretched wives whom you have wronged and
dishonoured, two of them are still living. I do not stipulate for
your return to either. They are sufficiently fortunate to be rid
of you forever. But this I insist upon, that you leave the country. As for taking the property of this wife or that, you must
consider yourself particularly fortunate that you escape the halter. You can take nothing. Your fate lies in these papers."

In an instant the desperate hands of the criminal had clutched
the documents where the other laid them down. He clutched
them, and sprang towards the door, but a single blow from the
powerful fist of young John Ramsay brought him to the floor. The
stranger quietly repossessed himself of the papers."

"You are insane, William Ragin," he remarked coolly—
"these are all copies of the originals, and even were they originals, their loss would be of little value while all the witnesses are
living. They are brought for your information—to show you on
what a perilous point you stand—and have been used only to base
the warrant upon which has been already issued for your arrest.
That warrant is even now in this village in the hands of the sheriff of the county. I have but to say that you are the man whom
he must arrest under it, and he does his duty. You are at my
mercy. I see that you feel that. Rise and sign this paper and
take your departure. If, after forty-eight hours, you are found
east of the Tombeckbe, you forfeit all the chances which it affords
you of escape. Rise, sir, and sign. I have no more words for you."

The criminal did as he was commanded—passively, as one in a stupor. The stranger then waved him to the door, and he took his departure without any more being spoken on either side. When he was gone—

"These papers," said Lamar, to old John Ramsay, "are yours. I leave them for your protection from this scoundrel. The proofs are all conclusive, and, with his re-appearance, you have but to seek the sheriff and renew the warrant."

The old man clasped the hands of the stranger and bedewed them with tears.

"You will stay with us while you are here. We owe you too much to suffer it otherwise. We have no other way of thanking you."

"I have another day's business here," said Lamar, "and will cheerfully partake your hospitality for that time. For the present I must leave you. I have an engagement with Mr. Atkins."

The engagement with Atkins, led the stranger to the grave of poor Ellen Ramsay and to that of Robert Anderson. They next visited the cottage of the widow Anderson, and obtained her consent to the use of the head board which the devoted youth had framed and inscribed, while himself dying, for the grave of his beloved. The next day was employed, with the consent of old Ramsay, in putting it up—an occasion which brought the villagers together as numerously as the burial of the poor girl had done. The events of the day had taken wind—the complete exposure of the wretch who had brought ruin and misery into the little settlement, was known to all, and deep were the imprecations of all upon his crime, and warm the congratulations at a development, which saved the venerable father from being spoiled and left in poverty in his declining years. But there is yet a finish to our story—another event, perhaps necessary to its finish, which, as it was the offspring of another day, we must reserve for another chapter.

CHAPTER III.

THAT night, while the little family at Ramsay's were sitting over their evening meal, Abram, one of the plantation negroes, appeared at the door of the apartment, and abruptly addressed young Ramsay after the following fashion :

" Look ya, Mass Jack, I want for see you out ya a minute."

Abram was the *driver* of the plantation—a sort of superintendant of details. He was a faithful negro, such as is to be found on every long established plantation at the South—shrewd, cool, sensible—perhaps forty years of age—honest, attentive to his business, and, from habit, assuming the interest which he managed to be entirely his own. His position gave him conse-quence, which he felt and asserted, but never abused. A trick of speaking very much what was uppermost in his mind, was the fruit of a just consciousness of duties well performed, leaving him in no fear of any proper authority. Young Ramsay rose instantly and obeyed the summons. With some little mystery in his manner, Abram conducted the youth from the piazza into the yard, and thence into the shadow of one of the gigantic shade trees by which the house was literally embowered. Here, looking around him with the air of one anxious neither to be seen nor overheard, he thrust a paper into the hands of John Ramsay with this inquiry—

" Dis ya money, Mass Jack,—good money ?"

" I will tell you when I look at it by the candle. Why ?—where did you get it ?"

" You look at 'em first—I tell you all 'bout 'em arterward. '

John did as was required, returned and reported the bank note—for it was such, and for twenty dollars—to be utterly worthless that, in short, of a broken bank.

" I bin tink so," said the negro.

" Where did you get it, Abram ?"

" Who you speck gib me, Mass Jack ?"

" I don't know !"

" Who but Mass Ned Stanton."

" Ha !—why—when did he give you this money ?"

" To-day—when you bin all busy wid de tomb stone of young
Missis. He come by de old creek field, call me out, say I must
come to em in de wood, and den he say to me dat he sorry for
see me ya working for Mossa. Him will help me git off work—I
shall be free man, if I will only go wid him, and bring off many
of the brack people as I kin. He promise me heap of tings, git
me 'nuff tobacco for las' a mont', gib me knife—see dis ya—and
dis money which you say no good money. I bin speck 'em for
bad when he tell me its twenty dollars. Twenty dollars is heap
money, I say to myself. Wha' for he gib me twenty dollars now.
Wha' for he consider my freedom, jes' now, and he nebber bin
tink 'pon 'em before. Someting's wrong, I say to myself, and
Mossa for know—but I neber let on to 'em I 'spec 'em. I say
' da's all right. I will come, Mass Ned. I will see you in de
bush to-night.' Den he shake my hand—say he always bin lub
me—will take me to country whay brack man is gentleman and
hab white wife, and is lawyer, and schoolmosser, and preacher,
and hab white man for dribe he carriage. I yerry em berry
well, but I never le' him see I laugh. But I hab my tongue ya
(thrust to one side of his jaws) and the white ob my eye grow
large as I look 'pon 'em. I know 'em of ole. I bin speck 'em
when he first come ya courting poor Miss Nelly. I no like 'em
den—I no like 'em now. But I mak' blieb I lub 'em too much.
Das for you now to fix 'em. He's for see me to-night by ole
Robin tree in de swamp. Wha' mus do—wha' mus say—how
you gwine fix 'em ?"

" You have done right, 'Bram. Before I say any thing, I will
consult my father, and a stranger who is with us."

" I yerry bout 'em. He's a man, I ya. Flora bin tell me
how he fix Ned Stanton."

" Well, I'll consult him and my father. Do you remain here
in the meantime. Do not let yourself be seen. Stanton *is* a villain, but we have found him out. Stanton is not his real name,
but Ragin."

" Ragin, eh ? Well, we must Ragin 'em. I'll wait 'pon you

va. But mak' haste—de time is pretty close, and he'll 'spec'
something ef I aint by de tree when he come."

John Ramsay re-entered the house, and, in few words, repeated the substance of the negro's story.

"The scoundrel's bent on being hung," was the exclamation
of Lamar, with something like a look of exultation.   "Let
'Bram encourage him, and give him a meeting for to-morrow
night, promising to bring all the negroes that he can. We shall
be at the meeting. 'Bram shall carry us, though we go as his
comrades, not as his superiors."

The scheme of Lamar was soon laid. Young Ramsay and
himself were to smut their faces, and, in negro habiliments, were
to impose upon the villain. Lamar promised that the sheriff
should take his hand at the game.

"Our mercy is thrown away upon such a thrice-dyed scoundrel. His destiny forces the task of vengeance upon us. Go to
Abram, and give him his cue."

CHAPTER IV.

THERE is a fatality about the wicked that, sooner or later, whaever may be their precautions and their adroitnesses, invariably brings about their confusion and defeat. The criminal in the present instance, was one who had enjoyed a long swing of good fortune—using these words only to mean that he had been able to gratify his wishes, of whatever sort, without yet having been made to pay the usual penalties. This very success is most commonly the source of final disaster. The fortunate man is apt to presume upon his good fortune—to hold himself, like Sylla, a sort of favourite with the capricious goddess, until he loses himself irrevocably in the blind presumption which his confidence provokes. Edward Stanton, for so we shall continue to call him, had been too often in straits like the present, and had too often emerged from them with profit, to fancy that he had much at hazard in the new game that he had determined to pursue. He had been temporarily daunted by the complete exposure of his career which had been made by Lamar, and felt, from all he saw and all he heard, that the chances were entirely up with him where he then stood. But he had not long gone from sight of his enemy, before his mind began once more to recover, and to unravel new schemes and contrivances for the satisfaction of his selfish passions. He was a person soon to cast aside his apprehensions, and to rise with new energies after defeat. It is a very great misfortune that this admirable quality of character should be equally shared, upon occasion, by the rogue and the ruffian, with the honest man and the noble citizen. Stanton was resolved to make the most of the forty-eight hours which were allowed him. He took for granted that, having attained his object, Lamar would be satisfied ;—he may have discovered, indeed, that the latter would return in another day to Georgia. We have seen, from the revelations of Abram, what direction his scheming mind was disposed to pursue. His plans were laid in a few minutes, and, while the family of Ramsay, its guest, and the people of the village generally, were raising the simple head board over the grave of his injured wife, the miserable wretch, totally insensible to all honourable or human feeling, was urging the ignorant negro to a desertion of the ancient homestead, in the vain hope of attaining that freedom with which, when acquired, he knew not well what to do. Of course, this was all a pretext of the swindler, by which to get the property within his grasp. He had but to cross the Tombeckbe with his unsuspecting companions, and they would have been sold, by public outcry, at the first popular gathering. His plans laid, his artifices all complete, he waited with anxiety the meeting with the negro. He had already taken his leave of the family with which he lodged, had mounted his horse, and turned his head towards the west, using particular care that his departure should be seen by several. He little fancied that his return to the neighbourhood by another route, and after night had set in, had also been perceived. But the vigilance of Lamar had arranged for this. Young Atkins had volunteered to observe the movements of Stanton, and, born a hunter, and familiar with all the woods for twenty miles round, he was able to report on the return of the fugitive, within half an hour of the moment when it took place. Concealing his horse in a neighbourng *bay*, ready for use in the first emergency, Stanton proceeded, at the appointed time, to the place of rendezvous.

Meanwhile, the preparations of Lamar were also in progress. The sheriff had been brought, after night-fall, to the house of old Ramsay. The coarse garments of the negro had been provided for himself and his deputy—for Lamar and the younger Ramsay. Young Atkins also insisted on going as a volunteer, and old Ramsay could with difficulty be persuaded to forbear accompanyig the party. The blood of the veteran blazed up as fiercely as it nad done twenty years before, when he heard the call for volunteers, from the lips of Andrew Jackson, to avenge the butcheries of Indian warfare. The good sense of Lamar succeeded in persuading him to leave the affair to younger men. Abram was of the party, and, with his assistance, a greasy preparation was procured, in which soot and oil were the chief ingredients, by which our free citizens were made to assume, in a very few moments, the dark and glossy outside of the African. Prime stout fellows were they—able field hands—such as would delight the unsuspecting eye of the kidnapper as soon as he beheld them. They were all armed with pistols—all but Abram, who carried however the knife—a formidable *couteau de chasse*, which had been one of the bribes of Stanton, presented to him with the bank note and tobacco, at their first interview. Abram undertook the conduct of the party. They were led forth secretly, in profoundest silence, by a circuitous path, to the swamp thicket, in the neighbourhood of which the meeting was to take place. It is needless to describe the route. Suffice it that they were there in season, snugly quartered, and waiting with due impatience for the signal. It was heard at last ;—a shrill whistle, thrice repeated, followed by the barking of a hound. To this Abram answered, going forth as he did so, and leaving the party in the close covert to which he had conducted them. The night was a bright star-light. The gleams, however, came but imperfectly through the thick foliage, and our conspirators could distinguish each other only by the sound of their voices. Their faces shone as glossily as the leaves, when suddenly touched by the far light of the stars. Gradually, they heard approaching footsteps. It was then that Lamar said, seizing the hand of young Ramsay,—

" No haste, now,—no rashness,—we must let the fellow hobble himself fairly."

Deep silence followed, broken only by the voice of the negro and his companion.

" You have brought them ?" said Stanton.

" Da's ya !" replied the black.

" How many ?"

" Some tree or four, 'side myself."

" Could you bring no more ?" asked the eager kidnapper.

" Hab no chance—you no gib me time 'nuff. Ef you leff 'em tell Saturday night now, and Sunday, I get 'em all."

" No !—no ! that's impossible. I dare not. These must de. Where are they ?"

" In de bush ! jes' ya ! But look ya, Mass Ned, you sure you gwine do wha' you promise ?"

" On my honour, 'Bram."

" You will take you Bible oat', Mass Ned ?"

" I swear it."

" Dis ya nigger I bring you is no common nigger, I tell you. Mossa hab heaby loss for lose 'em.   Wha' you 'spose he gwine say,—wha' he tink, when he get up to-morrow mornin', and can't find 'Bram and de rest ob 'em.   Wha' he gwine do ?"

" What can he do ?   We will have the start of him by twenty-five miles, and in one day more you will be free, 'Bram, your own master, and able to put him at defiance.   I will see to that."

" He will push arter us, Mass Ned,—and dese ya nigger in de bush—look ya, Mass Ned, dese all prime nigger.   Da's one on 'em, a gal ya, most purty nuff for white man wife.   You 'member little Suzy, Mass Ned ?"

" Don't I, 'Bram ?   Little Suzy is a pretty girl—pretty enough to be the wife of any man.   Bring her out, bring them all out, and let us be off.   We understand each other."

" Suzy is good gal, Mass Ned.   I want for see 'em doing prime when he git he freedom.   You will marry 'em yourself, wid parson ?"

" If she wishes it."

" He will wish 'em for true !   But wha' dis I yer 'em say 'bout you habing tree wife a'ready ?"

" No more of that, 'Bram."

" Wha' ! he aint true, den ?"

" A lie, 'Bram ! a black, a bloody lie !"

" What for den you let dat Georgy man run you out ob de country ?"

" Ha ! who told you this ?"

" I yer dem house sarbant talk ob 'em."

" They do not understand it.   I am not driven.   I choose to go."

" Well ! you know bes', but dat's wha' I yer dem say."

" No more, 'Bram !   Where are the people ?"

" Let de dog bark tree time, and dey come.   You kin bark like dog, Mass Ned.   Try for 'em."

The imitation was a good one.   Sounds were heard in the

bushes, and one by one the supposed negroes appeared in the star light. They looked natural enough, and the kidnapper approach-ed them with some interest.

"These are all men, are they not? Are there no women? Where's Little Suzy?"

"Ha! Mass Ned,—I speck its true wha' dem people say. You lub gal too much. I call little Suzy now, him take you 'bout de neck. Come ya, my people. Mass Ned hab make 'greement wid me to carry us all to fine country. He swear Bible 'oat to make we all free, and gib we plenty whiskey and tobacco. I tell 'em you's ready to go. You ready, eh?"

There was a general grunt of assent.

'Bram was disposed to be satirical. His dry chuckle accom-panied every syllable.

"Gib um you hand den on de bargain. Shake hand like brudderin. Ha! ha! I nebber bin speck to be brudder ob my young mossa. Shake hands, niggers, on de bargain."

"You have heard what 'Bram has said, my boys. I promise the same things to you. You shall go with me to a country where you shall be free. I will give you plenty of whiskey and tobacco. Here is my hand. Who is this—Zeke?"

The hand was clutched by Lamar, with a grasp that somewhat startled the criminal. The voice of the supposed negro in the next moment, terribly informed him of his danger.

"Villain!" exclaimed the Georgian, "I have you! You are sworn for the gallows! You shall not escape us now."

A short struggle followed—the doubtful light, and their rapid movements, not suffering the other persons around so to distin-guish between them as to know where to take hold. The crimi-nal put forth all his strength, which was far from inconsiderable. The combatants were nearly equally matched, but in the struggle they traversed a fallen tree, over which Lamar stumbled and fell, partly dragging his enemy with him to the ground. To save him-self only did he relax his hold. Of this Stanton nimbly availed himself. He recovered his feet, and, before the rest of the party could interfere, had gained a dozen paces on his way to the thicket. Once within its shadows, he might, with good heart and good for-tune, have baffled their pursuit. But this was not destined. He was intercepted by no less a person than Abram, who rolled himself suddenly like a huge ball in the path of the fugitive, and thus broke the fall which yet precipitated him to the ground. In the next moment, the negro had caught him by the leg, yelling at the same time to the rest of the party to come to his succour.

"Ah! dog it is you then to whom I owe all this."

Such was the speech, muttered through his closed teeth, with which Stanton declared his recognition of the assailant. His words were followed by a pistol shot. Abram gave a cry, released his hold, and leapt to his feet. Stanton had only half risen when the whole weight of the negro was again upon him.

"You shoot, eh! You shoot!" were the words of the black, shrieked rather than spoken. The party interfered. The whole affair had passed in a moment, quick as thought, and in far less time than has been occupied with the recital.

"Where is he, 'Bram?" demanded Lamar.

"I hab em ya, Mossa—he safe," responded the other with a groan.

"You are hurt?" said young Ramsay, inquiringly.

"One arm smash wid he pistol, Mass Jack."

His young master helped the fellow up, while Lamar and the sheriff, with young Atkins, prepared to secure the criminal.

"What is this! He is lifeless!" said the former, as he touched the body. "What have you done, 'Bram?"

"I don't know, Mossa. I hab my knife in my han', and when he shoot me, I so bex and I so scare, I don't know wha' I do wid em. I gib um he knife, I speck. It's he own knife."

Sure enough! the weapon was still sticking in the side of the criminal. The one blow was fatal, and his dying groan, if any was uttered, was drowned in the furious exclamation with which the negro accompanied the blow.

"It is a loss to the gallows," said Lamar, with an expression of chagrin.

"Better so!" replied young Ramsay.

"It saves me a very dirty job!" muttered the sheriff. We may add that he took care to pay the usual fees to Abram, who was otherwise well provided for by the Ramsay family, and still lives to relate the events of that night of conflict with the Snake of the Cabin.

OAKATIBBE,

OR THE CHOCTAW SAMPSON.

CHAPTER I.

It was in the year 182–, that I first travelled in the vallies of the great south-west. Circumstances, influenced in no slight degree by an " errant disposition," beguiled me to the Choctaw nation, which, at that time, occupied the greater part of the space below the Tennessee line, lying between the rivers Tombeckbe and Mississippi, as low, nearly, as the town of Jackson, then, as now, the capital of the State of Mississippi. I loitered for several weeks in and about this region, without feeling the loss or the weight of time. Yet, the reader is not to suppose that travelling at that day was so simple a matter, or possessed many, if any of the pleasant facilities of the present. *Au contraire :* It was then a serious business. It meant *travail* rather than *travel.* The roads were few and very hard to find. Indian foot-paths—with the single exception of the great military traces laid out by General Jackson, and extending from Tennessee to Lake Ponchar train—formed almost the only arteries known to the " Nation ;" and the portions of settled country in the neighbourhood, nominally civilized only, were nearly in the same condition. Some of the Indian paths, as I experienced, seemed only to be made for the perplexity of. the stranger. Like Gray's passages which " led to nothing," they constantly brought me to a stand. Some times they were swallowed up in swamps, and, in such cases, your future route upon the earth was to be discovered only by a deliberate and careful survey of the skies above. The openings in the trees over head alone instructed you in the course you were to pursue. You may readily imagine that this sort of progress was as little pleasant as edifying, yet, in some respects, it was not wanting in its attractions, also. To the young and ardent mind, obstacles of this nature tend rather to excite than to depress. They contain the picturesque in themselves, at times, and always bring out the moral in the man. "To learn to rough it," is an educational phrase, in the dialect of the new countries, which would be of great service, adopted as a rule of government for the young in all. To "coon a log"—a mysterious process to the uninitiated—swim a river—experiment, at a guess, upon the properties of one, and the proprieties of another route—parley with an Indian after his own fashion—not to speak of a hundred other incidents which the civilized world does not often present—will reconcile a lad of sanguine temperament to a number of annoyances much more serious than will attend him on an expedition through our frontier countries.

It was at the close of a cloudy day in November, that I came within hail of the new but rude plantation settlements of Colonel Harris. He had but lately transferred his interests to Mississippi, from one of the "maternal thirteen"—had bought largely in the immediate neighbourhood of the Choctaw nation, and had also acquired, by purchase from the natives, certain reserves within it, to which he chiefly owes that large wealth, which, at this day, he has the reputation of possessing. In place of the stately residence which now adorns his homestead, there was then but a miserable log-house, one of the most ordinary of the country, in which, unaccompanied by his family, he held his temporary abiding place. His plantation was barely rescued from the dominions of nature. The trees were girdled only the previous winter, for his first crop, which was then upon the ground, and an excellent crop it was for that immature condition of his fields. There is no describing the melancholy aspect of such a settlement, seen in winter, on a cloudy day, and in the heart of an immense forest, through which you have travelled for miles, without glimpse of human form or habitation. The worm-fence is itself a gloomy spectacle, and the girdled trees, erect but dead, the perishing skeletons of recent life, impress you with sensations not entirely unlike those which you would experience in going over some

13

battle-field, from which the decaying forms of man and horse have not yet been removed. The fences of Col. Harris were low in height, though of great extent. They were simply sufficient to protect the fields from the random assaults of cattle. Of his out-houses, the most respectable in size, solidity and security, was the corn crib. His negro-houses, like the log-house in which he himself dwelt, were only so many temporary shanties, covered with poles and thatched with bark and pine-straw. In short, every thing that met my eye only tended the more to frown upon my anticipations of a cheerful fireside and a pleasant arrangement of the creature-comforts. But my doubts and apprehensions all vanished at the moment of my reception. I was met by the proprietor with that ease and warmth of manner which does not seem to be conscious of any deficiencies of preparation, and is resolved that there shall be none which sincere hospitality can remedy. I was soon prepared to forget that there were deficiencies. I felt myself very soon at home. I had letters to Col. Harris, which made me particularly welcome, and in ten minutes we were both in full sail amongst all the shallows and deeps of ordinary conversation.

Not that we confined ourselves to these. Our discourse, after a little while, turned upon a circumstance which I had witnessed on riding through his fields and while approaching his dwelling, which struck me with considerable surprise, and disturbed, in some degree, certain pre-conceived opinions in my mind. I had seen, interspersed with his negro labourers, a goodly number of Indians of both sexes, but chiefly young persons, all equally and busily employed in cotton picking. The season had been a protracted one, and favourable, accordingly, to the maturing of great numbers of the bolls which an early and severe winter must have otherwise destroyed. The crop, in consequence, had been so great as to be beyond the ability, to gather in and harvest, of the "force" by which it was made. This, in the new and fertile vallies of the south-west, is an usual event. In ordinary cases, when this happens, it is the custom to buy other negroes from less productive regions, to consummate and secure the avails of labour of the original "force." The whole of these, united, are then addressed to the task of opening additional lands, which, should

they yield a. before, necessarily demand a second purchase of an
extra number to secure and harvest, in season, the surplus fruits
of their industry. The planter is very readily persuaded to make
this purchase so long as the seeming necessity shall re-occur;
and in this manner has he continued expanding his interests, increasing the volume of his lands, and incurring debt for these and
for his slaves, at exorbitant prices, in order to the production of a
commodity, every additional bag of which, disparages its own
value, and depreciates the productive power, in an estimate of
profit, of the industry by which it is produced. It will not be
difficult, keeping this fact in mind as a sample of the profligacy
of western adventure—to account, in part, for the insolvency and
desperate condition of a people in possession of a country naturally
the most fertile of any in the world.

The crop of Col. Harris was one of this description. It far
exceeded the ability of his "force" to pick it in; but instead of
buying additional slaves for the purpose, he conceived the idea
of turning to account the lazy Choctaws by whom he was surrounded. He proposed to hire them at a moderate compensation,
which was to be paid them weekly. The temptation of gain was
greedily caught at by these hungering outcasts, and, for a few
dollars, or an equivalent in goods, groceries, and so forth, some
forty-five of them were soon to be seen, as busy as might be, in
the prosecution of their unusual labours. The work was light
and easy—none could be more so—and though not such adepts
as the negro, the Indian women soon contrived to fill their bags
and baskets, in the course of the day. At dark, you might behold them trudging forward under their burdens to the log-house,
where the proprietor stood ready to receive them. Here he
weighed their burdens, and gave them credit, nightly, for the
number of pounds which they each brought in. The night of my
arrival was Saturday, and the value of the whole week's labour
was then to be summed up and accounted for. This necessarily
made them all punctual in attendance, and nothing could be
more amusing than the interest which they severally displayed as
Col. Harris took out his memorandum book, and proceeded to
make his entries. Every eye was fixed upon him, and an old Indian, who, though he did not work himself, represented the intereste

of a wife and two able-bodied daughters, planted himself directly
behind this gentleman, and watched, with looks of growing sagacity, every stroke that was made in this—to him—volume of
more than Egyptian mystery and hieroglyphics.   Meanwhile, the
squaws stood about their baskets with looks expressive of similar
interest, but at the same time of laudable patience.   The negroes in
the rear, were scarcely less moved by curiosity, though a contemptuous grin might be seen on nearly all their countenances,
as they felt their superiority in nearly every physical and intellectual respect, over the untutored savages.   Many Indians were
present who neither had nor sought employment.   Of those employed, few or none were of middle age.   But these were not
wanting to the assemblage.   They might be seen prowling about
the rest—watchful of the concerns of their wives, sons and
daughters, with just that sort and degree of interest, which the
eagle may be supposed to feel, who, from his perch on the tree-
top or the rock, beholds the fish-hawk dart into the water in pursuit of that prey which he meditates to rend from his jaws as soon
as he shall re-ascend into the air.   Their interest was decidedly
greater than that of the poor labourer.   It was in this manner that
these vultures appropriated the fruits of his industry, and there
was no remedy.   They commonly interfered, the moment it was
declared what was due to the *employée*, to resolve the pay into a
certain number of gallons of whiskey ; so many pounds of tobacco ; so much gunpowder and lead.   If the employer, as was
the case with Col. Harris, refused to furnish them with whiskey,
they required him to pay in money.   With this, they soon made
their way to one of those moral sinks, called a grog-shop, which
English civilization is always ready to plant, as its first, most familiar, and most imposing standard, among the hills and forests
of the savage.

   It may be supposed that this experiment upon the inflexibility
of Indian character and habit—for it was an experiment which
had been in trial only a single week—was a subject of no little
curiosity to me, as it would most probably be to almost every
person at all impressed with the humiliating moral and social de-
terioration which has marked this fast decaying people.   Could it
possibly be successful ?   Could a race, proud, sullen, incommuni

cative, wandering, be persuaded, even by gradual steps, and with
the hope of certain compensation, to renounce the wild satisfaction
afforded by their desultory and unconstrained modes of life ?
Could they be beguiled for a season into employments which,
though they did not demand any severe labours, at least required
pains-taking, regular industry, and that habitual attention to daily
recurring tasks, which, to their roving nature, would make life
a most monotonous and unattractive possession ? How far the
lightness of the labour and the simplicity of the employment, with
the corresponding recompense, would reconcile them to its tasks,
was the natural subject of my inquiry. On this head, my friend,
Col. Harris, could only conjecture and speculate like myself. His
experiment had been in progress but a few days. But our speculations led us to very different conclusions. He was a person of
very ardent character, and sanguine, to the last degree, of the
success of his project. He had no question but that the Indian,
even at his present stage, might be brought under the influence
of a judicious civilization. We both agreed that the first process
was in procuring their labour—that this was the preliminary step,
without taking which, no other could be made ; but how to bring
them to this was the question.

"They can be persuaded to this," was his conclusion. " Money, the popular god, is as potent with them as with our own people. They will do any thing for money. You see these now in
the field. They have been there, and just as busy, and in the
same number, from Monday last."

"How long will they continue ?"

"As long as I can employ and pay them."

"Impossible·! They will soon be dissatisfied. The men will
consume and squander all the earnings of the females and the
feeble. The very motive of their industry, money, to which you
refer, will be lost to them after the first payment. I am convinced that a savage people, not as yet familiar with the elements of
moral prudence, can only be brought to habitual labour, by the
one process of coercion."

"We shall see. There is no coercion upon them now, we they
work with wonderful regularity."

"This week will end it. Savages are children in all but physical respects.   To do any thing with them. you must place them in that position of responsibility, and teach them that law, without the due employment of which, any attempt to educate a child, must be an absurdity—you must teach them obedience.   They must he made to know, at the outset, that they know nothing— that they must implicitly defer to the superior.   This lesson they will never learn, so long as they possess the power, at any moment, to withdraw from his control."

"Yet, even were this to be allowed, there must be a limit. There must come a time when you will be required to emanci- pate them.   In what circumstances will you find that time? You cannot keep them under this coercion always; when will you set them free?"

"When they are fit for freedom."

"How is that to be determined?   Who shall decide their fitness?"

"Themselves; as in the case of the children of Israel.   The children of Israel went out from bondage as soon as their own intellectual advancement had been such as to enable them to produce from their own ranks a leader like Moses:—one whose genius was equal to that of the people by whom they had been educated, and sufficient for their own proper government there- after."

"But has not an experiment of this sort already been tried in our country?"

"Nay, I think not—I know of none."

"Yes: an Indian boy was taken in infancy from his parents, carried to one of the Northern States, trained in all the learning and habits of a Northern college and society, associated only with whites, beheld no manners, and heard no morals, bot those which are known to Christian communities.   His progress was satisfac- tory—he learned rapidly—was considered something of a prodigy, and graduated with eclât.   He was then left, with the same op- tion as the rest enjoyed, to the choice of a profession.   And what was his choice?   Do you not remember the beautiful little poem of Freneau on this subject?   He chose the buck-skin leggins, the moccasins, bow and arrows, and the wide, wild forests, where his people dwelt."

"Freneau's poem tells the story somewhat differently.   The

facts upon which it is founded, however, are, I believe, very much
as you tell them.   But what an experiment it was!   How very
silly !   They take a copper-coloured boy from his people, and car
ry him, while yet an infant, to a remote region.   Suppose, in order that the experiment may be fairly tried, that they withhold
from him all knowledge of his origin.   He is brought up precisely as the other lads around him.   But what is the first discovery
which he makes ?   That he is a copper-coloured boy—that he is,
alone, the only copper-coloured boy—that wherever he turns he
sees no likeness to himself.   This begets his wonder, then his curiosity, and finally his suspicion.   He soon understands—for his
suspicion sharpens every faculty of observation—that he is an
object of experiment.   Nay, the most cautious policy in the world
could never entirely keep this from a keen-thoughted urchin.
His fellow pupils teach him this.   He sees that, to them, he is an
object of curiosity and study.   They regard him, and he soon
regards himself, as a creature set apart, and separated, for some
peculiar purposes, from all the rest.   A stern and singular sense
of individuality and isolation is thus forced upon him.   He asks
—Am I, indeed, alone ?—Who am I ?—What am I ?—These inquiries naturally occasion others.   Does he read ?   Books give
him the history of his race.   Nay, his own story probably meets
his eye in the newspapers.   He learns that he is descended from
a nation dwelling among the secret sources of the Susquehannah.
He pries in all corners for information.   The more secret his
search, the more keenly does he pursue it.   It becomes the great
passion of his mind.   He learns that his people are fierce war.
riors and famous hunters.   He hears of their strifes with the
white man—their successful strifes, when the nation could send
forth its thousand bow-men, and the whites were few and feeble.
Perhaps, the young pale faces around him, speak of his people,
even now, as enemies ; at least, as objects of suspicion, and perhaps antipathy.   All these things tend to elevate and idealize, in
his mind, the history of his people.   He cherishes a sympathy, even
beyond the natural desires of the heart, for the perishing race
from which he feels himself, " like a limb, cast bleeding and
torn."   The curiosity to see his ancestry—the people of his tribe
and country—would be the most natural feeling of the white boy,

under similar circumstances—shall we wonder that it is the predominant passion in the bosom of the Indian, whose very complexion forces him away from any connection with the rest! My
idea of the experiment—if such a proceeding may be called an
experiment—is soon spoken.   As a statement of facts, I see nothing to provoke wonder.   The result was the most natural thing
in the world, and a man of ordinary powers of reflection might
easily have predicted it, precisely as it happened.   The only
wonder is, that there should be found, among persons of common
education and sagacity, men who should have undertaken such
an experiment, and fancied that they were busy in a moral and
philosophical problem."

    " Why, how would you have the experiment tried ?"

    " As it was tried upon the Hebrews, upon the Saxons—upon
every savage people who ever became civilized.   It cannot be
tried upon an individual : it must be tried upon a nation—at least
upon a community, sustained by no succour from without—having
no forests or foreign shores upon which to turn their eyes for
sympathy—having no mode or hope of escape—under the full
control of an already civilized people—and sufficiently numerous
among themselves, to find sympathy, against those necessary
rigours which at first will seem oppressive, but which will be the
only hopeful process by which to enforce the work of improvement.   They must find this sympathy from beholding others, like
themselves in aspect, form, feature and condition, subject to the
same unusual restraints.   In this contemplation they will be
content to pursue their labours under a restraint which they
cannot displace.   But the natural law must be satisfied.   There
must be opportunities yielded for the indulgence of the legitimate
passions.   The young of both sexes among the subjected people,
must commune and form ties in obedience to the requisitions of
nature and according to their national customs.   What, if the
Indian student, on whom the " experiment" was tried, had paid
his addresses to a white maiden !   What a revulsion of the moral
and social sense would have followed his proposition in the mind
of the Saxon damsel ;—and, were she to consent, what a commotion in the community in which she lived.   And this revulsion
and commotion would have been perfectly natural, and, accord-

ingly, perfectly proper. God has made an obvious distinction between certain races of men, setting them apart, and requiring them to be kept so, by subjecting them to the resistance and rebuke of one of the most jealous sentinels of sense which we possess—the eye. The prejudices of this sense, require that the natural barriers should be maintained, and hence it becomes necessary that the race in subjection, should be sufficiently numerous to enable it to carry out the great object of every distinct community, though, perchance, it may happen to be an inferior one. In process of time, the beneficial and blessing effects of labour would be felt and understood by the most ignorant and savage of the race. Perhaps, not in one generation, or in two, but after the fifth and seventh, as it is written, " of those who keep my commandments." They would soon discover that, though compelled to toil, their toils neither enfeebled their strength nor impaired their happiness—that, on the contrary, they still resulted in their increasing strength, health, and comfort ;—that their food, which before was precarious, depending on the caprices of the seasons, or the uncertainties of the chase, was now equally plentiful, wholesome and certain. They would also perceive that, instead of the sterility which is usually the destiny of all wandering tribes, and one of the processes by which they perish—the fecundity of their people was wonderfully increased. These discoveries—if time be allowed to make them—would tacitly reconcile them to that inferior position of their race, which is proper and inevitable, so long as their intellectual inferiority shall continue. And what would have been the effect upon our Indians—decidedly the noblest race of aborigines that the world has ever known—if, instead of buying their scalps at prices varying from five to fifty pounds each, we had conquered and subjected them ? Will any one pretend to say that they would not have increased with the restraints and enforced toils of our superior genius ?—that they would not, by this time, have formed a highly valuable and noble integral in the formation of our national strength and character ? Perhaps their civilization would have been comparatively easy— the Hebrews required four hundred years—the Britons and Saxons, possibly, half that time after the Norman Conquest. Differing in colour from their conquerors, though I suspect, with a natural genius superior to that of the ancient Britons, at the time of the Roman invasion under Julius Cæsar, the struggle between the two races must have continued for some longer time, but the union would have been finally effected, and then, as in the case of the Englishman, we should have possessed a race, in their progeny, which, in moral and physical structure, might have challenged competition with the world."

"Ay, but the difficulty would have been in the conquest."

"True, that would have been the difficulty. The American colonists were few in number and feeble in resource. The nations from which they emerged put forth none of their strength in sending them forth. Never were colonies so inadequately provided—so completely left to themselves; and hence the peculiar injustice and insolence of the subsequent exactions of the British, by which they required their colonies to support their schemes of aggrandizement and expenditure by submitting to extreme taxation. Do you suppose, if the early colonists had been powerful, that they would have ever deigned to treat for lands with the roving hordes of savages whom they found on the continent? Never! Their purchases and treaties were not for lands, but tolerance. They bought permission to remain without molestation. The amount professedly given for land, was simply a tribute paid to the superior strength of the Indian, precisely as we paid it to Algiers and the Musselmens, until we grew strong enough to whip them into respect. If, instead of a few ships and a few hundred men, timidly making their approaches along the shores of Manhattan, Penobscot and Ocracocke, some famous leader, like Æneas, had brought his entire people—suppose them to be the persecuted Irish—what a wondrous difference would have taken place. The Indians would have been subjected—would have sunk into their proper position of humility and dependence; and, by this time, might have united with their conquerors, producing, perhaps, along the great ridge of the Alleghany, the very noblest specimens of humanity, in mental and bodily stature, that the world has ever witnessed. The Indians were taught to be insolent by the fears and feebleness of the whites. They were flattered by fine words, by rich presents, and abundance of deference, until the ignorant savage, but a single degree above the

brute—who, until then, had never been sure of his porridge for
more than a day ahead—took airs upon himself, and became one
of the most conceited and arrogant lords in creation. The colonists grew wiser as they grew stronger; but the evil was already
done, and we are reaping some of the bitter fruits, at this day, of
seed unwisely sown in that. It may be that we shall yet see the
experiment tried fairly."

" Ah, indeed—where ?"

" In Mexico—by the Texians. Let the vain, capricious, ignorant, and dastardly wretches who now occupy and spoil the
face and fortunes of the former country, persevere in pressing
war upon those sturdy adventurers, and their doom is written. I
fear it may be the sword—I *hope* it may be the milder fate of
bondage and subjection. Such a fate would save, and raise them
finally to a far higher condition than they have ever before enjoyed. Thirty thousand Texians, each with his horse and rifle,
would soon make themselves masters of the city of Montezuma,
and then may you see the experiment tried upon a scale sufficiently extensive to make it a fair one. But your Indian student,
drawn from

" Susquehannah's farthest springs,"

and sent to Cambridge, would present you with some such moral
picture as that of the prisoner described by Sterne. His chief
employment, day by day, would consist in notching upon his stick,
the undeviating record of his daily suffering. It would be to him
an experiment almost as full of torture, as that of the Scottish
Boot, the Spanish Thumb-screw—or any of those happy devices
of ancient days, for impressing pleasant principles upon the mind,
by impressing unpleasant feelings upon the thews, joints and sinews.
I wish that some one of our writers, familiar with mental analysis,
would make this poem of Freneau, the subject of a story. I think
it would yield admirable material. To develope the thoughts and
feelings of an Indian boy, taken from his people, ere yet he has
formed such a knowledge of them, or of others, as to have begun
to discuss or to compare their differences—follow him to a college
such as that of Princeton or Cambridge—watch him within its
walls—amid the crowd, but not of it—looking only within him-

self, while all others are looking into him, or trying to do so—surrounded by active, sharp-witted lads of the Anglo-Norman race;
undergoing an hourly repeated series of moral spasms, as he hears
them wantonly or thoughtlessly dwell upon the wild and ignorant people from whom he is chosen;—listening, though without
seeming to listen, to their crude speculations upon the great problem which is to be solved only by seeing how well he can endure his spasms, and what use he will make of his philosophy if
he survives it—then, when the toils of study and the tedious restraints and troubles of prayer and recitation are got over, to behold and describe the joy with which the happy wretch flings by
his fetters, when he is dismissed from those walls which have witnessed his tortures—even supposing him to remain (which is very
unlikely,) until his course of study is pronounced to be complete
With what curious pleasure will he stop in the shadow of the first
deep forest, to tear from his limbs those garments which make
him seem unlike his people! How quick will be the beating at
his heart as he endeavours to dispose about his shoulders the
blanket robe in the manner in which it is worn by the chief warrior of his tribe! With what keen effort—should he have had
any previous knowledge of his kindred—will he seek to compel
his memory to restore every, the slightest, custom or peculiarity
which distinguished them when his eyes were first withdrawn
from the parental tribe; and how closely will he imitate their indomitable pride and lofty, cold, superiority of look and gesture,
as, at evening, he enters the native hamlet, and takes his seat in
silence at the door of the Council House, waiting, without a word,
for the summons of the Elders!"

"Quite a picture. I think with you, that, in good hands, such
a subject would prove a very noble one."

"But the story would not finish here. Supposing all this to
have taken place, just as we are told it did—supposing the boy to
have graduated at college, and to have flung away the distinction
—to have returned, as has been described, to his savage costume
—to the homes and habits of his people;—it is not so clear that he
will fling away all the lessons of wisdom, all the knowledge of facts,
which he will have acquired from the tuition of the superior race.
A natural instinct, which is above all lessons, must be complied

with ; but this done—and when .the first tumults of his blood have subsided, which led him to defeat the more immediate object of his social training—there will be a gradual resumption of the educational influence in his mind, and his intellectual habits will begin to exercise themselves anew. They will be provoked necessarily to this exercise by what he beholds around him. He will begin to perceive, in its true aspects, the wretchedness of that hunter-state, which, surveyed at a distance, appeared only the embodiment of stoical heroism and the most elevated pride. He will see and lament the squalid poverty of his people; which, his first lessons in civilization must have shown him, is due only to the mode of life and pursuits in which they are engaged. Their beastly intoxication will offend his tastes—their superstition and ignorance—the circumscribed limits of their capacity for judging of things and relations beyond the life of the bird or beast of prey—will awaken in him a sense of shame when he feels that they are his kindred. The insecurity of their liberties will awaken his fears, for he will instantly see that the great body of the people in every aboriginal nation are the veriest slaves in the world ; and the degrading exhibitions which they make in their filth and drunkenness, which reduce the man to a loathesomeness of aspect which is never reached by the vilest beast which he hunts or scourges, will be beheld by the Indian student in very lively contrast with all that has met his eyes during that novitiate among the white sages, the processes of which have been to him so humiliating and painful. His memory reverts to that period with feelings of reconciliation. The torture is over, and the remembrance of former pain, endured with manly fortitude, is comparatively a pleasure. A necessary reaction in his mind takes place ; and, agreeably to the laws of nature, what will, and what should follow, but that he will seek to become the tutor and the reformer of his people ? They themselves will tacitly raise him to this position, for the man of the forest will defer even to the negro who has been educated by the white man. He will try to teach them habits of greater method and industry—he will overthrow the altars of their false gods—he will seek to bind the wandering tribes together under one head and in one nation—he will prescribe uniform laws of govermnent.

He will succeed in some things—he will fail in others ; he will offend the pride of the self-conceited and the mulish—the priest-hood will be the first to declare against him—and he will be mur-dered most probably, as was Romulus, and afterwards deified. If he escapes this fate, he will yet, most likely, perish from mor-tification under failure, or, in consequence of those mental strifes which spring from that divided allegiance between the feelings belonging to his savage, and those which have had their origin in his christian schools—those natural strifes between the acquisi-tions of civilization on the one hand, and those instinct tendencies of the blood which distinguish his connection with the inferior race. In this conflict, he will, at length, when the enthusiasm of his youthful zeal has become chilled by frequent and unex-pected defeat, falter, and finally fail. But will there be nothing done for his people ? Who can say ? I believe that no seed falls without profit by the wayside. Even if the truth produces no immediate fruits, it forms a moral manure which fertilizes the otherwise barren heart, in preparation for the more favourable season. The Indian student may fail, as his teachers did, in realizing the object for which he has striven ; and this sort of failure, is, by the way, one of the most ordinary of human allot-ment. The desires of man's heart, by an especial Providence, that always wills him to act for the future, generally aim at something far beyond his own powers of performance. But the labour has not been taken in vain, in the progress of successive ages, which has achieved even a small part of its legitimate pur-poses. The Indian student has done for his people much more than the white man achieves ordinarily for his generation, if he has only secured to their use a single truth which they knew not before—if he has overthrown only one of their false gods—if he has smitten off the snaky head of only one of their superstitious prejudices. If he has added to their fields of corn a field of mil-let, he has induced one farther physical step towards moral im-provement. Nay, if there be no other result, the very deference which they will have paid him, as the _elevé_ of the white man, will be a something gained of no little importance, towards in-ducing their more ready, though still tardy, adoption of the laws and guidance of the superior race."

CHAPTER II.

I AM afraid that my reader will suffer quite as much under this long discussion, as did my excellent companion, Col. Harris. But he is not to suppose that all the views here expressed, were uttered consecutively, as they are above set down. I have simply condensed, for more easy comprehension, the amount of a conversation which lasted some two hours. I may add, that, at the close, we discovered, as is very often the case among disputants, there was very little substantial difference between us. Our dispute, if any, was rather verbal than philosophical. On the subject of his experiment, however, Col. Harris fancied, that, in employing some forty or fifty of the Indians, of both sexes, he had brought together a community sufficiently large for the purposes of a fair experiment. Still, I thought that the argument remained untouched. They were not subordinate; they were not subdued; they could still exercise a free and absolute will, in despite of authority and reason. He could resort to no method for compelling their obedience; and we know pretty well what will result —even among white men—from the option of vagrancy.

" But," I urged, " even if the objections which I have stated, fail of defeating your scheme, there is yet another agent of defeat working against it, in the presence of these elderly Indians, who do not join in the labour, and yet, according to your own showing, still prowl in waiting to snatch from the hands of the industrious all the fruits of their toil. The natural effect of this will be to discourage the industry of those who work; for, unless the labourer is permitted to enjoy a fair proportion of the fruits of his labour, it is morally impossible that he should long continue it."

Our conference was interrupted by the appearance of the labourers, Indians and Negroes, who now began to come in, bringing with them the cotton which they had severally gathered during the day. This was accumulated in the court-yard, before the dwelling; each Indian, man or woman, standing beside the bag or basket which contained the proofs of his industry. You may readily suppose, that, after the dialogue and discussion which is partially reported above, I felt no little interest in observing the proceedings. The parties present were quite numerous. I put the negroes out of the question, though they were still to be seen, lingering in the background, grinning spectators of the scene. The number of Indians, men and women, who had *that day* been engaged in picking, was thirty-nine. Of these, twenty-six were females; three, only, might be accounted men, and ten were boys —none over sixteen. Of the females the number of elderly and young women was nearly equal. Of the men, one was very old and infirm; a second of middle age, who appeared to be something of an idiot; while the third, whom I regarded for this reason with more consideration and interest than all the party beside, was one of the most noble specimens of physical manhood that my eyes had ever beheld. He was fully six feet three inches in height, slender but muscular in the extreme. He possessed a clear, upright, open, generous cast of countenance, as utterly unlike that sullen, suspicious expression of the ordinary Indian face, as you can possibly imagine. Good nature and good sense were the predominant characteristics of his features, and—which is quite as unusual with Indians when in the presence of strangers —he laughed and jested with all the merry, unrestrainable vivacity of a youth of Anglo-Saxon breed. How was it that so noble a specimen of manhood consented to herd with the women and the weak of his tribe, in descending to the mean labours which the warriors were accustomed to despise?

" He must either be a fellow of great sense, or he must be a coward. He is degraded."

Such was my conclusion. The answer of Col. Harris was immediate.

" He is a fellow of good sense, and very far from being a coward. He is one of the best Choctaws that I know."

" A man, then, to be a leader of his people. It is a singular proof of good sense and great mental flexibility, to find an Indian, who is courageous, voluntarily assuming tasks which are held to be degrading among the hunters. I should like to talk with this fellow when you are done. What is his name?"

"His proper name is Oakatibbé ; but that by which he is gen
erally known among us—his English name—is Slim Sampson, a
name which he gets on the score of his superior strength and
great slenderness. The latter name, in ordinary use, has completely superseded the former, even among his own people. It
may be remarked, by the way, as another proof of the tacit deference of the inferior to the superior people, that most Indians
prefer to use the names given by the whites to those of their own
language. There are very few among them who will not contrive, after a short intimacy with white men, to get some epithet
—which is not always a complimentary one—but which they
cling to as tenaciously as they would to some far more valuable
possession."

This little dialogue was whispered during the stir which followed the first arrival of the labourers. We had no opportunity
for more.

The rest of the Indians were in no respect remarkable. There
were some eight or ten women, and perhaps as many men, who
did not engage in the toils of their companions, though they did
not seem the less interested in the result. These, I noted, were
all, in greater or less degree, elderly persons. One was full
eight years old, and a strange fact for one so venerable, was the
most confirmed drunkard of the tribe. When the cotton pickers
advanced with their baskets, the hangers-on drew nigh also, deeply
engrossed with the prospect of reaping the gains from that industry which they had no mood to emulate. These, however, were
very moderate, in most cases. Where a negro woman picked
from one to two hundred weight of cotton, *per diem*, the Indian
woman, at the utmost, gathered sixty-five ; and the general average among them, did not much exceed forty-five. Slim Sampson's basket weighed eighty-six pounds—an amount considerably
greater than any of the rest—and Col. Harris assured me, that
his average during the week had been, at no time, much below
this quantity.

The proceedings had gone on without interruption or annoyance for the space of half an hour. Col. Harris had himself
weighed every basket, with scrupulous nicety, and recorded the
several weights opposite to the name of the picker, in a little memo-

randum book which he kept exclusively for this purpose; and it
was amusing to see with what pleasurable curiosity, the Indians,
men and women, watched the record which stated their several
accounts. The whole labour of the week was to be settled for
that night (Saturday), and hence the unusual gathering of those
whose only purpose in being present, was to grasp at the spoils.

Among these hawks was one middle-aged Indian—a stern,
sulky fellow, of considerable size and strength—whose skin was
even then full of liquor, which contributing to the usual insolence
of his character, made him at times very troublesome. He had
more than once, during the proceedings, interfered between Col.
Harris and his *employées*, in such a manner as to provoke, in the
mind of that gentleman, no small degree of irritation. The English name of this Indian, was Loblolly Jack. Loblolly Jack had
a treble motive for being present and conspicuous. He had
among the labourers, a wife and two daughters. When the bas
kets of these were brought forward to be weighed, he could no
longer be kept in the background, but, resolutely thrusting himself before the rest, he handled basket, book and steelyards in
turn, uttered his suspicions of foul play, and insisted upon a close
examination of every movement which was made by the proprietor. In this manner, he made it very difficult for him to proceed
in his duties; and his conduct, to do the Indians justice, seemed
quite as annoying to them as to Col. Harris. The wife frequently
expostulated with him, in rather bolder language than an Indian
squaw is apt to use to her liege lord; while Slim Sampson, after
a few words of reproach, expressed in Choctaw, concluded by
telling him in plain English, that he was "a rascal dog." He
seemed the only one among them who had no fear of the intruder
Loblolly Jack answered in similar terms, and Slim Sampson.
clearing the baskets at a single bound, confronted him with a
show of fight, and a direct challenge to it, on the spot where they
stood. The other seemed no ways loth. He recoiled a pace,
drew his knife—a sufficient signal for Slim Sampson to get his
own in readiness—and, thus opposed, they stood, glaring upon
each other with eyes of the most determined expression of malignity. A moment more—an additional word of provocation from
either—and blows must have taken place. But Col. Harris, a

man of great firmness, put himself between them, and calling to one of his negroes, bade him bring out from the house his double-barreled gun.

"Now," said he, " my good fellows, the first man of you that lifts his hand to strike, I'll shoot him down; so look to it. Slim Sampson, go back to your basket, and don't meddle in this business. Don't you suppose that I'm man enough to keep Loblolly Jack in order? You shall see."

It is not difficult for a determined white man to keep an Indian in subordination, so long as both of them are sober. A few words more convinced Loblolly Jack, who had not yet reached the reckless stage in drunkenness, that his wiser course was to give back and keep quiet, which he did. The storm subsided almost as suddenly as it had been raised, and Col. Harris resumed his occupation. Still, the Indian who had proved so troublesome before, continued his annoyances, though in a manner somewhat less audacious. His last proceeding was to get as nigh as he could to the basket which was about to be weighed—his wife's basket—and, with the end of a stick, adroitly introduced into some little hole, he contrived to press the basket downwards, and thus to add so much to the weight of the cotton, that his squaw promised to bear off the palm of victory in that day's picking. Nobody saw the use to which the stick was put, and for a few moments no one suspected it. Had the cunning fellow been more moderate, he might have succeeded in his attempt upon the steelyards; but his pressure increased with every approach which was made to a determination of the weight, and while all were wondering that so small a basket should be so heavy, Slim Sampson discovered and pointed out the trick to Col. Harris, who suddenly snatching the stick from the grasp of the Indian, was about to lay it over his head. But this my expostulation prevented ; and, after some delay, the proceedings were finally ended ; but in such a manner as to make my friend somewhat more doubtful than he had been before, on the subject of his experiment. He paid off their accounts, some in cloths and calicoes, of which he had provided a small supply for this purpose ; but the greater number, under the evil influence of the idle and the elder, demanded and received their pay in money.

CHAPTER III.

It was probably about ten o'clock that evening. We had fin ished supper, and Col. H. and myself had resumed the subject upon which we had been previously engaged. But the discus- sion was languid, and both of us were unquestionably lapsing into that state, when each readily receives an apology for retiring for the night, when we were startled from our drowsy tendencies by a wild and terrible cry, such as made me thrill instinctively with the conviction that something terrible had taken place. We start- ed instantly to our feet, and threw open the door. The cry was more distinct and piercing, and its painful character could not be mistaken. It was a cry of death—of sudden terror, and great and angry excitement. Many voices were mingled together—some expressive of fury, some of fear, and many of lamentation. The tones which finally prevailed over, and continued long after all others had subsided, were those of women.

" These sounds come from the shop of that trader. Those ras- cally Choctaws are drunk and fighting, and ten to one but some- t.. 's killed among them !" was the exclamation of Col. H. " These sounds are familiar to me. I have heard them once be- fore. They signify murder. It is a peculiar whoop which the Indians have, to denote the shedding of blood—to show that a crime has been committed."

The words had scarcely been uttered, before Slim Sampson came suddenly out into the road, and joined us at the door. Col. H. instantly asked him to enter, which he did. When he came fully into the light, we discovered that he had been drinking. His eyes bore sufficient testimony to the fact, though his drunken- ness seemed to have subsided into something like stupor. His looks were heavy, rather than calm. He said nothing, but drew nigh to the fireplace, and seated himself upon one corner of the hearth. I now discovered that his hands and hunting shirt were stained with blood. His eyes beheld the bloody tokens at the same time, and he turned his hand curiously over, and examined it by the fire-light.

"Kurnel," said he, in broken English, "me is one dog fool !'

"How, Sampson ?"

"Me drunk—me fight—me kill Loblolly Jack! Look ya ! Dis blood 'pon my hands. 'Tis Loblolly Jack blood! He dead ! I stick him wid de knife !"

"Impossible ! What made you do it ?"

"Me drunk ! Me dog fool !—Drink whiskey at liquor shop— hab money—buy whiskey—drunk come, and Loblolly Jack dead !"

This was the substance of the story, which was confirmed a few moments after, by the appearance of several other Indians, the friends of the two parties. From these it appeared that all of them had been drinking, at the shop of Ligon, the white man ; that, when heated with liquor, both Loblolly Jack and Slim Sampson had, as with one accord, resumed the strife which had been arrested by the prompt interference of Col. H. ; that, from words they had got to blows, and the former had fallen, fatally hurt, by a single stroke from the other's hand and knife.

The Indian law, like that of the Hebrews, is eye for eye, tooth for tooth, life for life. The fate of Slim Sampson was ordained He was to die on the morrow. This was well understood by himself as by all the rest. The wound of Loblolly Jack had proved mortal. He was already dead ; and it was arranged among the parties that Slim Sampson was to remain that night, if permitted, at the house of Col. H., and to come forth at early sunrise to execution. Col. H. declared his willingness that the criminal should remain in his house ; but, at the same time, disclaimed all responsibility in the business ; and assured the old chief, whose name was " Rising Smoke," that he would not be answerable for his appearance.

" He won't run," said the other, indifferently.

" But you will not put a watch over him—I will not suffer more than the one to sleep in my house."

The old chief repeated his assurance that Slim Sampson would not seek to fly. No guard was to be placed over him. He was expected to remain quiet, and come forth to execution at the hour appointed.

"He got for dead," continued Rising Smoke—"he know the law. He will come and dead like a man. Oakatibbé got big heart." Every word which the old fellow uttered went to mine.

What an eulogy was this upon Indian inflexibility! What confidence in the passive obedience of the warrior! After a little farther dialogue, they departed,—friends and enemies—and the unfortunate criminal was left with us alone. He still maintained his seat upon the hearth. His muscles were composed and calm —not rigid. His thoughts, however, were evidently busy; and, once or twice, I could see that his head was moved slowly from side to side, with an expression of mournful self-abandonment. I watched every movement and look with the deepest interest, while Col. H. with a concern necessarily deeper than my own, spoke with him freely, on the subject of his crime. It was, in fact, because of the affair of Col. H. that the unlucky deed was committed. It was true, that, for this, the latter gentleman was in no wise responsible; but that did not lessen, materially, the pain which he felt at having, however unwittingly, occasioned it. He spoke with the Indian in such terms of condolence as conventional usage among us has determined to be the most proper. He proffered to buy off the friends and relatives of the deceased, if the offence could be commuted for money. The poor fellow was very grateful, but, at the same time, told him that the attempt was useless. —The tribe had never been known to permit such a thing, and the friends of Loblolly Jack were too much his enemies, to consent to any commutation of the penalty.

Col. H., however, was unsatisfied, and determined to try the experiment. The notion had only suggested itself to him after the departure of the Indians. He readily conjectured where he should find them, and we immediately set off for the grogshop of Ligon. This was little more than a quarter of a mile from the plantation. When we reached it, we found the Indians, generally, in the worst possible condition to be treated with. They were, most of them, in the last stages of intoxication. The dead body of the murdered man was stretched out in the piazza, or gallery, half covered with a bear-skin. The breast was bare—

a broad, bold, manly bosom—and the wound, a deep narrow gash, around which the blood stood, clotted, in thick, frothy masses. The nearer relations of the deceased, were perhaps the most drunk of the assembly. Their grief necessarily entitled them to the greatest share of consolation, and this took the form of whiskey. Their love of excess, and the means of indulgence, encouraged us with the hope that their vengeance might be bought off without much difficulty, but we soon found ourselves very much deceived. Every effort, every offer, proved fruitless; and after vainly exhausting every art and argument, old Rising Smoke drew us aside to tell us that the thing was impossible.

"Oakatibbé hab for die, and no use for talk. De law is make for Oakatibbé, and Loblolly Jack, and me, Rising Smoke, and all, just the same. Oakatibbé will dead to-morrow."

With sad hearts, we left the maudlin and miserable assembly. When we returned, we found Slim Sampson employed in carving with his knife upon the handle of his tomahawk. In the space thus made, he introduced a small bit of flattened silver, which seemed to have been used for a like purpose on some previous occasion. It was rudely shaped like a bird, and was probably one of those trifling ornaments which usually decorate the stocks of rifle and shot-gun. I looked with increasing concern upon his countenance. What could a spectator—one unacquainted with the circumstances—have met with there? Nothing, surely, of that awful event which had just ta.ten place, and of that doom which now seemed so certainly to await him. He betrayed no sort of interest in our mission. His look and manner denoted his own perfect conviction of its inutility; and when we told him what had taken place, he neither answered nor looked up.

It would be difficult to describe my feelings and those of my companion. The more we reflected upon the affair, the more painful and oppressive did our thoughts become. A pain, little short of horror, coupled itself with every emotion. We left the Indian still beside the fire. He had begun a low chanting song just before we retired, in his own language, which was meant as a narrative of the chief events of his life. The death song—for such it was—is neither more nor less than a recital of those deeds which it will be creditable to a son or a relative to remember.

In this way the valor of their great men, and the leading events in their history, are transmitted through successive ages. He was evidently refreshing his own memory in preparation for the morrow. He was arranging the narrative of the past, in prope. form for the acceptance of the future.

We did not choose to disturb him in this vocation, and retired. When we had got to our chamber, H. who already had one boot off, exclaimed suddenly—" Look you, S'., this fellow ought not to perish in this manner. We should make an effort to save him. We must save him !"

" What will you do ?"

" Come—let us go back and try and urge him to flight. He can escape easily while all these fellows are drunk. He shall have my best horse for the purpose."

We returned to the apartment.

" Slim Sampson."

" Kurnel !" was the calm reply.

" There's no sense in your staying here to be shot."

" Ugh !" was the only answer, but in an assenting tone.

" You're not a bad fellow—you didn't mean to kill Loblolly . ack—it's very hard that you should die for what you didn't wish to do. You're too young to die. You've got a great many years to live. You ought to live to be an old man and have sons like yourself; and there's a great deal of happiness in this world, if a man only knows where to look for 'it. But a man that's dead is of no use to himself, or to his friends, or his enemies. Why should you die—why should you be shot ?"

" Eh ?"

" Hear me ; your people are all drunk at Ligon's—blind drunk —deaf drunk—they can neither see nor hear. They won't get sober till morning—perhaps not then. You've been across the Mississippi, hav'nt you ? You know the way ?"

The reply was affirmative.

" Many Choctaws live over the Mississippi now—on the Red River, and far beyond, to the Red Hills. Go to them—they will take you by the hand—they will give you one of their daughters to wife—they will love you—they will make you a chief. Fly, Sampson, fly o them—you shall have one of my horses, and be-

'fore daylight you will be down the country, among the white people, and far from your enemies—Go, my good fellow, it would be
a great pity that so brave a man should die."

This was the substance of my friend's exhortation. It was put
into every shape, and addressed to every fear, hope, or passion
which might possibly have influence over the human bosom. A
strong conflict took place in the mind of the Indian, the outward
signs of which were not wholly suppressible. He started to his
feet, trod the floor hurriedly, and there was a tremulous quickness
in the movement of his eyes, and a dilation of their orbs, which
amply denoted the extent of his emotion. He turned suddenly
upon us, when H. had finished speaking, and replied in language
very nearly like the following.

"I love the whites—I was always a friend to the whites. I
believe I love their laws better than my own. Loblolly Jack
laughed at me because I loved the whites, and wanted our people
to live like them. But I am of no use now. I can love them no
more. My people say that I must die. How can I live?"

Such was the purport of his answer. The meaning of it was
simple. He was not unwilling to avail himself of the suggestions
of my friend—to fly—to live—but he could not divest himself of
that habitual deference to those laws to which he had given implicit reverence from the beginning. Custom is the superior tyrant of all savage nations.

To embolden him on this subject, was now the joint object of
Col. H. and myself. We spared no argument to convince him
that he ought to fly. It was something in favour of our object, that
the Indian regards the white man as so infinitely his superior;
and, in the case of Slim Sampson, we were assisted by his own
inclinations in favour of those customs of the whites, which he had
already in part begun to adopt. We discussed for his benefit
that which may be considered one of the leading elements in
civilization—the duty of saving and keeping life as long as we
can—insisted upon the morality of flying from any punishment
which would deprive us of it; and at length had the satisfaction
of seeing him convinced. He yielded to our arguments and so-
licitations, accepted the horse, which he promised voluntarily to find
some early means to return, and, with a sigh   perhaps one of the

first proofs of that change of feeling and of principle which he
had just shown, he declared his intention to take the road instantly.

"Go to bed, Kurnel. Your horse will come back." We retired, and a few moments after heard him leave the house. I
am sure that both of us felt a degree of light-heartedness which
scarcely any other event could have produced. We could not
sleep, however. For myself I answer—it was almost dawn before I fell into an uncertain slumber, filled with visions of scuffling
Indians—the stark corse of Loblolly Jack, being the conspicuou
object, and Slim Sampson standing up for execution.

CHAPTER IV.

NEITHER Col. H. nor myself arose at a very early hour. Our first thoughts and feelings at waking were those of exultation. We rejoiced that we had been instrumental in saving from an ig-nominious death, a fellow creature, and one who seemed so worthy, in so many respects. Our exultation was not a little increased, as we reflected on the disappointment of his enemies; and we enjoyed a hearty laugh together, as we talked over the matter while putting on our clothes. When we looked from the window the area in front of the house was covered with Indians. They sat, or stood, or walked, all around the dwelling. The hour ap-pointed for the delivery of Slim Sampson had passed, yet they betrayed no emotion. We fancied, however, that we could dis-cern in the countenances of most among them, the sentiment of friendship or hostility for the criminal, by which they were sev-erally governed. A dark, fiery look of exultation—a grim an-ticipation of delight—was evident in the faces of his enemies; while, among his friends, men and women, a subdued concern and humbling sadness, were the prevailing traits of expression.

But when we went below to meet them—when it became known that the murderer had fled, taking with him the best horse f the proprietor, the outbreak was tremendous. A terrible yell went up from the party devoted to Loblolly Jack; while the friends and relatives of Slim Sampson at once sprang to their weapons, and put themselves in an attitude of defence. We had not foreseen the effects of our interposition and advice. We did not know, or recollect, that the nearest connection of the criminal, among the Indian tribes, in the event of his escape, would be re-quired to suffer in his place; and this, by the way, is the grand source of that security which they felt the night before, that flight would not be attempted by the destined victim. The aspect of affairs looked squally. Already was the bow bent and the toma-hawk lifted. Already had the parties separated, each going to

nis own side, and ranging himself in front of some one opponent.
The women sunk rapidly into the rear, and provided themselves
with billets or fence-rails, as they occurred to their hands ; while
little brats of boys, ten and twelve years old, kept up a continual
shrill clamour, brandishing aloft their tiny bows and *blow-guns,*
which were only powerful against the lapwing and the sparrow.
In political phrase, " a great crisis was at hand." The stealthier
chiefs and leaders of both sides, had sunk from sight, behind the
trees or houses, in order to avail themselves of all the arts of Indian strategy. Every thing promised a sudden and stern conflict.
At the first show of commotion, Col. H. had armed himself. I
had been well provided with pistols and bowie knife, before leaving home ; and, apprehending the worst, we yet took our places
as peace-makers, between the contending parties.

It is highly probable that all our interposition would have been
fruitless to prevent their collision ; and, though our position certainly delayed the progress of the quarrel, yet all we could have
hoped to effect by our interference would have been the removal
of the combatants to a more remote battle ground. But a circumstance that surprised and disappointed us all, took place, to settle
the strife forever, and to reconcile the parties without any resort to
blows. While the turmoil was at the highest, and we had des-
paired of doing any thing to prevent bloodshed, the tramp of a
fast galloping horse was heard in the woods, and the next moment
the steed of Col. H. made his appearance, covered with foam,
Slim Sampson on his back, and still driven by the lash of his rider
at the top of his speed. He leaped the enclosure, and was drawn
up still quivering in every limb, in the area between the opposing
Indians. The countenance of the noble fellow told his story. His
heart had smitten him by continual reproaches, at the adoption of
a conduct unknown in his nation; and which all its hered-
itary opinions had made cowardly and infamous. Besides, he
remembered the penalties which, in consequence of his flight, must
fall heavily upon his people. Life was sweet to him—very sweet!
He had the promise of many bright years before him. His mind
was full of honourable and—speaking in comparative phrase—
lofty purposes, for the improvement of himself and nation. We
have already sought to show that, by his conduct, he had **taken**

one large step in resistance to the tyrannous usages of custom, in order to introduce the elements of civilization among his people. But he could not withstand the reproaches of a conscience formed upon principles which his own genius was not equal to overthrow. His thoughts, during his flight, must have been of a very humbling character; but his features now denoted only pride, exultation and a spirit strengthened by resignation against the worst. By his flight and subsequent return, he had, in fact, exhibited a more lively spectacle of moral firmness, than would have been display-ed by his simple submission in remaining. He seemed to feel this. It looked out from his soul in every movement of his body. He leaped from his horse, exclaiming, while he slapped his breast with his open palm :

" Oakatibbé heard the voice of a chief, that said he must die. Let the chief look here—Oakatibbé is come !"

A shout went up from both parties. The signs of strife disap-peared. The language of the crowd was no longer that of threat-ening and violence. It was understood that there would be no re-sistance in behalf of the condemned. Col. H. and myself, were both mortified and disappointed. Though the return of Slim Sampson, had obviously prevented a combat à outrance, in which a dozen or more might have been slain, still we could not but re-gret the event. The life of such a fellow seemed to both of us, to be worth the lives of any hundred of his people.

Never did man carry with himself more simple nobleness. He was at once surrounded by his friends and relatives. The hostile party, from whom the executioners were to be drawn, stood look-ing on at some little distance, the very pictures of patience. There was no sort of disposition manifested among them, to hurry the proceedings. Though exulting in the prospect of soon shedding the blood of one whom they esteemed an enemy, yet all was dig-nified composure and forbearance. The signs of exultation were no where to be seen. Meanwhile, a conversation was carried on in low, soft accents, unmarked by physical action of any kind, between the condemned and two other Indians. One of these was the unhappy mother of the criminal—the other was his uncle. They rather listened to his remarks, than made any of their own. The dialogue was conducted in their own language. After a while this ceased, and he made a signal which seemed to be felt, rather than understood, by all the Indians, friends and enemies. All of them started into instant intelligence.   It was a sign that he was ready for the final proceedings.   He rose to his feet and they surrounded him.   The groans of the old woman, his mother, were now distinctly audible, and she was led away by the uncle, who, placing her among the other women, returned to the condemned, beside whom he now took his place.   Col. H. and myself, also drew nigh.   Seeing us, Oakatibbé simply said, with a smile :

"Ah, kurnel, you see, Injun man ain't strong like white man !"

Col. H. answered with emotion.

"I would have saved you, Sampson."

"Oakatibbé hab for dead !" said the worthy fellow, with another, but a very wretched smile.

His firmness was unabated.   A procession was formed, which was headed by three sturdy fellows, carrying their rifles conspicuously upon their shoulders.   These were the appointed executioners, and were all near relatives of the man who had been slain. There was no mercy in their looks.   Oakatibbé followed immediately after these.   He seemed pleased that we should accompany him to the place of execution.   Our way lay through a long avenue of stunted pines, which conducted us to a spot where an elevated ridge on either hand produced a broad and very prettily defined valley.   My eyes, in all this progress, were scarcely ever drawn off from the person of him who was to be the principal actor in the approaching scene.   Never, on any occasion, did I behold a man with a step more firm—a head so unbent—a countenance so sweetly calm, though grave—and of such quiet unconcern, at the obvious fate in view.   Yet there was nothing in his deportment of that effort which would be the case with most white men on a similar occasion, who seek to wear the aspect of heroism. He walked as to a victory, but he walked with a staid, even dignity, calmly, and without the flush of any excitement on his cheek. In his eye there was none of that feverish curiosity, which seeks for the presence of his executioner, and cannot be averted from the contemplation of the mournful paraphernalia of death.   His look was like that of the strong man, conscious of his inevitable doom, and prepared, as it is inevitable, to meet it with corresponding indifference.

The grave was now before us. It must have been prepared at the first dawn of the morning. The executioners paused, when they had reached a spot within thirty steps of it. But the condemned passed on, and stopped only on the edge of its open jaws. The last trial was at hand with all its terrors. The curtain was about to drop, and the scene of life, with all its hopes and promises and golden joys—even to an Indian golden—was to be shut forever. I felt a painful and numbing chill pass through my frame, but I could behold no sign of change in him. He now beckoned his friends around him. His enemies drew nigh also, but in a remoter circle. He was about to commence his song of death—the narrative of his performances, his purposes, all his living experience. He began a low chant, slow, measured and composed, the words seeming to consist of monosyllables only. As he proceeded, his eyes kindled, and his arms were extended. His action became impassioned, his utterance more rapid, and the tones were distinguished by increasing warmth. I could not understand a single word which he uttered, but the cadences were true and full of significance. The rise and fall of his voice, truly proportioned to the links of sound by which they were connected, would have yielded a fine lesson to the European teacher of school eloquence. His action was as graceful as that of a mighty tree yielding to and gradually rising from the pressure of a sudden gust. I felt the eloquence which I could not understand. I fancied, from his tones and gestures, the play of the muscles of his mouth, and the dilation of his eyes, that I could detect the instances of daring valour, or good conduct, which his narrative comprised. One portion of it, as he approached the close, I certainly could not fail to comprehend. He evidently spoke of his last unhappy affray with the man whom he had slain. His head was bowed—the light passed from his eyes, his hands were folded upon his heart, and his voice grew thick and husky. Then came the narrative of his flight. His glance was turned upon Col. H. and myself, and, at the close, he extended his hand to us both. We grasped it earnestly, and with a degree of emotion which I would not now seek to describe   He paused

The catastrophe was at hand. I saw him step back, so as to place himself at the very verge of the grave—he then threw open his breast—a broad, manly, muscular bosom, that would have sufficed for a Hercules—one hand he struck upon the spot above the heart, where it remained—the other was raised above his head. This was the signal. I turned away with a strange sickness. I could look no longer. In the next instant I heard the simultaneous report, as one, of the three rifles, and when I again looked, they were shoveling in the fresh mould, upon the noble form of one, who, under other more favouring circumstances, might have been a father to his nation.

JOCASSÉE.

A CHEROKEE LEGEND.

~~~~~~~~~~~~~~~~~~~

CHAPTER I.

" KEOWEE Old Fort," as the people in that quarter style it, is a fine antique ruin and relic of the revolution, in the district of Pendleton, South Carolina. The region of country in which we find it is, of itself, highly picturesque and interesting. The broad river of Keowee, which runs through it, though comparatively small as a stream in America, would put to shame, by its size not less than its beauty, one half of the far-famed and boasted rivers of Europe ;—and then the mountains, through and among which it winds its way, embody more of beautiful situation and romantic prospect, than art can well figure to the eye, or language convey to the imagination. To understand, you must see it. Words are of little avail when the ideas overcrowd utterance ; and even vanity itself is content to be dumb in the awe inspired by a thousand prospects, like Niagara, the ideals of a god, and altogether beyond the standards common to humanity.

It is not long since I wandered through this interesting region, under the guidance of my friend, Col. G——, who does the honours of society, in that quarter, with a degree of ease and unostentatious simplicity, which readily makes the visiter at home. My friend was one of those citizens to whom one's own country is always of paramount interest, and whose mind and memory, accordingly, have been always most happily employed when storing away and digesting into pleasing narrative those thousand little traditions of the local genius, which give life to rocks and valleys, and people earth with the beautiful colours and creatures

15

of the imagination. These, for the gratification of the spiritual seeker, he had forever in readiness ; and, with him to illustrate them, it is not surprising if the grove had a moral existence in my thoughts, and all the waters around breathed and were instinct with poetry. To all his narratives I listened with a satisfaction which book-stories do not often afford me. The more he told, the more he had to tell ; for nothing staled

" His infinite variety."

There may have been something in the style of telling his stories ; there was much, certainly, that was highly attractive in his manner of doing every thing, and this may have contributed not a little to the success of his narratives. Perhaps, too, my presence, upon the very scene of each legend, may have given them a life and a *vraisemblance* they had wanted otherwise.

In this manner, rambling about from spot to spot, I passed five weeks, without being, at any moment, conscious of time's progress. Day after day, we wandered forth in some new direction, contriving always to secure, and without effort, that pleasurable excitement of novelty, for which the great city labours in vain, spite of her varying fashions, and crowding, and not always innocent indulgences. From forest to river, from hill to valley, still on horseback,—for the mountainous character of the country forbade any more luxurious form of travel,—we kept on our way, always changing our ground with the night, and our prospect with the morning. In this manner we travelled over or round the Six Mile, and the Glassy, and a dozen other mountains ; and sometimes, with a yet greater scope of adventure, pushed off on a much longer ramble,—such as took us to the falls of the White Water, and gave us a glimpse of the beautiful river of Jocassée, named sweetly after the Cherokee maiden, who threw herself into its bosom on beholding the scalp of her lover dangling from the neck of his conqueror. The story is almost a parallel to that of the sister of Horatius, with this difference, that the Cherokee girl did not wait for the vengeance of her brother, and altogether spared her reproaches. I tell the story, which is pleasant and curious, in the language of my friend, from whom I first heard it.

" The Occonies and the Little Estatoees, or, rather, the Brown

Vipers and the Green Birds, were both minor tribes f the Cherokee nation, between whom, as was not unfrequently the case,
there sprung up a deadly enmity. The Estatoees had their town
on each side of the two creeks, which, to this day, keep their
name, and on the eastern side of the Keowee river. The Occonies occupied a much larger extent of territory, but it lay on the
opposite, or west side of the same stream. Their differences were
supposed to have arisen from the defeat of Chatuga, a favourite
leader of the Occonies, who aimed to be made a chief of the nation at large. The Estatoee warrior, Toxaway, was successful ;
and as the influence of Chatuga was considerable with his tribe,
he laboured successfully to engender in their bosoms a bitter dislike of the Estatoees. This feeling was made to exhibit itself on
every possible occasion. The Occonies had no word too foul by
which to describe the Estatoees. They likened them, in familiar
speech, to every thing which, in the Indian imagination, is accounted low and contemptible. In reference to war, they were
reputed women,—in all other respects, they were compared to
dogs and vermin ; and, with something of a Christian taste and
temper, they did not scruple, now and then, to invoke the devil
of their more barbarous creed, for the eternal disquiet of their
successful neighbours, the Little Estatoees, and their great chief,
Toxaway.

" In this condition of things there could not be much harmony ;
and, accordingly, as if by mutual consent, there was but little
intercourse between the two people. When they met, it was
either to regard one another with a cold, repulsive distance, or
else, as enemies, actively to foment quarrel and engage in strife.
But seldom, save on national concerns, did the Estatoees cross the
Keowee to the side held by the Occonies ; and the latter, more
numerous, and therefore less reluctant for strife than their rivals,
were yet not often found on the opposite bank of the same river.
Sometimes, however, small parties of hunters from both tribes,
rambling in one direction or another, would pass into the enemy's
territory ; but this was not frequent, and when they met, quarrel
and bloodshed were sure to mark the adventure.

" But there was one young warrior of the Estatoees, who did
not give much heed to this condition of parties, and who, moved

by an errant spirit, and wholly insensible to fear, would not hesitate, when the humour seized him, to cross the river, making quite as free, when he did so, with the hunting-grounds of the Occonies as they did themselves. This sort of conduct did not please the latter very greatly, but Nagoochie was always so gentle, and at the same time so brave, that the young warriors of Occony either liked or feared him too much to throw themselves often in his path, or labour, at any time, to arrest his progress.

" In one of these excursions, Nagoochie made the acquaintance of Jocassée, one of the sweetest of the dusky daughters of Occony. He was rambling, with bow and quiver, in pursuit of game, as was his custom, along that beautiful enclosure which the whites have named after her, the Jocassée valley. The circumstances under which they met were all strange and exciting, and well calculated to give her a power over the young hunter, to which the pride of the Indian does not often suffer him to submit. It was towards evening when Nagoochie sprung a fine buck from a hollow of the wood beside him, and just before you reach the ridge of rocks which hem in and form this beautiful valley. With the first glimpse of his prey flew the keen shaft of Nagoochie ; but, strange to say, though renowned as a hunter, not less than as a warrior, the arrow failed entirely and flew wide of the victim. Off he bounded headlong after the fortunate buck ; but though, every now and then getting him within range, —for the buck took the pursuit coolly,—the hunter still most unaccountably failed to strike him. Shaft after shaft had fallen seemingly hurtless from his sides ; and though, at frequent intervals, suffered to approach so nigh to the animal that he could not but hope still for better fortune, to his great surprise, the wary buck would dash off when he least expected it, bounding away in some new direction, with as much life and vigour as ever. What to think of this, the hunter knew not ; but such repeated disappointments at length impressed it strongly upon his mind, that the object he pursued was neither more nor less than an Occony wizard, seeking to entrap him ; so, with a due feeling of superstition, and a small touch of sectional venom aroused into action within his heart, Nagoochie, after the manner of his people promised a green bird—the emblem of his tribe—in sacrifice to the tutelar divinity of Estato, if he could only be permitted to overcome the potent enchanter, who had thus dazzled his aim and blunted his arrows. He had hardly uttered this vow, when he beheld the insolent deer mincingly grazing upon a beautiful tuft of long grass in the valley, just below the ledge of rock upon which he stood. Without more ado, he pressed onward to bring him within fair range of his arrows, little doubting at the moment that the Good Spirit had heard his prayer, and had granted his desire. But, in his hurry, leaping too hastily forward, and with eyes fixed only upon his proposed victim, his foot was caught by the smallest stump in the world, and the very next moment found him precipitated directly over the rock and into the valley, within a few paces of the deer, who made off with the utmost composure, gazing back, as he did so, in the eyes of the wounded hunter, for all the world, as if he enjoyed the sport mightily. Nagoochie, as he saw this, gravely concluded that he had fallen a victim to the wiles of the Occony wizard, and looked confidently to see half a score of Occonies upon him, taking him at a vantage. Like a brave warrior, however, he did not despond, but determining to gather up his loins for battle and the torture, he sought to rise and put himself in a state of preparation. What, however, was his horror, to find himself utterly unable to move : —his leg had been broken in the fall, and he was covered with bruises from head to foot.

" Nagoochie gave himself up for lost ; but he had scarcely done so, when he heard a voice,—the sweetest, he thought, he had ever heard in his life,—singing a wild, pleasant song, such as the Occonies love, which, ingeniously enough, summed up the sundry reasons why the mouth, and not the eyes, had been endowed with the faculty of eating. These reasons were many, but the last is quite enough for us According to the song, had the eyes, and not the mouth, been employed for this purpose, there would soon be a famine in the land, for of all gluttons, the eyes are the greatest. Nagoochie groaned aloud as he heard the song, the latter portion of which completely indicated the cause of his present misfortune. It was, indeed, the gluttony of the eyes which had broken his leg. This sort of allegory the Indians are fond of, and Jocassée knew all their legends. Certainly, thought

Nagoochie, though his leg pained him wofully at the time, 'certainly I never heard such sweet music, and such a voice.' The singer advanced as she sung, and almost stumbled over him.

" ' Who are you ?' she asked timidly, neither retreating nor advancing ; and, as the wounded man looked into her face, he blessed the Occony wizard, by whose management he deemed his leg to have been broken.

" ' Look !' was the reply of the young warrior, throwing aside the bearskin which covered his bosom,—' look, girl of Occony ! 'tis the *totem* of a chief ;' and the green bird stamped upon his left breast, as the badge of his tribe, showed him a warrior of Estato, and something of an enemy. But his eyes had no enmity, and then the broken leg ! Jocassée was a gentle maiden, and her heart melted with the condition of the warrior. She made him a sweet promise, in very pretty language, and with the very same voice the music of which was so delicious ; and then, with the fleetness of a young doe, she went off to bring him succour.

CHAPTER II.

" NIGHT, in the meanwhile, came on ; and the long howl of the wolf, as he looked down from the crag, and waited for the thick darkness in which to descend the valley, came freezingly to the ear of Nagoochie. ' Surely,' he said to himself, ' the girl of Occony will come back. She has too sweet a voice not to keep her word. She will certainly come back.' While he doubted, he believed. Indeed, though still a very young maiden, the eyes of Jocassée had in them a great deal that was good for little beside, than to persuade and force conviction ; and the belief in them was pretty extensive in the circle of her rustic acquaintance. All people love to believe in fine eyes, and nothing is more natural than for lovers to swear by them. Nagoochie did not swear by those of Jocassée, but he did most religiously believe in them ; and though the night gathered fast, and the long howl of the wolf came close from his crag, down into the valley, the young hunter of the green bird did not despair of the return of the maiden.

" She did return, and the warrior was insensible. But the motion stirred him ; the lights gleamed upon him from many torches ; he opened his eyes, and when they rested upon Jocassée they forgot to close again. She had brought aid enough, for her voice was powerful as well as musical ; and, taking due care that the totem of the green bird should be carefully concealed by the bearskin, with which her own hands covered his bosom, she had him lifted upon a litter, constructed of several young saplings, which, interlaced with withes, binding it closely together, and strewn thickly with leaves, made a couch as soft as the wounded man could desire. In a few hours, and the form of Nagoochie rested beneath the roof of Attakulla, the sire of Jocassée. She sat beside the young hunter, and it was her hand that placed the fever balm upon his lips and poured into his wounds and bruises the strong and efficacious balsams of Indian pharmacy.

"Never was nurse more careful of her charge. Day and night she watched by him, and few were the hours which she then required for her own pleasure or repose. Yet why was Jocassée so devoted to the stranger? She never asked herself so unnecessary a question; but as she was never so well satisfied, seemingly, as when near him, the probability is she found pleasure in her tendance. It was fortunate for him and for her, that her father was not rancorous towards the people of the Green Bird, like the rest of the Occonies. It might have fared hard with Nagoochie otherwise. But Attakulla was a wise old man, and a good; and when they brought the wounded stranger to his lodge, he freely yielded him shelter, and went forth himself to Chinabee, the wise medicine of the Occonies. The eyes of Nagoochie were turned upon the old chief, and when he heard his name, and began to consider where he was, he was unwilling to task the hospitality of one who might be disposed to regard him, when known, in an unfavourable or hostile light. Throwing aside, therefore, the habit of circumspection, which usually distinguishes the Indian warrior, he uncovered his bosom, and bade the old man look upon the totem of his people, precisely as he had done when his eye first met that of Jocassée.

"'Thy name? What do the people of the Green Bird call the young hunter?' asked Attakulla.

"'They name Nagoochie among the braves of the Estato: they will call him a chief of the Cherokee, like Toxaway,' was the proud reply.

"This reference was to a sore subject with the Occonies, and perhaps it was quite as imprudent as it certainly was in improper taste for him to make it. But, knowing where he was, excited by fever, and having—to say much in little—but an unfavourable opinion of Occony magnanimity, he was more rash than reasonable. At that moment, too, Jocassée had made her appearance, and the spirit of the young warrior, desiring to look big in her eyes, had prompted him to a fierce speech not altogether necessary. He knew not the generous nature of Attakulla; and when the old man took him by the hand, spoke well of the Green Bird, and called him his 'son,' the pride of Nagoochie was something humbled, while his heart grew gentler than ever. His 'son!'— that was the pleasant part; and as the thoughts grew more and more active in his fevered brain, he looked to Jocassée with such a passionate admiration that she sunk back with a happy smile from the flame-glance which he set upon her. And, day after day she tended him until the fever passed off, and the broken limb was set and had reknitted, and the bruises were all healed upon him. Yet he lingered. He did not think himself quite well, and she always agreed with him in opinion. Once and again did he set off, determined not to return, but his limb pained him, and he felt the fever come back whenever he thought of Jocassée; and so the evening found him again at the lodge, while the fever-balm, carefully bruised in milk, was in as great demand as ever for the invalid. But the spirit of the warrior at length grew ashamed of these weaknesses; and, with a desperate effort, for which he gave himself no little credit, he completed his determination to depart with the coming of the new moon. But even this decision was only effected by compromise. Love settled the affair with conscience, after his own fashion; and, under his direction, following the dusky maiden into the little grove that stood beside the cottage, Nagoochie claimed her to fill the lodge of a young warrior of the Green Bird. She broke the wand which he presented her, and seizing upon the torch which she carried, he buried it in the bosom of a neighbouring brook; and thus, after their simple forest ceremonial, Jocassée became the betrothed of Nagoochie.

CHAPTER III.

"But we must keep this secret to ourselves, for as yet it remained unknown to Attakulla, and the time could not come for its revealment until the young warrior had gone home to his people. Jocassee was not so sure that all parties would be so ready as herself to sanction her proceeding. Of her father's willingness, she had no question, for she knew his good nature and good sense; but she had a brother of whom she had many fears and misgivings. He was away, on a great hunt of the young men, up at Charashilactay, or the falls of the White Water, as we call it to this day—a beautiful cascade of nearly forty feet, the water of which is of a milky complexion. How she longed, yet how she dreaded, to see that brother! He was a fierce, impetuous, sanguinary youth, who, to these characteristics, added another still more distasteful to Jocassée;—there was not a man among all the Occonies who so hated the people of the Green Bird as Cheochee. What hopes, or rather what fears, were in the bosom of that maiden!

"But he came not. Day after day they looked for his return, and yet he came not; but in his place a runner, with a bearded stick, a stick covered with slips of skin, torn from the body of a wolf. The runner passed by the lodge of Attakulla, and all its inmates were aroused by the intelligence he brought. A wolf-hunt was commanded by Moitoy, the great war-chief or generalissimo of the Cherokee nation, to take place, instantly, at Charashilactay, where an immense body of wolves had herded together, and had become troublesome neighbours. Old and young, who had either taste for the adventure, or curiosity to behold it, at once set off upon the summons; and Attakulla, old as he was, and Nagoochie, whose own great prowess in hunting had made it a passion, determined readily upon the journey. Jocassée, too, joined the company,—for the maidens of Cherokee were bold spirits, as well as beautiful, and loved to ramble, particularly when, as in the present instance, they went forth in company with their lovers. Lodge after lodge, as they pursued their way, poured forth its inmates, who joined them in their progress, until the company had swollen into a goodly caravan, full of life, anxious for sport, and carrying, as is the fashion among the Indians, provisions of smoked venison and parched grain, in plenty, or many days.

"They came at length to the swelling hills, the long narrow valleys of the Keochee and its tribute river of Toxaway, named after that great chief of the Little Estatoees, of whom we have already heard something. At one and the same moment they beheld the white waters of Charashilactay, plunging over the precipice, and the hundred lodges of the Cherokee hunters. There they had gathered—the warriors and their women—twenty different tribes of the same great nation being represented on the ground ; each tribe having its own cluster of cabins, and rising up, in the midst of each, the long pole on which hung the peculiar emblem of the clan. It was not long before Nagoochie marshalled himself along with his brother Estatoees—who had counted him lost—under the beautiful green bird of his tribe, which waved about in the wind, over the heads of their small community.

" The number of warriors representing the Estato in that great hunt was inconsiderable—but fourteen—and the accession, therefore, of so promising a brave as Nagoochie, was no small matter. They shouted with joy at his coming, and danced gladly in the ring between the lodges—the young women in proper taste, and with due spirit, hailing, with a sweet song, the return of so handsome a youth, and one who was yet unmarried.

" Over against the lodges of the Estatoees, lay the more imposing encampment of the rival Occonies, who turned out strongly, as it happened, on this occasion. They were more numerous than any other of the assembled tribes, as the hunt was to take place on a portion of their own territory. Conscious of their superiority, they had not, you may be sure, forborne any of the thousand sneers and sarcasms which they were never at a loss to find when they spoke of the Green Bird warriors ; and of all their clan, none was so bitter, so uncompromising, generally, in look,

speech, and action, as Cheochee, the fierce brother of the beautiful Jocassée. Scorn was in his eye, and sarcasm on his lips, when
he heard the rejoicings made by the Estatoees on the return of
the long-lost hunter.

" ' Now wherefore screams the painted bird to-day ? why
makes he a loud cry in the ears of the brown viper that can strike ?'
he exclaimed contemptuously yet fiercely.

" It was Jocassée that spoke in reply to her brother, with the
quickness of woman's feeling, which they wrong greatly who hold
it subservient to the strength of woman's cunning. In her reply,
Cheochee saw the weakness of her heart.

" ' They scream for Nagoochie,' said the girl ; 'it is joy tha
the young hunter comes back that makes the green bird to sing
to-day.'

" ' Has Jocassée taken a tongue from the green bird, that she
screams in the ears of the brown viper ?   What has the girl to do
with the thoughts of the warrior ?   Let her go—go, bring drink to
Cheochee.'

" Abashed and silent, she did as he commanded, and brought
meekly to the fierce brother, a gourd filled with the bitter beverage
which the Cherokees love. She had nothing further to say on the
subject of the Green Bird warrior, for whom she had already so
unwarily spoken. But her words had not fallen unregarded
upon the ears of Cheochee, nor had the look of the fond heart
which spoke out in her glance, passed unseen by the keen eye of
that jealous brother. He had long before this heard of the great
fame of Nagoochie as a hunter, and in his ire he was bent to sur-
pass him. Envy had grown into hate, when he heard that this
great reputation was that of one of the accursed Estatoees ; and,
not satisfied with the desire to emulate, he also aimed to destroy.
This feeling worked like so much gall in his bosom ; and when
his eyes looked upon the fine form of Nagoochie, and beheld its
symmetry, grace, and manhood, his desire grew into a furious
passion which made him sleepless. The old chief, Attakulla, his
father, told him all the story of Nagoochie's accident—how Jocassée had found him ; and how, in his own lodge, he had been
nursed and tended. The old man spoke approvingly of Nagoochie ; and, the better to bring about a good feeling for her lover,

Jocassée humbled herself greatly to her brother,—anticipated his desires, and studiously sought to serve him. But all this failed to effect a favourable emotion in the breast of the malignant young savage towards the young hunter of the Green Bird. He said nothing, however, of his feelings; but they looked out and were alive to the sight, in every aspect, whenever any reference, however small, was made to the subject of his ire. The Indian passion is subtlety, and Cheochee was a warrior already famous among the old chiefs of Cherokee.

CHAPTER IV.

" The next day came the commencement of the great hunt, and the warriors were up betimes and active.   Stations were chosen, the keepers of which, converging to a centre, were to hem in the wild animal on whose tracks they were going.   The wolves were known to be in a hollow of the hills, near Charashilactay, which had but one outlet ; and points of close approximation across this outlet were the stations of honour ; for, goaded by the hunters to this passage, and failing of egress in any other, the wolf, it was well known, would be then dangerous in the extreme.   Well cal-culated to provoke into greater activity the jealousies between the Occonies and the Green Birds, was the assignment made by Moi-toy, the chief, of the more dangerous of these stations to these two clans.   They now stood alongside of one another, and the action of the two promised to be joint and corresponsive.   Such an ap-pointment, in the close encounter with the wolf, necessarily prom-ised to bring the two parties into immediate contact ; and such was the event.   As the day advanced, and the hunters, contract-ing their circles, brought the different bands of wolves into one, and pressed upon them to the more obvious and indeed the only outlet, the badges of the Green Bird and the Brown Viper—the one consisting of the stuffed skin and plumage of the Carolina par-rot, and the other the attenuated viper, filled out with moss, and winding, with erect head, around the pole, to the top of which it was stuck—were, at one moment, in the indiscriminate hunt, al-most mingled over the heads of the two parties.   Such a sight was pleasant to neither, and would, at another time, of a certainty, have brought about a squabble.   As it was, the Occonies drove their badge-carrier from one to the other end of their ranks, thus stu-diously avoiding the chance of another collision between the viper so adored, and the green bird so detested.   The pride of the Es-tatoees was exceedingly aroused at this exhibition of impertinence, and though a quiet people enough, they began to think that for bearance had been misplaced in their relations with their presuming and hostile neighbours. Had it not been for Nagoochie, who had his own reasons for suffering yet more, tne Green Birds would certainly have plucked out the eyes of the Brown Vipers, or tried very hard to do it; but the exhortations to peace of the young warrior, and the near neighbourhood of the wolf, quelled any open show of the violence they meditated; but, Indian-like, they determined to wait for the moment of greatest quiet, as that most fitted for taking away a few scalps from the Occony. With a muttered curse, and a contemptuous slap of the hand upon their thighs, the more furious among the Estatoees satisfied their present anger, and then addressed themselves more directly to the business before them.

"The wolves, goaded to desperation by the sight and sound of hunters strewn all over the hills around them, were now, snapping and snarling, and with eyes that flashed with a terrible anger, descending the narrow gully towards the outlet held by the two rival tribes. United action was therefore demanded of those who, for a long time past, had been conscious of no feeling or movement in common. But here they had no choice—no time, indeed, .o think. The fierce wolves were upon them, doubly furious at finding the only passage stuck full of enemies. Well and manfully did the hunters stand and seek the encounter with the infuriated beasts. The knife and the hatchet, that day, in the hand of Occony and Estato, did fearful execution. The Brown Vipers fought nobly, and with their ancient reputation. But the Green Birds were the hunters, after all; and they were now stimulated into double adventure and effort, by an honourable ambition to make up for all deficiencies of number by extra valour, and the careful exercise of all that skill in the arts of hunting for which they have always been the most renowned of the tribes of Cherokee. As, one by one, a fearful train, the wolves wound into sight along this or that crag of the gully, arrow after arrow told fearfully upon them, for there were no marksmen like the Estatoees. Nor did they stop at this weapon. The young Nagoochie, more than ever prompted to such audacity, led the way; and dashing into the very path of the teeth-gnashing and claw-rending enemy, he grappled in desperate fight the first that offered himself, and as the wide jaws of his hairy foe opened upon him, with a fearful plunge at his side, adroitly leaping to the right, he thrust a pointed stick down, deep, as far as he could send it, into the monster's throat, then pressing back upon him, with the rapidity of an arrow, in spite of all his fearful writhings he pinned him to the ground, while his knife, in a moment after, played fatally in his heart. Another came, and, in a second, his hatchet cleft and crunched deep into the skull of the angry brute, leaving him senseless, without need of a second stroke. There was no rivalling deeds of valour so desperate as this; and with increased bitterness of soul did Cheochee and his followers hate in proportion as they admired. They saw the day close, and heard the signal calling them to the presence of the great chief Moitoy, conscious, though superior in numbers, they could not at all compare in skill and success with the long-despised, but now thoroughly-hated Estatoees.

" And still more great the vexation, still more deadly the hate, when the prize was bestowed by the hand of Moitoy, the great military chief of Cherokee—when, calling around him the tribes, and carefully counting the number of their several spoils, consisting of the skins of the wolves that had been slain, it was found that of these the greater number, in proportion to their force, had fallen victims to the superior skill or superior daring of the people of the Green Bird. And who had been their leader? The rambling Nagoochie—the young hunter who had broken his leg among the crags of Occony, and, in the same adventure, no longer considered luckless, had won the young heart of the beautiful Jocassée.

" They bore the young and successful warrior into the centre of the ring, and before the great Moitoy. He stood up in the presence of the assembled multitude, a brave and fearless, and fine looking Cherokee. At the signal of the chief, the young maidens gathered into a group, and sung around him a song of compliment and approval, which was just as much as to say,— ' Ask, and you shall have.' He did ask; and before the people of the Brown Viper could so far recover from their surprise as to interfere, or well comprehend the transaction, the bold Nagoochie had led the then happy Jocassée into the presence of Moitoy and the multitude, and had claimed the girl of Occony to fill the green lodge of the Estato hunter.

"That was the signal for uproar and commotion. The Occonies were desperately angered, and the fierce Cheochee, whom nothing, not even the presence of the great war-chief, could restrain, rushed forward, and dragging the maiden violently from the hold of Nagoochie, hurled her backward into the ranks of his people ; then, breathing nothing but blood and vengeance, he confronted him with ready knife and uplifted hatchet, defying the young hunter in that moment to the fight.

"' E-cha-e-cha, e-herro—echa-herro-echa-herro,' was the warwhoop of the Occonies ; and it gathered them to a man around the sanguinary young chief who uttered it. ' Echa-herro, echa-herro,' he continued, leaping wildly in air with the paroxysm of rage which had seized him,—' the brown viper has a tooth for the green bird. The Occony is athirst—he would drink blood from the dog-heart of the Estato. E-cha-e-cha-herro, Occony.' And again he concluded his fierce speech with that thrilling roll of sound, which, as the so much dreaded warwhoop, brought a death feeling to the heart of the early pioneer, and made the mother clasp closely, in the deep hours of the night, the young and unconscious infant to her bosom. But it had no such influence upon the fearless spirit of Nagoochie. The Estato heard him with cool composure, but, though evidently unafraid, it was yet equally evident that he was unwilling to meet the challenger in strife. Nor was his decision called for on the subject. The great chief interposed, and all chance of conflict was prevented by his intervention. In that presence they were compelled to keep the peace, though both the Occonies and Little Estatoees retired to their several lodges with fever in their veins, and a restless desire for that collision which Moitoy had denied them. All but Nagoochie were vexed at this denial ; and all of them wondered much that a warrior, so brave and daring as he had always shown himself, should be so backward on such an occasion. It was true, they knew of his love for the girl of Occony ; but they never dreamed of such a feeling acquiring an influence over the hunter, of so paralyzing and unmanly a character. Even Nagoochie himself, as he listened to some of the speeches uttered

16

around him, and reflected upon the insolence of Cheochee—even he began to wish that the affair might happen again, that he might take the hissing viper by the neck. And poor Jocassée—what of her when they took her back to the lodges? She did nothing but dream all night of Brown Vipers and Green Birds in the thick of battle.

CHAPTER V.

" THE next day came the movement of the hunters, still under the conduct of Moitoy, from the one to the other side of the upper branch of the Keowee river, now called the Jocassée, but which, at that time, went by the name of Sarratay. The various bands prepared to move with the daylight; and, still near, and still in sight of one another, the Occonies and Estatoees took up their line of march with the rest. The long poles of the two, bearing the green bird of the one, and the brown viper of the other, in the hands of their respective bearers—stout warriors chosen for this purpose with reference to strength and valour—waved in parallel courses, though the space between them was made as great as possible by the common policy of both parties. Following the route of the caravan, which had been formed of the ancient men, the women and children, to whom had been entrusted the skins taken in the hunt, the provisions, utensils for cooking, &c., the great body of hunters were soon in motion for other and better hunting-grounds, several miles distant, beyond the river.

" The Indian warriors have their own mode of doing business, and do not often travel with the stiff precision which marks European civilization. Though having all one point of destination, each hunter took his own route to gain it, and in this manner asserted his independence. This had been the education of the Indian boy, and this self-reliance is one source of that spirit and character which will not suffer him to feel surprise in any situation. Their way, generally, wound along a pleasant valley, unbroken for several miles, until you came to Big-knob, a huge crag which completely divides it, rising formidably up in the midst, and narrowing the valley on either hand to a fissure, necessarily compelling a closer march for all parties than had heretofore been pursued. Straggling about as they had been, of course but little order was perceptible when they came together, in little groups, where the mountain forced their junction. One

of the Bear tribe found himself alongside a handful of the Fox-
es, and a chief of the Alligators plunged promiscuously int
the centre of a cluster of the Turkey tribe, whose own chief was
probably doing the proper courtesies among the Alligators. These
little crossings, however, were amusing rather than annoying, and
were, generally, productive of little inconvenience and no strife.
But it so happened that there was one exception to the accustomed harmony.   The Occonies and Estatoees, like the rest, had
broken up in small parties, and, as might have been foreseen,
when they came individually to where the crag divided the valley
into two, some took the one and some the other hand, and it was
not until one of the paths they had taken opened into a little plain
in which the woods were bald—a sort of prairie—that a party of
seven Occonies discovered that they had among them two of their
detested rivals, the Little Estatoees.   What made the matter
worse, one of these stragglers was the ill-fated warrior who had
been chosen to carry the badge of his tribe ; and there, high
above their heads—the heads of the Brown Vipers—floated that
detestable symbol, the green bird itself.

" There was no standing that.   The Brown Vipers, as if with
a common instinct, were immediately up in arms.   They grappled the offending stragglers without gloves.   They tore the green
bird from the pole, stamped it under foot, smothered it in the mud,
and pulling out the cone-tuft of its head, utterly degraded it in
their own as well as in the estimation of the Estatoees.   Not content with this, they hung the desecrated emblem about the neck
of the bearer of it, and, spite of all their struggles, binding the
arms of the two stragglers behind their backs, the relentless Vipers thrust the long pole which had borne the bird, in such a
manner between their alternate arms as effectually to fasten them
together.   In this manner, amidst taunts, blows and revilings,
they were left in the valley to get on as they might, while their
enemies, insolent enough with exultation, proceeded to join the
rest of their party.

CHAPTER VI.

" An hundred canoes were ready on the banks of the river Sarratay, for the conveyance to the opposite shore of the assembled Cherokees. And down they came, warrior after warrior, tribe after tribe, emblem after emblem, descending from the crags around, in various order, and hurrying all with shouts, and whoops and songs, grotesquely leaping to the river's bank, like so many boys just let out of school. Hilarity is, indeed, the life of nature! Civilization refines the one at the expense of the other, and then it is that no human luxury or sport, as known in society, stimulates appetite for any length of time. We can only laugh in the woods—society suffers but a smile, and desperate sanctity, with the countenance of a crow, frowns even at that.

" But, down, around, and gathering from every side, they came —the tens and the twenties of the several tribes of Cherokee. Grouped along the banks of the river, were the boats assigned to each. Some, already filled, were sporting in every direction over the clear bosom of that beautiful water. Moitoy himself, at the head of the tribe of Nequassée, from which he came, had already embarked; while the venerable Attakulla, with Jocassée, the gentle, sat upon a little bank in the neighbourhood of the Occony boats, awaiting the arrival of Cheochee and his party. And why came they not? One after another of the several tribes had filled their boats, and were either on the river or across it. But two clusters of canoes yet remained, and they were those of the rival tribes—a green bird flaunted over the one, and a brown viper, in many folds, was twined about the pole of the other.

" There was sufficient reason why they came not. The strife had begun ;—for, when, gathering his thirteen warriors in a little hollow at the termination of the valley through which they came, Nagoochie beheld the slow and painful approach of the two stragglers upon whom the Occonies had so practised—when he saw the green bird, the beautiful emblem of his tribe, disfigured and defiled—there was no longer any measure or method in his mad-ness. There was no longer a thought of Jocassée to keep him back ; and the feeling of ferocious indignation which filled his bosom was the common feeling with his brother warriors. They lay in wait for the coming of the Occonies, down at the foot of the Yellow Hill, where the woods gathered green and thick. They were few—but half in number of their enemies—but they were strong in ardour, strong in justice, and even death was pref-erable to a longer endurance of that dishonour to which they had already been too long subjected. They beheld the approach of the Brown Vipers, as, one by one, they wound out from the gap of the mountain, with a fierce satisfaction. The two parties were now in sight of each other, and could not mistake the terms of their encounter. No word was spoken between them, but each began the scalp-song of his tribe, preparing at the same time his weapon, and advancing to the struggle.

" ' The green bird has a bill,' sang the Estatoees ; ' and he flies like an arrow to his prey.'

" ' The brown viper has poison and a fang,' responded the Oc-conies ; ' and he lies under the bush for his enemy.'

" ' Give me to clutch the war-tuft,' cried the leaders of each party, almost in the same breath.

" ' To taste the blood,' cried another.

" ' And make my knife laugh in the heart that shrinks,' sung another and another.

" ' I will put my foot on the heart,' cried an Occony.

" ' I tear away the scalp,' shouted an Estato, in reply ; while a joint chorus from the two parties, promised—

" ' A dog that runs, to the black spirit that keeps in the dark.'

" ' *Echa-herro, echa-herro, echa-herro*,' was the grand cry, or fearful warwhoop, which announced the moment of onset and the beginning of the strife.

" The Occonies were not backward, though the affair was commenced by the Estatoees. Cheochee, their leader, was quite as brave as malignant, and now exulted in the near prospect of that sweet revenge, for all the supposed wrongs and more certain rivalries which his tribe had suffered from the Green Birds. Nor was this more the feeling with him than with his tribe. Disposing

.hemselves, therefore, in readiness to receive the assault, they rejoiced in the coming of a strife, in which, having many injuries
to redress, they had the advantages, at the same time, of position
and numbers.

" But their fighting at disadvantage was not now a thought with
the Little Estatoees. Their blood was up, and like all usually
patient people, once aroused, they were not so readily quieted.
Nagoochie, the warrior now, and no longer the lover, led on the
attack. You should have seen how that brave young chief went
into battle—how he leapt up in air, slapped his hands upon his
thighs in token of contempt for his foe, and throwing himself open
before his enemies, dashed down his bow and arrows, and waving
his hatchet, signified to them his desire for the conflict, à l'outrance,
and, which would certainly make it so, hand to hand. The Occonies took him at his word, and throwing aside the long bow, they
bounded out from their cover to meet their adversaries. Then
should you have seen that meeting—that first rush—how they
threw the tomahawk—how they flourished the knife—how the
brave man rushed to the fierce embrace of his strong enemy—and
how the two rolled along the hill in the teeth-binding struggle of
death.

" The tomahawk of Nagoochie had wings and a tooth. It flew
and bit in every direction. One after another, the Occonies went
down before it, and still his fierce war cry of ' Echa-mal-Occony,'
preceding every stroke, announced another and another victim.
They sank away from him like sheep before the wolf that is
hungry, and the disparity of force was not so great in favour of
the Occonies, when we recollect that Nagoochie was against them.
The parties, under his fierce valour, were soon almost equal in
number, and something more was necessary to be done by the
Occonies before they could hope for that favourable result from
the struggle which they had before looked upon as certain. It
was for Cheochee now to seek out and to encounter the gallant
young chief of Estato. Nagoochie, hitherto, for reasons best
known to himself, had studiously avoided the leader of the Vipers ; but he could no longer do so. He was contending, in
close strife, with Okonettee, or the One-Eyed—a stout warrior of
the Vipers—as Cheochee approached him. In the next moment,

the hatchet of Nagoochie entered the skull of Okonettee. The One-Eyed sunk to the ground, as if in supplication, and, seizing the legs of his conqueror, in spite of the repeated blows which descended from the deadly instrument, each of which was a death, while his head swam, and the blood filled his eyes, and his senses were fast fleeting, he held on with a death-grasp which nothing could compel him to forego. In this predicament, Cheochee confronted the young brave of Estato. The strife was short, for though Nagoochie fought as bravely as ever, yet he struck in vain, while the dying wretch, grappling his legs, disordered, by his convulsions, not less than by his efforts, every blow which the strong hand of Nagoochie sought to give. One arm was already disabled, and still the dying wretch held on to his legs. In another moment, the One-Eyed was seized by the last spasms of death, and in his struggles, he dragged the Estato chief to his knees. This was the fatal disadvantage. Before any of the Green Bird warriors could come to his succour, the blow was given, and Nagoochie lay under the knee of the Brown Viper. The knife was in his heart, and the life not yet gone, when the same instrument encircled his head, and his swimming vision could behold his own scalp waving in the grasp of his conqueror. The gallant spirit of Nagoochie passed away in a vain effort to utter his song of death—the song of a brave warrior conscious of many victories.

———

" Jocassée looked up to the hills when she heard the fierce cry of the descending Vipers. Their joy was madness, for they had fought with—they had slain, the bravest of their enemies. The intoxication of tone which Cheochee exhibited, when he told the story of the strife, and announced his victory, went like a death-stroke to the heart of the maiden. But she said not a word—she uttered no complaint—she shed no tear. Gliding quietly into the boat in which they were about to cross the river, she sat silent, gazing, with the fixedness of a marble statue, upon the still dripping scalp of her lover, as it dangled about the neck of his conqueror. On a sudden, just as they had reached the middle of the stream, she started, and her gaze was turned once more backward upon the banks they had left, as if, on a sudden, some object of interest had met her sight,—then, whether by accident or design, with look still intent in the same direction, she fell over the side, before they could save or prevent her, and was buried in the deep waters of Sarratay for ever. She rose not once to the surface. The stream, from that moment, lost the name of Sarratay, and both whites and Indians, to this day, know it only as the river of Jocassée. The girls of Cherokee, however, contend that she did not sink, but walking 'the waters like a thing of life,' that she rejoined Nagoochie, whom she saw beckoning to her from the shore. Nor is this the only tradition. The story goes on to describe a beautiful lodge, one of the most select in the valleys of Manneyto, the hunter of which is Nagoochie of the Green Bird, while the maiden who dresses his venison is certainly known as Jocassée."

THE GIANT'S COFFIN,

OR THE FEUD OF HOLT AND HOUSTON.

A TALE OF REEDY RIVER.

CHAPTER I.

In 1766, the beautiful district of Greenville, in South Carolina,
—which is said to have had its name in consequence of the ver-
dant aspect which it bore in European eyes,—received its first
white settlers from Virginia and Pennsylvania. Among these
early colonists were the families of Holt and Houston,—represented by two fearless borderers, famous in their day as Indian
hunters;—men ready with the tomahawk and rifle, but not less
distinguished, perhaps, for the great attachment which existed between them. Long intercourse in trying periods—the habit of
referring to each other in moments of peril—constant adventures
in company—not to speak of similar tastes and sympathies in numerous other respects, had created between them a degree of affection, which it would be difficult, perhaps, to find among persons
of more mild and gentle habits. Each had his family—his wife
and little ones—and, traversing the mountain paths which lie between Virginia and the Carolinas, they came in safety to the
more southern of the last-named colonies. Charmed with the appearance of the country, they squatted down upon the borders of
Reedy River, not very far from the spot now occupied by the
pleasant town of Greenville. Family division, for the present,
there was none. Congeniality of tastes, the isolation of their

abodes, the necessity of concentration against the neighbouring Indian nation of Cherokees, kept them together; and, continuing the life of the hunter, rather than that of the farmer, John Holt and Arthur Houston pursued the track of bear, deer, and turkey, as before, with a keenness of zest which, possibly, derived its impulse quite as much from attachment to one another, as from any great fondness for the pursuit itself.

Meanwhile, their families, taking fast hold upon the soil, began to flourish together after a fashion of their own. Flourish they did, for the boys thrived, and the girls grew apace. But tradition has preserved some qualifying circumstances in this history, by which it would seem that their prosperity was not entirely without alloy. The sympathies between *Mesdames* Holt and Houston were not, it appears, quite so warm and active as those which distinguished the intercourse of their respective husbands. Civil enough to one another in the presence of the latter, they were not unfrequently at " *dagger-draw*" in their absence. The husbands were not altogether ignorant of this condition of things at home, but they had their remedy; and there is little doubt that, like some other famous sportsmen of my acquaintance, they became happy hunters only when there was no longer any hope that they could become happy husbands. Now, as quarrels most commonly owe their spirit and excellence to the presence of spectators, we may assume that some portion of the virulence of our two wives underwent diminution from the absence of those before whom it might hope to display itself with appropriate eloquence; and the wrath of the dames, only exhibited before their respective children, was very apt to exhale in clouds, and slight flashes, and an under-current of distant thunder. Unhappily, however, the evil had consequences of which the weak mothers little thought, and the feud was entailed to the children, who, instead of assimilating, with childish propensities, in childish sports, took up the cudgels of their parents, and under fewer of the restraints,—arising from prudence, and the recognition of mutual necessities,—by which the dames were kept from extreme issues, they played the aforesaid cudgels about their mutual heads, with a degree of earnestness that very frequently rendered necessary the interposition of their superiors.

The miserable evil of this family feud fell most heavily upon the natures of the two eldest boys, one a Holt, the other a Houston,—spoiling their childish tempers, impressing their souls with fearful passions, and embittering their whole intercourse.

At this period young Houston has reached the age of fourteen and Holt of twelve years of age. The former was a tall, slender, and very handsome youth; the latter was short, thickset, and of rather plain, unpromising appearance. But he was modest, gentle, and subdued in temper, and rather retiring and shy. The former, on the contrary, was bold, vain, and violent—the petted boy of his mother, insolent in his demands, and reckless in his resentments—a fellow of unbending will, and of unmeasured impulses. He had already gone forth as a hunter with his father; he had proved his strength and courage; and he longed for an opportunity to exercise his youthful muscle upon his young companion, with whom, hitherto,—he himself could not say how or why—his collisions had fallen short of the extremities of personal violence. For such an encounter the soul of young Houston yearned; he knew that Holt was not wanting in strength—he had felt that in their plays together; but he did not doubt that his own strength, regularly put forth, was greatly superior.

One day the boys had gone down together to the banks of Reedy River to bathe. There they met a deformed boy of the neighbourhood, whose name was Acker. In addition to his deformity, the boy was an epileptic, and such was his nervous sensibility, that, merely to point a finger at him in mischief, was apt to produce in him the most painful sensations. Sometimes, indeed, the pranks of his playmates, carried too far, had thrown him into convulsions. This unhappy lad had but just recovered from a sickness produced by some such practices, and this fact was well known to the boys. Disregarding it, however, John Houston proceeded to amuse himself with the poor boy. Holt, however, interposed, and remonstrated with his companion, but without effect. Houston persisted, until, fairly tired of the sport, he left the diseased boy in a dreadful condition of mental excitement and bodily exhaustion. This done, he proceeded to bathe.

Meanwhile, with that sort of cunning and vindictiveness which often distinguishes the impaired intellect of persons subject to such infirmities, the epileptic boy watched his opportunity, and stole down, unobserved, to the river's edge, among the rocks, where the boys had placed their clothes. There he remained in waiting, and when John Houston appeared to dress himself, and was stooping down for his garments, the epileptic threw himself violently upon him, bore him to the ground, and, grasping a heavy rock, would have beaten out the brains of the offending lad, but for the timely assistance of Arthur Holt, who drew off the assailant, deprived him of his weapon, and gave his comrade a chance to recover, and place himself in a situation to defend himself.

But Acker, the epileptic boy, was no longer in a condition to justify the hostility of any enemy. His fit of frenzy had been succeeded by one of weeping, and, prostrate upon the ground, he lay convulsed under most violent nervous agitation. While he remained in this state, John Houston, who had now partially dressed himself, furious with rage at the indignity he had suffered, and the danger he had escaped, prepared to revenge himself upon him for this last offence; and, but for Arthur Holt, would, no doubt, have subjected the miserable victim to a severe beating. But the manly nature of Arthur resented and resisted this brutality. He stood between the victim and his persecutor.

" You shall not beat him, John—it was your own fault. You begun it."

" I will beat you then," was the reply.

" No! you shall not beat me, either."

" Ha! Take that!"

The blow followed on the instant. A first blow, and in the eye, too, is very apt to conclude an ordinary battle. But this was to be no ordinary battle. Our young hero was stunned by the blow;—the fire flashed from the injured eye;—but the unfairness of the proceeding awakened a courage which had its best sources in the moral nature of the boy; and, though thus taken at advantage, he closed in with his assailant, and, in this manner, lessened the odds at which he otherwise must have fought with one so much taller and longer in the arms than himself. In the fling that followed, John Houston was on his back. His conqueror suffered him to rise.

" Let us fight no more, John," he said, on relaxing his hold;
" I don't want to fight with you."

The answer, on the part of the other, was a renewal of the assault. Again was he thrown, and this time with a considerable
increase of severity. He rose with pain. He felt his hurts.
The place of battle was stony ground. Fragments of rock
were at hand. Indignant and mortified at the result of the second struggle—aiming only at vengeance—the furious boy snatch-
ed up one of these fragments, and once more rushed upon his
companion. But this time he was restrained by a third party—
no less than his own father—who, unobserved, had emerged from
the neighbouring thicket, and, unseen by the combatants, had witnessed the whole proceeding. The honourable nature of the old
hunter recoiled at the conduct of his son. He suddenly took the
lad by the collar, wrested the stone from him, and laying a heavy
hickory rod some half dozen times over his shoulders, with no
moderate emphasis, sent him home, burning with shame, and
breathing nothing but revenge.

CHAPTER II.

IN the space of five years after this event, the two fathers yielded their scalps to the Cherokees, and upon the young men, now stretching to manhood, devolved the task of providing for their families. The patriarchal sway was at an end, and, with it, all those restraining influences by which the external show of peace had been kept up. It was to be a household in common no longer. But a short time had elapsed, when a domestic storm of peculiar violence determined the dames to separate for ever; and, while the family of Holt, under the management of young Arthur, remained at the old settlement near Reedy River, the Houstons proceeded to Paris Mountain, some seven miles off,—in the neighbourhood of which may be found, at this day, some traces of their rude retreat. The settlement at Reedy River, meanwhile, had undergone increase. New families had arrived, and the first foundations were probably then laid of the flourishing village which now borders the same lovely stream. The sons grew up, but not after the fashion of their fathers. In one respect only did John Houston resemble his parent—he was a hunter. Arthur Holt, on the other hand, settled down into a methodical, hard-working farmer, who, clinging to his family fireside, made it cheerful, and diffused the happiest influences around it. He grew up strong rather than handsome, good rather than conspicuous; and, under his persevering industry and steady habits, his mother's family, now his own, reached a condition of comfort before unknown. The family of young Houston, by which we mean his mother, sister, and a younger brother, did not flourish in like degree. Yet Houston had already acquired great reputation as a hunter. In the woods he seemed literally to follow in his father's footsteps. He had his accomplishments also. He was certainly the handsomest youth in all the settlements; of a bold carriage, lofty port, free, open, expressive countenance, tall of person and graceful of movement.

It was some qualification of these advantages that the *morale* of John Houston was already something more than questionable in the public opinion of the settlement.   His tastes were vicious, —his indulgences in strong drink had more than once subjected him to humiliating exposures, but as yet they had produced cau- tion rather than dislike among his associates.   Among the wo- men, however, they were not suspected to exist, or, if known or suspected, weighed very little against the graces of a fine person, a dashing, easy carriage, and a free " gift of the gab," which left him quite as unrivalled among the debaters as he was among the dancers.

Among the families settled down upon Reedy River, was that of Marcus Heywood, a Virginia cavalier, a fine hearty gentle- man of the old school, polished and precise, who had seen better days, and was disposed very much to insist upon them.   He brought with him into the little colony a degree of taste and refinement, of which, before his coming, the happy little neigh- bourhood knew nothing ; but, unhappily for all parties, he sur- vived too short a time after his arrival, to affect very favourably, or very materially, the sentiments and manners of those about him.   He left his widow, a lady of fifty, and an only daughter of sixteen, to lament his loss.   Mrs. Heywood was a good wo- man, an excellent housewife, a kind matron, and all that is exem- plary at her time of life ; but Leda Heywood, her daughter, was a paragon ;—in such high terms is she described by still-worship- ing tradition, and the story that comes down to us, seems, in some respects, to justify the warmth of its eulogium.   At the period of her father's death, Leda was only sixteen ; but she was tall, well- grown, and thoughtful beyond her years.   The trying times in which she lived—frequent travel—the necessity of vigilance— the duties which naturally fall upon the young in new countries —conspired to bring out her character, and to hurry to maturity an intellect originally prompt and precocious.   Necessity had forced thought into exercise, and she had become acute, ob- servant, subdued in bearing, modest in reply, gentle, full of wo- manly solicitude, yet so calm in her deportment that, to the su- perficial observer, she wore an aspect,—quite false to the fact— of great coldness and insensibility.   Her tastes were excellent ;

17

she sang very sweetly—and when you add to the account of her merits, that she was really very lovely, a fair, blue-eyed, graceful creature,—you need not wonder that one day she became a heroine! A heroine! poor Leda! Bitterly, indeed, must she have wept, in after times, the evil fortune that doomed her to be a heroine!

But Leda was a belle before she became a heroine. This was, perhaps, the more unfortunate destiny of the two. She was the belle of Reedy River, called by hunter, and shepherd, and farmer, "the blue-eyed girl of Reedy River," to whom all paid an involuntary tribute, to whom all came as suitors, and, with the rest, who but our two acquaintances, John Houston and Arthur Holt. At first they themselves knew not that they were rivals, but the secret was one of that sort which very soon contrived to reveal itself. It was then that the ancient hate of John Houston revived, in all its fury. If Arthur Holt was not conscious of the same feelings exactly, he was yet conscious of an increased dislike of his old companion. With that forbearance which, whether the fruit of prudence or timidity, Arthur Holt had always been careful to maintain in his intercouse with his former associate, he now studiously kept aloof from him as much as possible. Not that this reserve and caution manifested itself in any unmanly weakness. On the contrary, no one could have appeared more composed, when they met, than Arthur Holt. It is true that, in the actual presence of Leda Heywood, he was rather more embarrassed than his rival. The reader will not need to be reminded that we have already described him as being naturally shy. This bashfulness showed badly in contrast with the deportment of John Houston. If the difference between the manner of the two young men, in approaching their mistress, was perceptible to herself and others, it was little likely to escape the eyes of one who, like John Houston, was rendered equally watchful both by hate and jealousy. But, unconscious of any bashfulness himself, he could not conceive the influence of this weakness in another. He committed the grievous error of ascriting the disquiet and nervous timidity of Arthur Holt to a very different origin; and fondly fancied that it arose from a secret dread which the young man felt of his rival. We shall not say what degree of influence this notion might have had, in determining his own future conduct towards his rival.

Some months had passed away, since the death of Colonel Heywood, in this manner, and the crowd of suitors had gradually given way to the two to whom our own attention has been more particularly turned. Events, meanwhile, had been verging towards a very natural crisis; and the whisper, on all hands, determined that Leda Heywood was certainly engaged, and to John Houston. This whisper, as a matter of course, soon reached the ears of the man whom it was most likely to annoy.

Arthur Holt could not be said to hope, for, in truth, Leda Heywood had given him but little encouragement; still he was not willing to yield in despair, for, so far as he himself had observed, she had never given any encouragement to his rival. At all events, there was a way of settling the matter, which the stout-hearted fellow determined to take at the earliest moment. He resolved to propose to Leda, a measure which he would sooner have adopted, but for a delicate scruple arising from the fact that he had made himself particularly useful to her mother, who, in her widowhood, and in straitened circumstances, was very glad to receive the help and friendly offices of the young farmer. These scruples yielded, however, to the strength of his feelings; and one evening he had already half finished his toilet with more than usual care, in order to the business of a formal declaration, when, to his own surprise and that of his family, John Houston abruptly entered the humble homestead. It was the first visit which he had paid since the separation of the two families, and Arthur saw at a glance that it had its particular object. After a few moments, in which the usual civilities were exchanged, John Houston, rising as he spoke, said abruptly to Arthur—

"You seem about to go out, and perhaps we may be walking in the same direction. If so, I can say what I have to say, while we're on the road together."

"I am about to go to see the Widow Heywood."

"Very good.! our road lies the same way."

The tones of Houston were more than usually abrupt as he spoke, and there was a stern contracting of the brow, and a fierce flashing of the eye, while he looked upon the person he addressed, which did not escape the observation of Arthur, and excited the apprehensions of his mother. On some pretence, she drew her son into her chamber ere he went forth, and in few, but earnest words, insisted that John Houston meant harm.

"If you will go with him, Arthur, take this pistol of your father's in your bosom, and keep a sharp look-out upon him. Man never meant evil if John Houston does not mean it now."

We pass over her farther remonstrances. They made little impression upon Arthur, but, to quiet her, he put the weapon into his bosom—half ashamed—as he did so—of a concession that seemed to look like cowardice.

The two young men set out together, and the eyes of the anxious mother followed them as long as they were in sight. They took the common path, which led them down to the river, just below the falls. When they had reached the opposite shore, and before they had ascended the rocks by which it is lined, John Houston, who had led, turned suddenly upon his companion, and thus addressed him:

"Arthur Holt, you may wonder at my coming to see you to-day, for I very well know that there is no love lost between us. You like me as little as I like you. Nay, for that matter, I don't care how soon you hear it from my lips,—I hate you, and I shall always hate you! We were enemies while we were boys,—we are enemies now that we are men; and I suppose we shall be enemies as long as we live. Whether we are to fight upon it, is for you to say."

Here he paused and looked eagerly into the eyes of his companion. The latter regarded him steadily, but returned no answer. He evidently seemed to await some farther explanation of the purpose of one who had opened his business with an avowal so startling and ungracious. After a brief pause, Houston proceeded:

"The talk is that you're a-courting Leda Heywood—that you mean to offer yourself to her—and when I see how finely you've rigged yourself out for it to-night, I'm half inclined to believe you're foolish enough to be thinking of it. Arthur Holt, this must not be! You must have nothing to do with Leda Heywood."

He paused again—his eyes keenly searching those of his rival.

The latter still met his glance with a quiet sort of determination, which betrayed nothing of the effect which the words of the other might have produced upon his mind. Houston was annoyed. Impatiently, again, he spoke, as follows:

"You hear me,—you hear what I say?"

"Yes, I hear you, John Houston."

"Well!—"

"Well!—you want my answer, I suppose? You shall have it! This it is. If *you* are a madman or a fool, that is no reason why I should not do as I please!"

The other was about to interrupt him,—but Holt persisted:

"Let me finish, John Houston. I heard you patiently—now, hear me! I am no fighting man, and as heaven is above us, I have no wish to quarrel; but I am ready to fight whenever I can't do better. As for being bullied by you, that is out of the question. I am not afraid of you, and never was, as you should have known before this, and as you may know whenever the notion suits you to try. I am now, this very moment, going to see Leda Heywood, and I mean to ask her hand."

"That you shall never do!" exclaimed the other, whose passions had been with difficulty kept down so long—"That, by the Eternal! you shall never do!"—and as he spoke, drawing a knife from his belt, he rushed upon Arthur Holt, with a promptness and fury that left the latter in no doubt of the bloody and desperate purposes of his foe. But the coolness of the young farmer was his safeguard in part, and to the weapon; so thoughtfully furnished him by his mother, he was indebted for the rest. He had kept a wary watch upon the movements of Houston's eye, and read in its glance the bloody purpose of his soul, the moment ere he struck. Retreating on one side, he was ready, when the latter turned a second time upon him, with his presented pistol.

"It is well for both of us, perhaps," said he, quietly, as he cocked and held up the weapon to the face of the approaching Houston, "that this pistol was put into my hands by one who knew you better than I did; or you might this moment have my blood upon your soul. Let us now part, John Houston. If you are bent to go from this to Widow Heywood's,—the path is open to you,—go! I will return home, an I seek some other time, when there's no chance of our meeting; for I neither wish to kill you nor to be killed by you. Which will you do—go forward or return? Take your choice—I yield the path to you."

The fury of the baffled assassin may be imagined. It is not easy to describe it. But he was in no condition of mind to visit Leda Heywood, and, after exhausting himself in ineffectual threatenings, he dashed once more across the foaming torrents of Reedy River, leaving Arthur Holt free to pursue his way to the cottage of his mistress. This he did, with a composure which the whole exciting scene, through which he had passed, had entirely failed to disturb. Indeed, the events of this interview appeared to have the effect, only, of strengthening the resolve of the young farmer, for, to confess a truth, the good fellow was somewhat encouraged—by certain expressions which had dropped from Houston, in his fury,—to hope for a favourable answer to his suit. We may as well say, in this place, that the frenzy of the latter had been provoked by similar stories reaching his ears to those which had troubled Arthur.

When they separated, and Arthur Holt went forward to the cottage of Widow Heywood, it was with a new and most delightful hope awakened in his bosom.

CHAPTER III.

BUT he was doomed to disappointment. He was rejected,—
tenderly, but firmly. Leda Heywood was not for him; and
resigning himself to the denial, with the instincts of a man by
nature strong, and inured by trial to disappointments, Arthur
Holt retired from the field of Love, to cultivate more certain
fruits in those of Ceres and Pomona. Had the mind of the young
farmer been morbidly affected, his mortification would have been
heightened by subsequent events. Three days afterwards, Leda
Heywood accepted the hand of his enemy, John Houston! Philosophers will continue to seek in vain for the cause of that
strange perversity, by which the tastes, even of the finest women,
are sometimes found to be governed. There is a mystery here
beyond all solution. The tastes and sympathies of Leda Heywood
and John Houston did not run together;—there was, in reality,
no common ground, whether of the affections or of the sentiments,
upon which they could meet. But he sought, and wooed, and
won her;—they were married; and, to all but Arthur Holt. the
wonder was at an end after the customary limits of the ninth day.
The wonder, in this case, will be lessened to the reader if two or
three things were remembered. Leda Heywood was very young,
and John Houston very handsome. Of the wild passions of the
latter she knew little or nothing. She found him popular—the
favourite of the damsels around her, and this fact, alone, will account for the rest. But we must not digress in speculations of
this nature. The parties were married, and the honeymoon, in all
countries and climates, is proverbially rose-coloured. The only
awkward thing is, that, in all countries, it is but a monthly moon.
The wedding took place. The honeymoon rose, but set somewhat earlier than usual. With the attainment of his object, the
passion of John Houston very soon subsided, and we shall make
a long story conveniently short by saying, in this place, that it
was not many weeks before Leda Heywood (or as we must now

call her,) Leda Houston, began to weep over the ill-judged pre
cipitation with which she had joined herself to a man whose vio
lent temper made no allowances for the feelings, the sensibilities,
and tastes of others.   No longer restrained by the dread of losing
his object, his brutalities shocked her delicacy, while his fierce
passions awoke her fears.   She soon found herself neglected and
abused, and learned to loathe the connection she had formed, and
to weep bitter tears in secret.   To all this evil may be added the
pressure of poverty, which now began to be more seriously felt
than ever.   The hunter life, always uncertain, was still more so,
in the case of one like John Houston, continually led into indulgences which unfitted him, sometimes for days together, to go
into the woods.   Carousing at the tavern with some congenial
natures, he suffered himself to be little disturbed by home cares;
and the privations to which his wife had been subjected even, before her marriage, were now considerably increased.   It will be
remembered that the Widow Heywood was indebted (perhaps
even more than she then knew) to the generous care of Arthur
Holt.   Her resources from this quarter were necessarily withdrawn on the marriage of her daughter with Houston, not so
much through any diminution of the young farmer's sympathy
for the objects of his bounty, as from a desire to withdraw from
any connexion or communion, direct or indirect, with the family
of his bitterest foe.   Knowing the fierce, unreasoning nature of
Houston, he was unwilling to expose to his violence the innocent
victims of his ill habits—a consequence which he very well knew
would follow the discovery of any services secretly rendered
them by Holt.   But these scruples were soon compelled to give
way to a sense of superior duty.   It soon came to his knowledge
that the unhappy women — mother and daughter — were frequently without food.   John Houston, abandoned to vicious habits
and associates, had almost entirely left his family to provide for
themselves.   He was sometimes absent for weeks—would return
home, as it appeared, for no purpose but to vent upon his wife and
mother-in-law the caprices of his ill-ordered moods, and then depart, leaving them hopeless of his aid.   In this condition, the
young farmer came again to their rescue.   The larder was provided regularly and bountifully.   But Leda knew not at first

whence this kindly succor came. She might have suspected—nay, did suspect—but Arthur Holt proceeded so cautiously, that his supplies came to the house with the privity of Widow Heywood only.

To add to Leda's sorrows, two events now occurred within a few months of each other, and both in less than sixteen months after her marriage, which were calculated to increase her burthen, and to lessen, in some respect, her sources of consolation : the birth of a son and the death of her mother. These events drew to her the assistance of neighbours, but the most substantial help came from Arthur Holt. It was now scarcely possible to conceal from Leda, as he had hitherto done, his own direct agency in the support of her family. She was compelled to know it, and—which was still more mortifying to her spirit—conscious as she was of the past—she was compelled to receive it. Her husband's course was not materially improved by events which had so greatly increased the claims and the necessities of his wife. The child, for a time, appealed to his pride. It was fine boy, who was supposed and said to resemble himself. This pleased him for a while, but did not long restrain him from indulgences, which, grateful to him from the first, had now acquired over him all the force of habit. He soon disappeared from his home, and again, for long and weary periods, left the poor Leda to all the cares and solitude, without the freedom, of widowhood.

But a circumstance was about to occur, which suddenly drew his attention to his home. Whether it was that some meddlesome neighbour informed him of the assistance which his wife derived from Arthur Holt, or that he himself had suddenly awakened to the inquiry as to the source of her supplies, we cannot say ; but certain it is that the suspicions of his evil nature were aroused ; and he who would not abandon his low and worthless associates for the sake of duty and love, was now prompted to do so by his hate. He returned secretly to the neighbourhood of his home, and put himself in a place of concealment.

The cottage of the Widow Heywood was within three quarters of a mile of Reedy River, on the opposite side of which stood the farm of Arthur Holt. This space the young farmer was accustomed nightly to cross, bearing with him the commodity, whether of flour, honey, milk, meat, or corn, which his benevolence prompted him to place on the threshold of his sad and suffering neighbour. There was a little grove of chestnut and other forest trees, that stood about two hundred yards from Leda's cottage. A part of this grove belonged to their dwelling; the rest was unenclosed. Through this grove ran one of the lines of fence which determined the domain of the cottage. On both sides of the fence, in the very centre of this thicket, there were steps, gradually rising, from within and without, to its top,—a mode of constructing a passage frequent in the country, which, having all the facilities of a gateway, was yet more permanent, and without its disadvantages. To this point came Arthur Holt nightly. On these steps he laid his tribute, whether of charity or a still lingering love, or both, and, retiring to the thicket, he waited, sometimes for more than an hour, until he caught a glimpse of the figure of Leda, descending through the grove, and possessing herself of the supply. This done, and she departed; the young farmer, sighing deeply, would turn away unseen, unsuspected, perhaps, and regain his own cottage.

On these occasions *the two never met*. The Widow Heywood, on her deathbed, had confided to her daughter the secret of her own interviews with Arthur, and he, to spare himself as well as Leda, the pain of meeting, had appointed his own and her hour of coming, differently. Whether she, at any time, suspected his propinquity, cannot be conjectured. That she was touched to the heart by his devotion, cannot well be questioned.

For five weary nights did the malignant and suspicious eyes of John Houston, from a contiguous thicket, watch these proceedings with feelings of equal hate and mortification. Filled with the most foul and loathsome anticipations—burning to find victims—to detect, expose, destroy—he beheld only a spectacle which increased his mortification. He beheld innocence superior to misfortune—love that did not take advantage of its power—a benevolence that rebuked his own worthlessness and hardness of heart—a purity on the part of both the objects of his jealousy, which mocked his comprehension, as it was so entirely above any capacity of his own, whether of mind or heart, to appreciate.

It was now the fifth night of his watch. He began to despair of his object. He had seen nothing to give the least confirmation to his suspicions. His wife had appeared only as she was, as pure as an angel;—his ancient enemy not less so. He was furious that he could find no good cause of fury, and weary of a watch which was so much at variance with his habits. He determined that night to end it. With the night, and at the usual hour, came the unfailing Arthur. He placed his bowl of milk upon the steps, his sack of meal, a small vessel of butter, and a neat little basket of apples. For a moment he lingered by the fence, then slipping back, adroitly ensconced himself in a neighbouring thicket, from whence he could see every movement of the fair sufferer by whom they were withdrawn. This last movement of the young farmer had not been unseen by the guilty husband. Indeed, it was this part of the proceeding which, more than any thing beside, had forced upon him the conviction that the parties did not meet. She came, and she, too, lingered by the steps, before she proceeded to remove the provisions. Deep was the sigh that escaped her—deeper than usual were her emotions. She sank upon one of the steps—she clasped her hands convulsively—her lips moved—she was evidently breathing a spontaneous prayer to heaven, at the close of which she wept bitterly, the deep sobs seeming to burst from a heart that felt itself relieved by this mournful power of expression.

Was it the echo of her own sighs—her sobs—that came to her from the thicket? She started, and with wild eye gazing around her, proceeded with all haste to gather up her little stores. But in this she was prevented. The answering sigh, the sob,—coming from the lips of his hated rival and ancient enemy, had gone, hissingly, as it were, into the very brain of John Houston. He darted from his place of concealment, dashed the provisions from the hands of his wife, and, with a single blow, smote her to the earth, while he cried out to Holt in the opposite thicket, some incoherent language of insults and opprobrium. The movement of the latter was quite as prompt, though not in season to prevent the unmanly blow. He sprang forward, and, grasping the offender about the body, lifted him with powerful effort from the earth, upon which he was about to hurl him again with all the fury of indignant manhood, when Leda leapt to her feet, and interposed. At the sound of her voice, the very tones of which declared her wish, Arthur released his enemy, but with no easy effort. The latter, regaining his feet, and recovering in some degree his composure, turned to his wife and commanded her absence.

"I cannot go—I will not—while there is a prospect of blood-shed," was her firm reply.

"What! you would see it, would you? Doubtless, the sight of my blood would delight your eyes! But hope not for it!—Arthur Holt, are you for ever to cross my path, and with impunity? Shall there never be a settlement between us? Is the day of reckoning never to come? Speak! Shall we fight it out here, in the presence of this woman, or go elsewhere, where there will be no tell-tale witnesses? Will you follow me?"

"Go not,—follow him not,—Arthur Holt. Go to your home! I thank you, I bless you for what you have done for me and mine ;—for the mother who looks on us from heaven,—for the child that still looks to me on earth. May God bless you for your charity and goodness! Go now, Arthur Holt—go to your own home—and look not again upon mine. Once more, God's blessings be upon you! May you never want them."

There was a warmth, an earnestness, almost a violence in the tone and manner of this adjuration, so new to the usually meek and calm deportment of his wife, that seemed, on a sudden, to confound the brutal husband. He turned on her a vacant look of astonishment. He was very far from looking for such bold-ness—such audacity—in that quarter. But his forbearance was not of long duration, and he was already beginning a fierce and almost frenzied repetition of his blasphemies, when the subdued, but firm answer of Arthur Holt again diverted his attention. The good sense of the young farmer made him at once sensible of the danger to the unhappy woman of using any language calculated to provoke the always too prompt brutality of the husband, and, stifling his own indignation with all his strength, he calmly prom-ised compliance with her requisitions.

"There are many reasons," he added, "why there should be no strife between John Houston and myself; we were boys together, our fathers loved one another; we have slept in the same bed."

"That shall not be your excuse, Arthur Holt," exclaimed the other, interrupting him; "you shall not escape me by any such pretences. My father's name shall not shelter your cowardice."

"Cowardice!"

"Ay, cowardice! cowardice! What are you but an unmanly coward!"

There was a deep, but quiet struggle, in the breast of Arthur, to keep down the rising devil in his mood; but he succeeded, and turning away, he contented himself with saying simply:

"*You* know that I am no coward, John Houston—nobody better than yourself. You will take good heed how you approach such cowardice as mine."

"Do you dare me!"

"Yes!"

"No! no!" cried the wife, again flinging herself between them. Away, Arthur Holt, why will you remain when you see what I am doomed to suffer?"

"I go, Leda, but I dread to leave you in such hands. God have you in his holy keeping!"

CHAPTER IV.

WE pass over a period of eighteen months. In this time John Houston had sold out the little cottage near Reedy River, and had removed his wife to the residence of his mother near Paris Mountain. Why he had not adopted this measure on the demise of Widow Heywood is matter of conjecture only. His own mother was now dead, and it was the opinion of those around, that it was only after this latter event that he could venture upon a step which might seem to divide the sceptre of household authority—a point about which despotical old ladies are apt to be very jealous. His household was as badly provided for as ever, but some good angel, whose presence might have been suspected, still watched over the wants of the suffering wife, and the hollow of an ancient chestnut now received the stores which we have formerly seen placed upon the rude blocks near the thicket fence in Greenville. Whether John Houston still suspected the interference of his hated playmate we cannot say. The prudent caution of the latter availed so that they did not often meet, and never under circumstances which could justify a quarrel. But events were ripening which were to bring them unavoidably into collision. We are now in the midst of the year 1776. The strife had already begun, of Whig and Tory, in the upper part of South Carolina. It happened some time in 1774 that the afterwards notorious Moses Kirkland stopped one night at the dwelling of John Houston. This man was already busy in stirring up disaffection to the popular party of the State. He was a man of loose, vicious habits, and irregular propensities. He and John Houston were kindred spirits ; and the hunter was soon enlisted under his banners. He was out with Kirkland in the campaign of 1775, when the Tories were dispersed and put down by the decisive measures of General Williamson and William Henry Drayton. It so happened that Arthur Holt made his appearance in the field, also for the first time, in the army of Williamson

The two knew that they were now opponents as they had long been enemies. But they did not meet. The designs of Kirkland were baffled, his troops dispersed, and the country settled down into a condition of seeming quiet. But it was a seeming quiet only. The old wounds festered, and when, in 1780, the metropolis of the State fell into the hands of the British, yielding to captivity nearly the whole of its military power, the Tories resumed their arms and impulses with a fury which long forbearance had heightened into perfect madness. Upon the long and melancholy history of that savage warfare which followed, we need not dwell. The story is already sufficiently well known. It is enough to say that John Houston distinguished himself by his cruelties. Arthur Holt threw by the plough, and was one of Butler's men for a season. With the decline of British power in the lower, the ascendancy in the upper country finally passed over to the Whigs. Both parties were now broken up into little squads of from ten to fifty persons ;—the Tories, the better to avoid pursuit, the Whigs, the better to compass them in all their hiding-places.

It was a cold and cheerless evening in the month of November that Arthur Holt, armed to the teeth, stopped for the night, with a party of eleven men, at a cottage about fourteen miles from his own dwelling on the banks of Reedy River.

An hour had not well elapsed, before Arthur Holt found some one jerking at his shoulder. He opened his eyes and recognised the epileptic of whom mention was made in the early part of our narrative. Acker was still an epileptic, and still, to all appearance, a boy ;—he was small, decrepit, pale, and still liable to the shocking disease, the effects of which were apparent equally in his withered face and shrivelled person. But he was not without intelligence, and his memory was singularly tenacious of benefits and injuries Eagerly challenging the attention of Arthur Holt he proceeded to tell him that John Houston had only two hours before been seen with a party of seven, on his way to the farm at Paris Mountain, where, at that very moment, he might in all probability be found. By this time the troopers, accustomed to sudden rousings, were awake and in possession of the intelligence. It was greedily listened to by all but Arthur Holt. John Houston

was particularly odious in his own neighbourhood. Several of
the inhabitants had fallen victims to his brutality and hate. To
take him, living or dead,—to feed the vengeance for which they
thirsted,—was at once the passion of the party. It was with
some surprise that they found their leader apathetic and disposed
to fling doubt upon the information.

"I know not how you could have seen John Houston, Peter
Acker, with seven men, when we left him behind us, going below, and crossing at Daniel's Ford on the Ennoree, only two days
ago."

"'Twas him I seed, Captain, and no other. Don't you think I
knows John Houston? Oughtn't I to know him? Wasn't it he
that used to beat me, and duck me in the water? I knows him.
'Twas John Houston, I tell you, and no other person."

"You are mistaken, Peter—you must be mistaken. No horse
could have brought him from the Ennoree so soon."

"He's on his own horse, the great bay. 'Tis John Houston,
and you must catch him and hang him."

One of the party, a spirited young man, named Fletchall, now
said :

"Whether it's Houston and his men or not, Captain Holt, we
should see who the fellows are. Acker ought to know Houston,
and though we heard of him on the Ennoree, we may have
heard wrong. It's my notion that Acker is right; and every
man of Reedy River, that claims to be a man, ought to see to it."

There was a sting in this speech that made it tell. They did
not understand the delicacy of their Captain's situation, nor could
he explain it. He could only sigh and submit. Buckling on his
armour, he obeyed the necessity, and his eager troop was soon in
motion for the cottage of Houston at Paris Mountain. There, two
hours before, John Houston had arrived. He had separated from
his companions. It was not affection for his wife that brought
Houston to his home. On the contrary, his salutation was that
of scorn and suspicion. He seemed to have returned, brooding
on some dark imagination or project. When his wife brought
his child, and put him on his knees, saying with a mournful look
of reproach, "You do not even ask for your son !" the reply, betraying the foulest of fancies—"How know I that he is !" showed

too plainly the character of the demon that was struggling in his soul. The miserable woman shrunk back in horror, while his eyes, lightened by a cold malignant smile, pursued her as if in mockery. When she placed before him a little bread and meat, he repulsed it, exclaiming: " Would you have me fed by your Arthur ?" And when she meekly replied by an assurance that the food did not come from him, his answer, " Ay, but I am not so sure of the sauce !" indicated a doubt so horrible, that the poor woman rushed from the apartment with every feeling and fibre of her frame convulsed. Without a purpose, except to escape from suspicions by which she was tortured, she had turned the corner of the enclosure, hurrying, it would seem, to a little thicket, where her sorrows would be unseen, when she suddenly encountered Arthur Holt, with a cocked pistol in his grasp. The troopers had dismounted and left their horses in the woods. They were approaching the house cautiously, on foot, and from different quarters. The object was to effect a surprise of the Tory ,— since, armed and desperate, any other more open mode of approach might, even if successful, endanger valuable life. The plan had been devised by Arthur. He had taken to himself that route which brought him first to the cottage. His object was explained in the few first words with Leda Houston.

" Arthur Holt ! — you here !" was her exclamation, as she started at his approach.

" Ay ; and your husband is here !"

" No, no !" was the prompt reply.

" Nay, deny not ! I would save him—away ! let him fly at once. We shall soon be upon him !"

A mute but expressive look of gratitude rewarded him, while, forgetting the recent indignities to which she had been subjected, Leda hurried back to the cottage and put Houston in possession of the facts. He started to his feet, put the child from his knee, though still keeping his hand upon its shoulder, and glaring upon her with eyes of equal jealousy and rage, he exclaimed—

" Woman ! you have brought my enemy upon me !"

To this charge the high-souled woman made no answer, but her form became more erect, and her cheek grew paler, while her exquisitely chiselled lips were compressed with the effort to

18

keep down her stifling indignation. She approached him as if
to relieve him of the child; but he repulsed her, and grasping
the little fellow firmly in his hands, with no tenderness of hold,
he lifted him to his shoulder, exclaiming—

"No! he shares my danger! he goes with me. He is at least
your child—he shall protect me from your—"

The sentence was left unfinished as he darted through the
door! With a mother's scream she bounded after him, as he
took his way to the edge of the little coppice in which his horse
was fastened. The agony of a mother's soul lent wings to her
feet. She reached him ere he could undo the fastenings of his
horse, and, seizing him by his arm, arrested his progress.

"What!" he exclaimed; "you would seize—you would deliver me!"

"My child! my child!" was her only answer, as she clung
to his arm, and endeavoured to tear the infant from his grasp.

"He goes with me! He shall protect me from the shot!"

"You will not, cannot risk his precious life."

"Do I not risk mine?"

"My son—your son!"

"Were I sure of that!"

"God of heaven! help me! Save him! save him!"

But there was no time for parley. A pistol-shot was fired
from the opposite quarter of the house, whether by accident, or
for the purpose of alarm, is not known, but it prompted the
instant movement of the ruffian, who, in order to extricate himself from the grasp of his wife, smote her to the earth, and in
the midst of the child's screams hurried forward with his prize.
To reach the coppice, to draw forth and mount his horse, was
the work of an instant only. The life of the hunter and the
partisan had made him expert enough in such performances.
Mounted on a splendid bay, of the largest size and greatest
speed, he lingered but a moment in sight, the child conspicuously
elevated in his grasp, its head raised above his left shoulder, while one
of its little arms might be seen stretching towards his mother, now
rising from the earth. At this instant Arthur Holt made his appearance. From the wood, where he had remained as long as he
might, he had beheld the brutal action of his enemy. It was the

second time that he had witnessed such a deed, and his hand now convulsively grasped and cocked his pistol, as he rushed forward to revenge it. But the unhappy woman rose in time to prevent him. Her extended arms were thrown across his path. He raised the deadly weapon above them.

" Would you shoot! oh, my God! would you shoot! Do you not see my child! my child!"

The action of Arthur was suspended at the mother's words; and, lifting the child aloft with a powerful arm, as if in triumph and defiance, the brutal father, putting spurs to his horse, went off at full speed. A single bound enabled the noble animal to clear the enclosure, and, appearing but a single moment upon the hillside, the mother had one more glimpse of her child, whose screams, in another moment, were drowned in the clatter of the horse's feet. She sunk to the ground at the foot of Arthur, as his comrades leapt over the surrounding fence.

CHAPTER V.

Pursuit under present circumstances was pretty much out of the question—yet Arthur Holt determined upon it. John Houston was mounted upon one of the most famous horses of the country. He had enjoyed a rest of a couple of hours before the troopers came upon him. The steeds of the latter, at all times inferior, were jaded with the day's journey. Any attempt at direct pursuit would, therefore, in all probability, only end in driving the Tory out of the neighbourhood, thus increasing the chances of his final escape. This was by no means the object of the party, and when Arthur ordered the pursuit, some of his men remonstrated by showing, or endeavouring to show, that such must be the effect of it. Arthur Holt, however, had his own objects. But his commands were resisted by no less a person than Leda herself.

"Do not pursue, Arthur, for my sake, do not pursue. My child!—he will slay my child if you press him hard. He is desperate. You know him not. Press him not, for my sake,—for the child's sake,—but let him go free."

The entreaty, urged strenuously and with all those tears and prayers which can only flow from a mother's heart, was effectual—at least to prevent that direct pursuit which Arthur had meditated. But, though his companions favoured the prayers of the wife and mother, they were very far from being disposed to let the Tory go free. On the contrary, when, a little after, they drew aside to the copse for the purpose of farther consultation, Arthur Holt found, to his chagrin, that his course with regard to Houston was certainly suspected. His comrades assumed a decision in the matter which seemed to take the business out of his hands. Young Fletchall did not scruple to say, that he was not satisfied with the spirit which Arthur had shown in the pursuit; and the hints conveyed by more than one, in the course of the discussion, were of such a nature, that the mortified Arthur

.nrew up his command; a proceeding which seemed to occasion no regret or dissatisfaction. Fletchall was immediately invested with it, and proceeded to exercise it with a degree of acuteness and vigour which soon satisfied the party of his peculiar fitness for its duties. His plan was simple but comprehensive. He said: " We cannot press the pursuit, or we drive him off; but we can so fix it as to keep him where he is. If we do not press him, he will keep in the woods, near abouts, till he can find some chance of getting the child to the mother again. There's no doubt an understanding between them. She knows where to find him in the woods, or he'll come back at night to the farm. We must put somebody to watch over all her movements. Who will that be ?"

The question was answered by the epileptic, Acker, who, o asked, had hung upon the skirts of the party.

" I will watch her !"

" You !"

" Yes ! I'm as good a one as you can get."

" Very well ! but suppose you have one of your fits, Acker !'

" I won't have one now for two weeks. My time's over for this month."

" Well, in two weeks, I trust, his time will be over too. We will get some twenty more fellows and make a ring round him. That's my plan. Don't press, for I wouldn't have him hurt the child; but mark him when he aims to pass the ring."

The plan thus agreed on, with numerous details which need not be given here, was immediately entered upon by all parties. Arthur Holt alone took no share in the adventure. The design was resolved upon even without his privity, though the general object could not be concealed from his knowledge. On throwing up his commission he had withdrawn from his comrades, under a show of mortification, which was regarded as sufficiently natural by those around him to justify such a course. He returned to his farm on Reedy River, but he was no indifferent or inactive spectator of events.

Meanwhile, John Houston had found a temporary retreat some six miles distant from the dwelling of his wife. It was a spot seemingly impervious, in the density of its woods, to the steps of man. A small natural cavity in a hillside had been artificially deepened, in all probability, by the bear, who had left it as a heritage to the hunter to whom he had yielded up his ears. The retreat was known to the hunter only. He had added, from time to time, certain little improvements of his own. Cells were opened on one side, and then the other. These were strewn with dried leaves and rushes, and, at the remote inner extremity, a fourth hollow had been prepared so as to admit of fire, the smoke finding its way through a small and simple opening at the top. All around this rude retreat the woods were dense, the hunter being at particular pains to preserve it as a place of secrecy and concealment. Its approach was circuitous, and the very entrance upon it, one of those happy discoveries, by which nature is made to accomplish the subtlest purposes of art. Two gigantic shafts, shooting out from the same root, had run up in diverging but parallel lines, leaving between them an opening through which, at a moderate bound, a steed might make his way. On each side of this mighty tree the herbage crowded closely ; the tree itself seemed to close the passage. and behind it care was taken, by freely scattering brush and leaves, to remove any traces of horse or human footsteps. In this place John Houston found refuge. To this place, in the dead of night, the unhappy Leda found her way. How she knew of the spot may be conjectured only. But, prompted by a mother's love and a mother's fears, she did not shrink from the task of exploring the dreary forest alone. Here she found her miserable husband, and was once more permitted to clasp her infant to her bosom. The little fellow slept soundly upon the rushes, in one of the recesses of the cave. The father sat at the entrance, keeping watch over him. His stern eye looked upon the embrace of mother and child with a keen and painful interest ; and when the child, awakened out of sleep, shrieking with joy, clung to the neck of the mother, sobbing her name with a convulsive delight, he turned from the spectacle with a single sentence, muttered through his closed teeth, by which we may see what his meditations had been—" Had the brat but called me father !" The words were unheard by the mother, too full of joy to be conscious of any thing but her child and her child's recovery

When, however, before the dawn of day, she proposed to leave
him and take the child with her, she was confounded to meet
with denial.

"No!" said the brutal father. "He remains with me. If he
is my child, he shall remain as my security and yours. Hear
me, woman! Your ruffians have not pursued me; your Arthur
Holt knows better than to press upon me; but I know their aims.
They have covered the outlets. They would make my captivity
secure. I wish but three days; in that time, Cunningham will
give them employment, and I shall walk over them as I please.
But, during that time, I shall want food for myself and horse—
perhaps you will think there is some necessity for bringing food
to the child. I do not object to that. Bring it then yourself,
nightly, and remember, **the first show of treachery seals his
fate!**"

He pointed to the child as he spoke.

"Great God!" she exclaimed. "Are **you a man, John
Houston**! Will you keep the infant from me!"

"Ay!—you should thank heaven that I do not keep you from
him also. But away! Bring the provisions! Be faithful, and
you shall have the child. But, remember! if I am entrapped,
he dies!"

We pass over the horror of the mother. At the dawn of day,
as she was hurrying, but not unseen, along the banks of Reedy
River, she was encountered by Arthur Holt.

"I went to your house at midnight, Leda, to put you on your
guard," was the salutation of the farmer. "I know where you
have been, and can guess what duty is before you. I must also
tell you its danger."

He proceeded to explain to her the watch that was put upon
her movements, and the *cordon militaire* by which her husband
was surrounded.

"What am I to do!" was her exclamation, as, wringing her
hands, the tears for the first time flowed freely from her eyes.

"I will tell you! Go not back to your cottage, till you can
procure the child. Go now to the stone heap on the river bank
below, which they call the 'Giant's Coffin.' There, in an hour
from now, I will bring you a basket of provisions. The place

is very secret, and before it is found out that you go there, you will have got the child. Nightly, I will fill the basket in the same place, which, at the dawn, you can procure. Go now, before we are seen, and God be with you !"

They separated—the young farmer for his home, and Leda for the gloomy vault which popular tradition had dignified with the title of the " Giant's Coffin." This was an Indian giant, by the way, whose exploits, in the erection of Table Mountain, for gymnastic purposes, would put to shame the inferior feats of the devil, under direction of Merlin or Michael Scott. But we have no space in this chapter for such descriptions. Enough if we give some idea of the sort of coffin and the place of burial which the giant selected for himself, when he could play his mountain pranks no longer. The coffin was a vaulted chamber of stone, lying at the river's edge, and liable to be overflowed in seasons of freshet. It took its name from its shape. Its area was an oblong square, something more than twelve feet in length, and something less than five in breadth. Its depth at the upper end was about six feet, but it sloped gradually down, until, at the bottom, the ends lay almost even with the surrounding rocks. The inner sides were tolerably smooth and upright—the outer presented the appearance of huge boulders, in no way differing from the ordinary shape and externals of such detached masses. The separate parts had evidently, at one period, been united. Some convulsion of nature had fractured the mass, and left the parts in a position so relative, that tradition might well be permitted to assume the labours of art in an achievement which was really that of nature alone. To complete the fancied resemblance of this chamber to a coffin, it had a lid ; a thin layer of stone, detached from the rest, which, as the earth around it had been loosened and washed away by the rains, had gradually slid down from the heights above, and now in part rested upon the upper end of the vault. The boys at play, uniting their strength, had succeeded in forcing it down a foot or more, so that it now covered, securely from the weather, some four or five feet of the " Giant's Coffin." It was at this natural chamber that Arthur Holt had counselled Leda Houston to remain, until he could bring the promised supply of provisions. This he did, punctually, at the time appointed, and continued to do until it ceased to be necessary ; to this spot did the wretched wife and mother repair before dawn of every morning, bearing her burden with all the uncomplaining meekness of a broken heart. We must suppose, in the meantime, that the cordon has been drawn around the tract of country in which it was known that Houston harboured. The news was spread, at the same time, that an attack might be expected from Bloody Bill Cunningham, or some of his men ; and the consequence was, that the country was every where in arms and vigilant. A feeling of pity for Leda Houston, who was generally beloved, alone prevented the more daring young men from pressing upon the fugitive, hunting him, with dog and fire, and bringing the adventure to a fierce and final issue. Meanwhile, the epileptic, Acker, was active in the business which he had undertaken. He was partially successful—but of his proceedings we must speak at another moment.

The situation of Leda Houston was in no ways improved by the diligence, the patience, the devotion which she displayed in her servitude. She did not seem to make any progress in subduing the inexorable nature of her husband. She was permitted to be with and to feed her child ; to clasp him to her bosom when she slept, and to watch over his sleep with that mixed feeling of hope and fear, which none but a mother knows. But these were all her privileges. The brutal father, still insinuating base and unworthy suspicions, declared that the child should remain, a pledge of her fidelity, and a partial guaranty for his own safety.

Four days had now elapsed in this manner. On the morning of the fifth, at a somewhat later hour than usual, she re-appeared with her basket, and, having set down her stores, proceeded to tell her husband of the arrival of a certain squad of troopers, " Butler's men," known for the fierce hostility with which they hunted the men of " Cunningham." The tidings gave him some concern. He saw in it the signs of a dogged determination of the neighbourhood to secure him at all hazards ; since, from what he knew of the present condition of the war, these men could be required in that quarter only for some such purpose

They were wanted elsewhere. "Did you see them?" was the question, which she answered in the negative. "Who told you then of their arrival?" She was silent! Her countenance underwent a change. "Woman! you have spoken with Holt! These are his provisions!" With a blow of his foot he struck the basket from her hand, and, in his fury, trampled upon the scattered stores. It was with difficulty that the unhappy woman gathered up enough to pacify the hunger of the child. That day was passed in sullen and ferocious silence on his part—on hers in mute caresses of her boy. His darker suspicions were in full force, and darker thoughts came with them. "Could I but know!" he muttered. "The child has my mouth and nose; but the forehead, the hair, the eyes,—are *his!*" Convulsed with terrible fancies, the miserable man hurried to the entrance of the cavern, and throwing himself upon the earth, leaned back, and looked up through the leafy openings at the bits of sky that were suffered to appear above. In this gloomy mood and posture, hours passed by as moments. It was midnight. A change of weather was at hand. The stars were hidden—the sky overcast with clouds, while the winds, seeming to subside, were moaning through the woods as one in a deep and painful sleep. The sound, the scene, were congenial with the outlaw's soul. It was full of angry elements that only waited the signal to break forth in storm. Suddenly, he was roused from his meditations by the cessation of all sounds from within the cave. The mother slept there, she had been playing with the child, and he upon her bosom. Nature, in her case, had sunk, in spite of sorrow, under fatigue. And she slept deeply, her slumbers broken only by a plaintive moaning of those griefs that would not sleep. With a strange curiosity Houston seated himself quietly beside the pair, while his eyes keenly perused the calm and innocent features of the child. Long was the study, and productive of conflicting emotions. It was interrupted with a start, and his eyes involuntarily turned, with ever a less satisfied expression, upon the features of his wife.

But it was not to watch or to enjoy the beauty which he beheld, that John Houston now bent his dark brows over the sleeping countenance of his wife. The expression in his looks was that of a wild and fearful curiosity suddenly aroused. She had spoken in her sleep. She had uttered a word—a name—which, of all others, was most likely, from any lips, to awaken his most angry emotions,—from her lips, most terrible. The name was that of Arthur Holt,—and she still murmured. The ears of the suspicious husband were placed close to her lips, that none of the whispered sounds might escape him. He heard enough to open to him a vista, at the extremity of which his diseased imagination saw the worst shapes of hate and jealousy. With the pressing thought in her memory of the tasks before her, she spoke of the little basket—the bread—the bottle of milk, the slender slices of ham or venison—which she had been accustomed to receive and bring. Then came the two words, " Giant's Coffin," and the quick fancy of the outlaw, stimulated by hate and other passions. immediately reached, at a bound, the whole narrative of her dependence upon Holt and her meetings with him at the " Giant's Coffin !"

A dark smile passed over his countenance. It was the smile of a demon, who is at length, after long being baffled, in possession of his prey. Leda slept on—soundly slept—for nature had at length coerced the debtor, and compelled her rights—and the hour was approaching when it was usual for her to set out on her nightly progress. The resolution came, quick as lightning, to the mind of the ruffian. He rose stealthily from the rushes, —drew his pistols from his belt, silently examined the flints, and, looking at the knife in his bosom, stole forth from the cavern. With a spirit exulting with the demoniac hope of assuring himself of a secret long suspected, and of realizing a vengeance long delayed,—and familiar, night and day, with every step in his progress, he hurried directly across the country to the banks of Reedy River. The night, by this time, had become tempestuous. Big drops of rain already began to fall; but these caused no delay to the hardy outlaw. He reached the river, and, moving now with cautious steps from rock to rock, he approached the " Giant's Coffin" with the manner of one who expects to find a victim and an enemy. One hand grasped a pistol, the other a knife!—and, stealing onward with the pace of the Indian, he hung over the sides of the "Coffin," and peered into its dark chamber with his keenest eyes. It was untenanted. "I am too soon," he muttered. "Well! I can wait!" And where better to await the victim—where more secure from detection—than in the vault which lay before him!—one half covered from the weather and shut in from all inspection,—that alone excepted, for which he had come prepared. The keen gusts of wind which now came across the stream laden with rain, was an additional motive to this movement. He obeyed the suggestion, passed into the mouth of the "Coffin;" and, crouching from sight, in a sitting posture, in the upper or covered part of the chamber, he sat with the anxiety of a passion which did not, however, impair its patience, awaiting for his foe.

He had not reached this position unseen or unaccompanied. We have already intimated that Acker, the epileptic, had made some progress in his discoveries. With the singular cunning, and the wonderful acuteness which distinguish some of the faculties, where others are impaired in the same individual, he had contrived, unseen and unsuspected, to track Leda Houston to the place of her husband's concealment. He had discovered the periods of her incoming and departure, and, taking his rest at all other periods, he was always prepared to renew his surveillance at those moments when the wife was to go forth. He had barely resumed his watch, on the night in question, when he was surprised to see Houston himself and not his wife emerging from the cave. He followed cautiously his footsteps. Light of foot, and keeping at convenient distance, his espionage was farther assisted by the wind, which, coming in their faces, effectually kept all sounds of pursuit from the ears of the outlaw. His progress was not so easy when the latter emerged from the woods, and stood upon the banks of the river. His approach now required more caution; but, stealing on from shrub to shrub, and rock to rock, Acker at length stood—or rather crouched—upon the brink of the river also, and at but small distance from the other. But of this distance he had ceased to be conscious. He was better informed, however, when, a moment after, he heard a dull, clattering, but low sound, which he rightly conjectured to have been caused by some pressure upon the lower lid of the Coffin, which, being somewhat pendulous, was apt to vibrate slightly, in spite of its great length and weight, under any pressure from above. This sound apprised Acker of the exact whereabouts of the outlaw, and his keen eyes at length detected the dim outline of the latter's form, as he stood upon the lid of the Coffin, the moment before he disappeared within its recesses. Encouraged to advance, by the disappearance of the other, the Epileptic did so with extreme caution. He was favoured by the hoarse tumbling of the water as it poured its way among the rocks, and by the increasing discords of the wind and rain, which now came down in heavy showers. As he crawled from rock to rock, with the stealthy movement of a cat along some precipitous ledge, shrinking and shivering beneath the storm, his own desire for shelter led him suddenly to the natural conclusion that Houston had found his within the vault. The ideas of Acker came to him slowly ; but, gradually, as he continued to approach, he remembered the clattering of the Coffin-lid,—he remembered how, in his more youthful days, the boys, with joint strength, had forced it to its present place, and he conceived the sudden purpose of making the Coffin of the Giant, that also of the deadly enemy whose boyish persecutions he had neither forgot nor forgiven. To effect his present object, which, suddenly conceived, became for the time an absorbing thirst, a positive frenzy, in his breast,—he concentrated all his faculties, whether of mind or of body, upon his task. His pace was deliberate, and, so stealthy, that he reached the upper end of the Coffin, laid himself down beside it, and, applying his ear to one of the crevices, distinctly heard the suppressed breathings of the man within. Crawling back, he laid his hands lightly and with the greatest care upon the upper and heavier end of the stone. His simple touch, so nicely did it seem to be balanced, caused its vibration ; and with the first consciousness of its movement, Houston, whom we must suppose to have been lying down, raising his pistol with one hand, laid the other on one of the sides of the vault, with the view, as it was thought, to lift himself from his recumbent position. He did so just as the huge plate of stone was set in motion, and the member was caught and closely wedged between the mass and the side of the

Coffin upon which it rested.   A slight cry broke from the outlaw.
The fingers were crushed, the hand was effectually secured.   But
for this, so slow was the progress of the stone, that it would
have been very easy for Houston to have scrambled out before the
vault was entirely closed in.   Slowly, but certainly, the lid went
down.   Ignorant of the peculiar occasion of the outlaw's groans,
the Epileptic answered them with a chuckle, which, had the
former been conscious, would have taught him his enemy.   But
he had fainted.   The excruciating agony of his hurt had been
too much for his strength.   Acker finished his work without
interruption ; then piling upon the plate a mountain of smaller
stones, he dashed away in the direction of Holt's cottage.   Here
he encountered the young farmer, busy, as was usual about that
hour, in making up his little basket of provisions.   A few words
from the Epileptic sufficed to inform him that they were no longer
necessary—that Houston was gone—fled—utterly escaped, and
now, in all probability, beyond pursuit.   Such was the tale he
told.   He had his policy in it.   The characteristic malignant
cunning which had prompted him to the fearful revenge which
he had taken upon his enemy, was studious now to keep it
from being defeated.   To have told the truth, would have been
to open the " Giant's Coffin," to undo all that had been done,
and once more let free the hated tyrant upon whose head he had
visited the meditated retribution of more than twenty years.
Acker well knew the generous nature of the young farmer, and
did not doubt that, if he declared the facts, Arthur would have
proceeded at once to the rescue of the common enemy.   He
suppressed all show of exultation, made a plausible story—it
matters not of what sort—by which to account for the flight of
Houston ; and, the consequence was, that, instead of proceeding
as before to the " Giant's Coffin," Arthur Holt now prepared to
set out for the " Hunter's Cave."   But the day had broke in
tempest.   A fearful storm was raging.   The windows of heaven
were opened, the rain came down in torrents, and the wind went
forth with equal violence, as if from the whole four quarters of
the earth.   The young farmer got out his little wagon, and
jumping in, Acker prepared to guide him to the place of retreat.
    " The river is rising fast, Peter," was the remark of Arthur

ns he caught a glimpse of the swollen stream as it foamed along its way.

"Yes!" said the other, with a sort of hiccough, by which he suppressed emotions which he did not venture to declare: "Yes! I reckon 'twon't be many hours afore it fills the 'Coffin.'"

"If it keeps on at this rate," returned the other, "one hour will be enough to do that."

"Only one, you think?"

"Yes! one will do!"

Another hiccough of the Epileptic appropriately finished the dialogue.

CHAPTER VI.

LEDA awakened from her deep sleep to find herself alone with the child. She was startled and alarmed at the absence of her husband; but as the child was left—the great, and we may add, the only, object for which she could have borne so much—she was satisfied. On assuring herself of the departure of Houston from the cave, she would unhesitatingly have taken hers also— but the storm was now raging without, and, persuaded that her husband had taken advantage of its violence to cross the barriers, she gathered up the fragments of the last night's supper, and was busy in giving her boy his little breakfast, when roused by the voice of Arthur Holt. The story of the Epileptic was soon told—as he had related it to Arthur. In this story, as there was nothing improbable, both parties put implicit faith; and, cloaking mother and child as well as he might, the young farmer bore them through the close thicket to the place, some three hundred yards without, where, on account of the denseness of the wood, he had been compelled to leave the wagon. The horse of Houston, the "Big Bay," was next brought forth, but as Acker could neither be persuaded to mount, or take him in charge, he was restored to the covert until a better opportunity for removing him. To the surprise of the young farmer, the Epileptic was equally firm in refusing to go with him in the wagon. "I don't mind the rain," said he, "it can't hurt me." "He will get his death," said Leda. "Not he," replied Arthur, as Acker scampered through the woods; "the water always helps him in his fits." While the wagon took one course, he took another. Little did they suspect his route. A terrible feeling carried him back to Reedy River—to a pitiless watch above that natural tomb in which he had buried his living victim.

Meanwhile, what of Houston? When he recovered his consciousness, the vault had been closed upon him; the flat mass, once set in motion, had slid down the smooth edges of the upright sides with uninterrupted progress, and now lay above him, shutting out light almost equally with hope. But a faint glimmering reached the interior of the cell, from a crevice on one side, where, in consequence of some inequality of the edges, the lid had not settled fairly down upon it. It was the side opposite to that in which his fingers had been crushed, and where the stone still maintained its hold upon the mutilated member. He heard the whistling of the wind, the hoarse rush of the waters, and the heavy fall of the rain without, and a shuddering sense of his true situation rushed instantly upon his soul. For a moment he sank back, appalled, oppressed ; but the numbing pain of his injured hand and wrist, up to his elbow, recalled him to the necessity of effort. Houston was a man of strong will and great energies. Though at the first moment of consciousness oppressed and overcome, the outlaw soon recovered himself. It was necessary that he should do something for his extrication. The light shut out, if not entirely the air, is one of those fearful facts to rouse a man in his situation and of his character, to all his energies. But the very first movement was one to awaken him still more sensibly to his dangers. Having arisen to grasp the sides of the vault, which, in the place where he had laid his hand was fully five feet high, his position when fixed there, was that of a man partially supended in the air. His right hand could barely touch the floor of the chamber. His left was utterly useless. In this position he could not even exert the strength which he possessed ; and, after an ineffectual effort, he sank back again in momentary consternation. The horror of that moment, passed in thought,—the despair which it occasioned—was the parent of new strength. He came to a terrible decision. To avail himself of his right hand, it was necessary that he should extricate the other. He had already tried to do so, by a vain effort at lifting the massive lid of his coffin. The heavy plate no longer vibrated upon a pivot. It had sunk into a natural position, which each upright evenly maintained. The hand was already lost to him. He resolved that it should not render the other useless. With a firmness which might well excite admiration, he drew the *couteau de chasse* from his bosom, and deliberately smote off the mutilated

19

fingers at the joints; dividing the crushed parts—bone and tendon, —from the uninjured,—falling heavily back upon the stone floor the moment the hand was freed. But this time he had not fainted, though the operation tended to restore the hand, which had been deadened by the pressure and pain of its position, to something like sensibility. But such pain was now but slightly felt; and, wrapping the hand up in his handkerchief, he prepared with due courage for the difficult task before him. But the very first effort almost convinced him of its hopelessness. In vain did he apply the strength of his muscular arm, the force of his broad shoulders, his sinewy and well-supported frame. Forced to crouch in his narrow limits, it was not possible for him to apply, to advantage, the strength which he really possessed; and, from the extreme shallowness of his cell in the lower extremity, he was unable to address his efforts to that part where the stone was thinnest. At the upper part, where he *could* labour, the mass was greatly thicker than the rest; and it was the weight of this mass, rather than the strength of Acker,—the momentum once given it from above,—that carried the plate along to the foot of the plane. His exertions were increased as his strength diminished—the cold sweat poured from his brow,—and, toiling against conviction—in the face of his increasing terrors,—he at length sunk back in exhaustion. From time to time, at brief intervals, he renewed his toils, each time with new hope, each time with a new scheme for more successful exertion. But the result was, on each occasion, the same; and, yielding to despair, he threw himself upon the bottom of his cell and called death to his relief.

While thus prostrate, with his face pressed upon the chilling pavement, he suddenly starts, almost to his feet, and a new terror seizes upon his soul. He is made conscious of a new and pressing danger. Is it the billows of the river—the torrents swollen above their bounds—that beat against the walls of his dungeon? Is it the advancing waters that catch his eye glimmering faint at his feet, as they penetrate the lower crevice of the coffin? A terrible shudder shook his frame! He cannot doubt this new danger, and he who, a moment before, called upon death to relieve him from his terrors, now shouts, under worse terrors, at the prospect of his near approach in an unexpected shape. It is necessary that he should employ all his strength—that he should make other and more desperate efforts. He rises, almost erect. He applies both arms—the maimed as well as the sound,—almost unconscious of the difference, to the lid of his tomb. "Buried alive!" he cries aloud—"Buried alive!" and at each cry, his sinewy arms shoot up—his broad shoulders are raised:—his utmost powers, concentrated upon the one point, in the last effort of despair, must surely be successful. His voice shouts with his straining sinews. He feels the mass above him yielding. Once more—and once again,—and still he is encouraged. The lid vibrates—he could not be deceived,—but oh! how slightly. Another trial—he moves it as before, but as his strength fails, his efforts relax,—and it sinks down heavily in its place. Breathless, he crouches in his cell. He listens! Is it a footstep? — It is a movement! — the stones fall about the roof of his narrow dwelling. A human agency is above. "Hurrah!" he cries—"Hurrah! Throw off the stone—crush it—break it! There is no time to be lost!" For a moment he fancies that the movement above is one intended for his relief. But what mean these rolling stones? A new apprehension possesses him in the very moment of his greatest hope. He rises. Once more he extends his arms, he applies his shoulders; but he labours now in vain. His strength is not less—his efforts are not more feebler—in this than in his former endeavours. He cannot doubt the terrible truth! New stones have been piled above his head. He is doomed! His utmost powers fail to move the mass from its place. His human enemy is unrelenting. He cries to him in a voice of equal inquiry and anguish.

"Who is there? what enemy? who? Speak to me! who is above me? Who? Who!"

Can it be? He is answered by a chuckle—a fell, fiendish laugh—the most terrible sort of answer. Can it be that a mortal would so laugh at such a moment? He tries to recall those to whom he has given most occasion for vindictiveness and hate. He names "Arthur Holt!" He is again answered by a chuckle, and now he knows his enemy.

"God of heaven!" he exclaims, in the bitter anguish of his discovery, "and can it be that I am doomed to perish by this most miserable of all my foes!"

Once more he rushes against the mass above him, but this time with his head alone. He sinks down stunned upon the floor, and is aroused by the water around him. Inch by inch it rises. He knows the character of the stream. It will be above him, unless he is relieved, in less than an hour. The proud and reckless outlaw is humbled. He condescends to entreat the wretched creature to whom he owes his situation. He implores forgiveness—he promises reward. He begs—he threatens—he execrates. He is answered by a chuckle as before; the Epileptic sits upon his coffin-lid, and the doomed man can hear his heels without, as they beat time with the winds and waters, against the sides of his tomb. Meanwhile, the water presses in upon him—he feels its advance around him—it is now about his knees—in another moment it is every where. It has gradually ascended the plane—it now spreads over the entire floor of his dungeon. He grasps his pistols, which he had laid down beside him, and applies their muzzles to his head. He is too late. They are covered with water, and refuse fire. His knife is no longer to be found. It had dropped from his right hand when he smote off the fingers of the left, and had probably rolled down the plane to the bottom, where, covered with water, it is impossible to recover it. Hope within, and hope from without, have failed him equally; and, except in prayer, there is no refuge from the pang of death. But prayer is not easy to him who has never believed in the efficacy of its virtues. How can he pray to be forgiven, who has never been taught to forgive. He tries to pray! The Epileptic without, as he stoops his ear, can catch the fragmentary plea, the spasmodic adjuration, the gasping, convulsive utterance, from a throat around which the waters are already wreathing with close and unrelaxing grasp. Suddenly the voice ceases—there is a hoarse murmur—the struggle of the strong man among the waters, which press through the crevices between the lid and the sides of the dungeon. As the convulsion ceases, the Epileptic starts to his feet, with a terror which he had not felt before; and, looking wildly behind him as he ran, bounded up the sides of the neigh-bouring hills.

Thus ends our legend of the "Giant's Coffin." Tradition does not tell us of the farther fortunes of Leda Houston. Some pages of the chronicle have dropped. It is very certain, however, that Arthur Holt, like Benedick, lived to be a married man, and died the father of several children—the descendants of some of whom still live in the same region. Of the "Coffin" itself, some frag-ments, and, it is thought, one of the sides, may be shown, but it was "blown up" by the very freshet which we have described, and the body of Houston drifted down to the opposite shore. It was not till long after that Acker confessed the share which he had in the manner of his death and burial.

SERGEANT BARNACLE,

OR THE RAFTSMAN OF THE EDISTO.

Short be the shrift and sure the cord.—SCOTT.

CHAPTER I.

THE pretty little settlement of Orangeburg, in South Carolina, was an old and flourishing establishment before the Revolution. It was settled, as well as the contiguous country, by successive troops of German Palatines, who brought with them all the sober industry, and regular perseverance, characteristic of their country. They carried the cultivation of indigo in Carolina to a degree of perfection, on which they prospered, thriving, without much state, and growing great in wealth, without provoking the attention of their neighbours to the fact. To this day their descendants maintain some of these characteristics, and, in a time of much cry and little wool, when it is no longer matter of mortification for a vain people to confess a want of money, they are said to respond to the "I O U," of their more needy acquaintance, by knocking the head out of a flour barrel, and unveiling a world of specie, which would renovate the credit of many a mammoth bank. The good old people, their ancestors, were thrifty in other respects; clean and comfortable in their houses; raising abundance of pigs and poultry; rich in numerous children, whom they reared up in good works and godliness, with quite as much concern, to say no more, as they addressed to worldly objects. They lived well—knew what surprising moral benefits accrue from a due attent's to creature comforts; and, if they spent little money upon foreign luxuries, it was only because they had learned to domesticate so many of their own.

Home, indeed, was emphatically their world, and they found a world in it. Frank hospitality, and the simple sorts of merriment which delight, without impairing the unsophisticated nature, were enjoyed among them in full perfection; and, from Four Holes to Poplar Springs, they were emphatically one and the same, and a very happy people.

Our present business lies in this region, at a period which we may state in round numbers, as just five years before the Revolution. The ferment of that event, as we all know, had even then begun—the dispute and the debate, and the partial preparation—but the details and the angry feeling had been slow in reaching our quiet farmers along the Upper Edisto. The people were not good English scholars, preserving, as they did in many places, the integrity of the unbroken German. Here and there, it had suffered an English cross, and, in other places, particularly in the village, the English began to assert the ascendancy. But of newspapers they saw nothing, unless it were the venerable South Carolina Gazette, which did little more than tell them of the births, marriages and deaths in the royal family, and, at melancholy intervals, of the arrival in Charleston of some broad-bottomed lugger from Bremen, or other kindred ports in Faderland. The events which furnished materials to the village publican and politician, were of a sort not to extend their influence beyond their own ten-mile horizon. Their world was very much around them, and their most foreign thoughts and fancies still had a savour of each man's stable-yard. They never interfered in the slightest degree with the concerns of Russia or Constantinople, and I verily believe that if they had happened to have heard that the Great Mogul were on his last legs, and knew the secret of his cure, they would have hesitated so long before advising him of its nature, that the remedy would come too late to be of any service. And this, understand me, not because of any lack of Christian bowels, but simply because of a native modesty, which made them reluctant to meddle with any matters which did not obviously and immediately concern themselves. They were, certainly, sadly deficient in that spirit of modern philanthropy which seems disposed to meddle with nothing else. Their hopes and fears, strifes and excitements, were all local. At worst a

village scandal, or farm-yard jealousy—a squabble between two
neighbours touching a boundary line, or cattle pound, which ended in an arbitration and a feast, in which cherry and domestic
grape—by no means the simple juice of either—did the duty of
peacemakers, and were thrice blessed accordingly. Sometimes
—a more serious matter—the tall lad of one household would fail
to make the proper impression upon the laughing damsel of another, and this would produce a temporary family estrangement,
until Time, that great consoler, would furnish to the injured
heart of the sufferer, that sovereignest of all emollients—indifference! Beyond such as these, which are of occurrence in the
best regulated and least sophisticated of all communities, there
were precious few troubles among our people of the North Edisto,
which they could not easily overcome.

But the affair which I am about to relate, was an exception to
the uniform harmlessness and simplicity of events among them,
and the better to make the reader understand it, I must take him
with me this pleasant October evening, to a snug farm-house in
the Forks of Edisto—a part of the country thus distinguished, as
it lies in the crotch formed by the gradual approach of the two
branches of Edisto river, a few miles above the spot of their final
junction. Our farmer's name is Cole. He is not rich, but not
poor—one of those substantial, comfortable men of the world,
who has just enough to know what to do with it, and just
little enough to fancy that if he could get more he should
know what to do with that also. His farm, consisting of five or
six hundred acres, is a competence, but a small part of which is
cleared and in cultivation. He has but two slaves, but he has
two strapping sons, one of twelve, the other of fourteen, who
work with the slaves, and upon whom, equally with them, he bestows the horse-whip when needed, with as bountiful a hand as
he bestows the hommony. But if he counts but precious little
of gold and silver among his treasures, he has some treasures
which, in those days of simplicity, were considered by many to
be much more precious than any gold or silver. Like Jephthah,
Judge of Israel, he has a daughter—nay, for that matter, he has
two of them, and one of them, the eldest, is to be married this
very evening. Philip Cole was no Judge of Israel, but he loved

his daughters not the less, and the whole country justified his love. The eyes of the lads brightened, and their mouths watered at the bare mention of their names, and the sight of them generally produced such a commotion in the hearts of the surrounding swains, that, as I have heard averred a hundred times by tradition, they could, on such occasions, scarcely keep their feet. Keep their feet they could not, on such nights as the present, when they were not only permitted to see the lasses, but to dance it with them merrily. Dorothy Cole, the eldest, was as fine a specimen of feminine mortality, as ever blossomed in the eyes of love ; rather plumpish, but so well made, so complete, so brightly eyed, and so rosily cheeked, that he must be a cold critic indeed, who should stop to look for flaws—to say, here something might be pared off, and here something might be added. Such fine women were never made for such foolish persons. But Margaret, the younger, a girl of sixteen, was unexceptionable. She was her sister in miniature. She was beautiful, and faultless in her beauty, and so graceful, so playful, so pleasantly arch, and tenderly mischievous—so delightful, in short, in all her ways, that in looking upon her you ceased to remember that Eve had fallen —you still thought of her in Eden, the queen of its world of flowers, as innocent and beautiful as the very last budding rose amongst them. At all events, this was the opinion of every body for ten miles round, from Frank Leichenstein, the foreign gentleman—a German on his travels—to Barnacle Sam, otherwise Samuel Moore, a plain raftsman of the Edisto.

The occasion, though one of gaiety, which brought the company together, was also one of gloom. On this night the fair Dorothy would cease to be a belle. All hopes, of all but She, were cut off by her lately expressed preference for a farmer from a neighbouring district, and the young men assembled to witness nuptials which many of them looked on with envy and regret. But they bore, as well as they might, with the mortification which they felt. Love does not often kill in modern periods, and some little extra phlegm may be allowed to a community with an origin such as ours. The first ebullitions of public dissatisfaction had pretty well worn off before the night of the wedding, and, if the beauty of the bride, when she stood up that night to receive the fatal ring, served to reawaken the ancient flame in the breasts of any present, its violence was duly overcome in the reflection that the event was now beyond recall, and regrets utterly unavailing. The frolic which succeeded, the good cheer, the uproar, and the presence of numerous other damsels, all in their best, helped in no small degree to lessen the discontent and displeasure of the disappointed. Besides, there was the remaining sister, Margaret, a host in herself, and so gay, and so good natured, so ready to dance and sing, and so successful in the invention of new modes of passing time merrily, that, before the bride disappeared for the night, she was half chagrined to discover that nobody—unless her new-made husband—now looked to where she stood. Her sway was at an end with the hopes of her host of lovers.

CHAPTER II.

THE revels were kept up pretty late. What with the ceremony,
the supper, the dancing, and the sundry by-plays which are common to all such proceedings, time passed away without the proper consciousness of any of the parties. But all persons present
were not equally successful or equally happy. It was found, after a while, that though Margaret Cole smiled, and talked, and played, and danced with every body, there was yet one young fellow
who got rather the largest share of her favours. What rendered
this discovery particularly distressing was the fact that he was a
stranger and a citizen. His name was Wilson Hurst, a genteel
looking youth, who had recently made his appearance in the
neighbourhood, and was engaged in the very respectable business
of a country store. He sold calicoes and ribbons, and combs,
and dimity, and the thousand other neat, nice matters, in which
the thoughts and affections of young damsels are supposed to be
quite too much interested. He was no hobnail, no coarse unman-
·nered clown ; but carried himself with an air of decided *ton*, as
if he knew his position, and was resolute to make it known to
all around him. His manner was calculated to offend the more
rustic of the assembly, who are always, in every country, rather
jealous of the citizen ; and the high head which he carried, the
petty airs of fashion which he assumed, and his singular success
with the belle of the Forks, all combined to render the conceited
young fellow decidedly odious among the male part of the assembly. A little knot of these might have been seen, toward the
small hours, in earnest discussion of this subject, while sitting in
the piazza they observed the movements of the unconscious pair,
through a half opened window. We will not listen at present to
their remarks, which we may take for granted were sufficiently
bitter ; but turn with them to the entrance, where they have discovered a new arrival. This was a large man, seemingly rather

beyond the season of youth, who was now seen advancing up the narrow avenue which led to the house.

"It's Barnacle Sam!" said one.

"I reckon," was the reply of another.

"It's he, by thunder!" said a third, "wonder what he ll say to see Margaret and this city chap? He's just in time for it. They're mighty close."

"Reckon he'll bile up again. Jest be quiet now, till he comes."

From all this we may gather that the person approaching is an admirer of the fair Margaret. His proximity prevented all further discussion of this delicate subject, and the speakers at once surrounded the new comer.

"Well, my lads, how goes it? demanded this person, in a clear, manly accent, as he extended a hand to each. "Not too late, I reckon, for a fling on the floor, but I had to work hard for it, I reckon. Left Charleston yesterday when the sun was on the turn; but I swore I'd be in time for one dash with Margaret"

"Reckon you've walked for nothing, then," said one with a significant shake of the head to his fellows.

"For nothing! and why do you think so?"

"Well, I don't know, but I reckon Margaret's better satisfied to sit down jest now. She don't seem much inclined to foot it with any of us."

"That's strange for Margaret," said the new comer; "but I'll see how my chance stands, if so be the fiddle has a word to say in my behalf. She aint sick, fellows?"

"Never was better—but go in and try your luck."

"To be sure I will. It'll be bad luck, indeed, when I set my heart on a thing, and walk a matter of seventy miles after it, if I couldn't get it then, and for no reason that I can see; so here goes."

With these words, the speaker passed into the house, and was soon seen by his companions—who now resumed their places by the window—in conversation with the damsel. There was a frank, manly something in the appearance, the face, carriage and language of this fellow, that, in spite of a somewhat rude exterior and coarse clothing, insensibly commanded one's respect. It was very evident that those with whom he had spoken, had accorded

him theirs—that he was a favourite among them—and indeed, we
may say, in this place, that he was a very general favourite. He
was generous and good natured, bold, yet inoffensive, and so
liberal that, though one of the most industrious fellows in the
world, and constantly busy, he had long since found that his
resources never enabled him to lay by a copper against a rainy
day. Add to these moral qualities, that he was really a fine
looking fellow, large and well made, with a deep florid complexion,
black hair, good forehead and fine teeth, and we shall wonder to
find that he was not entirely successful with the sex. That he
was not an economist, and was a little over the frontier line of
forty, were perhaps objections, and then he had a plain, direct
way of speaking out his mind, which was calculated, sometimes,
to disturb the equanimity of the very smoothest temper.

It was perceived by his companions that Margaret answered
him with some evident annoyance and embarrassment, while they
beheld, with increasing aversion, the supercilious air of the
stranger youth, the curl of his lips, the simpering, half-scornful
smile which they wore, while their comrade was urging his
claims to the hand of the capricious beauty. The application of
the worthy raftsman—for such was the business of Barnacle Sam
—proved unavailing. The maiden declined dancing, pleading
fatigue. The poor fellow said that he too was fatigued, " tired
down, Miss Margaret, with a walk of seventy miles, only to have
the pleasure of dancing with you." The maiden was inexorable
and he turned off to rejoin his companions. The immoderate
laughter in which Margaret and the stranger youth indulged,
immediately after Barnacle Sam's withdrawal, was assumed by
his companions to be at his expense. This was also the secret
feeling of the disappointed suitor, but the generous fellow disclaimed any such conviction, and, though mortified to the very
heart, he studiously said every thing in his power to excuse the
capricious girl to those around him. She had danced with several
of them, the hour was late, and her fatigue was natural enough.
But the malice of his comrades determined upon a test which
should invalidate all these pleas and excuses. The fiddle was
again put in requisition, and a Virginia reel was resolved upon.
Scarcely were the parties summoned to the floor, before Margaret

made her appearance as the partner of young Hurst. Poor Barnacle walked out into the woods, with his big heart ready to break.
It was generally understood that he was fond of Margaret, but
how fond, nobody but himself could know. She, too, had been
supposed willing to encourage him, and, though by no means a
vain fellow, he was yet very strongly impressed with the belief
that he was quite as near to her affections as any man he knew.
His chagrin and disappointment may be imagined ; but a lonely
walk in the woods enabled him to come back to the cottage, to
which he was drawn by a painful sort of fascination, with a face
somewhat calmed, and with feelings, which, if not subdued, were
kept in proper silence and subjection. He was a strong-souled
fellow, who had no small passions. He did not flare up and make
a fuss, as is the wont of a peevish nature, but the feeling and
the pain were the deeper in due proportion to the degree of
restraint which he put upon them. His return to the cottage was
the signal to his companions to renew their assaults upon his temper. They found a singular satisfaction in making a hitherto
successful suitor partake of their own frequent mortifications.
But they did not confine their efforts to this single object. They
were anxious that Barnacle Sam should be brought to pluck a
quarrel with the stranger, whose conceited airs had so ruffled the
feathers of self-esteem in all of their crests. They dilated accordingly on all the real or supposed insolences of the new comer
—his obvious triumph—his certain success—and that unbearable
volley of merriment, which, in conjunction with Margaret Cole,
he had discharged at the retreating and baffled applicant for her
hand. Poor Barnacle bore with all these attempts with great
difficulty. He felt the force of their suggestions the more readily,
because the same thoughts and fancies had already been traversing his own brain. He was not insensible to the seeming indignity which the unbecoming mirth of the parties had betrayed on
his retiring from the field, and more than once a struggling devil
in his heart rose up to encourage and enforce the suggestions
made by his companions. But love was stronger in his soul than
hate, and served to keep down the suggestions of anger. He
truly loved the girl, and though he felt very much like trouncing the

presumptuous stranger, he subdued this inclination entirely on her account.

"No! no! my lads," said he, finally, "Margaret's her own mistress, and may do as she pleases. She's a good girl and a kind one, and if her head's turned just now by this stranger, let's give her time to get it back in the right place. She'll come right, I reckon, before long. As for him, I see no fun in licking him, for that's a thing to be done just as soon as said. If he crosses me, it'll do then—but so long as she seems to have a liking for him, so long I'll keep my hands off him, if so be he'll let me."

"Well," said one of his comrades, "I never thought the time would come when Barnacle Sam would take so much from any man."

"Oh hush! Peter Stahlen; you know I take nothing that I don't choose to take. All that know me, know what I am, and they'll all think rightly in the matter; and those that don't know me may think just what they please. So good night, my lads. I'll take another turn in the woods to freshen me."

CHAPTER III

WE pass over much of the minor matter in this history. We forbear the various details, the visitings and wanderings, the doings of the several parties, and the scandal which necessarily kept all tongues busy for a season. The hope so confidently expressed by Barnacle Sam, that the head of his beauty, which had been turned by the stranger, would recover its former sensible position after certain days, did not promise to be soon realized. On the contrary, every succeeding week seemed to bring the maiden and her city lover more frequently together; to strengthen his assurance, and increase his influence over her heart. All his leisure time was consumed either at her dwelling or in rambles with her alone, hither and thither, to the equal disquieting of maid and bachelor. *They*, however, had eyes for nobody but one another—lived, as it were, only in each other's regards, and, after a month of the busiest idleness in which he had ever been engaged, Barnacle Sam, in very despair, resumed his labours on the river by taking charge of a very large fleet of rafts. The previous interval had been spent in a sort of gentlemanly watch upon the heart and proceedings of the fair Margaret. The result was such as to put the *coup de grace* to all his own fond aspirations. But this effect was not brought about but at great expense of pride and feeling. His heart was sore and soured. His temper underwent a change. He was moody and irritable—kept aloof from his companions, and discouraged and repulsed them when they approached him. It was a mutual relief to them and himself when he launched upon the river in his old vocation. But his vocation, like that of Othello, was fairly gone. He performed his duties punctually, carried his charge in safety to the city, and evinced, in its management, quite as much skill and courage as before. But his performances were now mechanical—therefore carried on doggedly, and with no portion of his former spirit. There was now no catch of song, no famous shout or whistle, to be heard by the far

mer on the bank, as the canoe or the raft of Barnacle Sam round
ed the headlands.   There was no more friendly chat with the
wayfarer—no more kind, queer word, such as had made him the
favourite of all parties before.   His eye was now averted—his
countenance troubled—his words few—his whole deportment, as
well as his nature, had undergone a change ; and folks pointed
to the caprice of Margaret Cole as the true source of all his misfortunes.   It is, perhaps, her worst reproach that she seemed to
behold them with little concern or commiseration, and, exulting in
the consciousness of a new conquest over a person who seemed to
rate himself very much above his country neighbours, she suffered
herself to speak of the melancholy which had seized upon the
soul of her former lover with a degree of scorn and irreverence
which tended very much to wean from her the regard of the most
intimate and friendly among her own sex.

Months passed away in this manner, and but little of our raftsman was to be seen.   Meanwhile, the manner of Wilson Hurst
became more assured and confident.   In his deportment toward
Margaret Cole there was now something of a lordly condescension, while, in hers, people were struck with a new expression of
timidity and dependence, amounting almost to suffering and grief.
Her face became pale, her eye restless and anxious, and her step
less buoyant.   In her father's house she no longer seemed at
home.   Her time, when not passed with her lover, was wasted
in the woods, and at her return the traces of tears were still to be
seen upon her cheeks.   Suspicion grew active, scandal busied
herself, and the young women, her former associates, were the
first to declare themselves not satisfied with the existing condition
of things.   Their interest in the case soon superseded their
charity ;

> " For every wo a tear may claim,
>   Except an erring sister's shame."

Conferences ensued, discussions and declarations, and at length
the bruit reached the ears of her simple, unsuspecting parents.
The father was, when roused, a coarse and harsh old man.   Margaret was his favourite, but it was Margaret in her glory, not
Margaret in her shame.   His vanity was stung, and in the inter-

view to which he summoned the unhappy girl, his anger, which soon discovered sufficient cause of provocation, was totally without the restraints of policy or humanity.

A traditionary account—over which we confess there hangs some doubt—is given of the events that followed. There were guests in the dwelling of the farmer, and the poor girl was conducted to a neighbouring outhouse probably the barn. There, amid the denunciations of the father, the reproaches of the mother, and the sobs, tears and agonies of the victim, a full acknowledgment was extorted of her wretched state. But she preserved one secret, which no violence could make her deliver. She withheld the name of him to whom she owed all her misfortunes. It is true, this name was not wanting to inform any to whom her history was known, by whom the injury was done; but of all certainty on this head, derived from her own confession, they were wholly deprived. Sitting on the bare floor, in a state of comparative stupor, which might have tended somewhat to blunt and disarm the nicer sensibilities, she bore, in silence, the torrent of bitter and brutal invective which followed her developments. With a head drooping to the ground, eyes now tearless, hands folded upon her lap—self-abandoned, as it were—she was suffered to remain. Her parents left her and returned to the dwelling, having closed the door, without locking it, behind them. What were their plans may not be said; but, whatever they were, they were defeated by the subsequent steps taken, in her desperation of soul, by the deserted and dishonoured damsel.

CHAPTER IV.

WE still continue to report the tradition, though it does not appear that the subsequent statements of the affair were derived from any acknowledged witness. It appears that, after the night had set in, Margaret Cole fled from the barn in which she had been left by her parents. She was seen, in this proceeding, by her little brother, a lad of eight years old. Catching him by the arm as they met, she exclaimed—" Oh, Billy, don't tell, don't tell, if you love me!" The child kept the secret until her flight was known, and the alarm which it occasioned awakened his own apprehensions. He described her as looking and speaking very wildly; so much so as to frighten him. The hue and cry was raised, but she was not found for several hours after, and then— but we must not anticipate.

It appears—and we still take up the legend without being able to show the authorities—it appears that, as soon as she could hope for concealment, under cover of the night, she took her way through unfrequented paths in the forest, running and walking, toward the store of Wilson Hurst. This person, it appears, kept his store on the road-side, some four miles from the village of Orangeburg, the exact spot on which it stood being now only conjectured. A shed-room, adjoining the store, he occupied as his chamber. To this shed-room she came a little after midnight, and tapping beneath the window, she aroused the inmate. He rose, came to the window, and, without opening it, demanded who was there. Her voice soon informed him, and the pleading, pitiful, agonizing tones, broken and incoherent, told him all her painful story. She related the confession which she had made to her parents, and implored him at once to take her in and fulfil those promises by which he had beguiled her to her ruin. The night was a cold and cheerless one in February—her chattering teeth appealed to his humanity, even if her condition had not invoked his justice. Will it be believed that the wretch refused her?

He seemed to have been under the impression that she was accompanied by her friends, prepared to take advantage of his confessions ; and, under this persuasion, he denied her asseverations —told her she was mad—mocked at her pleadings, and finally withdrew once more, as if to his couch and slumbers.

We may fancy what were the feelings of the unhappy woman. It is not denied to imagination, however it may be to speech, to conjecture the terrible despair, the mortal agony swelling in her soul, as she listened to the cold-blooded and fiendish answer to her poor heart's broken prayer for justice and commiseration. What an icy shaft must have gone through her soul, to hearken to such words of falsehood, mockery and scorn, from those lips which had once pleaded in her ears with all the artful eloquence of love—and how she must have cowered to the earth, as if the mountains themselves were falling upon her as she heard his retiring footsteps—he going to seek those slumbers which she has never more to seek or find. That was death—the worst death— the final death of the last hope in her doomed and desolated heart. But one groan escaped her—one gasping sigh—the utterance, we may suppose of her last hope, as it surrendered up the ghost— and then, all was silence !

CHAPTER V.

THAT one groan spoke more keenly to the conscience of the miserable wretch within than did all her pleadings. The deep, midnight silence which succeeded was conclusive of the despair of the wretched girl It not only said that she was alone, abandoned of all others—but that she was abandoned by herself. The very forbearance of the usual reproaches—her entire submission to her fate—stung and goaded the base deceiver, by compelling his own reflections, on his career and conduct, to supply the place of hers. He was young, and, therefore, not entirely reckless. He felt that he lacked manliness—that courage which enables a man to do right from feeling, even where, in matters of principle, he does not appreciate the supremacy of virtue. Some miserable fears that her friends might still be in lurking, and, as he could not conjecture the desperation of a big heart, full of feeling, bursting with otherwise unutterable emotions, he flattered himself with the feeble conclusion, that, disappointed in her attempts upon him, the poor deluded victim had returned home as she came. Still, his conscience did not suffer him to sleep. He had his doubts. She might be still in the neighbourhood—she might be swooning under his window. He rose. We may not divine his intentions. It may have been—and we hope so for the sake of man and humanity—it may have been that he rose repentant, and determined to take the poor victim to his arms, and do all the justice to her love and sufferings that it yet lay in his power to do. He went to the window, and leant his ear down to listen. Nothing reached him but the deep soughing of the wind through the branches, but even this more than once startled him with such a resemblance to human moaning that he shuddered at his place of watch. His window was one of those unglazed openings in the wall, such as are common in the humbler cottages of a country where the cold is seldom of long duration, and where the hardy habits of the people render them comparatively careless of those agents of comfort which would protect against it. It was closed, not very snugly, by a single shutter, and fastened by a small iron hook within. Gradually, as he became encouraged by the silence, he raised this hook, and, still grasping it, suffered the window to expand so as to enable him to take into his glance, little by little, the prospect before him. The moon was now rising above the trees, and shedding a ghastly light upon the unshadowed places around. The night was growing colder, and in the chill under which his own frame shivered, he thought of poor Margaret and her cheerless walk that night. He looked down for her immediately beneath the window, but she was not there, and for a few moments his eyes failed to discover any object beyond the ordinary shrubs and trees. But as his vision became more and more accustomed to the indistinct outlines and shadowy glimpses under which, in that doubtful light, objects naturally presented themselves, he shuddered to behold a whitish form gleaming fitfully, as if waving in the wind, from a little clump of woods not forty yards from the house. He recoiled, closed the window with trembling hands, and got down upon his knees—but it was to cower, not to pray—and he did not remain in this position for more than a second. He then dressed himself, with hands that trembled too much to allow him, without much delay, to perform this ordinary office. Then he hurried into his shop—opened the door, which he as instantly bolted again, then returned to his chamber—half undressed himself, as if again about to seek his bed—resumed his garments, re-opened the window, and gazed once more upon the indistinct white outline which had inspired all his terrors. How long he thus stood gazing, how many were his movements of incertitude, what were his thoughts and what his purposes, may not be said—may scarcely be conjectured. It is very certain that every effort which he made to go forth and examine more closely the object of his sight and apprehensions, utterly failed—yet a dreadful fascination bound him to the window. If he fled to the interior and shut his eyes, it was only for a moment. He still returned to the spot, and gazed, and gazed, until the awful ghost of the unhappy girl spoke out audibly, to his ears, and filled his soul with the most unmitigated horrors.

CHAPTER VI.

But the sound of horses' feet, and hurrying voices, aroused him to the exercise of his leading instinct—that of self-preservation. His senses seemed to return to him instantly under the pressure of merely human fears. He hurried to the opposite apartment, silently unclosed the outer door, and stealing off under cover of the woods, was soon shrouded from sight in their impenetrable shadows. But the same fascination which had previously led him to the fatal window, now conducted him into that part of the forest which contained the cruel spectacle by which his eyes had been fixed and fastened. Here, himself concealed, crouching in the thicket, he beheld the arrival of a motley crowd—white and black—old Cole, with all the neighbours whom he could collect around him and gather in his progress. He saw them pass, without noticing, the object of their search and his own attention—surround his dwelling—heard them shout his name, and finally force their way into the premises. Torches were seen to glare through the seams and apertures of the house, and, at length, as if the examination had been in vain, the party reappeared without. They gathered in a group in front of the dwelling, and seemed to be in consultation. While they were yet in debate, the hoofs of a single horse, at full speed, were heard beating the frozen ground, and another person was added to the party. It did not need the shout with which this new comer was received by all, to announce to the skulking fugitive that, in the tall, massive form that now alighted among the rest, he beheld the noble fellow whose love had been rejected by Margaret for his own—Barnacle Sam. It is remarkable that, up to this moment, a doubt of his own security had not troubled the mind of Hurst; but, absorbed by the fearful spectacle which, though still unseen by the rest, was yet ever waving before his own spell-bound eyes, he had foregone all farther considerations of his own safety. But the appearance of this man, of whose character, by this time, he had full knowledge, had dis-pelled this confidence ; and, with the instinct of hate and fear, shuddering and looking back the while, he silently rose to his feet, and stealing off with as much haste as a proper caution would justify, he made his way to one of the landings on the river, where he found a canoe, with which he put off to the opposite side. For the present, we leave him to his own course and conscience, and return to the group which we left behind us, and which, by this time, has realized all the horrors natural to a full discovery of the truth.

The pocr gin. was found suspended, as we have already in part described, to the arm of a tree, but a little removed from the dwelling of her guilty lover, the swinging boughs of which had been used commonly for fastening horses. A common handkerchief, torn in two, and lengthened by the union of the parts, provided the fatal means of death for the unhappy creature. Her mode of procedure had been otherwise quite as simple as successful. She had mounted the stump of a tree which had been left as a horse-block, and which enabled her to reach the bough over which the kerchief was thrown. This adjusted, she swung from the stump, and passed in a few moments—with what remorse, what agonies, what fears, and what struggles, we will not say—from the vexing world of time to the doubtful empire of eternity ! We dare not condemn the poor heart, so young, so feeble, so wronged, and, doubtless, so distraught ! Peace to her spirit !

It would be idle to attempt to describe the tumult, the wild uproar and storm of rage, which, among that friendly group, seemed for a season to make them even forgetful of their grief. Their sorrow seemed swallowed up in fury. Barnacle Sam was alone silent. His hand it was that took down the lifeless body from the accursed tree—upon his manly bosom it was borne. He spoke but once on the occasion, in reply to those who proposed to carry it to the house of the betrayer. " No ! not there ! not there !" was all he said, in tones low—almost whispered—yet so distinctly heard, so deeply felt, that the noisy rage of those around him was subdued to silence in the sterner grief which they expressed. And while the noble fellow bore away the victim, with arms as fond, and a solicitude as tender, as if the lifeless form could still feel, and the cold defrauded heart could still respond to love, the

violent hands of the rest applied fire to the dwelling of the sedu-
cer, and watched the consuming blaze with as much delight as
they would have felt had its proprietor been involved within its
flaming perils. Such, certainly, had he been found, would have
been the sudden, and perhaps deserved judgment to which their
hands would have consigned him. They searched the woods for
him, but in vain. They renewed the search for him by daylight,
and traced his footsteps to the river. The surrounding country
was aroused, but, prompted by his fears, and favoured by his fortune, he had got so completely the start of his enemies that he
eluded all pursuit ; and time, that dulls even the spirit of revenge,
at length served to lessen the interest of the event in the minds
of most of the survivors. Months went by, years followed—the
old man Cole and his wife sunk into the grave ; hurried prematurely,
it was thought, by the dreadful history we have given ; and of all
that group, assembled on the fatal night we have just described,
but one person seemed to keep its terrible aspect forever fresh before his eyes—and that was Barnacle Sam.

He was a changed man. If the previous desertion and caprice
of the wretched Margaret, who had paid so heavy a penalty for
the girlish injustice which she had inflicted on his manly heart,
had made him morose and melancholy, her miserable fate increased this change in a far more surprising degree. He still, it is
true, continued the business of a raftsman, but, had it not been for
his known trustworthiness, his best friends and admirers would
have certainly ceased altogether to give him employment. He
was now the creature of a moodiness which they did not scruple
to pronounce madness. He disdained all sort of conference with
those about him, on ordinary concerns, and devoting himself to the
Bible, he drew from its mystic, and to him unfathomable, resources, constant subjects of declamation and discussion. Its thousand
dark prophecies became unfolded to his mind. He denounced the
threatened wrath of undesignated ages as already at the door—
called upon the people to fly, and shouted wildly in invocation of
the storm. Sometimes, these moods would disappear, and, at such
times, he would pass through the crowd with drooping head and
hands, the humbled and resigned victim to a sentence which seemed destined for his utter annihilation. The change in his physi-

cal nature had been equally great and sudden. His hair, though long and massive, suddenly became white as snow ; and though his face still retained a partial fulness, there were long lines and heavy seams upon his cheeks, which denoted a more than common struggle of the inner life with the cares, the doubts, and the agonies of a troubled and vexing existence. After the lapse of a year, the more violent paroxysms of his mood disappeared, and gave place to a settled gloom, which was not less significant than his former condition of an alienated mind. He was still devoted to religion—that is to say, to that study of religious topics, which, among ignorant or thoughtless people, is too apt to be mistaken for religion. But it was not of its peace, its diffusing calm, its holy promise, that he read and studied. His favourite themes were to be found among the terrible judgments, the fierce vengeances, the unexampled woes, inflicted, or predicted, in the prophetic books of the Old Testament. The language of the prophets, when they denounced wrath, he made his own language ; and when his soul was roused with any one of these subjects, and stimulated by surrounding events, he would look the Jeremiah that he spoke—his eyes glancing with the frenzy of a flaming spirit—his lips quivering with his deep emotions—his hands and arms spread abroad, as if the phials of wrath were in them ready to be emptied—his foot advanced, as if he were then dispensing judgment—his white hair streaming to the wind, with that meteor-likeness which was once supposed to be prophetic of " change, perplexing monarchs." At other times, going down upon his rafts, or sitting in the door of his little cabin, you would see him with the Bible on his knee—his eyes lifted in abstraction, but his mouth working, as if he then busied himself in calculation of those wondrous problems, contained in the " times and half times," the elucidation of which, it is supposed, will give us the final limit accorded to this exercise of our human toil in the works of the devil.

CHAPTER VII.

T was while his mind was thus occupied, that the ferment of colonial patriotism drew to a head. The Revolution was begun, and the clamours of war and the rattle of arms resounded through the land. Such an outbreak was the very event to accord with the humours of our morbid raftsman. Gradually, his mind had grasped the objects and nature of the issue, not as an event simply calculated to work out the regeneration of a decaying and impaired government, but as a sort of purging process, the great beginning of the end, in fact, by which the whole world was to be again made new. The exaggerated forms of rhetoric in which the orators of the time naturally spoke, and in which all stump orators are apt to speak, when liberty and the rights of man are the themes—and what themes, in their hands, do not swell into these? —happily chimed in with the chaotic fancies and confused thoughts which filled the brain of Barnacle Sam. In conveying his rafts to Charleston, he took every opportunity of hearing the great orators of that city—Gadsden, Rutledge, Drayton and others—and imbued with what he had heard, coupling it, in singular union, with what he had read—he proceeded to propound to his wondering companions, along the road and river, the equally exciting doctrines of patriotism and religion. In this way, to a certain extent, he really proved an auxiliary of no mean importance to a cause, to which, in Carolina, there was an opposition not less serious and determined, as it was based upon a natural and not discreditable principle. Instead now of avoiding the people, and of dispensing his thoughts among them only when they chanced to meet, Barnacle Sam now sought them out in their cabins. Returning from the city after the disposal of his rafts, his course lay, on foot, a matter of seventy miles through the country. On this route he loitered and lingered, went into by-places, and sought in lonely nooks, and " every bosky bower," " from side to side," the rustics of whom he either knew or heard. His own history, by this time, was pretty well known throughout the country, and he was generally received with open hands and that sympathy, which was naturally educed wherever his misfortunes were understood. His familiarity with the Bible, his exemplary life, his habits of self-denial, his imposing manner, his known fearlessness ot heart; these were all so many credentials to the favour of a simple and unsophisticated people. But we need dwell on this head no longer. Enough, in this place, to say that, on the first threat of the invader against the shores of Carolina, Barnacle Sam leapt from his rafts, and arrayed himself with the regiment of William Thompson, for the defence of Sullivan's Island. Of his valour, when the day of trial came, as little need be said. The important part which Thompson's riflemen had to play at the eastern end of Sullivan's Island, while Moultrie was rending with iron hail the British fleet in front, is recorded in another history. That battle saved Carolina for two years, but, in the interregnum which followed, our worthy raftsman was not idle. Sometimes on the river with his rafts, earning the penny which was necessary to his wants, he was more frequently engaged in stirring up the people of the humbler classes, by his own peculiar modes of argument, rousing them to wrath, in order, as he conclusively showed from Holy Writ, that they might " escape from the wrath to come." This logic cost many a tory his life; and, what with rafting, preaching and fighting, Barnacle Sam was as busy a prophet as ever sallied forth with short scrip and heavy sandal on the business of better people than himself.

During the same period of repose in Carolina from the absolute pressure of foreign war, and from the immediate presence of the foreign enemy, the city of Charleston was doing a peculiar and flourishing business. The British fleets covering all the coast, from St. Augustine to Martha's Vineyard, all commerce by sea was cut off, and a line of wagons from South, and through North Carolina, to Virginia and Pennsylvania, enabled the enterprising merchants of Charleston to snap their fingers at the blockading squadrons. The business carried on in this way, though a tedious, was yet a thriving one; and it gave many a grievous pang to patriotism, in the case of many a swelling tradesman, when the final investment of the Southern States com-

pelled its discontinuance. Many a Charleston tory owed his defection from principle, to this unhappy turn in the affairs of local
trade. It happened on one occasion, just before the British army
was ordered to the South, that General Huger, then in command
of a fine regiment of cavalry, somewhere near Lenud's Ferry on
the Santee, received intelligence which led him to suspect the
fidelity of a certain caravan of wagons which had left the city
some ten or twelve days before, and was then considerably advanced on the road to North Carolina. The intelligence which
caused this suspicion, was brought to him by no less a person
than our friend Barnacle Sam, who was just returning from one
of his ordinary trips down the Edisto. A detachment of twenty
men was immediately ordered to overtake the wagons and sift
them thoroughly, and under the guidance of Barnacle, the detachment immediately set off. The wagons, eleven in number,
were overhauled after three days' hard riding, and subjected to
as close a scrutiny as was thought necessary by the vigilant officer in command. But it did not appear that the intelligence
communicated by the raftsman received any confirmation. If
there were treasonable letters, they were concealed securely, or
seasonably destroyed by those to whom they were entrusted ; and
the search being over, and night being at hand, the troops and
the persons of the caravan, in great mutual good humour, agreed
to encamp together for the night. Fires were kindled, the wagons wheeled about, the horses were haltered and fed, and all
things being arranged against surprise, the company broke up into
compact groups around the several fires for supper and for sleep.
The partisan and the wagoner squatted, foot to foot, in circles the
most equal and sociable, and the rice and bacon having been
washed down by copious draughts of rum and sugar, of which
commodities the Carolinas had a copious supply at the time of the
invasion—nothing less could follow but the tale and the song,
the jest and the merry cackle, natural enough to hearty fellows,
under such circumstances of equal freedom and creature comfort.
As might be guessed from his character, as we have described it,
Barnacle Sam took no part in this sort of merriment. He mixed
with none of the several groups, but, with his back against a tree,
with crossed hands, and chin upon his breast, he lay soundly

wrapt in contemplation, chewing that cud of thought, founded
upon memory, which is supposed to be equally sweet and bitter.
In this position he lay, not mingling with any of the parties, perhaps unseen of any, and certainly not yielding himself in any
way to the influences which made them temporarily happy. He
was in a very lonely and far removed land of his own. He had
not supped, neither had he drank, neither had he thirsted, nor
hungered, while others indulged. It was one peculiarity of his
mental infirmities that he seemed, whenever greatly excited by
his own moods, to suffer from none of the animal wants of nature. His position, however, was not removed from that of the
rest. Had his mind been less absorbed in its own thoughts
—had he willed to hear—he might have been the possessor
of all the good jokes, the glees and every thoughtless or
merry word, which delighted those around him. He lay between two groups, a few feet only from one, in deep shadow,
which was only fitfully removed as some one of those around
the fire bent forward or writhed about, and thus suffered the
ruddy glare to glisten upon his drooping head or broad manly
bosom. One of these groups—and that nearest him—was composed entirely of young men. These had necessarily found each
other out, and, by a natural attraction, had got together in the
same circle. Removed from the restraints and presence of their
elders, and after the indulgence of frequent draughts from the
potent beverage, of which there was always a supply adequate to
the purposes of evil, their conversation soon became licentious ;
and, from the irreverent jest, they soon gave way to the obscene
story. At length, as one step in vice, naturally and inevitably,—
unless promptly resisted—impels another—the thoughtless repro
bates began to boast of their several experiences in sin. Each
strove to outdo his neighbour in the assertion of his prowess, and
while some would magnify the number of their achievements,
others would dilate in their details, and all, at the expense of poor,
dependent woman. It would be difficult to say—nor is it important—at what particular moment, or from what particular circumstance, Barnacle Sam was induced to give any attention to
what was going on. The key-note which opened in his own soul
all its dreadful remembrances of horror, was no doubt to be found

in some one word, some tone, of undefinable power and import, which effectually commanded his continued attention, even though it was yielded with loathing and against the stomach of his sense. He listened with head no longer drooping, eyes no longer shut, thought no longer in that far and foreign world of memory. Memory, indeed, was beginning to recover and have a present life and occupation. Barnacle Sam was listening to accents which were not unfamiliar to his ear. He heard one of the speakers, whose back was turned upon him, engaged in the narrative of his own triumphs, and every syllable which he uttered was the echo of a dreadful tale, too truly told already. The story was not the same—not identical in all its particulars—with that of poor Margaret Cole ; but it was her story. The name of the victim was not given—and the incidents were so stated, that, without altering the results, all those portions were altered which might have placed the speaker in a particularly base or odious position. He had conquered, he had denied his victim the only remedy in his power—for was he to confide in a virtue, which he had been able to overcome ?—and she had perished by her own hands. This was the substance of his story ; but this was not enough for the profligate, unless he could show how superior were his arts of conquest, how lordly his sway, how indifferent his love, to the misery which it could occasion ; a loud and hearty laugh followed, and, in the midst of the uproar, while every tongue was conceding the palm of superiority to the narrator, and his soul was swelling with the applause for which his wretched vanity had sacrificed decency and truth, a heavy hand was laid upon his shoulder, and his eyes, turning round upon the intruder, encountered those of Barnacle Sam !

" Well, what do you want ?" demanded the person addressed. It was evident that he did not recognize the intruder. How could he ? His own mother could not have known the features of Barnacle Sam, so changed as he was, from what he had been, by wo and misery.

" You ! I want you ! You are wanted, come with me !"

The other hesitated and trembled. The eye of the raftsman was upon him. It was the eye of his master—the eye of fate. It was not in his power to resist it. It moved him whither it would. He rose to his feet. He could not help but rise. He was stationary for an instant, and the hand of Barnacle Sam rested upon his wrist. The touch appeared to smite him to the bone. He shuddered, and it was noted that his other arm was extended, as if in appeal to the group from which he had risen. Another look of his fate fixed him. He shrunk under the full, fierce, compelling glance of the other. He shrunk, but went forward in silence, while the hand of the latter was still slightly pressed upon his wrist.

CHAPTER VIII.

NEVER was mesmeric fascination more complete. The rafts. man seemed to have full confidence in his powers of compulsion, ror he retained his grasp upon the wrist of the profligate, but a single moment after they had gone from the company.

"Come! Follow!" said the conductor, when a few moments more had elapsed, finding the other beginning to falter.

"Where must I go? Who wants me?" demanded the criminal, with a feeble show of resolution.

"Where must you go—who wants you; oh! man of little faith—does the soldier ask of the officer such a question—does the sinner of his judge? of what use to ask, Wilson Hurst, when the duty must be done—when there is no excuse and no appeal. Come!"

"Wilson Hurst! Who is it calls me by that name? I will go no farther."

The raftsman who had turned to proceed, again paused, and stooping, fixed his keen eyes upon those of the speaker so closely that their mutual eyebrows must have met. The night was starlighted, and the glances from the eyes of Barnacle Sam flashed upon the gaze of his subject, with a red energy like that of Mars. "Come!" he said, even while he looked. "Come, miserable man, the judgment is given, the day of favour is past, and lo! the night cometh—the night is here."

"Oh, now I know you, now I know you—Barnacle Sam!" exclaimed Hurst, falling upon his knees. "Have mercy upon me —have mercy upon me!"

"It is a good prayer," said the other, "a good prayer—the only prayer for a sinner, but do not address it to me. To the Judge, man, to the Almighty Judge himself! Pray, pray! I will give you time. Pour out your heart like water. Let it run upon the thirsty ground. The contrite heart is blessed though it be

21

doomed. You cannot pray too much—you cannot pray enough. In the misery of the sinner is the mercy of the Judge."

"And will you spare me ? Will you let me go if I pray ?' demanded the prostrate and wretched criminal with eagerness.

"How can I ? I, too, am a sinner. I am not the judge. I am but the officer commanded to do the will of God. He has spoken this command in mine ears by day and by night. He has commanded me at all hours. I have sought for thee, Wilson Hurst, for seven weary years along the Edisto, and the Congaree and Santee, the Ashley, and other rivers. It has pleased God to weary me with toil in this search, that I might the better understand how hard it is for the sinner to serve him as he should be served ! ' For I thy God am a jealous God !' He knew how little I could be trusted, and he forced me upon a longer search and upon greater toils. I have wearied and I have prayed; I have toiled and I have travelled; and it is now, at last, that I have seen the expected sign, in a dream, even in a vision of the night. Oh, Father Almighty, I rejoice, I bless thee, that thou hast seen fit to bring my labours to a close—that I have at length found this favour in thy sight. Weary have been my watches, long have I prayed. I glad me that I have not watched and prayed vainly, and that the hour of my deliverance is at hand. Wilson Hurst, be speedy with thy prayers. It is not commanded that I shall cut thee off suddenly and without a sign. Humble thyself with speed, make thyself acceptable before the Redeemer of souls, for thy hour is at hand."

"What mean you ?" gasped the other

"Judgment ! Death !" And, as he spoke, the raftsman looked steadfastly to the tree overhead, and extended his arm as if to grasp the branches. The thought which was in his mind was immediately comprehended by the instinct of the guilty man. He immediately turned to fly. The glimmering light from the fires of the encampment could still be seen fitfully flaring through the forest.

Whither would you go ?" demanded the raftsman, laying his nand upon the shoulder of the victim. "Do you hope to fly from the wrath of God, Wilson Hurst ? Foolish man, waste not the moments which are precious. Busy thyself in prayer. Thou canst not hope for escape. Know that God hath sent me against thee, now, on this very expedition, after, as I have told thee, after a weary toil in search of thee for a space of seven years. Thou hast had all that time for repentance while I have been tasked vainly to seek thee even for the same period of time. But late, as I went out from the city, there met me one near Dorchester, who bade me set forth in pursuit of the wagon-train for the north, but I heeded not his words, and that night, in a vision, I was yet farther commanded. In my weak mind and erring faith, me-thought I was to search among these wagons for a traitor to the good cause of the colony. Little did I think to meet with thee, Wilson Hurst. But when I heard thy own lips openly denounce thy sins ; when I heard thee boastful of thy cruel deed to her who was the sweetest child that ever Satan robbed from God's blessed vineyard—then did I see the purpose for which I was sent —then did I understand that my search was at an end, and that the final judgment was gone forth against thee. Prepare thyself, Wilson Hurst, for thy hour is at hand."

" I will not. You are mad ! I will fight, I will halloo to our people," said the criminal, with more energetic accents and a greater show of determination. The other replied with a coolness which was equally singular and startling.

" I have sometimes thought that I *was* mad ; but now, that the Lord hath so unexpectedly delivered thee into my hands, I know that I am not. Thou may'st fight, and thou may'st halloo, but I cannot think that these will help thee against the positive com-mandment of the Lord. Even the strength of a horse avails not against him for the safety of those whom he hath condemned. Prepare thee, then, Wilson Hurst, for thy hour is almost up."

He laid his hand upon the shoulder of the criminal as he spoke. The latter, meanwhile, had drawn a large knife from his pocket, and though Barnacle Sam had distinguished the movement and suspected the object, he made no effort to defeat it.

" Thou art armed," said he, releasing, as he spoke, his hold upon the shoulder of Hurst. " Now, shalt thou see how certainly the Lord hath delivered thee into my hands, for I will not strive against thee until thou hast striven. Use thy weapon upon me Lo ! I tand unmoved before thee ! Strike boldly and see what

thou shalt do, for I tell thee thou hast no hope.   Thou art doomed, and I am sent this hour to execute God's vengeance against
thee.''

The wretch took the speaker at his word, struck with tolerable
boldness and force, twice, thrice upon the breast of the raftsman,
who stood utterly unmoved, and suffering no wound, no hurt of
any sort.   The baffled criminal dropped his weapon, and scream-
ed in feeble and husky accents for help.   In his tremour and timidity, he had, after drawing the knife from his pocket, utterly
forgotten to unclasp the blade.   He had struck with the blunted
handle of the weapon, and the result which was due to so simple
and natural a cause, appeared to his cowardly soul and excited
imagination as miraculous.   It was not less so to the mind of Barnacle Sam.

" Did I not tell thee !   Look here, Wilson Hurst, look on this,
and see how slight a thing in the hand of Providence may yield
defence against the deadly weapon.   This is the handkerchief by
which poor Margaret Cole perished.   It has been in my bosom
from the hour I took her body from the tree.   It has guarded my
life against thy steel, though I kept it not for this.   God has commanded me to use it in carrying out his judgment upon thee.''

He slipt it over the neck of the criminal as he spoke these
words.   The other, feebly struggling, sunk upon his knees.   His
nerves had utterly failed him.   The coward heart, still more enfeebled by the coward conscience, served completely to paralyze the
common instinct of self-defence.   He had no strength, no manhood.   His muscles had no tension, and even the voice of supplication died away, in sounds of a faint and husky terror in his
throat—a half-stifled moan, a gurgling breath—and ——

CHAPTER IX.

WHEN Barnacle Sam returned to the encampment he was alone. He immediately sought the conductor of the wagons, and, without apprising him of his object, led him to the place of final conference between himself and Hurst. The miserable man was found suspended to a tree, life utterly extinct, the body already stiff and cold. The horror of the conductor almost deprived him of utterance. " Who has done this ?" he asked.

" The hand of God, by the hand of his servant, which I am! The judgment of Heaven is satisfied. The evil thing is removed from among us, and we may now go on our way in peace. I have brought thee hither that thou may'st see for thyself, and be a witness to my work which is here ended. For seven weary years have I striven in this object. Father, I thank thee, that at the last thou hast been pleased to command that I should behold it finished !"

These latter words were spoken while he was upon his knees, at the very feet of the hanging man. The conductor, availing himself of the utter absorption in prayer of the other, stole away to the encampment, half-apprehensive that he himself might be made to taste of the same sharp judgment which had been administered to his companion. The encampment was soon roused and the wagoners hurried in high excitement to the scene. They found Barnacle Sam still upon his knees. The sight of their comrade suspended from the tree, enkindled all their anger. They laid violent hands upon his executioner. He offered no resistance, but showed no apprehension. To what lengths their fury would have carried them may only be conjectured, but they had found a rope, had fitted the noose, and in a few moments more they would, in all probability, have run up the offender to the same tree from which they had cut down his victim, when the timely appearance of the troopers saved him from such a fate. The *esprit de corps* came in seasonably for his preservation. It was in vain that the wagoners pointed to the suspended man—in vain that Barnacle Sam avowed his handiwork—"He is one of us," said the troopers ; and the slightest movement of the others toward hostility was resented with a handling so rough, as made it only a becoming prudence to bear with their loss and abuses, as they best might.   The wonder of all was, as they examined the body of the victim, how it was possible for the executioner to effect his purpose.   Hurst was a man of middle size, rather stoutly built, and in tolerably good case.   He would have weighed about one hundred and thirty.   Barnacle Sam was of powerful frame and great muscle, tall and stout, yet it seemed impossible, unless en- dued with superhuman strength, that, unaided, he could have achieved his purpose ; and some of the troopers charitably sur- mised that the wagoner had committed suicide ; while the wagon- ers, in turn, hurried to the conclusion that the executioner had found assistance among the troopers.   Both parties overlooked the preternatural strength accruing, in such a case, from the ex- cited moral and mental condition of the survivor.   They were not philosophers enough to see that, believing himself engaged upon the work of God, the enthusiast was really in possession of attri- butes, the work of a morbid imagination, which seemed almost to justify his pretensions to a communion with the superior world. Besides, they assumed a struggle on the part of the victim.   They did not conjecture the influence of that spell by which the domi- nant spirit had coerced the inferior, and made it docile as the squirrel which the fascination of the snake brings to its very jaws, in spite of all the instincts which teach it to know how fatal is the enemy that lurks beneath the tree.   The imbecile Hurst, con- scious as it were of his fate, seems to have so accorded to the commands of his superior, as to contribute, in some degree, to his designs.   At all events, the deed was done ; and Barnacle Sam never said that the task was a hard one.

It was reserved for an examination of the body to find a full military justification for the executioner, and to silence the clam- ours of the wagoners.   A screw bullet was found admirably folded in the knot of his neck kerchief, which, it seems, was not with- drawn from his neck when the kerchief of Margaret Cole was employed for a more deadly purpose.   In this bullet was a note in cypher, addressed to Clinton, at New York, describing the actual condition of Savannah, evidently from the hands of some one in that quarter. In a few months after this period Savannah was in possession of the British.

Barnacle Sam was tried for the murder of Hurst before a civil tribunal, and acquitted on the score of insanity ; a plea put in for him, in his own spite, and greatly to his mortification. He retired from sight, for a space after this verdict, and remained quiet until a necessity arose for greater activity on the part of the patriots at home. It was then that he was found among the partisans, always bold and fearless, fighting and suffering manfully to the close of the war.

It happened, on one occasion, that the somewhat celebrated Judge Burke, of South Carolina, was dining with a pleasant party at the village of Orangeburg. The judge was an Irish gentleman of curious humour, and many eccentricities. He had more wit than genius, and quite as much courage as wisdom. The bench, indeed, is understood to have been the reward of his military services during the Revolution, and his bulls in that situation are even better remembered than his deeds in the other. But his blunders were redeemed by his humour, and the bar overlooked his mistakes in the enjoyment of his eccentricities. On the present occasion the judge was in excellent mood, and his companions equally happy, if not equally humorous with himself The cloth had been removed, and the wine was in lively circulation, when the servant announced a stranger, who was no other than Barnacle Sam. Our ancient was known to the judge and to several of the company. But they knew him rather as the brave soldier, the successful scout, the trusty spy and courier, than as the unsuccessful lover and the agent of God's judgment against the wrong doer. His reception was kind ; and the judge, taking for granted that he came to get a certificate for bounty lands, or a pension, or his seven years' pay, or something of that sort, supposed that he should get rid of him by a prompt compliance with his application. No such thing. He had come to get a reversal of that judgment of the court by which he had been pronounced insane. His acquittal was not an object of his concern. In bringing his present wish to the knowledge of the judge he had perforce to tell his story. This task we have already sufficiently performed. It was found that, though by no means obtrusive or earnest, the good fellow was firm in his application, and the judge, in one of his best humours, saw no difficulty in obliging him.

"Be plaised, gentlemen," said he, "to fill your glasses. Our revision of the judgment in the case of our excellent friend, Sergeant Barnacle, shall be no dry joke. Fill your glasses, and be raisonably ripe for judgment. Sit down, Sergeant Barnacle, sit down, and be plaised to take a drhap of the crathur, though you leave no other crathur a drhap. It sames to me, gentlemen of the jury, that our friend has been hardly dealt with. To be found guilty of insanity for hanging a tory and a spy—a fellow actually bearing despatches to the enemy—sames a most extraordinary judgment; and it is still more extraordinary, let me tell you, that a person should be suspected of any deficiency of sense who should lay hands on a successful rival. I think this hanging a rival out of the way an excellent expadient; and the only mistake which, it sames to me, our friend Sergeant Barnacle has made, in this business, was in not having traed him sooner than he did."

"I sought him, may it please your honour, but the Lord did not deliver him into my hands until his hour had come," was the interruption of Barnacle Sam.

"Ah! I see! You would have hung him sooner if you could. Gentlemen of the jury, our friend, the sergeant, has shown that he would have hung him sooner if he could. The only ground, *then*, upon which, it sames to me, that his sanity could have been suspected, is thus cleared up; and we are made to say that our worthy friend was not deficient in that sagacity which counsels us to execute the criminal before he is guilty, under the good old rule that prevention is better than cure—that it is better to hang thirty rogues before they are proved so, rayther than to suffer one good man to come to avil at their hands."

It is needless to say that the popular court duly concurred with the judge's humorous reversal of the former decision; and Barnacle Sam went his way, perfectly satisfied as to the removal of all stain from his sanity of mind.

THOSE OLD LUNES!

OR, WHICH IS THE MADMAN?

" I am but mad, North—North-West: when the wind is southerly, I know
a hawk from a handsaw."—HAMLET.

CHAPTER I.

WE had spent a merry night of it. Our stars had paled their
not ineffectual fires, only in the daylight; and while Dan Phœbus
was yet rising, " jocund on the misty mountain's top," I was busy
in adjusting my foot in the stirrup and mounting my good steed
" Priam," to find my way by a close cut, and through narrow
Indian trails, to my lodgings in the little town of C.—, on the very
borders of Mississippi. There were a dozen of us, all merry
larks, half mad with wine and laughter, and the ride of seven
miles proved a short one. In less than two hours, I was snugly
snoozing in my own sheets, and dreaming of the twin daughters
of old Hansford Owens.

Well might one dream of such precious damsels. Verily, they
seemed, all of a sudden, to have become a part of my existence.
They filled my thoughts, excited my imagination, and,—if it be
not an impertinence to say any thing of the heart of a roving lad
of eighteen,—then were they at the very bottom of mine.—Both of
them, let me say,—for they were twins, and were endowed with
equal rights by nature. I was not yet prepared to say what was
the difference, if any, between their claims. One was fair, the
other brown; one pensive, the other merry as the cricket of
Venus. Susannah was meek as became an Elder's daughter;
Emmeline so mischievous, that she might well have worried the

meekest of the saints in the calendar from his propriety and position. I confess, though I thought constantly of Susannah, I always looked after Emmeline the first. She was the brunette—
one of your flashing, sparkling, effervescing beauties,—perpetu-
ally running over with exultation—brimfull of passionate fancies
that tripped, on tiptoe, half winged, through her thoughts. She
was a creature to make your blood bound in your bosom,—to
take you entirely off your feet, and fancy, for the moment, that
your heels are quite as much entitled to dominion as your head.
Lovely too,—brilliant, if not absolutely perfect in features—she
kept you always in a sort of sunlight. She sung well, talked
well, danced well—was always in air—seemed never herself to
lack repose, and, it must be confessed, seldom suffered it to any
body else. Her dancing was the crowning grace and glory. She
was no Taglioni—not an Ellsler—I do not pretend that. But she
was a born *artiste*. Every motion was a study. Every look
was life. Her form subsided into the sweetest luxuriance of attitude, and rose into motion with some such exquisite buoyancy,
as would become Venus issuing from the foam. Her very affec-
tations were so naturally worn, that you at length looked for them
as essential to her charm. I confess—but no! Why should I
do any thing so foolish?

Susannah was a very different creature. She was a fair girl
—rather pale, perhaps, when her features were in repose. She
had rich soft flaxen hair, and dark blue eyes. She looked rather
than spoke. Her words were few, her glances many. She was
not necessarily silent in silence. On the contrary, her very silence had frequently a significance, taken with her looks, that
needed no help from speech. She seemed to look through you at
a glance, yet there was a liquid sweetness in her gaze, that disarmed it of all annoyance. If Emmeline was the glory of the
sunlight—Susannah was the sovereign of the shade. If the song
of the one filled you with exultation, that of the other awakened
all your tenderness. If Emmeline was the creature for the
dance,—Susannah was the wooing, beguiling Egeria, who could
snatch you from yourself in the moments of respite and repose.
For my part, I felt that I could spend all my mornings with the
former, and all my evenings with the latter. Susannah with her

large, blue, tearful eyes, and few, murmuring and always gentle accents, shone out upon me at nightfall, as that last star that watches in the vault of night for the coming of the sapphire dawn.

So much for the damsels. And all these fancies, not to say feelings, were the fruit of but three short days acquaintance with their objects. But these were days when thoughts travel merrily and fast—when all that concerns the fancies and the affections, are caught up in a moment, as if the mind were nothing but a congeries of instincts, and the sensibilities, with a thousand delicate antennæ, were ever on the grasp for prey.

Squire Owens was a planter of tolerable condition. He was a widower, with these two lovely and lovable daughters—no more. But, bless you! Mine was no calculating heart. Very far from it. Neither the wealth of the father, nor the beauty of the girls, had yet prompted me to think of marriage. Life was pleasant enough as it was. Why burden it? Let well enough alone, say I. I had no wish to be happier. A wife never entered my thoughts. What might have come of being often with such damsels, there's no telling; but just then, it was quite enough to dance with Emmeline, and muse with Susannah, and—*vive la bagatelle!*

I need say nothing more of my dreams, since the reader sufficiently knows the subject. I slept late that day, and only rose in time for dinner, which, in that almost primitive region, took place at 12 o'clock, M. I had no appetite. A herring and soda water might have sufficed, but these were matters foreign to the manor. I endured the day and headache together, as well as I could, slept soundly that night, with now the most ravishing fancies of Emmeline, and now the pleasantest dreams of Susannah, one or other of whom still usurped the place of a bright particular star in my most capacious fancy. Truth is, in those heydey days, my innocent heart never saw any terrors in polygamy. I rose a new man, refreshed and very eager for a start. I barely swallowed breakfast when Priam was at the door. While I was about to mount, with thoughts filled with the meek beauties of Susannah, —I was arrested by the approach of no less a person than Ephraim Strong, the village blacksmith.

"You're guine to ide, I see."

" Yes."

" To Squire Owens, I reckon."

" Right."

" Well, keep a sharp look out on the road, for there's news come down that the famous Archy Dargan has broke Hamilton gaol."

" And who's Archy Dargan ?"

" What! don't know Archy ? Why, he's the madman that's been shut up there, it's now guine on two years."

" A madman, eh ?"

" Yes, and a mighty sevagerous one at that. He's the cunningest white man going. Talks like a book, and knows how to get out of a scrape,—is jest as sensible as any man for a time, but, sudden, he takes a start, like a shying horse, and before you knows where you are, his heels are in your jaw. Once he blazes out, it's knife or gun, hatchet or hickory—any thing he can lay hands on. He's kill'd two men already, and cut another's throat a'most to killing. He's an ugly chap to meet on the road, so look out right and left."

" What sort of man is he ?"

" In looks ?"

" Yes !"

" Well, I reckon, he's about your heft. He's young and tallish, with a fair skin, brown hair, and a mighty quick keen blue eye, that never looks steddily nowhere. Look sharp for him. The sheriff with his ' spose-you-come-and-take-us'—is out after him, but he's mighty cute to dodge, and had the start some twelve hours afore they missed him."

CHAPTER II.

THE information thus received did not disquiet me. After the momentary reflection that it might be awkward to meet a madman, out of bounds, upon the highway, I quickly dismissed the matter from my mind. I had no room for any but pleasant meditations. The fair Susannah was now uppermost in my dreaming fancies, and, reversing the grasp upon my whip, the ivory handle of which, lined with an ounce or two of lead, seemed to me a sufficiently effective weapon for the worst of dangers, I bade my friendly blacksmith farewell, and dashed forward upon the high road. A smart canter soon took me out of the settlement, and, once in the woods, I recommended myself with all the happy facility of youth, to its most pleasant and beguiling imaginings. I suppose I had ridden a mile or more—the story of the bedlamite was gone utterly from my thought—when a sudden turn in the road showed me a person, also mounted, and coming towards me at an easy trot, some twenty-five or thirty yards distant. There was nothing remarkable in his appearance. He was a plain farmer or wood-man, clothed in simple homespun, and riding a short heavy chunk of an animal, that had just been taken from the plough. The rider was a spare, long-legged person, probably thirty years or thereabouts. He looked innocent enough, wearing that simple, open-mouthed sort of countenance, the owner of which, we assume, at a glance, will never set any neighbouring stream on fire. He belonged evidently to a class as humble as he was sim-ple,—but I had been brought up in a school which taught me that the claims of poverty were quite as urgent upon courtesy as those of wealth. Accordingly, as we neared each other, I prepared to bestow upon him the usual civil recognition of the highway. What is it Scott says—I am not sure that I quote him rightly—

> " When men in distant forests meet,
> They pass not as in peaceful street."

And, with the best of good humour, I rounded my lips into a smile, and got ready my salutation. To account somewhat for its effect when uttered, I must premise that my own personal appearance at this time, was rather wild and impressive. My face was full of laughter, and my manners of buoyancy. My hair was very long, and fell in masses upon my shoulder, unrestrained by the cap which I habitually wore, and which, as I was riding under heavy shade trees, was grasped in my hand along with my riding whip As the stranger drew nigh, the arm was extended, cap and whip lifted in air, and with free, generous lungs, I shouted —"good morning, my friend,—how wags the world with you to-day ?"

The effect of this address was prodigious. The fellow gave no answer,—not a word, not a syllable—not the slightest nod of the head,—*mais, tout au contraire*. But for the dilating of his amazed pupils, and the dropping of the lower jaw, his features might have been chiselled out of stone. They wore an expression amounting to consternation, and I could see that he caught up his bridle with increased alertness, bent himself to the saddle, half drew up his horse, and then, as if suddenly resolved, edged him off, as closely as the woods would allow, to the opposite side of the road. The undergrowth was too thick to allow of his going into the wood at the spot where we encountered, or he certainly would have done so. Somewhat surprised at this, I said something, I cannot now recollect what, the effect of which was even more impressive upon him than my former speech. The heads of our horses were now nearly parallel—the road was an ordinary wagon track, say twelve feet wide—I could have brushed him with my cap as we passed, and, waving it still aloft, he seemed to fancy that such was my intention,—for, inclining his whole body on the off side of his nag, as the Cumanche does when his aim is to send an arrow at his enemy beneath his neck—his heels thrown back, though spurless, were made to belabour with the most surprising rapidity, the flanks of his drowsy animal. And, not without some effect The creature dashed first into a trot, then into a canter, and finally into a gallop, which, as I was bound one way and he the other, soon threw a considerable space between us.

" The fellow's mad !" was my reflection and speech, as, wheeling my horse half about, I could see him looking backward, and driving his heels still into the sides of his reluctant hack. The next moment gave me a solution of the matter. The simple countryman had heard of the bedlamite from Hamilton jail. My bare head, the long hair flying in the wind, my buoyancy of manner, and the hearty, and, perhaps, novel form of salutation with which I addressed him, had satisfied him that I was the person. As the thought struck me, I resolved to play the game out, and, with a restless love of levity which has been too frequently my error, I put the whip over my horse's neck, and sent him forward in pursuit. My nag was a fine one, and very soon the space was lessened between me and the chase. As he heard the footfalls behind, the frightened fugitive redoubled his exertions. He laid himself to it, his heels paddling in the sides of his donkey with redoubled industry And thus I kept him for a good mile, until the first houses of the settlement grew visible in the distance. I then once more turned upon the path to the Owens', laughing merrily at the rare chase, and the undisguised consternation of the countryman The story afforded ample merriment to my fair friends Emmeline and Susannah. "It was so ridiculous that one of my appearance should be taken for a madman. The silly fellow deserved the scare." On these points we were all perfectly agreed. That night we spent charmingly. The company did not separate till near one o'clock. We had fun and fiddles. I danced by turns with the twins, and more than once with a Miss Gridley, a very pretty girl, who was present. Squire Owens was in the best of humours, and, no ways loth, I was made to stav all night.

CHAPTER III.

A NEW day of delight dawned upon us with the next. Our breakfast made a happy family picture, which I began to think it would be cruel to interrupt. So snugly did I sit beside Emmeline, and so sweetly did Susannah minister at the coffee urn, and so patriarchally did the old man look around upon the circle, that my meditations were all in favour of certain measures for perpetuating the scene. The chief difficulty seemed to be, in the way of a choice between the sisters.

> " How happy could one be with either,
> Were t'other dear charmer away."

I turned now from one to the other, only to become more bewildered. The lively glance and playful remark of Emmeline, her love smiling visage, and buoyant, unpremeditative air, were triumphant always while I beheld them ; but the pensive, earnest look of Susannah, the mellow cadences of her tones, seemed always to sink into my soul, and were certainly remembered longest. Present, Emmeline was irresistible ; absent, I thought chiefly of Susannah. Breakfast was fairly over before I came to a decision. We adjourned to the parlour,—and there, with Emmeline at the piano, and Susannah with her Coleridge in hand –her favourite poet—I was quite as much distracted as before. The bravura of the one swept me completely off my feet. And when I pleaded with the other to read me the touching poem of " Genevieve "—her low, subdued and exquisitely modulated utterance, so touching, so true to the plaintive and seductive sentiment, so harmonious even when broken, so thrilling even when most checked and hushed, was quite as little to be withstood. Like the ass betwixt two bundles of hay, my eyes wandered from one to the other uncertain where to fix. And thus passed the two first hours after breakfast.

The third brought an acquisition to our party. We heard the

trampling of horses' feet in the court below, and all hurried to the
windows, to see the new comer. We had but a glimpse of him—
a tall, good-looking personage, about thirty years of age, with
great whiskers, and a huge military cloak. Squire Owens met
him in the reception room, and they remained some half hour or
three quarters together. It was evidently a business visit. The
girls were all agog to know what it was about, and I was mortified to think that Emmeline was now far less eager to interest me
than before. She now turned listlessly over the pages of her music book, or strummed upon the keys of her piano, with the air of
one whose thoughts were elsewhere. Susannah did not seem so
much disturbed,—she still continued to draw my attention to the
more pleasing passages of the poet; but I could see, or I fancied,
that even she was somewhat curious as to the coming of the stranger. Her eyes turned occasionally to the parlour door at the slightest approaching sound, and she sometimes looked in my face with
a vacant eye, when I was making some of my most favourable
points of conversation.

At length there was a stir within, a buzz and the scraping of
feet. The door was thrown open, and, ushered by the father, the
stranger made his appearance. His air was rather *distingué*.
His person was well made, tall and symmetrical. His face was
martial and expressive. His complexion was of a rich dark
brown; his eye was grey, large, and restless—his hair thin, and
dishevelled. His carriage was very erect; his coat, which was
rather seedy, was close buttoned to his chin. His movements were
quick and impetuous, and seemed to obey the slightest sound,
whether of his own, or of the voices of others. He approached
the company with the manner of an old acquaintance; certainly,
with that of a man who had always been conversant with the best
society. His ease was unobtrusive,—a polite deference invariably distinguishing his deportment whenever he had occasion to
address the ladies. Still, he spoke as one having authority.
There was a lordly something in his tones,—an emphatic assurance in his gesture,—that seemed to settle every question; and,
after a little while, I found that, hereafter, if I played on any fiddle at all, in that presence, it was certainly not to be the first.
Emmeline and Susannah had ears for me no longer. There was

22

a something of impatience in the manner of the former whenever I spoke, as if I had only interrupted much pleasanter sounds; and, even Susannah, the meek Susannah, put down her Coleridge upon a stool, and seemed all attention, only for the imposing stranger.

The effect upon the old man was scarcely less agreeable. Col. Nelson,—so was the stranger called—had come to see about the purchase of his upper mill-house tract—a body of land containing some four thousand acres, the sale of which was absolutely ne-cessary to relieve him from certain incumbrances. From the conversation which he had already had with his visitor, it ap-peared that the preliminaries would be of easy adjustment, and Squire Owens was in the best of all possible humours. It was nothing but Col. Nelson,—Col. Nelson   The girls did not seem to need this influence, though they evidently perceived it; and, in the course of the first half hour after his introduction, I felt myself rapidly becoming *de trop*. The stranger spoke in passion-ate bursts,—at first in low tones,—with halting, hesitating man-ner, then, as if the idea were fairly grasped, he dilated into a tor-rent of utterance, his voice rising with his thought, until he start-ed from his chair and confronted the listener. I cannot deny that there was a richness in his language, a warmth and colour in his thought, which fascinated while it startled me. It was only when he had fairly ended that one began to ask what had been the prov-ocation to so much warmth, and whether the thought to which we had listened was legitimately the growth of previous suggestions. But I was in no mood to listen to the stranger, or to analyze what he said. I found my situation quite too mortifying—a mortification which was not lessened, when I perceived that neither of the two damsels said a word against my proposed departure. Had they shown but the slightest solicitude, I might have been reconciled to my temporary obscuration. But no! they suffered me to rise and declare my purpose, and made no sign. A cold courtesy from them, and a stately and polite bow from Col. Nelson, ac-knowledged my parting salutation, and Squire Owens attended me to the threshold, and lingered with me till my horse was got in readiness. As I dashed through the gateway, I could hear the rich voice of Emmeline swelling exultingly with the tones of her piano, and my fancy presented me with the images of Col. Nelson, hanging over her on one hand, while the meek Susannah on the other, was casting those oblique glances upon him which had so frequently been addressed to me. "Ah! pestilent jades," I exclaimed in the bitterness of a boyish heart; "this then is the love of woman."

CHAPTER IV.

CHEWING such bitter cud as this, I had probably ridden a good mile, when suddenly I heard the sound of human voices, and looking up, discovered three men, mounted, and just in front of me. They had hauled up, and were seemingly awaiting my approach. A buzzing conversation was going on among them. " That's he !" said one. " Sure ?" was the question of another. A whistle at my very side caused me to turn my head, and as I did so, my horse was caught by the bridle, and I received a severe blow from a club above my ears, which brought me down, almost unconscious, upon the ground. In an instant, two stout fellows were upon me, and busy in the praiseworthy toil of roping me, hands and feet, where I lay. Hurt, stung, and utterly confounded by the surprise, I was not prepared to suffer this indignity with patience. I made manful struggle, and for a moment succeeded shaking off both assailants. But another blow, taking effect upon my temples, and dealt with no moderate appliance of hickory, left me insensible. When I recovered consciousness, I found myself in a cart, my hands tied behind me, my head bandaged with a red cotton handkerchief, and my breast and arms covered with blood. A stout fellow rode beside me in the cart, while another drove, and on each side of the vehicle trotted a man, well armed with a double-barrelled gun.

" What does all this mean ?" I demanded. " Why am I here? Why this assault ? What do you mean to do with me ?"

" Don't be obstropolous," said one of the men. " We don't mean to hurt you ; only put you safe. We had to tap you on the head a little, for your own good."

" Indeed !" I exclaimed, the feeling of that unhappy tapping upon the head, making me only the sorer at every moment—" but will you tell me what this is for, and in what respect did my good require that my head should be broken ?"

" It might have been worse for you, where you was onbeknown," replied the spokesman,—"but we knowd your situation, and sarved you off easily. Be quiet now, and———"

"What do you mean—what is my situation?"

"Well, I reckon we know. Only you be quiet, or we'll have to give you the skin."

And he held aloft a huge wagon whip as he spoke. I had sufficient proof already of the unscrupulousness with which my companions acted, not to be very chary of giving them farther provocation, and, in silent misgiving, I turned my head to the opposite side of the vehicle. The first glance in this quarter revealed to me the true history of my disaster, and furnished an ample solution of the whole mystery. Who should I behold but the very fellow whom I had chased into town the day before. The truth was now apparent. I had been captured as the stray bedlamite from Hamilton jail. It was because of this that I had been "tapped on the head—only for my own good." As the conjecture flashed upon me, I could not avoid laughter, particularly as I beheld the still doubtful and apprehensive visage of the man beside me. My laughter had a very annoying effect upon all parties. It was a more fearful sign than my anger might have been. The fellow whom I had scared, edged a little farther from the cart, and the man who had played spokesman, and upon whom the whole business seemed to have devolved, now shook his whip again—"None of that, my lad," said he, "or I'll have to bruise you again. Don't be obstroplous."

"You've taken me up for a madman, have you?" said I.

"Well, I reckon you ought to know what you are. There's no disputing it."

"And this silly fellow has made you believe it?"

"Reckon!"

"You've made a great mistake."

"Don't think it."

"But you have: Only take me to C——, and I'll prove it by General Cocke, himself, or Squire Humphries, or any body in the town."

"No! no! my friend,—that cock won't fight. We aint misdoubting at all, but you're the right man. You answer all the descriptions, and Jake Sturgis here, has made his affidavy that you chased him, neck and neck, as mad as any blind puppy in a dry September, for an hour by sun yesterday.   We don't want no more proof."

"And where do you mean to carry me?" I enquired, with all the coolness I was master of.

"Well, we'll put you up in a pen we've got a small piece from here; and when the sheriff comes, he'll take you back to your old quarters at Hamilton jail, where I reckon they'll fix you a little tighter than they had you before.   We've sent after the sheriff, and his 'spose-you-come-and-take-us,' and I reckon they'll be here about sun-down."

CHAPTER V.

HERE was a "sitiation" indeed. Burning with indignation, I
was yet sufficiently master of myself to see that any ebullition of
rage on my part, would only confirm the impressions which they
had received of my insanity. I said little therefore, and that little was confined to an attempt to explain the chase of yesterday,
which Jake Sturgis had made the subject of such a mischievous
"affidavy." But as I could not do this without laughter, I incurred the danger of the whip. My laugh was ominous.—Jake
edged off once more to the roadside; the man beside me, got his
bludgeon in readiness, and the potent wagon whip of the leader
of the party, was uplifted in threatening significance. Laughter
was clearly out of the question, and it naturally ceased on my
part, as I got in sight of the "*pen*" in which I was to be kept secure. This structure is one well known to the less civilized regions of the country. It is a common place of safe keeping in
the absence of gaols and proper officers. It is called technically
a "bull pen," and consists of huge logs, roughly put together,
crossing at right angles, forming a hollow square,—the logs too
massy to be removed, and the structure too high to be climbed,
particularly if the prisoner should happen to be, like myself, fairly tied up hand and foot together. I relucted terribly at being
put into this place. I pleaded urgently, struggled fiercely, and
was thrust in neck and heels without remorse; and, in sheer hopelessness and vexation, I lay with my face prone to the earth, and
half buried among the leaves, weeping, I shame to confess it, the
bitter tears of impotence and mortification.

Meantime, the news of my capture went through the country;
—not *my* capture, mark me, but that of the famous madman,
Archy Dargan, who had broke Hamilton jail. This was an
vent, and visitors began to collect. My captors, who kept watch
on the outside of my den, had their hands full in answering questions. Man, woman and child, Squire and ploughboy, and, finally,

dames and damsels, accumulated around me, and such a throng of eyes as pierced the crevices of my log dungeon, to see the strange monster by whom they were threatened, now disarmed of his terrors, were,—to use the language of one of my keepers—"a power to calkilate." This was not the smallest part of my annoyance. The logs were sufficiently far apart to suffer me to see and to be seen, and I crouched closer to my rushes, and buried my face more thoroughly than ever, if possible, to screen my dishonoured visage from their curious scrutiny. This conduc mightily offended some of the visitors.

"I can't see his face," said one.

"Stir him with a long pole!"—and I was greatly in danger of being treated as a surly bear, refusing to dance for his keeper; since one of mine seemed very much disposed to gratify the spectator, and had actually begun sharpening the end of a ten foot hickory, for the purpose of pricking me into more sociableness. He was prevented from carrying his generous design into effect by the suggestion of one of his companions.

"Better don't, Bosh; if ever he should git out agen, he'd put his ear mark upon you."

"Reckon you're right," was the reply of the other, as he laid his rod out of sight.

Meanwhile, the people came and went, each departing visitor sending others. A couple of hours might have elapsed leaving me in this humiliating situation, chained to the stake, the beast of a bear garden, with fifty greedy and still dissatisfied eyes upon me. Of these, fully one fourth were of the tender gender; some pitied me, some laughed, and all congratulated themselves that I was safely laid by the heels, incapable of farther mischief. It was not the most agreeable part of their remarks, to find that they all universally agreed that I was a most frightful looking object. Whether they saw my face or not, they all discovered that I glared frightfully upon them, and I heard one or two of them ask in under tones, "did you see his teeth—how sharp!" I gnashed them with a vengeance all the while, you may be sure.

CHAPTER VI.

THE last and worst humiliation was yet to come—that which put me for a long season out of humour with all human and wo-man nature. Conscious of an unusual degree of bustle without, I was suddenly startled by sounds of a voice that had been once pleasingly familiar. It was that of a female, a clear, soft, trans-parent sound, which, till this moment, had never been associated in my thoughts with any thing but the most perfect of all mortal melodies. It was now jangled harsh, like "sweet bells out of tune." The voice was that of Emmeline. "Good heavens!" I exclaimed to myself—' can she be here?" In another instant, I heard that of Susannah—the meek Susannah,—she too was among the curious to examine the features of the bedlamite, Archy Dar-gan."

"Dear me," said Emmeline, "is he in that place?"

"What a horrid place!" said Susannah.

"It's the very place for such a horrid creature," responded Emmeline.

"Can't he get out, papa?" said Susannah. "Isn't a mad per-son very strong?"

"Oh! don't frighten a body, Susannah, before we have had a peep," cried Emmeline; "I declare I'm afraid to look—do, Col. Nelson, peep first and see if there's no danger."

And there was the confounded Col. Nelson addressing his eyes to my person, and assuring his fair companions, my Emmeline, my Susannah, that there was no sort of danger,—that I was evi-dently in one of my fits of apathy.

"The paroxysm is off for the moment, ladies,—and even if he were violent, it is impossible that he should break through the pen. He seems quite harmless—you may look with safety."

"Yes, he's mighty quiet now, Miss,"—said one of my keepers encouragingly, "but it's all owing to a close sight of my whip. He was a-guine to be obstroplous more than once, when I shook it over him—he's usen to it, I reckon. You can always tell when the roaring fit is coming on—for he breaks out in such a dreadful sort of laughing."

"Ha! Ha!—he laughs does he—Ha! Ha!" such was the somewhat wild interruption offered by Col. Nelson himself. If my laugh produced such an effect upon my keeper, his had a very disquieting effect upon me. But, the instinctive conviction that Emmeline and Susannah were now gazing upon me, prompted me with a sort of fascination, to lift my head and look for them. I saw their eyes quite distinctly. Bright treacheries! I could distinguish between them—and there were those of Col. Nelson beside them—the three persons evidently in close propinquity.

"What a dreadful looking creature!" said Susannah.

"Dreadful!" said Emmeline, "I see nothing so dreadful in him. He seems tame enough. I'm sure, if that's a madman, I don't see why people should be afraid of them."

"Poor man, how bloody he is!" said Susannah.

"We had to tap him, Miss, a leetle upon the head, to bring him quiet. He's tame and innocent now, but you should see him when he's going to break out. Only just hear him when he laughs."

I could not resist the temptation. The last remark of my keeper fell on my ears like a suggestion, and suddenly shooting up my head, and glaring fiercely at the spectators, I gave them a yell of laughter as terrible as I could possibly make it.

"Ah!" was the shriek of Susannah, as she dashed back from the logs. Before the sounds had well ceased, they were echoed from without, and in more fearful and natural style from the practised lungs of Col. Nelson. His yells following mine, were enough to startle even me.

"What!" he cried, thrusting his fingers through the crevice, 'you would come out, would you,—you would try your strength with mine. Let him out,—let him out! I am ready for him, breast to breast, man against man, tooth and nail, forever and forever. You can laugh too, but—Ha! Ha! Ha!—what do you say to that? Shut up, shut up, and be ashamed of yourself. Ha! Ha! Ha!"

There was a sensation without. I could see that Emmeline

recoiled from the side of her companion.   He had thrown himself
into an attitude, had grappled the logs of my dungeon, and
exhibited a degree of strange emotion, which, to say the least,
took every body by surprise.   My chief custodian was the first to
speak.

"Don't be scared, Mr.—there's no danger—he can't get out."

"But I say let him out—let him out.   Look at him, ladies—
look at him.   You shall see what a madman is—you shall see
how I can manage him.   Hark ye, fellow,—out with him at once.
Give me your whip—I know all about his treatment.   You shall
see me work him.   I'll manage him,—I'll fight with him, and
laugh with him too—how we shall laugh—Ha! Ha! Ha!"

His horrible laughter,—for it was horrible—was cut short by
an unexpected incident.   He was knocked down as suddenly as
I had been, with a blow from behind, to the astonishment of all
around.   The assailant was the sheriff of Hamilton jail, who had
just arrived and detected the fugitive, Archy Dargan—the most
cunning of all bedlamites, as he afterwards assured me,—in the
person of the handsome Col. Nelson.

"I knew the scamp by his laugh—I heard it half a mile," said
the sheriff, as he planted himself upon the bosom of the prostrate
man, and proceeded to leash him in proper order.   Here was a
concatenation accordingly.

"Who hev' I got in the pen?" was the sapient inquiry of my
captor—the fellow whose whip had been so potent over my imagination.

"Who?   Have you any body there?" demanded the sheriff.

"I reckon!—We cocht a chap that Jake made affidavy was
the madman."

"Let him out then, and beg the man's pardon.   I'll answer for
Archy Dargan."

My appearance before the astonished damsels was gratifying to
neither of us.   I was covered with mud and blood,—and they
with confusion.

"Oh! Mr. ———, how could we think it was you, such a
fright as they've made you."

Such was Miss Emmeline's speech after her recovery.   Susannah's was quite as characteristic.

"I am so very sorry, Mr. ———."

"Spare your regrets, ladies," I muttered ungraciously, as I leapt on my horse. "I wish you a very pleasant morning."

"Ha! Ha! Ha!" yelled the bedlamite, writhing and bounding in his leash—"a very pleasant morning."

The damsels took to their heels, and went off in one direction quite as fast as I did in the other. Since that day, dear reader, I have never suffered myself to scare a fool, or to fall in love with a pair of twins; and if ever I marry, take my word for it, the happy woman shall neither be a Susannah, nor an Emmeline.

THE LAZY CROW.

A STORY OF THE CORNFIELD

~~~~~~~~~~~~~~~~~~~~~~~~

CHAPTER I.

WE were on the Savannah river when the corn was coming up; at the residence of one of those planters of the middle country, the staid, sterling, old-time gentlemen of the last century, the stock of which is so rapidly diminishing. The season was advanced and beautiful; the flowers every where in odour, and all things promised well for the crops of the planter. Hopes and seed, however, set out in March and April, have a long time to go before ripening, and when I congratulated Mr. Carrington on the prospect before him, he would shake his head, and smile and say, in a quizzical inquiring humour, " wet or dry, cold or warm, which shall it be? what season shall we have? Tell me that, and I will hearken with more confidence to your congratulations. We can do no more than plant the seed, scuffle with the grass, say our prayers, and leave the rest to Him without whose blessing no labour can avail."

" There is something more to be done, and of scarcely less importance it would seem, if I may judge from the movements of Scipio—kill or keep off the crows."

Mr. Carrington turned as I spoke these words; we had just left the breakfast table, where we had enjoyed all the warm comforts of hot rice-waffles, journey-cake, and glowing biscuit, not to speak of hominy and hoe-cake, without paying that passing acknowledgment to dyspeptic dangers upon which modern physicians so earnestly insist. Scipio, a sleek, well-fed negro, with a round, good-humoured face, was busy in the corner of the apartment;

one hand employed in grasping a goodly fragment of bread, half-concealed in a similar slice of fried bacon, which he had just received from his young mistress ;—while the other carefully selected from the corner, one of half-a-dozen double-barrelled guns, which he was about to raise to his shoulder, when my remark turned the eye of his master upon him.

" How now, Scipio, what are you going to shoot ?" was the inquiry of Mr. Carrington.

" Crow, sa ; dere's a dratted ugly crow dat's a-troubling me, and my heart's set for kill 'um."

" One only ; why Scip, you're well off if you hav'n't a hundred. Do they trouble you very much in the pine land field ?"

" Dare's a plenty, sa ; but dis one I guine kill, sa, he's wuss more nor all de rest. You hab good load in bote barrel, mossa ?"

" Yes, but small shot only. Draw the loads, Scip, and put in some of the high duck ; you'll find the bag in the closet. These crows will hardly let you get nigh enough, Scipio, to do them any mischief with small shot."

" Ha ! but I will trouble dis black rascal, you see, once I set eye 'pon um. He's a cussed ugly nigger, and he a'n't feared I can git close 'nough, mossa."

The expression of Scipio's face, while uttering the brief declaration of war against the innumerable, and almost licensed pirates of the cornfield, or rather against one in particular, was full of the direst hostility. His accents were not less marked by malignity, and could not fail to command our attention.

" Why, you seem angry about it, Scipio ; this crow must be one of the most impudent of his tribe, and a distinguished character."

" I'll 'stinguish um, mossa,—you'll see. Jist as you say, he's a mos' impudent nigger. He no feared of me 't all. When I stan' and look 'pon him, he stan' and look 'pon me. I tak' up dirt and stick, and trow at um, but he no scare. When I chase um, he fly dis way, he fly dat, but he nebber gone so far, but he can turn round and cock he tail at me, jist when he see me 'top. He's a mos' cussed sassy crow, as ebber walk in a cornfield."

" But Scip, you surprise me. You don't mean to say that it is one crow in particular that annoys you in this manner."

"De same one ebbery day, mossa; de same one;" was the reply.

"How long has this been ?

"Mos' a week now, massa; ebber sence las' Friday."

"Indeed! but what makes you think this troublesome crow always the same one, Scipio? Do you think the crows never change their spies ?"

"Enty, I know um, mossa; dis da same crow been trouble me, ebber since las' Friday. He's a crow by hese'f, mossa. I nebber see him wid t'oder crows he no hab complexion ob t'oder crow, yet he's crow, all de same."

"Is he not black like all his tribe ?"

"Yes, he black, but he ain't black like de t'oder ones. Dere's someting like a grey dirt 'pon he wing. He's black, but he no pot black—no jet;—he hab dirt, I tell you, mossa, on he wing, jis' by de skirt ob he jacket—jis yer;" and he lifted the lappel of his master's coat as he concluded his description of the bird that troubled him.

"A strange sort of crow indeed, Scipio, if he answers your description. Should you kill him, be sure and bring him to me I can scarcely think him a crow."

"How, no crow, mossa? Enty, I know crow good as any body! He's a crow, mossa,—a dirty, black nigger ob a crow and I'll shoot um t'rough he head, sure as a gun. He trouble me too much; look hard 'pon me as ef you bin gib um wages for obersee. Nobody ax um for watch me, see wha' I do! Who mak' him obersheer?"

"A useful crow, Scipio; and now I think of it, it might be just as well that you shouldn't shoot him. If he does such good service in the cornfield as to see that you all do your work, I'll make him my overseer in my absence!"

This speech almost astounded the negro. He dropped the butt of the gun upon the floor, suffered the muzzle to rest in the hollow of his arm, and thus boldly expostulated with his master against so strange a decision.

"No shoot um, mossa; no shoot crow dat's a-troubling you. Dickens, mossa, dat's too foolish now, I mus' tell you; and to tell you de blessed trut', ef you don't shoot dis lazy crow I tell you ob, or le' me shoot 'um, one or t'oder, den you

mus' take Scip out ob de cornfiel', and put 'noder nigger in
he place.   I can't work wid dat ugly ting, looking at me so
sassy.   When I turn. he turn; if I go to dis hand, why, he's
dere ; if I change 'bout, and go t'oder hand, dere's de critter, jis de same.   He nebber git out ob de way, 'till I run at um
wid stick."

"Well, well, Scipio, kill your crow, but be sure and bring him
in when you do so.   You may go now."

"I hab um to-night for you, mossa, ef God spare me.   Look
ya, young missis, you hab any coffee lef' in de pot; I tanks
you."

Jane Carrington,—a gentle and lovely girl of seventeen—who
did the honours of the table, supplied Scipio's wants, and leaving
him to the enjoyment of his mug of coffee, Mr. C. and myself
walked forth into the plantation.

The little dialogue just narrated had almost entirely passed out
of my mind, when, at evening, returning from his labours in the
cornfield, who should make his appearance but Scipio.   He came
to place the gun in the corner from which he had taken it; but
he brought with him no trophies of victory.   He had failed to
scalp his crow.   The inquiry of his master as to his failure,
drew my attention to the negro, who had simply placed the weapon in the rest, and was about to retire, with a countenance, as
I thought, rather sullen and dissatisfied, and a hang-dog, sneaking manner, as if anxious to escape observation.   He had utterly lost that air of confidence which he had worn in the morning.

"What, Scipio ! no crow ?" demanded his master.

"I no shoot, sa," replied the negro, moving off as he spoke
as if willing that the examination should rest there.   But Mr.
Carrington, who was something of a quiz, and saw that the poor
fellow laboured under a feeling of mortified self-conceit, was not
unwilling to worry him a little further.

"Ah, Scip, I always thought you a poor shot, in spite of your
bragging; now I'm sure of it.   A crow comes and stares you
but of countenance, walks round you, and scarcely flies when
you pelt him, and yet, when the gun is in your hands, you do
nothing.   How's that ?"

"I tell you, mossa, I no bin shoot. Ef I bin shoot, I bin hurt um in he head for true; but dere' no use for shoot, tel you can get shot, enty? Wha' for trow 'way de shot?—you buy 'em, —he cos' you money; well, you hab money for trow 'way? No! Wha' c 'ip's a big rascal for true, ef he trow '-- you money. Dat's trow 'way you money, wha's trow 'way you shot,—wha's trow you corn, you peas, you fodder, you hog-meat, you chickens and eggs. Scip nebber trow 'way you property, mossa; nobody nebber say sich ting."

"Cunning dog—nobody accuses you, Scipio. I believe you to be as honest as the rest, Scipio, but haven't you been throwing away time; haven't you been poking about after this crow to the neglect of your duty. Come, in plain language, did you get through your task to-day?"

"Task done, mossa; I finish um by tree 'clock."

"Well, what did you do with the rest of your time? Have you been at your own garden, Scipio?"

"No, sa; I no touch de garden."

"Why not? what employed you from three o'clock?"

"Dis same crow, mossa; I tell you, mossa, 'tis dis same dirty nigger ob a crow I bin looking arter, ebber since I git over de task. He's a ting da's too sassy and aggrabates me berry much. I follow um. el de sun shut he eye, and nebber can git shot. Ef I bin git shot, I nebber miss um, mossa, I tell you."

"But why did you not get a shot? You must have bungled monstrously, Scipio, not to succeed in getting a shot at a bird that is always about you. Does he bother you less than he did before, now that you have the gun?"

"I spec' he mus' know, mossa, da's de reason; but he bodder me jis' de same. He nebber leff me all day I bin in de corn-field, but he nebber come so close for be shoot. He say to he sef, dat gun good at sixty yard, in Scip hand; I stan' sixty, I stan' a hundred; ef he shoot so far, I laugh at 'em. Da's wha' he say."

"Well, even at seventy or eighty yards, you should have tried him, Scipio. The gun that tells at sixty, will be very apt to tell at seventy or eighty yards, if the nerves be good that hold it, and the eye close. Try him even at a hundred, Scipio, rather than lose your crow; but put in your biggest shot."

23

CHAPTER II.

THE conference ended with this counse. of the maste   The fellow promised to obey, and the next morning he sallied forth with the gun as before. By this time, both Mr. Carrington and myself had begun to take some interest in the issue thus tacitly made up between the field negro and his annoying visiter. The anxiety which the former manifested, to destroy, in particular, one of a tribe, of which the corn-planter has an aversion so great as to prompt the frequent desire of the Roman tyrant touching his enemies, and make him wish that they had but one neck that a single blow might despatch them—was no less ridiculous than strange ; and we both fell to our fancies to account for an hostility, which could not certainly be accounted for by any ordinary anxiety of the good planter on such an occasion. It was evident to both of us that the imagination of Scipio was not inactive in the strife, and, knowing how exceeding superstitious the negroes generally are, (and indeed, all inferior people,) after canvassing the subject in various lights, without coming to any rational solution, we concluded that the difficulty arose from some grotesque fear or fancy, with which the fellow had been inspired, probably by some other negro, on a circumstance as casual as any one of the thousand by which the Roman augur divined, and the soothsayer gave forth his oracular responses. Scipio had good authority for attaching no small importance to the flight or stoppage of a bird ; and, with this grave justification of his troubles, we resolved to let the matter rest till we could join the negro in the cornfield, and look for ourselves into the condition of the rival parties.

This we did that very morning. " 'Possum Place,"—for such had been the whimsical name conferred upon his estate by the proprietor, in reference to the vast numbers of the little animal, nightly found upon it, the opossum, the meat of which a sagacious negro will always prefer to that of a pig,—lay upon the Santee swamp, and consisted pretty evenly of reclaimed swamp-land, in which he raised his cotton, and fine high pine-land hammock, on which he made his corn.   To one of the fields of the latter we made our way about mid-day, and were happy to find Scipio in actual controversy with the crow that troubled him.   Controversy is scarce the word, but I can find no fitter at this moment. The parties were some hundred yards asunder.   The negro was busy with his hoe, and the gun leaned conveniently at hand on a contiguous and charred pine stump, one of a thousand that dotted he entire surface of the spacious field in which he laboured. The crow leisurely passed to and fro along the alleys, now lost among the little hollows and hillocks, and now emerging into sight, sometimes at a less, sometimes at a greater distance, but always with a deportment of the most lord-like indifference to the world around him.   His gait was certainly as stately and as lazy as that of a Castilian the third remove from a king and the tenth from a shirt.   We could discover in him no other singularity but this marked audacity ; and both Mr. Carrington's eyes and mine were stretched beyond their orbits, but in vain, to discover that speck of " gray dirt upon he wing," which Scipio had been very careful to describe with the particularity of one who felt that the duty would devolve on him to brush the jacket of the intruder. We learned from the negro that his sooty visiter had come alone as usual,—for though there might have been a sprinkling of some fifty crows here and there about the field, we could not perceive that any of them had approached to any more familiarity with the one that annoyed him, than with himself.   He had been able to get no shot as yet, though he did not despair of better fortune through the day ; and, in order to the better assurance of his hopes, the poor fellow had borne what he seemed to consider the taunting swagger of the crow all around him, without so much as lifting weapon, or making a single step towards him.

"Give me your gun," said Mr. Carrington.   "If he walks no faster than now, I'll give him greater weight to carry."

But the lazy crow treated the white man with a degree of deference that made the negro stare.   He made off at full speed with the first movement towards him, and disappeared from sight in a few seconds. We lost him seemingly among the willows and fern of a little bay that lay a few hundred yards beyond us.

"What think you of that, Scip?" demanded the master. "I've done more with a single motion than you've done for days, with all your poking and pelting. He'll hardly trouble you in a hurry again, though, if he does, you know well enough now, how to get rid of him."

"The negro's face brightened for an instant, but suddenly changed, while he replied,—

"Ah, mossa, when you back turn, he will come 'gen—he dah watch you now."

Sure enough,—we had not proceeded a hundred yards, before the calls of Scipio drew our attention to the scene we had left. The bedevilled negro had his hand uplifted with something of an air of horror, while a finger guided us to the spot where the lazy crow was taking his rounds, almost in the very place from whence the hostile advance of Mr. Carrington had driven him; and with a listless, lounging strut of aristocratic composure, that provoked our wonder quite as much as the negro's indignation.

"Let us see it out," said Mr. C., returning to the scene of action. "At him, Scipio; take your gun and do your best."

But this did not seem necessary. Our return had the effect of sending the sooty intruder to a distance, and, after lingering some time to see if he would reappear while we were present, but without success, we concluded to retire from the ground. At night, we gathered from the poor negro that our departure was the signal for the crow's return. He walked the course with impunity, though Scipio pursued him several times, and towards the close of day, in utter desperation, gave him both barrels, not only without fracturing a feather, but actually, according to Scip's story, without occasioning in him the slightest discomposure or alarm. He merely changed his place at each onset, doubled on his own ground, made a brief circuit, and back again to the old station, looking as impudently, and walking along as lazily as ever.

CHAPTER III.

Some days passed by and I saw nothing of Scipio. It appears, however, that his singular conflict with the lazy crow was carried on with as much pertinacity on the one side, and as little patience on the other, as before. Still, daily, did he provide himself with the weapon and munitions of war, making as much fuss in loading it, and putting in shot as large as if he purposed warfare on some of the more imposing occupants of the forest, rather than a simple bird, so innocent in all respects except the single one of corn-stealing, as the crow. A fact, of which we obtained possession some time after, and from the other negroes, enlightened us somewhat on the subject of Scipio's own faith as to the true character of his enemy. In loading his gun, he counted out his shot, being careful to get an odd number. In using big buck he numbered two sevens for a load; the small buck, three; and seven times seven duck shot, when he used the latter, were counted out as a charge, with the studious nicety of the jeweller at his pearls and diamonds. Then followed the mystic process of depositing the load within the tube, from which it was to issue forth in death and devastation. His face was turned from the sunlight; the blaze was not suffered to rest upon the bore or barrel; and when the weapon was charged, it was carried into the field only on his left shoulder. In spite of all these preparations, the lazy crow came and went as before. He betrayed no change of demeanour; he showed no more consciousness of danger; he submitted to pursuit quietly, never seeming to hurry himself in escaping, and was quite as close an overseer of Scipio's conduct, as he had shown himself from the first. Not a day passed that the negro failed to shoot at him; always, however, by his own account, at disadvantage, and never, it appears, with any success. The consequence of all this was, that Scipio fell sick. What with the constant annoyance of the thing, and a too excitable imagination, Scipio, a stout fellow nearly six feet high, and half as many broad, laid himself at length in his cabin, at the end of the week, and was placed on the sick-list accordingly. But as a negro will never take physic if he can help it, however ready he may be to complain, it was not till Sunday afternoon, that Jane Carrington, taking her customary stroll on that day to the negro quarters, ascertained the fact. She at once apprised her father, who was something of a physician, (as every planter should be,) and who immediately proceeded to visit the invalid. He found him without any of the customary signs of sickness. His pulse was low and feeble, rather than full or fast ; his tongue tolerably clean ; his skin not unpleasant, and, in all ordinary respects Scipio would have been pronounced in very good condition for his daily task, and his hog and hominy. But he was an honest fel- low, and the master well knew that there was no negro on his plantation so little given to " playing 'possum," as Scipio. He complained of being very unwell, though he found it difficult to designate his annoyances, and say where or in what respect his ail- ing lay. Questions only confused and seemed to vex him, and, though really skilful in the cure of such complaints as ordinarily occur on a plantation, Mr. Carrington, in the case before him, was really at a loss. The only feature of Scipio's disease that was apparent, was a full and raised expression of the eye, that seemed to swell out whenever he spoke, or when he was required to direct his attention to any object, or answer to any specific in- quiry. The more the master observed him, the more difficult it became to utter an opinion, and he was finally compelled to leave him for the night, without medicine, judging it wiser to let na- ture take the subject in hand until he could properly determine in what respect he suffered. But the morrow brought no allevi- ation of Scipio's sufferings. He was still sick as before—inca- pable of work,—indeed, as he alleged, unable to leave his bed, though his pulse was a little exaggerated from the night previous, and exhibited only that degree of energy and fulness, which might be supposed natural to one moved by sudden physical ex- citement. His master half-suspected him of shamming, but the lugubrious expression of the fellow's face, could scarcely be as- sumed for any purpose, and was to all eyes as natural as could be. He evidently thought himself in a bad way. I suggested some simple medicine, such as salts or castor oil—any thing, indeed, which could do no harm, and which could lessen the patient's apprehensions, which seemed to increase with the evident inability of his master to give him help. Still he could scarcely tell where it hurt him; his pains were every where, in head, back, shoulder, heels, and strange to say, at the tips of his ears. Mr. C. was puzzled, and concluded to avoid the responsibility of such a case, by sending for the neighbouring physician.

Dr. C——, a very clever and well-read man, soon made his appearance, and was regularly introduced to the patient. His replies to the physician were as little satisfactory as those which he had made to us; and, after a long and tedious cross examination by doctor and master, the conclusion was still the same. Some few things, however, transpired in the inquiry, which led us all to the same inference with the doctor, who ascribed Scipio's condition to some mental hallucination. While the conversation had been going on in his cabin—a dwelling like most negro houses, made with poles, and the chinks stopped with clay,—he turned abruptly from the physician to a negro girl that brought him soup, and asked the following question.

"Who bin tell Gullah Sam for come in yer yesserday?"

The girl looked confused, and made no answer.

"Answer him," said the master.

"Da's him—why you no talk, nigger?" said the patient authoritatively. "I ax you who bin tell Gullah Sam for come in yer yesserday?"

"He bin come?" responded the girl with another inquiry.

"Sure, he bin come—enty I see um wid he dirty gray jacket, like dirt on a crow wing. He tink I no see um—he 'tan dere in dis corner, close de chimney, and look wha's a cook in de pot. Oh, how my ear bu'n—somebody's a talking bad tings 'bout Scipio now."

There was a good deal in this speech to interest Mr. Carrington and myself; we could trace something of his illness to his strife with the crow; but who was Gullah Sam? This was a question put both by the doctor and myself, at the same moment.

"You no know Gullah Sam, enty? Ha! better you don't

know 'um—he's a nigger da's more dan nigger—wish he min'
he own bis'ness."

With these words the patient turned his face to the wall of his
habitation, and seemed unwilling to vouchsafe us any farther
speech. It was thought unnecessary to annoy him with farther
inquiries, and, leaving the cabin we obtained the desired information from his master.

"Gullah Sam," said he, " is a native born African from the
Gold Coast, who belongs to my neighbour, Mr. Jamison, and was
bought by his father out of a Rhode Island slaver, some time before the Revolution. He is now, as you may suppose, rather an
old man ; and, to all appearances, would seem a simple and silly
one enough ; but the negroes all around conceive him to be a great
conjurer, and look upon his powers as a wizard, with a degree of
dread, only to be accounted for by the notorious superstition of ignorance. I have vainly endeavoured to overcome their fears and
prejudices on this subject ; but the object of fear is most commonly, at the same time, an object of veneration, and they hold on to
the faith which has been taught them, with a tenacity like that
with which the heathen clings to the idol, the wrath of which he
seeks to deprecate, and which he worships only because he fears.
The little conversation which we have had with Scipio, in his
partial delirium, has revealed to me what a sense of shame has
kept him from declaring before. He believes himself to be bewitched by Gullah Sam, and, whether the African possesses any
power such as he pretends to or not, is still the same to Scipio, if
his mind has a full conviction that he does, and that he has become its victim. A superstitious negro might as well be bewitched, as to fancy that he is so."

"And what do you propose to do ?" was my inquiry.

"Nay, that question I cannot answer you. It is a work of
philosophy, rather than of physic, and we must become the masters of the case, before we can prescribe for it. We must note
the fancies of the patient himself, and make these subservient to
the cure. I know of no other remedy."

CHAPTER IV.

THAT evening, we all returned to the cabin of Scipio. We found him more composed—sane, perhaps, would be the proper word—than in the morning, and, accordingly, perfectly silent on the subject of Gullah Sam. His master took the opportunity of speaking to him in plain language.

"Scipio, why do you try to keep the truth from me? Have you ever found me a bad master, that you should fear to tell me the truth?"

"Nebber say sich ting! Who tell you, mossa, I say you bad?" replied the negro with a lofty air of indignation, rising on his arm in the bed.

"Why should you keep the truth from me?" was the reply.

"Wha' trut' I keep from you, mossa?"

"The cause of your sickness, Scipio. Why did you not tell me that Gullah Sam had bewitched you?"

The negro was confounded.

"How you know, mossa?" was his demand.

"It matters not," replied the master, "but how came Gullah Sam to bewitch you?"

"He kin 'witch den, mossa?" was the rather triumphant demand of the negro, who saw, in his master's remark, a concession to his faith, which had always been withheld before. Mr. Carrington extricated himself from the dilemma with sufficient promptness and ingenuity.

"The devil has power, Scipio, over all that believe in him. If you believe that Gullah Sam can do with you what he pleases, in spite of God and the Saviour, there is no doubt that he can; and God and the Saviour will alike give you up to his power, since, when you believe in the devil, you refuse to believe in them. They have told you, and the preacher has told you, and I have told you, that Gullah Sam can do you no sort of harm, if you will refuse to believe in what he tells you. Why then do you believe in that miserable and ignorant old African, sooner than in God and the preacher, and myself?"

"I can't help it, mossa—de ting's de ting, and you can't change 'um. Dis Gullah Sam—he wus more nor ten debble—I jis' laugh at 'um t'oder day—tree week 'go, when he tumble in de hoss pond, and he shake he finger at me, and ebber since he put he bad mout' pon me. Ebber sence dat time, dat ugly crow bin stand in my eyes, whichebber way I tu'n. He hab gray dirt on he wing, and enty dere's a gray patch on Gullah Sam jacket? Gullah Sam hab close 'quaintan' wid dat same lazy crow da's walk roun' me in de cornfield, mossa. I bin tink so from de fuss; and when he 'tan and le' me shoot at 'um, and no 'fraid, den I sartain."

"Well, Scipio," said the master, "I will soon put an end to Sam's power. I will see Mr. Jamison, and will have Sam well flogged for his witchcraft. I think you ought to be convinced that a wizard who suffers himself to be flogged, is but a poor devil after all."

The answer of the negro was full of consternation.

"For Chris' sake, mossa, I beg you do no sich ting. You lick Gullah Sam, den you lose Scipio for eber and eber, amen. Gullah Sam nebber guine take off de bad mout' he put on Scip, once you lick em. De pains will keep in de bones—de leg will dead, fuss de right leg, den de lef, one arter t'oder, and you nigger will dead, up and up, till noting lef for dead but he head. He head will hab life, when you kin put he body in de hole, and cubbur um up wid du't. You mus' try n'oder tings, mossa, for get you nigger cure—you lick Gullah Sam, 'tis kill um for ebber."

A long conversation ensued among us, Scipio taking occasional part in it; for, now that his secret was known, he seemed somewhat relieved, and gave utterance freely to his fears and superstitions; and determined for and against the remedies which we severally proposed, with the authority of one, not only more deeply interested in the case than any one beside, but who also knew more about it. Having unscrupulously opposed nearly every plan, even in its inception, which was suggested, his master, out of all patience, at last exclaimed,

" Well, Scipio, it seems nothing will please you.   What would
you have ? what course shall I take to dispossess the devil, and
send Gullah Sam about his business ?"

After a brief pause, in which the negro twisted from side to
side of his bed, he answered as follows :

" Ef you kin trow way money on Scip, mossa, dere's a way I
tink 'pon, dat'll do um help, if dere's any ting kin help um now,
widout go to Gullah Sam. But it's a berry 'spensive way, mossa."

" How much will it cost ?" demanded the master.   " I am not
unwilling to pay money for you, either to cure you when you are
sick, as you ought to know by my sending for the doctor, or by
putting more sense into your head than you seem to have at present.   How much money do you think it will take to send the
devil out of you ?"

" Ha ! mossa, you no speak 'spectful 'nough.   Dis Gullah Sam
hard to move ; more dan de lazy crow dat walk in de cornfield.
He will take money 'nough ; mos' a bag ob cotton in dese hard
times."

" Pshaw—speak out, and tell me what you mean !" said the
now thoroughly impatient master.

" Dere's an old nigger, mossa, dat's an Ebo,—he lib ober on
St. Matt'ew's, by de bluff, place of Major Thompson. He's mighty
great hand for cure bad mout'.   He's named 'Tuselah, and he's
a witch he sef, worse more nor Gullah Sam.   Gullah Sam fear'd
um—berry fear'd um.   You send for 'Tuselah, mossa, he cos'
vou more nor twenty dollars.   Scipio git well for sartin, and you
nebber yerry any more 'bout dat sassy crow in de cornfield."

" If I thought so," replied Mr. Carrington, looking round upon
us, as if himself half ashamed to give in to the suggestions of the
negro ; " if I thought so, I would certainly send for Methuselah.
But really, there's something very ridiculous in all this."

" I think not," was my reply.   " Your own theory will sustain
you, since, if Scipio's fancy makes one devil, he is equally assured, by the same fancy, of the counter power of the other."

" Besides," said the doctor, " you are sustained by the prov-
erb, ' set a thief to catch a thief.'   The thing is really curious.
I shall be anxious to see how the St. Matthew's wizard overcomes
him of Santee ; though, to speak truth, a sort of sectional interest

in my own district, would almost tempt me to hope that he may be defeated. This should certainly be my prayer, were it not that I have some commiseration for Scipio. I should be sorry to see him dying by inches."

" By feet rather," replied his master with a laugh. " First the right leg, then the left, up and up, until life remains to him in his head only. But, you shall have your wish, Scipio. I will send a man to-morrow by daylight to St. Matthew's for Methuselah, and if he can overcome Gullah Sam at his own weapons, I shall not begrudge him the twenty dollars."

" Tenks, mossa, tousand tenks," was the reply of the invalid ; his countenance suddenly brightening for the first time for a week, as if already assured of the happy termination of his affliction. Meanwhile, we left him to his cogitations, each of us musing to himself, as well on the singular mental infirmities of a negro, at once sober, honest, and generally sensible, and that strange sort of issue which was about to be made up, between the respective followers of the rival principles of African witchcraft, the Gullah and the Ebo fetishes.

CHAPTER V.

The indulgent master that night addressed a letter to the owner of Methuselah, stating all the circumstances of the case, and soliciting permission for the wizard, of whom such high expectations were formed, or fancied, to return with the messenger, who took with him an extra horse that the journey might be made with sufficient despatch. To this application a ready assent was given, and the messenger returned on the day after his departure, attended by the sage personage in question.

Methuselah was an African, about sixty-five years of age, with a head round as an owl's, and a countenance quite as grave and contemplative. His features indicated all the marked characteristics of his race, low forehead, high cheek bone, small eyes, flat nose, thick lips, and a chin sharp and retreating. He was not more than five feet high, and with legs so bowed that—to use Scipio's expression, when he was so far recovered as to be able again to laugh at his neighbour,—a yearling calf might easily run between them without grazing the *calf*. There was nothing promising in such a person but his sententiousness and gravity, and Methuselah possessed these characteristics in remarkable degree. When asked—

"Can you cure this fellow?" his answer, almost insolently expressed, was,—

" I come for dat."

" You can cure people who are bewitched?"

" He no dead?"

" No."

" Belly well; I cure em;—can't cure dead nigger."

There was but little to be got out of such a character by examination, direct or cross; and attending him to Scipio's wigwam, we tacitly resolved to look as closely into his proceedings as we could, assured, that in no other way could we possibly hope to arrive at any knowledge of his *modus operandi* in so curious a case.

Scipio was very glad to see the wizard of St. Matthew's, and pointing to a chair, the only one in his chamber, he left us to the rude stools, of which there happened to be a sufficient supply.

" Well, brudder," said the African abruptly, " wha's matter ?"

" Ha, Mr. 'Tuselah, I bin hab berry bad mout' put 'pon me."

" I know dat—you eyes run water—you ears hot—you hab knee shake—you trimble in de joint."

" You hit um ; 'tis jis' dém same ting.   I hab ears bu'n berry muc'i," and thus encouraged to detail his symptoms, the garrulous Scipio would have prolonged his chronicle to the crack of doom, but that the wizard valued his time too much, to suffer any unnecessary eloquence on the part of his patient.

" You see two tings at a time ?" asked the African.

" How ! I no see," replied Scipio, not comprehending the question, which simply meant, do you ever see double ?   To this, when explained, he answered in a decided negative.

" 'Tis a man den, put he bad mout' 'pon you," said the African.

" Gor-a-mighty, how you knew dat ?" exclaimed Scipio.

" Hush, my brudder—wha' beas' he look like ?"

" He's a d—n black nigger ob a crow—a dirty crow, da's lazy for true."

" Ha ! he lazy—you sure he ain't lame ?'

" He no lame."

Scipio then gave a close description of the crow which had pestered him, precisely as he had given it to his master, as recorded in our previous pages.   The African heard him with patience, then proceeded with oracular gravity.

" 'Tis old man wha's trouble you !"

" Da's a trute !"

" Hush, my brudder.   Whay you bin see dis crow ?'

" Crow in de cornfiel', Mr. 'Tuselah ; he can't come in de house."

" Who bin wid you all de time ?"

" Jenny—de gal—he 'tan up in de corner now."

The magician turned and looked upon the person indicated by Scipio's finger—a little negro girl, probably ten years old.   Then turning again to Scipio, he asked,

" You bin sick two, tree, seben day, brudder—how long you bin on you bed ?"

" Since Saturday night—da's six day to-day."

" And you hab nobody come for look 'pon you, since you bin on de bed, but dis gal, and de buckrah ?"

Scipio confessed to several of the field negroes, servants of his own master, all of whom he proceeded to describe in compliance with the requisitions of the wizard, who, as if still unsatisfied, bade him, in stern accents, remember if nobody else had been in the cabin, or, in his own language, had " set he eye 'pon you."

The patient hesitated for awhile, but the question being repeated, he confessed that in a half-sleep or stupor, he had fancied seeing Gullah Sam looking in upon him through the half-opened door ; and at another time had caught glimpses, in his sleep, of the same features, through a chink between the logs, where the clay had fallen.

" Ha ! ha !" said the wizard, with a half-savage grin of mingled delight and sagacity—" I hab nose,—I smell. Well, brudder, I mus' gib you physic,—you mus' hab good sweat to-night, and smood skin to-morrow."

Thus ended the conference with Scipio. The man of mystery arose and left the hovel, bidding us follow, and carefully fastening the door after him.

This done, he anointed some clay, which he gathered in the neighbourhood, with his spittle, and plastered it over the lintel. He retired with us a little distance, and when we were about to separate, he for the woods, and we for the dwelling-house, he said in tones more respectful than those which he employed to Mr. Carrington on his first coming,

" You hab niggers, mossa—women is de bes'—dat lub for talk too much ?"

" Yes, a dozen of them."

" You sen' one to de plantation where dis Gullah Sam lib, but don't sen' um to Gullah Sam ; sen' um to he mossa or he missis ; and borrow someting—any ting—old pot or kettle—no matter if you don't want 'em, you beg um for lend you. Da's 'nough."

Mr. Carrington would have had the wizard's reasons for this wish, but finding him reluctant to declare them,. he promised his consent, concluding, as was perhaps the case, that the only object was to let Gullah Sam know that a formidable enemy had taken the field against him, and in defence of his victim.* This would seem to account for his desire that the messenger should be a woman, and one " wha' lub for talk too much." He then obtained directions for the nearest path to the swamp, and when we looked that night into the wigwam of Scipio, we found him returned with a peck of roots of sundry sorts, none of which we knew, prepared to make a decoction, in which his patient was to be immersed from head to heels. Leaving Scipio with the contemplation of this steaming prospect before him, we retired for the night, not a little anxious for those coming events which cast no shadow before us, or one so impenetrably thick, that we failed utterly to see through it.

* Since penning the above conjecture, I remember a story which was related to me several years ago, by a venerable country lady of South Carolina, who, to the merit of telling a good story well, added the equally commendable merit of always believing the story which she told—in which it was insisted upon, in these controversies between rival wizards, and, if I mistake not, in all cases where witch or wizard aimed to operate, that, to obtain complete success, it was necessary that they should succeed in borrowing something out of the house which was to be the scene of their diablerie. In this story, though a mere boy at the time, I can well remember the importance attached by a mother to the instructions which she gave her daughter, on going abroad, to lend nothing out of the house, under any circumstances, or to any body, during her absence. She had scarcely disappeared,—the story went on to relate, —before an old woman of the neighbourhood, whose intentions were already suspected, came to borrow a sieve. The girl, without admitting her into the house, for the door had been locked by the provident mother, answered her demand through the window by an unvarying refusal. Baffled in her aim by the child's firmness, the prayers and entreaties of the applicant were changed into the bitterest abuse and execrations; clearly showing, whatever might have been her pretensions or powers of evil, the devilish malignity of purpose which she entertained

CHAPTER VI.

In the morning, strange to say, we found Scipio considerably better, and in singularly good spirits. The medicaments of the African, or more likely the pliant imagination of the patient him-self, had wrought a charm in his behalf; and instead of groan-ing at every syllable, as he had done for several days before, he now scarcely uttered a word that was not accompanied by a grin. The magician seemed scarcely less pleased than his patient, par-ticularly when he informed us that he had not only obtained the article the woman was sent to borrow, but that Gullah Sam had been seen prowling, late at night, about the negro houses, without daring, however, to venture nigh that of the invalid—a forbear-ance which the necromancer gave us to understand, was entirely involuntary, and in spite of the enemy's desire, who was baffled and kept away by the spell contained in the ointment which he had placed on the lintel, in our presence the evening before. Still, half-ashamed of being even quiescent parties merely to this sol-emn mummery, we were anxious to see the end of it, and our African promised that he would do much towards relieving Scipio from his enchantment, by the night of the same day. His spells and fomentations had worked equally well, and Scipio was not only more confident in mind, but more sleek and strong in body. With his own hands, it appears, that the wizard had rub-bed down the back and shoulders of his patient with corn-shucks steeped in the decoction he had made, and, what was a more strange specific still, he had actually subjected Scipio to a smart-er punishment, with a stout hickory, than his master had given him for many a year. This, the poor fellow not only bore with Christian fortitude, but actually rejoiced in, imploring addi-tional strokes when the other ceased. We could very well un-derstand that Scipio deserved a whipping for laughing at an aged man, because he fell into the water, but we failed to ascertain from the taciturn wizard, that this was the rationale of an appli

24

catiou which a negro ordinarily is never found to approve. This over, Scipio was again put to bed, a green twig hung over the door of his cabin within, while the unctuous plaster was renewed freshly on the outside. The African then repeated certain uncouth sounds over the patient, bade him shut his eyes and go to sleep, in order to be in readiness and go into the fields by the time the sun was turning for the west.

"What," exclaimed Mr. Carrington, "do you think him able to go into the field to-day? He is very weak; he has taken little nourishment for several days."

"He mus' able," returned the imperative African; "he 'trong 'nough. He mus' able—he hab for carry gun."

With these words the wizard left us without deigning any explanation of his future purposes, and, taking his way towards the swamp, he was soon lost to our eyes in the mighty depth of its shrouding recesses.

When he returned, which was not till noon, he came at once to the mansion-house, without seeking his patient, and entering the hall where the family was all assembled, he challenged our attention as well by his appearance as by his words. He had, it would seem, employed himself in arranging his own appearance while in the swamp; perhaps, taking one of its thousand lakes or ponds for his mirror. His woolly hair, which was very long, was plaited carefully up, so that the ends stuck out from his brow, as pertly and pointedly as the tails of pigs, suddenly aroused to a show of delightful consciousness on discovering a forgotten corn-heap. Perhaps that sort of tobacco, known by the attractive and characteristic title of "pigtail," would be the most fitting to convey to the mind of the reader the peculiar form of plait which the wizard had adopted for his hair. This mode of disposing of his matted mop, served to display the tattooed and strange figures upon his temples,—the certain signs, as he assured us, of princely rank in his native country. He carried a long wand in his hand, freshly cut and peeled, at one end of which he had tied a small hempen cord. The skin of the wand was plaited round his own neck. In a large leaf he brought with him a small portion of some stuff which he seemed to preserve very carefully, but which appeared to us to be nothing more than coarse sand or gravel. To this he added a small portion of salt, which he obtained from the mistress of the house, and which he stirred together in our presence until the salt had been lost to the eye in the sand or gravel, or whatever might have been the article which he had brought with him. This done, he drew the shot from both barrels of the gun, and in its place, deposited the mixture which he had thus prepared.

"Buckrah will come 'long now. Scipio guine looka for de crow."

Such were his words, which he did not wait to hear answered or disputed, but taking the gun, he led the way towards the wigwam of Scipio. Our anxiety to see the conclusion of the adventure, did not suffer us to lose any time in following him. To our surprise, we found Scipio dressed and up ; ready, and it would seem perfectly able, to undertake what the African assigned him. The gun was placed in his hands, and he was told to take his way to the cornfield as usual, and proceed to work. He was also informed by the wizard, with a confidence that surprised us, that the lazy crow would be sure to be there as usual ; and he was desired to get as close as he could, and take good aim at his head in shooting him.

"You sure for hit um, brudder," said the African ; "so, don't 'tan too long for look. Jis' you git close, take you sight, and gib um bot' barrel. But fuss, 'fore you go, I mus' do someting wid you eye."

The plaster was taken from the door, as Scipio passed through it, re-softened with the saliva of the wizard, who, with his finger, described an arched line over each of the patient's eyes.

"You go 'long by you'sef now, brudder, and shoot de crow when you see um. He's a waiting for you now, I 'spec'."

We were about to follow Scipio to the field, but our African kept us back ; and leading the way to a little copse that divided it from the swamp, he took us to its shelter, and required us to remain with him out of sight of the field, until some report from Scipio or his gun, should justify us in going forth.

CHAPTER VII.

HERE we remained in no little anxiety for the space of nearly two hours, in which time, however, the African showed no sort of impatience, and none of that feverish anxiety which made us restless in body and eager, to the last degree, in mind. We tried to fathom his mysteries, but in vain. He contented himself with assuring us that the witchcraft which he used, and that which he professed himself able to cure, was one that never could affect the white man in any way. He insisted that the respective gods of the two races were essentially very different; as different as the races themselves. He also admitted that the god of the superior race was necessarily equal to the task of governing both, while the inferior god could only govern the one —that of taking charge of his, was one of those small businesses, with which it was not often that the former would soil his hands. To use his own phrase, "there is a god for de big house, and another for de kitchen."

While we talked over these topics, and strove, with a waste of industry, to shake the faith of the African in his own peculiar deities and demons, we heard the sound of Scipio's gun—a sound that made us forget all nicer matters of theology, and set off with full speed towards the quarter whence it came. The wizard followed us slowly, waving his wand in circles all the way, and pulling the withes from his neck, and casting them around him as he came. During this time, his mouth was in constant motion, and I could hear at moments, strange, uncouth sounds breaking from his lips. When we reached Scipio, the fellow was in a state little short of delirium. He had fired both barrels, and had cast th gun down upon the ground after the discharge. He was wringing his hands above his head in a sort of phrensy of joy, and at our approach he threw himself down upon the earth, laughing with the delight of one who has lost his wits in a dream of pleasure.

" Where's the crow ?" demanded his master.

" I shoot um—I shoot um in he head—enty I tell yc , mossa, I will hit um in he head ? Soon he poke he nose ober ᴅᵉ ground, I gib it to um. Hope he bin large shot. He gone t'rough he head,—t'rough and t'rough. Ha! ha! ha! If dat crow be Gullah Sam! if Gullah Sam be git in crow jacket, ho, mossa! he nebber git out crow jacket 'till somebody skin um. Ha! ha! ho! ho! ho! ki! ki! ki! ki! la! ki! Oh, mossa, wonder how Gullah Sam feel in crow jacket!"

It was in this strain of incoherent exclamation, that the invalid gave vent to his joyful paroxysm at the thought of having put a handful of duck shot into the hide of his mortal enemy. The unchristian character of his exultation received a severe reproof from his master, which sobered the fellow sufficiently to enable us to get from him a more sane description of his doings. He told us that the crow had come to bedevil him as usual, only— and the fact became subsequently of considerable importance,— that he had now lost the gray dirt from his wing, which had so peculiarly distinguished it before, and was now as black as the most legitimate suit ever worn by crow, priest, lawyer, or physician. This change in the outer aspect of the bird had somewhat confounded the negro, and made him loth to expend his shot, for fear of wasting the charmed charge upon other than the genuine Simon Pure. But the deportment of the other—lazy, lounging, swaggering, as usual—convinced Scipio in spite of his eyes, that his old enemy stood in fact before him ; and without wasting time, he gave him both barrels at the same moment.

" But where's the crow ?" demanded the master.

" I knock um ober, mossa ; I see um tumble ; 'speck you find um t'oder side de cornhill."

Nothing could exceed the consternation of Scipio, when, on reaching the designated spot, we found no sign of the supposed victim. The poor fellow rubbed his eyes, in doubt of their visual capacities, and looked round aghast, for an explanation, to the wizard who was now approaching, waving his wand in long sweeping circles as he came, and muttering, as before, those strange uncouth sounds, which we relished as little as we understood. He did not seem at all astonished at the result of Scipio's shot, but abruptly asked of him—" Whay's de fus' water, brudder Scip ?"

" De water in de bay, Mass 'Tuselah," was the reply ; the speaker pointing as he spoke to the little spot of drowned land on the very corner of the field, which, covered with thick shoots of the small sweet bay tree,—the magnolia glauca,—receives its common name among the people from its almost peculiar growth.

" Push for de bay ! push for de bay !" exclaimed the African, " and see wha' you see. Run, Scip ; run, nigger—see wha' lay in de bay !"

These words, scarcely understood by us, set Scipio in motion. At full speed he set out, and, conjecturing from his movement, rather than from the words of the African, his expectations, off we set also at full speed after him. Before we reached the spot, to our great surprise, Scipio emerged from the bay, dragging behind him the reluctant and trembling form of the aged negro, Gullah Sam. He had found him washing his face, which was covered with little pimples and scratches, as if he had suddenly fallen into a nest of briars. It was with the utmost difficulty we could prevent Scipio from pummelling the dreaded wizard to death.

" What's the matter with your face, Sam ?" demanded Mr. Carrington.

" Hab humour, Mass Carrington ; bin trouble berry mosh wid break out in de skin."

" Da shot, mossa—da shot. I hit um in crow jacket ; but whay's de gray di't ? Ha ! mossa, look yer ; dis de black coat ob Mass Jim'son dat Gullah Sam hab on. He no wear he jacket with gray patch. Da's make de diff"rence."

The magician from St. Matthew's now came up, and our surprise was increased when we saw him extend his hand, with an appearance of the utmost good feeling and amity, to the rival he had just overcome.

" Well, brudder Sam, how you come on ?"

The other looked at him doubtfully, and with a countenance in which we saw, or fancied, a mingling expression of fear and hostility ; the latter being evidently restrained by the other. H·

gave his hand, however, to the grasp of Methuselah, but said no thing.

"I will come take supper wid you to-night, brudder Sam," continued the wizard of St. Matthew's, with as much civility as if he spoke to the most esteemed friend under the sun. "Scip, boy, you kin go to you mossa work—you quite well ob dis bus'ness."

Scipio seemed loth to leave the company while there appeared something yet to be done, and muttered half aloud,

"You no ax Gullah Sam, wha' da' he bin do in de bay."

"Psha, boy, go 'long to you cornfiel'—enty I know," replied Methuselah. "Gullah Sam bin 'bout he own bus'ness, I s'pose. Brudder, you kin go home now, and get you tings ready for supper. I will come see you to-night."

It was in this manner that the wizard of St. Matthew's was disposed to dismiss both the patient and his persecutor; but here the master of Scipio interposed.

"Not so fast, Methuselah. If this fellow, Sam, has been playing any of his tricks upon my people, as you seem to have taken for granted, and as, indeed, very clearly appears, he must not be let off so easily. I must punish him before he goes."

"You kin punish um more dan me?" was the abrupt, almost stern inquiry of the wizard.

There was something so amusing as well as strange in the whole business, something so ludicrous in the wo-begone visage of Sam, that we pleaded with Mr. Carrington that the whole case should be left to Methuselah; satisfied that as he had done so well hitherto, there was no good reason, nor was it right, that he should be interfered with. We saw the two shake hands and part, and ascertained from Scipio that he himself was the guest of Gullah Sam, at the invitation of Methuselah, to a very good supper that night of pig and 'possum. Scipio described the affair as having gone off very well, but he chuckled mightily as he dwelt upon the face of Sam, which, as he said, by night, was completely raw from the inveterate scratching to which he had been compelled to subject it during the whole day. Methuselah the next morning departed, having received, as his reward, twenty dollars from the master, and a small pocket Bible from the young mistress of the negro; and to this day, there is not a negro in the surrounding

country—and many of the whites are of the same way of thinking—who does not believe that Scipio was bewitched by Gullah
Sam, and that the latter was shot in the face, while in the shape
of a common crow in the cornfield, by the enchanted shot provided by the wizard of St. Matthew's for the hands of the other.

The writer of this narrative, for the sake of vitality and dramatic force, alone, has made himself a party to its progress. The
material has been derived as much from the information of others,
as from his own personal experience ; though it may be as well to
add, that superstition among the negroes is almost as active to
this day, in the more secluded plantations, as it was prior to the
revolution. Nor is it confined to the negro only. An instance
occurred only a few years ago,—the facts of which were given
me by a gentleman of unquestionable veracity,—in which one of
his poor, uneducated white neighbours, labouring under a protracted, and perhaps, novel form of disease, fancied himself the
victim of a notorious witch or wizard in his own district, and
summoned to his cure the rival wizard of another. Whether the
controversy was carried in the manner of that between Gullah
Sam and Methuselah, I cannot say ; nor am I sure that the conquest was achieved by the wizard summoned. My authorities
are no less good than various, for the *procès nécromantique*, as de-
tailed above. It may be that I have omitted some of the mummery that seemed profane or disgusting ; for the rest

> " I vouch not for the truth, d'ye see,
> But tell the tale as 'twas told to me '

CALOYA;

OR, THE LOVES OF THE DRIVER

~~~~~~~~~~~~~~~~~

CHAPTER I.

WHEN I was a boy, it was the custom of the Catawba Indians —then reduced to a pitiful remnant of some four hundred persons, all told—to come down, at certain seasons, from their far homes in the interior, to the seaboard, bringing to Charleston a little stock of earthen pots and pans, skins and other small matters, which they bartered in the city for such commodities as were craved by their tastes, or needed by their condition. They did not, however, bring their pots and pans from the nation, bu descending to the low country empty-handed, in groups or families, they squatted down on the rich clay lands along the Edisto raised their poles, erected their sylvan tents, and there established themselves in a temporary abiding place, until their simple potteries had yielded them a sufficient supply of wares with which to throw themselves into the market. Their productions had their value to the citizens, and, for many purposes, were considered by most of the worthy housewives of the past generation, to be far superior to any other. I remember, for example, that it was a confident faith among the old ladies, that okra soup was always inferior if cooked in any but an Indian pot; and my own impressions make me not unwilling to take sides with the old ladies on this particular tenet. Certainly, an iron vessel is one of the last which should be employed in the preparation of this truly southern dish. But this aside. The wares of the Indians were not ill made, nor unseemly to the eye. They wrought with much cleaner hands than they usually carried; and if their vases were sometimes unequal in their proportions, and uncouth in their forms, these defects were more than compensated by their freedom from flaws and their general capaciousness and strength.   Wanting, perhaps, in the loveliness and perfect symmetry of Etruscan art, still they were not entirely without pretensions of their own   The ornamental enters largely into an Indian's idea of the useful, and his taste pours itself out lavishly in the peculiar decorations which he bestows upon his wares.   Among his first purchases when he goes to the great city, are vermilion, umber, and other ochres, together with sealing wax of all colours, green, red, blue and yellow.   With these he stains his pots and pans until the eye becomes sated with a liberal distribution of flowers, leaves, vines and stars, which skirt their edges, traverse their sides, and completely illuminate their externals.   He gives them the same ornament which he so judiciously distributes over his own face, and the price of the article is necessarily enhanced to the citizen, by the employment of materials which the latter would much rather not have at all upon his purchases.   This truth, however, an Indian never will learn, and so long as I can remember, he has still continued to paint his vessels, though he cannot but see that the least decorated are those which are always the first disposed of. Still, as his stock is usually much smaller than the demand for it, and as he soon gets rid of it, there is no good reason which he can perceive why he should change the tastes which preside over his potteries.

Things are greatly altered now-a-days, in these as in a thousand other particulars.   The Catawbas seldom now descend to the seaboard.   They have lost the remarkable elasticity of character which peculiarly distinguished them among the aboriginal nations, and, in declining years and numbers, not to speak of the changing circumstances of the neighbouring country, the ancient potteries are almost entirely abandoned.   A change has taken place among the whites, scarcely less melancholy than that which has befallen the savages.   Our grandmothers of the present day no longer fancy the simple and rude vessels in which the old dames took delight.   We are for Sêvre's Porcelain, and foreign goods wholly, and I am saddened by the reflection that I have seen the last of the Indian pots.   I am afraid, henceforward, that my okra soup will only be made in vessels from Brummagem; nay, even now, as it comes upon the table, dark, dingy and discoloured to my eye, I think I see unequivocal tokens of metallic influence upon the mucilaginous compound, and remember with a sigh, the glorious days of Catawba pottery.   New fashions, as usual, and conceited refinements, have deprived us of old pleasures and solid friends.   A generation hence, and the fragment of an Indian pot will be a relic, a treasure, which the lover of the antique will place carefully away upon the upper shelf of the *sanctum*, secure from the assaults of noisy children and very tidy housekeepers, and honoured in the eyes of all worthy-minded persons, as the sole remaining trophy of a time when there was perfection in one, at least, of the achievements of the culinary art. I am afraid that I have seen the last of the Indian pots!

But let me avoid this melancholy reflection.   Fortunately, my narrative enables me to do so.   It relates to a period when this valuable manufacture was in full exercise, and, if not encouraged by the interference of government, nor sought after by a foreign people, was yet in possession of a patronage quite as large as it desired.   To arrive at this important period we have only to go back twenty years—a lapse made with little difficulty by most persons, and yet one which involves many and more trying changes and vicissitudes than any of us can contemplate with equanimity. The spring season had set in with the sweetest of countenances, and the Catawbas, in little squads and detachments, were soon under way with all their simple equipments on their backs for the lower country.   They came down, scattering themselves along the Edisto, in small bodies which pursued their operations independently of each other.   In this distribution they were probably governed by the well known policy of the European Gipseys, who find it much easier, in this way, to assess the several neighbourhoods which they honour, and obtain their supplies without provoking apprehension and suspicion, than if they were, *en masse* to concentrate themselves on any one plantation.   Their camps might be found in famed loam-spots, from the Eutaws down to Parker's Ferry, on the Edisto, and among the numerous swamps that lie at the head of Ashley River, and skirt the Wassamasaw country.   Harmless usually, and perfectly inoffensive, they were seldom repelled or resisted, even when they made their camp contiguously to a planter's settlements; though, at such periods, the proprietor had his misgivings that his poultry yard suffered from other enemies than the Wild-cat, and his hogs from an assailant as unsparing as the Alligator. The overseer, in such cases, simply kept a sharper lookout than ever, though it was not often that any decisive consequences followed his increased vigilance. If the Indians were at any time guilty of appropriation, it was not often that they suffered themselves to be brought to conviction. Of all people, they, probably, are the most solicitous to obey the scripture injunction, and keep the right hand from any unnecessary knowledge of the doings of the left.

CHAPTER II.

ONE morning, early in this pleasant season, the youthful pro.
prietor of a handsome plantation in the neighbourhood of the Ashley River, might have been seen taking his solitary breakfast, at
a moderately late hour, in the great hall of his family mansion.
He was a tall, fine-looking young man, with quick, keen, lively
gray eyes, that twinkled with good humour and a spirit of playful
indulgence. A similar expression marked his features in general,
and lessened the military effect of a pair of whiskers, of which
the display was too lavish to be quite becoming. He had but
recently come into possession of his property, which had been
under the guardianship of an uncle. His parents had been cut
off by country fever while he was yet a child, and, as an only son,
he found, at coming of age, that his estates were equally ample
and well managed. He was one of those unfortunate young
bachelors, whose melancholy loneliness of condition is so apt to
arrest the attention, and awaken the sympathies of disinterested
damsels, and all considerate mothers of unappropriated daughters,
who are sufficiently well-informed in scripture authority, to know
that " it is not meet for man to be alone." But young Col. Gillison was alone, and continued, in spite of good doctrine, to be
alone for several long years after. Into the causes which led to
this strange and wilful eccentricity, it forms no part of our object
to inquire. Our story does not so much concern the master of
the plantation as one of his retainers, whom the reader will please
to imagine that he has seen, more than once, glancing his eye impatiently from the piazza through the window, into the apartment,
awaiting the protracted moment when his young master should
descend to his breakfast. This was a stout negro fellow, of port-
ly figure and not uncomely countenance. He was well made
and tall, and was sufficiently conscious of his personal attractions,
to take all pains to exhibit them in the most appropriate costume
and attitude. His pantaloons were of very excellent nankin, and

his coat, made of seersucker, was one of the most picturesque known to the southern country. It was fashioned after the Indian hunting shirt, and formed a very neat and well-fitting frock, which displayed the broad shoulders and easy movements of Mingo—for that was the negro's name—to the happiest advantage.

Mingo was the driver of the estate. The driver is a sort of drill-sergeant to the overseer, who may be supposed to be the Captain. He gets the troops in line, divides them into squads, sees to their equipments, and prepares them for the management and command of the superiors. On the plantation of Col. Gillison, there was at this time no overseer; and, in consequence, the import-ance of Mingo was not a little increased, as he found himself acting in the highest executive capacity known to his experience. Few persons of any race, colour, or condition, could have had a more elevated idea of their own pretensions than our present subject. He trod the earth very much as its Lord—the sovereign shone out in every look and movement, and the voice of supreme authority spoke in every tone. This feeling of superiority im-parted no small degree of grace to his action, which, accordingly, would have put to shame the awkward louting movements of one half of those numbed and cramped figures which serve at the emasculating counters of the trading city. Mingo was a Her-cules to the great majority of these; and, with his arms akimbo, his head thrown back, one foot advanced, and his hands, at inter-vals, giving life to his bold, and full-toned utterance, he would startle with a feeling not unlike that of awe, many of those bent, bowed and mean-looking personages who call themselves freemen, and yet have never known the use, either of mind or muscle, in one twentieth part the degree which had been familiar to this slave.

At length, after a delay which evidently did not diminish the impatience of Mingo, his young master descended to the breakfast room. His appearance was the signal for the driver to enter the same apartment, which he accordingly did without pause or preparation.

"Well, Mingo," said the young man, with lively tones—"what's the word this morning? Your face seems full of news! and now that I consider you closely, it seems to have smitten your

body also. You look fuller than I have ever seen you before
Out with your burden, man, before you burst.   What sow's lit-
tered—what cow's cast her calf—how many panels in the fence
are burnt—how many chickens has the hawk carried off this
morning?   What! none of these?" he demanded, as the shake
of the head, on the part of his hearer, which followed every distinct suggestion of the speaker, disavowed any subject of complaint from those current evils which are the usual subject of a
planter's apprehension.   "What's the matter, then, Mingo?"

"Matter 'nough, Mossa, ef we don't see to it in time," responded Mingo, with a becoming gravity.   "It's a needcessity," a driver's English is sometimes terribly emphatic, "it's a needcessity,
Sir, to see to other cattle, besides hogs and cows.   The chickens
too, is intended to, as much as they wants; and *I* ha'nt lost a
panel by fire, eber sence Col. Parker's hands let the fire get 'way
by Murray's Thick.   There, we did lose a smart chance, and
put us back mightily, I reckon ; but that was in old mossa's time,
and we had Mr. Groning, den, as the obershar—so, you see, Sir,
I couldn't be considered bound 'sponsible for that; sence I've had
the management, there ha'nt been any loss on my plantation of
any kind.   My fences ha'nt been burn, my cattle's on the rise,
and as for my hogs and chickens, I reckon there's not a plantation on the river that kin make so good a count at Christmas.
But——"

"Well, well, Mingo," said the youthful proprietor, who knew
the particular virtue of the driver, and dreaded that his tongue
should get such headway as to make it unmanageable—"if
there's no loss, and no danger of loss—if the hogs and chickens
are right, and the cattle and the fences—we can readily defer
the business until after breakfast. Here, boy, hand up the coffee."

"Stop a bit, Mossa—it aint right—all aint right—" said the
impressive Mingo—"it's a business of more transaction and de-
portance than the cattle and the fences—it's——"

"Well, out with it then, Mingo—there's no need for a long
preamble.   What is the trouble?"

"Why, Sir, you mus' know," began the driver, in no degree
pleased to be compelled to give his testimony in any but his own
fashion, and drawling out his accents accordingly, so as to in-

crease the impatience of his master, and greatly to elongate the sounds of his own voice—sounds which he certainly esteemed to be among the most musical in nature.——" You mus' know den, Sir, that Limping Jake came to me a while ago, tells me as how, late last night, when he was a-hunting 'possum, he came across an Indian camp, down by the ' Red Gulley.' They had a fire, and was a-putting up the poles, and stripping the bark to cover them. Jake only seed two of them ; but it's onpossible that they'll stick at that. Before we know anything, they'll be spreading like varmints all about us, and putting hands and teeth on every thing, without so much as axing who mout be the owner."

" Well, Mingo, what of all this ?" demanded the master, as the driver came to a pause, and looked volumes of increased dignity, while he concluded the intelligence which he meant to be as-tounding.

" Wha' of all this, Mossa !—Why, Sir, de'rs 'nough of it. Ef the hogs and the chickens did'nt go before, they'll be very apt to go now, with these red varmints about us."

" Surely, if you don't look after them ; but that's your busi-ness, Mingo. You must see to the poultry houses yourself, at night, and keep a close watch over these squatters so long as they are pleased to stay."

" But, Mossa, I aint gwine to let 'em stay ! To my idee, that's not the wisdom of the thing. Now, John Groning, the obershar of old mossa—though I don't much reprove of his onderstanding in other expects, yet he tuk the right reason, when he druv them off, bag and baggage, and wouldn't let hoof nor hide of 'em stretch off upon the land. I ha'nt seen these red varmints, myself, but I come to let you know, that I was gwine out to asperse, and send 'em off, under the shake of a cowhide, and then there's no farther needcessity to keep a look out upon them. I'm not willing to let such critters hang about *my* plantation."

The reader has already observed, that an established driver speaks always of his charge as if it were a possession of his own. With Mingo, as with most such, it was *my* horse, *my* land, *my* ox, and *my* ass, and all that is *mine*. His tone was much subdued, as he listened to the reply of his master, uttered in accents some-thing sterner than he had been wont to hear.

" I'm obliged to you, Mingo, for coming to inform me of your intentions.   Now, I command you to do nothing of this sort.   Let these poor devils remain where they are, and do you attend to your duty, which is to see that they do no mischief.   If I mistake not, the ' Red Gulley' is the place where they have been getting their clay ever since my grandfather settled this plantation."

" That's a truth, Sir, but——"

" Let them get it there still.   I prefer that they should do so, even though I may lose a hog now and then, and suffer some decrease in the fowl yard.   I am pleased that they should come to the accustomed place for their clay——"

" But, Sir, only last year, John Groning druv 'em off."

" I am the better pleased then, at the confidence they repose in me.   Probably they know that John Groning can no longer drive them off.   I am glad that they give me an opportunity to treat them more justly.   They can do me little harm, and as their fathers worked in the same holes, I am pleased that they, too, should work there.   I will not consent to their expulsion for such small evils as you mention.   But I do not mean, Mingo, that they shall be suffered to infest the plantation, or to do any mischief. You will report to me, if you see any thing going wrong, and to do this while they stay ; you will look very closely into their proceedings.   I, myself, will have an eye upon them, and if there be but two of them, and they seem sober, I will give them an allowance of corn while they stay."

" Well, but Mossa, there's no needcessity for that, and considering that the Corn-House aint oberfull—"

" No more at present, Mingo.   I will see into the matter during the day.   Meanwhile, you can ride out to the ' Red Gulley,' see these people, and say to them, from me, that, so long as they behave themselves civilly, they may remain.   I am not satisfied that these poor wretches should be denied camping ground and a little clay, on a spot which their people once possessed exclusively.   I shall probably see them after you, and will then be better able to determine upon their deserts."

25

CHAPTER III

MINGO retired from the conference rather chap-fallen. He was not so well satisfied with the result of his communication. He had some hope to commend himself more than ever to his youthful master by the zeal and vigilance which he had striven to display. Disappointed in this hope, he was still further mortified to perceive how little deference was shown him by one, whose youthful judgment he hoped to direct, and of whose inexperience he had possibly some hope to take advantage. He loved to display his authority, and sometimes seemed absolutely to fancy himself the proprietor, whose language of command he had habituated himself to employ ; on the present occasion, he made his way from the presence of his master with no complacent feelings, and his displeasure vented itself very unequivocally upon a favourite hound who lay at the foot of the outer steps, and whom he kicked off with a savage satisfaction, and sent howling to his kennel. A boy coming to him with a message from the kitchen, was received with a smart application of his wagon whip, and made to follow the example, if he did not exactly imitate the peculiar music of the hound. Mingo certainly made his exit in a rage. Half an hour after, he might have been seen, mounted on his marsh tacky, making tracks for the " Red Gulley," determined, if he was not suffered to expel the intruders, at least, to show them that it was in his power, during their stay, to diminish very considerably the measure of their satisfaction. His wrath —like that of all consequential persons who feel themselves in the wrong, yet lack courage to be right—was duly warmed by nursing ; and, pregnant with terrible looks and accents, he burst upon the little encampment at " Red Gulley," in a way that " was a caution" to all evil doers !

The squatters had only raised one simple habitation of poles, and begun a second which adjoined it. The first was covered in with bushes, bark and saplings ; the second was slightly advanced, and the hatchet lay before it, in waiting for the hand by which it was to be completed. The embers of a recent fire were strewed in front of the former, and a lean cur—one of those gaunt, far sighted, keen nosed animals which the Indians employed; dock tailed, short haired, bushy eyed—lay among the ashes, and did not offer to stir at the appearance of the terror-breathing Mingo. Still, though he moved not, his keen eyes followed the movements of the Driver with as jealous a glance as those of his owner would have done; while the former alighted from his horse, peered around the wigwam, and finally penetrated it. Here he saw nobody, and nothing to reward his scrutiny. Reappearing from the hut, he hallooed with the hope of obtaining some better satisfaction, but his call was unanswered. The dog alone raised his head, looked up at the impatient visitor, and, as if satisfied with a single glance, at once resumed his former luxurious position. Such stolidity, bad enough in an Indian, was still more impertinent in an Indian dog; and, forgetting every thing but his consequence, and the rage with which he had set out from home, Mingo, without more ado, laid his lash over the animal with no measured violence of stroke. It was then that he found an answer to his challenge. A clump of myrtles opened at a little distance behind him, and the swarthy red cheeks of an Indian man appeared through the aperture, to which his voice summoned the eyes of the assailant.

" You lick dog," said the owner, with accents which were rather soft and musical than stern, " dog is good, what for you lick dog ?"

Such a salutation, at the moment, rather startled the imperious driver; not that he was a timid fellow, or that his wrath had in the least degree abated; but that he was surprised completely. Had the voice reached him from the woods in front, he would have been better prepared for it; but, coming from the rear, his imagination made it startling, and increased its solemnity. He turned at the summons, and, at the same moment, the Indian, making his way through the myrtles, advanced toward the negro. There was nothing in his appearance to awaken the apprehensions of the latter. The stranger was small and slight of person, and evidently beyond the middle period of life. Intemperance, too, the great curse of the Indian who has long been a dweller in contact with the Anglo-Saxon settler—(the French, *par parenthese,* seem to have always civilized the Indian without making him a drunkard)—had made its ravages upon his form, and betrayed it-self in every lineament of his face. His step, even while he approached the negro, was unsteady from the influence of liquor ; and as all these signs of feebleness became obvious to the eye of Mingo, his courage, and with it his domineering insolence of char-acter, speedily returned to him.

"Lick dog !" he exclaimed, as he made a movement to the Catawba, and waved his whip threateningly, " lick dog, and lick Indian too."

"Lick Indian—get knife !" was the quiet answer of the savage, whose hand, at the same instant, rested upon the horn handle of his *couteau de chasse*, where it stuck in the deerskin belt that girdled his waist.

" Who's afeard ?" said Mingo, as he clubbed his whip and threw the heavy loaded butt of it upon his shoulder. The slight frame of the Indian moved his contempt only ; and the only cir-cumstance that prevented him from instantly putting his threat into execution, was the recollection of that strange interest which his master had taken in the squatters, and his positive command that they should not be ill treated or expelled. While he hesita-ted, however, the Catawba gave him a sufficient excuse, as he fancied, for putting his original intention into execution. The threatening attitude, partial advance of the foe, together with the sight of the heavy handled whip reversed and hanging over him, had, upon the mind of the savage, all the effect of an absolute assault. He drew his knife in an instant, and flinging himself forward to the feet of the negro, struck an upright blow with his weapon, which would have laid the entrails of his enemy open to the light, but for the promptitude of the latter, who, receding at the same instant, avoided and escaped the blow. In the next moment, levelling his whip at the head of the stooping Indian, he would most probably have retorted it with fatal effect, but for an unlooked for interruption. His arms were both grappled by some one from behind, and, for the perilous moment, effectually pre-vented from doing any harm. With some difficulty, he shook off the last comer, who, passing in front, between the hostile parties, proved to be an Indian woman.

CHAPTER IV.

BEFORE this discovery was fairly made, the wrath of Mingo had been such as to render him utterly forgetful of the commands of his master. He was now ready for the combat to the knife; and had scarcely shaken himself free from his second assailant, before he advanced with redoubled resolution upon the first. He, by the way, equally aroused, stood ready, with closed lips, keen eye and lifted knife, prepared for the encounter. All the peculiarities of the Indian shone out in the imperturbable aspect, composed muscles, and fiery gleaming eyes of the now half-sobered savage; who, as if conscious of the great disparity of strength between himself and foe, was mustering all his arts of war, all his stratagems and subtleties, to reduce those inequalities from which he had every thing to apprehend. But they were not permitted to fight. The woman now threw herself between them; and, at her appearance, the whip of Mingo fell from his shoulder, and his mood became instantly pacific. She was the wife of the savage, but certainly young enough to have been his daughter. She was decidedly one of the comeliest squaws that had ever enchanted the eyes of the Driver, and her life-darting eyes, the emotion so visible in her face, and the boldness of her action, as she passed between their weapons, with a hand extended toward each, was such as to inspire him with any other feelings than those which possessed him towards the squatters. Mingo was susceptible of the tender influences of love. As brave as Julius Cæsar, in his angry mood, he was yet quite as pliant as Mark Antony in the hour of indulgence; and the smile of one of the ebon damsels of his race, at the proper moment, has frequently saved her and others from the penalties incurred by disobedience of orders, or unfinished tasks. Nor were his sentiments towards the sex confined to those of his master's plantation only. He penetrated the neighbouring estates with the excursive and reck-less nature of the Prince of Troy, and, more than once, in consequence of this habit, had the several plantations rung with wars, scarcely less fierce, though less protracted than those of Ilium. His success with the favoured sex was such as to fill him with a singular degree of confidence in his own prowess and personal attractions. Mingo knew that he was a handsome fellow, and fancied a great deal more. He was presumptuous enough— surely there are no white men so !—to imagine that it was scarcely possible for any of the other sex, in their sober senses, to withstand him. This impression grew singularly strong, as he gazed upon the Indian woman. So bright an apparition had not met his eyes for many days. His local associations were all staling—the women he was accustomed to behold, had long since lost the charm of novelty in his sight—and, with all his possessions, Mingo, like Alexander of Macedon, was still yearning for newer conquests. The first glance at the Indian woman, assured his roving fancies that they had not yearned in vain. He saw in her a person whom he thought destined to provoke his jaded tastes anew, and restore his passions to their primitive ascendancy The expression of his eye softened as he surveyed her. War fled from it like a discomfited lion ; and if love, squatting quietly down in his place, did not look altogether so innocent as the lamb, he certainly promised not to roar so terribly. He now looked nothing but complacence on both the strangers ; on the woman because of her own charms ; on the man because of the charms which he possessed in her. But such was not the expression in the countenance of the Indian. He was not to be moved by the changes which he beheld in his enemy, but still kept upon him a wary watch, as if preparing for the renewal of the combat. There was also a savage side-glance which his keen fiery eyes threw upon the woman, which seemed to denote some little anger towards herself. This did not escape the watchful glance of our gay Lothario, who founded upon it some additional hope of success in his schemes. Meanwhile, the woman was not idle nor silent. She did not content herself with simply going between the combatants, but her tongue was active in expostulation with her sovereign, in a dialect not the less musical to the ears of Mingo because he did not understand a word of it. The tones were sweet, and he felt that they counselled peace and good will to the warrior. But the latter, so far as he could comprehend the expression of his face, and the mere sounds of his brief, guttural replies, had, like Sempronius, a voice for war only. Something, too, of a particular harshness in his manner, seemed addressed to the woman alone. Her answers were evidently those of deprecation and renewed entreaty ; but they did not seem very much to influence her Lord and master, or to soften his mood. Mingo grew tired of a controversy in which he had no share, and fancied, with a natural self-complacency, that he could smooth down some of its difficulties.

"Look yer, my friend," he exclaimed, advancing, with extended hand, while a volume of condescension was written upon his now benignant features—"Look yer, my friend, it's no use to be at knife-draw any longer. I didn't mean to hurt you when I raised the whip, and as for the little touch I gin the dog, why that's neither here nor there. The dog's more easy to squeal than most dogs I know. Ef I had killed him down to the brush at his tail eend, he could'nt ha' holla'd more. What's the sense to fight for dogs ? Here—here's my hand—we won't quarrel any longer, and, as for fighting, I somehow never could fight when there was a woman standing by. It's onbecoming, I may say, and so here's for peace between us. Will you shake ?"

The proffered hand was not taken. The Indian still kept aloof with the natural caution of his race ; but he seemed to relax something of his watchfulness, and betrayed less of that still and deliberate anxiety which necessarily impresses itself upon the most courageous countenance in the moment of expected conflict. Again the voice of the woman spoke in tones of reconciliation, and, this time, words of broken English were audible, in what she said, to the ears of the Driver. Mingo fancied that he had never heard better English—of which language he considered himself no humble proficient—nor more sweetly spoken by any lips. The savage darted an angry scowl at the speaker in return, uttered but a single stern word in the Catawba, and pointed his finger to the wigwam as he spoke. Slowly, the woman turned away and disappeared within its shelter. Mingo began to be impatient of the delay, probably because of her departure, and proceeded, with more earnestness than before, to renew his propo-

sition for peace. The reply of the Indian, betrayed all the tena.
city of his race in remembering threats and injuries.

"Lick dog, lick Indian; lick Indian, get knife—hah!"

"Who's afeard!" said the Driver. "Look yer, my friend:
'taint your knife, let me tell you, that's gwine to make me turn
tail on any chicken of your breed. You tried it, and what did
you git? Why, look you, if it hadn't been for the gripe of the
gal—maybe she's your daughter, mout-be your sister?—but it's
all one—ef it hadn't been her gripe which fastened my arm, the
butt of my whip would have flattened you, until your best friend
couldn't ha' said where to look for your nose. You'd ha' been
all face after that, smooth as bottom land, without e'er a snag or
a stump; and you'd have passed among old acquaintance for
any body sooner than yourself. But I'm no brag dog—nor I
don't want to be a biting dog, nother; when there's nothing to
fight for. Let's be easy. P'rhaps you don't feel certain whose
plantation you're on here. Mout be if you know'd, you'd find
out it wa'nt altogether the best sense to draw knife on Mingo
Gillison.—Why, look you, my old boy, I'm able to say what I
please here—I makes the law for this plantation—all round
about, so far as you can see from the top of the tallest of them
'ere pine trees, I'm the master! I look 'pon the pine land field,
and I say, 'Tom, Peter, Ned, Dick, Jack, Ben, Toney, Sam—
boys—you must 'tack that field to-morrow.' I look 'pon the
swamp field, and I say to 'nother ten, 'boys, go there!'—high
land and low land, upland and swamp, corn and cotton, rice and
rye, all 'pen 'pon me for order; and jis' as Mingo say, jis' so
they do. Well, wha' after dat! It stands clear to the leetlest
eye, that 'taint the best sense to draw knife on Mingo Gillison;
here, on he own ground. 'Spose my whip can't do the mischief,
it's a needcessity only to draw a blast out of this 'ere horn, and
there'll be twenty niggers 'pon you at once, and ebery one of dem
would go off wid 'he limb. But I ain't a hard man, my fren', ef
you treat me softly. You come here to make your clay pots and
pans. Your people bin use for make 'em here for sebenty
nine—mout-be forty seben year—who knows? Well, you can
make 'em here, same as you been usen to make 'em, so long as
you 'habe you'self like a gemplemans. But none of your

knife-work, le' me tell you.   I'll come ebery day and look 'pon you.   'Mout-be, I'll trade with you for some of your pots. Clay-pot is always best for bile hom'ny."

We have put in one paragraph the sum and substance of a much longer discourse which Mingo addressed to his Indian guest.   The condescensions of the negro had a visible effect upon the squatter, the moment that he was made to comprehend the important station which the former enjoyed; and when the Indian woman was fairly out of sight, Richard Knuckles, for such was the English name of the Catawba, gradually restored his knife to his belt, and the hand which had been withheld so long, was finally given in a gripe of amity to the negro, who shook it as heartily as if he had never meditated towards the stranger any but the most hospitable intentions.   He was now as affectionate and indulgent, as he had before shown himself hostile; and the Indian, after a brief space, relaxed much of the *hauteur* which distinguishes the deportment of the Aborigines.   But Mingo was pained to observe that Richard never once asked him into his wigwam, and, while he remained, that the squaw never once came out of it.   This reserve betokened some latent apprehension of mischief; and the whole thoughts of our enamoured Driver were bent upon ways and means for overcoming this austerity, and removing the doubts of the strangers.   He contrived to find out that Caloya—such was the woman's name—was the wife of the man; and he immediately jumped to a conclusion which promised favourably for his schemes.   "An ole man wid young wife!" said he, with a complacent chuckle, "Ah, ha! he's afeard!—well, he hab' good 'casion for fear'd, when Mingo Gillison is 'pon de ground."

CHAPTER V.

But though warmed with these encouraging fancies, our conceited hero found the difficulties to be much more numerous and formidable than he had anticipated. The woman was as shy as the most modest wife could have shown herself, and no Desdemona could have been more certainly true to her liege lord. Mingo paid no less than three visits that day to the wigwam, and all without seeing her, except at his first coming, when she was busied with, but retired instantly from, her potteries, in which Richard Knuckles took no part, and seemingly no interest. Lazy, like all his race, he lay in the sun, on the edge of the encampment, with an eye but half open, but that half set directly upon the particular movements of his young wife. Indians are generally assumed to be cold and insensible, and some doubts have been expressed, whether their sensibilities could ever have been such as to make them open to the influence of jealousy. These notions are ridiculous enough; and prove nothing half so decidedly as the gross ignorance of those who entertain them. Something, of course, is to be allowed for the natural differences between a civilized and savage people. Civilization is prolific, barbarism sterile. The dweller in the city has more various appetites and more active passions than the dweller in the camp; and the habits of the hunter, lead, above all things, to an intense gathering up of all things in self; a practice which tends, necessarily, to that sort of independence which is, perhaps, neither more nor less than one aspect of barrenness. But, while the citizen is allowed to have more various appetites and intenser passions in general, the Indian is not without those which, indeed, are essential to constitute his humanity. That he can love, is undeniable—that he loves with the ardour of the white, may be more questionable. That he can love, however, with much intensity, may fairly be inferred from the fact that his hate is subtle and is nourished with traditional tenacity and reverence.

But the argument against the sensibility of the savage, in his savage state, even if true, would not apply to the same animal in his degraded condition, as a borderer of the white settlements. Degraded by beastly habits, and deprived by them of the fiercer and warlike qualities of his ancestors, he is a dependent, (and jealousy is a creature of dependence)—a most wretched dependent, and that, too, upon his women—she who, an hundred years ago, was little other than his slave, and frequently his victim.   In his own feebleness, he learns to esteem her strength ; and, in due degree with his own degradation, is her rise into importance in his sight.   But it does not matter materially to our present narrative, whether men should, or should not agree, as to the sensibilities of the savage to the tender passion.   It is probable, that few warlike nations are very susceptible of love ; and as for the middle ages, which might be urged as an exception to the justice of this remark, Sismondi is good authority to show that Burke had but little reason to deplore their loss : " *Helas ! cet heroisme universel nous avons nomme la chevalerie, n'exista jamais comme fictions brillantes !*"   There were no greater brutes than the warriors of the middle ages.

Richard Knuckles, whether he loved his young wife or not, was certainly quite as jealous of her as Othello was of his. Not, perhaps, so much of her affections as of her deference ; and this, by the way, was also something of the particular form of jealousy under which the noble Moor suffered.   The proud spirit chafes that another object should stand for a moment between his particular sunlight and himself.   His jealousy had been awakened long before, and this led to his temporary separation from his tribe.   Caloya, it may be added, yielded, without a murmur, to the caprices of her lord, to whom she had been given by her father.   She was as dutiful as if she loved him ; and, if conduct alone could be suffered to test the quality of virtue, her affection for him was quite as earnest, pure and eager, as that of the most devoted woman.   That she could not love him, is a conclusion only to be drawn from the manifest inequalities between them. He was old and brutal—a truly worthless, sottish savage—while she, if not a beauty, was yet comely to the eye, very youthful, and, in comparison with Indian squaws in general, remarkably tidy in person, and good humoured in disposition.

Our hero, Mingo, was not only persuaded that she could not love Knuckles, but he equally soon became convinced that she could be made to love himself. He left no opportunity untried to effect this desirable result ; and, after a most fatiguing trial, he succeeded so far in a part of his scheme as to beguile the husband into good humour if not blindness. Returning towards nightfall to the camp, Mingo brought with him a "chunk-bottle" of whiskey, the potency of which, over the understanding of an Indian, he well knew ; and displaying his treasure to Knuckles, was invited by him, for the first time, with a grunt of cordiality, to enter the wigwam of the squatters. The whiskey while it lasted convinced Knuckles, that he had no better friend in the world than Mingo Gillison, and he soon became sufficiently blinded by its effects, to suffer the frequent and friendly glances of the Driver towards his wife, without discovering that they were charged with any especial signs of intelligence. Yet never was a more ardent expression of wilful devotion thrown into human eyes before. Mingo was something of an actor, and many an actor might have taken a goodly lesson of his art from the experienced Driver. He was playing Romeo, an original part always, to his own satisfaction. Tenderness, almost to tears, softened the fiery ardour of his glance, and his thick lips grew doubly thick, in the effort to throw into them an expression of devoted languor. But all his labour seemed to go for nothing —nay, for something worse than nothing—in the eyes of the faithful wife. If her husband *could* not see the arts of the amorous negro, she *would* not see them ; and when, at supper, it sometimes became necessary that her eyes should look where the lover sat, the look which she gave him was stony and inexpressive —cold to the last degree ; and, having looked, it would be averted instantly with a haste, which, to a less confident person would have been vastly discouraging and doubtful. As it was, even the self-assured Mingo was compelled to acknowledge, in his mental soliloquy that night as he made his way homeward, that, so far his progress was not a subject of brag, and scarcely of satisfaction. The woman, he felt, had resisted his glances, or, which was much worse, had failed to see them.   But this was owing, so he fancied, entirely to her caution and the natural dread which she had of her fiercely minded sovereign.   Mingo retired to his couch that night to plan, and to dream of plans, for overcoming the difficulties in the way of his own, and, as he persisted in believing, the natural desires of Caloya.   It may be stated in this place, that, under the new aspects which the squatters had assumed in his eyes, he did not think it necessary to make any very copious statement of his proceedings to his master ; but, after the fashion of certain public committees, when in difficulty among themselves, he wisely concluded to report progress and beg permission to sit again.

CHAPTER VI.

" DEM 'ere Indians," he said the next morning to his master— "dem 'ere Indians—der's only two ob 'em come yet, sir—I aint altogether sure about 'em—I has'n't any exspecial 'spicion, sir, from what I seed yesterday, that they's very honest in particklar, and then agen, I see no reasons that they aint honest. It mout be, they might steal a hen, sir, if she was reasonable to come at—it mout be, they mout eben go deeper into a hog ;—but then agen, it mout'n't be after all, and it wouldn't be right justice to say, tell a body knows for certain. There's no telling yet, sir. An Indian, as I may say, naterally, is honest or he aint honest ;—and there's no telling which, sir, 'tell he steals something, or tell he goes off without stealing ;—and so all that kin be done, sir, is to find out if he's a thief, or if he's not a thief; and I think, sir, I'm in a good way to git at the rights of the matter before worse comes to worser. As you say, Mossa, it's my business to see that you ain't worsened by 'em."

Without insisting that Col. Gillison entirely understood the ingenious speech of his driver, we can at least assert, with some confidence, that he was satisfied with it. Of an indolent disposition, the young master was not unwilling to be relieved from the trouble of seeing himself after the intruders ; and though he dismissed the amorous Mingo with an assurance, that he would take an early opportunity to look into their camp, the cunning driver, who perhaps guessed very correctly on the subject of his master's temperament, was fully persuaded that his own movements would suffer no interruption from the command or supervision of the other. Accordingly, sallying forth immediately after breakfast, he took his way to the encampment, where he arrived in time to perceive some fragments of a Catawba *dejeûné*, which, while it awakened his suspicions, did not in any measure provoke his appetite. There were numerous small well-picked bones, which might have been those of a squirrel, as Richard Knuckles somewhat gratuitously alleged, or which might have been those of one of his master's brood-hens, as Mingo Gillison half suspected. But, though he set forth with a declared resolve not to suffer his master's interests to be "worsened," our driver did not seem to think it essential to this resolution to utter his suspicions, or to search more narrowly into the matter. He seemed to take for granted that Richard Knuckles had spoken nothing but the truth, and he himself showed nothing but civility. He had not made his visit without bringing with him a goodly portion of whiskey in his flask, well knowing that no better medium could be found for procuring the confidence and blinding the jealous eyes of the Indian. But he soon discovered that this was not his true policy, however much he had fancied in the first instance that it might subserve it. He soothed the incivilities of the Catawba, and warmed his indifference by the liquor, but he, at the same time, and from the same cause, made him stationary in the camp. So long as the whiskey lasted, the Indian would cling to the spot, and when it was exhausted he was unable to depart. The prospect was a bad one for the Driver that day in the camp of the squatters, since, though the woman went to *her* tasks without delay, and clung to them with the perseverance of the most devoted industry, the Hunter was neither able nor willing to set forth upon his. The bow was unbent and unslung, lying across his lap, and he, himself, leaning back against his tree, seemed to have no wish beyond the continued possession of the genial sunshine in which he basked. In vain did Mingo, sitting beside him, cast his wistful eyes towards the woman who worked at a little distance, and whom, while her husband was wakeful, he did not venture to approach. Something, he thought, might be done by signs, but the inflexible wife never once looked up from the clay vessel which her hands were employed to round —an inflexibility which the conceited negro ascribed not so much to her indifference to his claims, as to her fears of her savage husband. We must not forget to say that the tongue of the Driver was seldom silent, however much his thoughts might be confused and his objects baffled. He had a faith in his own eloquence, not unlike that of the greater number of our young and promising statesmen; and did not doubt, though he could not speak to the woman directly, that much that he did say would s.ill reach her senses, and make the desired impression. With this idea, it may be readily supposed that he said a great many things which were much better calculated to please her, than to meet the assent of her husband.

"Now," for example, continuing a long dissertation on the physiological and psychological differences between his own and the Indian race, in which he strove to prove to the satisfaction of the Catawba, the infinite natural and acquired superiorities of the former,—"Now," said he, stretching his hand forth towards the toiling woman, and establishing his case, as he thought conclusively, by a resort to the *argumentum ad hominem*—"now, you see, if that 'ere gal was my wife instead of your'n, Knuckles, do you think I'd let her extricate herself here in a br'iling sun, working her fingers off, and I lying down here in the grass a-doing nothing and only looking on? No! I'd turn in and give her good resistance; 'cause why, Knuckles? 'Cause, you see, it's not, I may say, a 'spectable sight to see the woman doing all the work what's a needcessity, and the man a-doing nothing. The woman warn't made for hard work at all. My women I redulges—I never pushes 'em—I favours them all that I kin, and it goes agin me mightily, I tell you, when it's a needcessity to give 'em the lash. But I scores the men like old Harry. I gives them their desarbings; and if so be the task ain't done, let them look out for thick jackets. 'Twont be a common homespun that'll keep off my cuts. I do not say that I overwork my people. That's not the idee. My tasks is a'most too easy, and there's not a nigger among 'em that can't get through, if he's exposed that way, by tree o'clock in de day. The women has their task, but they're twice as easy, and then I don't open both eyes when I'm looking to see if they've got through 'em. 'Tain't often you hear my women in trivilation ; and, I know, it stands to reason what I'm telling you, that a black Gentlemen is always more 'spectable to a woman than an Indian. Dere's your wife now, and dere's. you. She ain't leff her business since I bin here, and you haint gone to your'n, nor you ain't gin her a drop of the whiskey. Not to say that a gal so young as that ought to drink whiskey and chaw tobacco—but for the sake of compliment now, 'twas only right that you should ha' ax her

to try a sup.   But then for the working.   You ain't offered to resist her ; you ain't done a stroke since breakfast.   Ef you was
under me, Knuckles, I'd a laid this green twig over your red jacket in a way that would ha' made a 'possum laugh.''

" Eh !'' was the only exclamation of the half drunken Indian,
at this characteristic conclusion of the negro's speech ; but, though
Knuckles said nothing that could denote his indignation at the irreverent threat, which, though contingent only, was excessively
annoying to the *amour propre* of the Catawba, there was a gleam
of angry intelligence which flashed out for a moment from his
eyes and his thin lips parted to a grin that showed his white teeth
with an expression not unlike that of a wolf hard pressed by one
more daring cur than the rest.   Either Mingo did not see this, or
he thought too lightly of the prowess of his companion to heed it.
He continued in the same strain and with increasing boldness.

" Now I say, Knuckles, all that's onbecoming.   A woman's a
woman, and a man's a man.   A woman has her sort of work,
and it's easy.   And a man has his sort of work, and that's hard.
Now, here you make this poor gal do your work and her own too.
That's not fair, it's a despisable principle, and I may say, no man's
a gempleman that believes it.   Ha'n't I seed, time upon time, Indian men going along, stiff and straight as a pine tree, carrying
nothing but a bow and arrow, and mout be, a gun ; and, same
time, the squaws walking a most double under the load.   That's
a common ex-servation.   Iv'e seed it a hundred times.   Is that
'spectful or decent to the fair seck ?   I say no, and I'll stand by, and
leave it to any tree gentlemen of any complexion, ef I ain't right.''

It was well, perhaps, for the maintenance of peace between the
parties, that Knuckles was too drunk and too ignorant to comprehend all that was spoken by the Driver.   The leading idea, however, was sufficiently clear for his comprehension, and to this he
answered with sufficient brevity and phlegm.

" Indian woman is good for work—Indian man for hunt; woman
is good for hab children ; man for shoot—man for fight.   The
Catawba man is very good for fight ;'' and as the poor, miserable
creature spoke, the fire of a former and a better day, seemed to
kindle his cheeks and give lustre to his eye.   Probably, the
memory of that traditional valour which distinguished the people

to which he belonged in a remarkable degree, in comparison
with the neighbouring nations, came over his thoughts, and
warned him with something like a kindred sentiment with those
which had been so long forgotten by his race.

"Oh go 'long!" said the negro. "How you talk, Knuckles!
wha make you better for fight more dan me? Ki, man! Once
you stan' afore Mingo, you tumble. Ef I was to take you in my
arms and give you one good hug, Lor' ha' massy 'pon you!
You'd neber feel yourself after that, and nothing would be lef' of
you for you wife to see, but a long greasy mark, most like a little
old man, yer, 'pon my breast and thighs. I never seed the Indian yet that I could'nt lick, fair up and down, hitch cross, or big
cross, hand over, hand under, arm lock and leg lock, in seventeen and nine minutes, by the sun. You don't know, Knuckles,
else you would'nt talk so foolish. Neber Indian kin stan' agen
black man, whedder for fight or work. That's the thing I'm
talking 'bout. You can't fight fair and you can't work. You
aint got strengt' for it. All your fighting is bush fighting and
behind tree, and you' woman does the work. Now, wha' make
you lie down here, and not go 'pon you' hunting? That's 'cause
you're lazy. You come look at my hands, see 'em plough, see
'em hoe, see 'em mak' ditch, cut tree, split rail, buil' house—
when you see dem, you'll see wha' I call man. I would'nt give
tree snap of a finger for any pusson that's so redolent as an Indian. They're good for nothing but eat."

"Catawba man is good for fight!" sullenly responded the Indian to a speech which the negro soon found to have been impru-
dently concerted and rashly spoken, in more respects than one.
"Nigger man and squaw is good for work!" continued the other
disdainfully, his thin lips curling into an expression of scorn
which did not escape the eyes of Mingo, obtuse as his vanity
necessarily made him. "Catawba man is a free man, he can
sleep or he can hunt," pursued the savage, retorting decidedly
upon the condition of the slave, but without annoying the sleek,
well fed and self-complacent driver. "Nigger man ain't free
man—he must work, same like Indian squaw."

"Oh, skion! Oh! skion! wha's all dat, Knuckles? You don't
know wha' you say. Who make you free? wha' make you

free ? How you show you got freedom, when here you expen' 'pon poor woman for work your pot, and half de time you got not'ing to put in 'em. Now, I is free man! Cause, you see my pot is always full, and when I does my work like a gempleman,— who cares? I laughs at mossa jist the same as I laughs at you. You free eh?—you! Whay you hab coat like mine? Whay, you hab breeches? Why, Knuckles, you aint decent for stan' 'fore you wife. Dat's trut' I'm telling you. How you can be free when you aint decent? How you can be free when you no work? How you can be free when you half-starbing all de time? When you aint got blanket to you' back—when you aint got fat 'pon you rib. When here, you expen' 'pon my land to get the mud-stuff for you' pots and pans! Psho, psho, Knuckles, you don't know wha' you talk 'bout. You aint hab sensible notion of dem tings wha make free pusson. Nebber man is freeman, ef he own arm can't fill he stomach. Nebber man is freeman if he own work can't put clothes 'pon he back. Nebber man is free-man—no, nor gempleman neider, when he make he purty young wife do all de work, him lying same time, wid he leg cross and he eye half shut, in de long grass smelling ob de sunshine. No, no, Knuckles, you must go to you' work, same as I goes to mine, ef you wants people to desider you a freeman. Now you' work is hunting—my work is for obersee my plantation. It's a trut', your work aint obermuch—'taint wha' gempleman kin call work altogedder, but nebber mind, it's someting. Now, wha for you no go to you' work? Come, I gwine to mine. You strike off now 'pon your business. I reckon you' wife can make he pots, same as ef we bin' stan' look 'pon 'em. Woman don't like to be obershee, and when I tink 'pon de seck, I don't see any needces-sity for it."

The Indian darted a fierce glance at the authoritative negro, and simply exclaiming, "Eh! Eh!" rose from his position, and tottering towards the spot where the woman was at work, uttered a few brief words in her ear which had the immediate effect of sending her out of sight, and into the hovel. He then returned quietly to his nest beneath the tree. Mingo was somewhat an-noyed by the conviction that he had overshot his object, and had provoked the always eager suspicions of the savage. Knuckles oetrayed no sort of intention to go on the hunt that day ; and his fierce glances, even if he had no words to declare his feelings, sufficiently betrayed to the negro the jealousies that were awakened in his mind.   The latter felt troubled.   He fancied that, in the pursuit of his desires, were the woman alone concerned, he should have no difficulty, but he knew not what to do with the man.   To scare him off was impossible—to beguile him from his treasure seemed equally difficult, and, in his impatience, the dogmatical driver, accustomed to have his will instantly obeyed, could scarcely restrain himself from a second resort to the whip.   A moment's reflection brought a more prudent resolution to his mind, and seeing that the squatters were likely to go without food that day, he determined to try the effect which the presentation of a flitch of his master's bacon would have, upon the jealousy of the husband, and the affections of the wife.   With this resolution, he retired from the ground, though without declaring his new and gracious purpose to either of the parties whom it was intended especially to benefit.

CHAPTER VII.

THE flitch was brougnt, boiled, and laid before the squatters.
It was accompanied by a wholesome supply of corn bread; and
this liberality, which had, for its sanction, in part, the expressed
determination of the master, had for its effect, the restoration of
Mingo to that favour in the mind of the savage, which his imprudent opinions had forfeited. Even a jealous Indian, when so very
hungry as our Catawba, and so utterly wanting in resources of
his own, cannot remain insensible to that generosity, however
suspicious, which fills his larder with good cheer in the happy
moment. He relaxed accordingly, Mingo was invited into the
hovel, and made to partake of the viands which he had provided.
A moderate supply of whiskey accompanied the gift, enough to
give a flavour to the meal, yet not enough to produce intoxication.
Mingo was resolved henceforth, to do nothing which would keep
himself and Knuckles from an uninterrupted pursuit of their sev
eral game. But while the meal lasted, he saw but few results,
beyond the thawing of Knuckles, which promised him success in
his object. Caloya was, if possible, more freezing than ever.
She never deigned him the slightest acknowledgment for his numerous civilities, which were not merely profitless, but which
had the additional disadvantage of attracting the eyes, and finally
re-awakening the jealous apprehensions of Knuckles; still, the
good cheer was so good, and the facility with which it had been
procured, so very agreeable to a lazy Indian, that he swallowed
his dissatisfaction with his pottage, and the meal passed over
without any special outbreak. Mingo, so near the object of his
desire, was by no means disposed to disputation with her husband,
and contented himself with only an occasional burst of declamation, which was intended rather for her ears than for those of her
lord. But he strove to make amends for their forbearance, by addressing the most excruciating glances across the table to the fair

—glances which she did not requite with favour, and which she did not often seem to see.

Mingo was in hopes, when dinner was over, that Knuckles would take up his bow and arrows, and set forth on the hunt. To this he endeavoured, in an indirect manner, to urge the savage. He told him that game was plenty in the neighbouring woods and swamps—that deer might be found at all hours, and even proceeded to relate several marvellous stories of his own success, which failed as well to persuade as to deceive the hunter. The whiskey being exhausted by this time, and his hunger being pacified, the jealous fit of the latter returned upon him with all the vigour of an ague. " Why," he asked himself, " should this negro steal his master's bacon to provide Richard Knuckles with a dinner ? Because Richard Knuckles has a young wife, the youngest and handsomest of the whole tribe. Why should he urge me to go hunting, and take such pains to show me where the buck stalks, and the doe sleeps, but that he knows I must leave my doe behind me ? Why should he come and sit with me half a dozen times a day, but that he may see and sit with my young wife also ?" An Indian reasons very much like every body else, and jumps very rationally to like conclusions. The reserve of Knuckles grew with his reflections, and Mingo had sense enough to perceive that he could hope for no successful operations that day. The woman was sent from the presence, and her husband began to exhibit very decided symptoms of returning sulks. He barely answered the civilities of the driver, and a savage grin displayed his white teeth, closely clenched, whenever his thin lips parted to reply. The parting speech of the negro was not precisely the D. I. O. of the rattle-dandy of fashionable life, but was very much like it. If he did not swear like a trooper at bidding adieu, he marked every step on his way homewards with a most bitter oath.

But success is no ripe fruit to drop at the first opening of the mouth of the solicitous. Mingo was not the person to forego his efforts, and he well knew from old experience, that a woman is never so near won, as when she seems least willing. He was not easily given to despair, however he might droop, and he next day, and the next, and the next found him still a frequent visitor at the camp of Knuckles; and still he provided the corn, the bacon, and the whiskey, and still he found the Catawba a patient recipient of his favours.   The latter saw no reason to leave home to hunt venison when his larder was so easily provided, and the former could not, but at some discredit, discontinue the liberal practices which he had so improvidently begun.

But if Knuckles was not unwilling to be fed after this fashion, he was not altogether insensible to some of the conditions which it implied.   He could not but perceive that the negro had his objects, and those objects his jealous blood had led him long before to conjecture with sufficient exactness.   He raged inwardly with the conviction that the gallant, good looking, and always well dressed Driver sought to compass his dishonour; and he was not without the natural fears of age and brutality that, but for his own eminent watchfulness, he might be successful. As there was no equality in the conditions of himself and wife, there was but little confidence between them—certainly none on his part;—and his suspicions—schooled into silence in the presence of Mingo, as well because of the food which he brought, as of the caution which the great physical superiority of the latter was calculated to inspire—broke out with unqualified violence when the two were alone together.   The night of the first day when Mingo provided the table of the squatters so bountifully, was distinguished by a concussion of jealousy, on the part of Knuckles, which almost led the poor woman to apprehend for her life.   The effects of the good cheer and the whiskey had subsided and the departure of Mingo was the signal for the domestic storm.

"Hah! hah! nigger is come for see Ingin wife.   Ingin wife is look 'pon nigger—hah?"

It was thus that he begun the warfare.   We have endeavoured to put into the Indian-English, as more suitable to the subject, and more accessible to the reader, that dialogue which was spoken in the most musical Catawba.   The reply of the woman, though meekly expressed, was not without its sting.

"Ingin man eats from nigger hand, drinks from nigger bottle, and sits down by nigger side in the sunshine.   Is Caloya to say, nigger go to the cornfield—Ingin man go look for meat?"

The husband glared at the speaker with fiery eyes, while his teeth gleamed maliciously upon her, and were suddenly gnashed in violence, as he replied :

" Hah ! Ingin man must not look pon his wife ! Hah ! Ingin woman says—' go hunt, man, go—that no eyes may follow nigger when he crawls through the bush. Hah !' "

" Caloya is blind when the nigger comes to the camp. Caloya looks not where he lies in the sunshine with the husband of Caloya. Is Enefisto (the Indian name for Knuckles) afraid of nigger ?—is he afraid of Caloya ?—let us go : Caloya would go to her people where they camp by the Edisto."

" Hah ! What said Chickawa, to Caloya ? Did he say, come to our people where they camp by the Edisto ? Wherefore should Caloya go beside the Edisto—Hah ?"

This question declared another object of the husband's jealousy. The woman's reply was as wild as it was immediate.

" Caloya sees not Chickawa—she sees not the nigger—she sees the clay and she sees the pans—and she sees Enefisto—Enefisto has said, and her eyes are shut to other men."

" Caloya lies !"

" Ah !"

" Caloya lies !"

The woman turned away without another word, and re-entering the miserable wigwam, slunk out of sight in the darkest corner of it. Thither she was pursued by the inveterate old man, and there, for some weary hours, she suffered like language of distrust and abuse without uttering a sentence either of denial or deprecation. She shed no tears, she uttered no complaints, nor did her tormentor hear a single sigh escape from her bosom ; yet, without question, her poor heart suffered quite as much from his cruelty and injustice, as if her lips had betrayed all the extravagant manifestations known to the sorrows of the civilized.

CHAPTER VIII.

IT is at least one retributive quality of jealousy, to torment the mind of the tormentor quite as much, if not more, than it does that of the victim. The anger of Richard Knuckles kept him awake the better part of the night; and, in his wakefulness, he meditated little else than the subject of his present fears. The indirect reproaches of his wife stung him, and suggested, at the same time, certain additional reasons for his suspicions. He reflected that, while he remained a close sentinel at home, it was impossible that he should obtain sufficient evidence to convict the parties whom he suspected, of the crime which he feared; for, by so doing, he must deprive the sooty Paris, who sought his hovel, of every opportunity for the prosecution of his design. With that morbid wilfulness of temper which marks the passions of man aroused beyond the restraints of right reason, he determined that the negro should have his opportunity; and, changing his plans, he set forth the next morning before day-peep, obviously for the purpose of hunting. But he did not remain long absent. He was fortunate enough just after leaving his cabin to shoot a fat wild turkey from his roost, on the edge of a little *bay* that stood about a mile from his camp; and with this on his shoulder, he returned stealthily to its neighbourhood, and, hiding himself in the covert, took such a position as enabled him to keep a keen watch over his premises and all the movements of Caloya. Until ten o'clock in the day he saw nothing to produce dissatisfaction or to alarm his fears. He saw the patient woman come forth according to custom, and proceed instantly to the " Red Gulley," where she resumed her tasks, which she pursued with quite as much industry, and, seemingly, much more cheerfulness than when she knew that he was watching. Her lips even broke forth into song while she pursued her tasks, though the strain was monotonous and the sentiment grave and melancholy. At ten o'clock, however, Knuckle's ague returned as he saw the negro make his appearance with wonted punctuality. The Indian laid his heaviest shaft upon the string of his bow, and awaited the progress of events. The movements of Mingo were made with due circumspection. He did not flatter himself, at first, that the field was clear, and looked round him with grave anxiety in momentary expectation of seeing the husband. His salutation of the wife was sufficiently distant and deferential. He began by asking after the chief, and received an answer equally cold and unsatisfactory. He gathered from this answer, however, that Knuckles was absent; but whether at a distance or at hand, or for how long a period, were important items of intelligence, which, as yet, he failed to compass; and it was only by a close cross-examination of the witness that he arrived at the conclusion, that Knuckles nad at length resumed the duties of the hunter. Even this conclusion reached him in a negative and imperfect form.

"Shall Ingin woman say to Ingin man, when he shall hunt and where, and how long he shall be gone?" demanded the woman in reply to the eager questioning of the negro.

"Certainly not, most angelical!" was the elevated response of the black, as his lips parted into smiles, and his eyes shot forth the glances of warmer admiration than ever. The arrow of Knuckles trembled meanwhile upon the string.

"Certainly not, most angelical!—but Ingin man, ef he lob and respects Indian woman, will tell her all about his consarns without her axing. I'm sure, most lubly Caloya, ef you was wife of mine, you should know all my outgivings and incomings, my journeyings and *backslidings*, to and fro,—my ways and my wishes;—there shouldn't be nothing that I wouldn't let you know. But there's a mighty difference, you see, twixt an old husband and a young one. Now, an old man like Knuckles, he's mighty close—he don't talk out his mind like a young fellow that's full of infections—a young fellow like me, that knows how to look 'pon a handsome young wife, and treat her with proper respectableness. Do you think now, ef you was wife of mine, that I'd let you do all that work by yourself? No! not for all the pots and jars twixt this and Edisto forks! Ef I did ask you to do the pans, and round 'em, and smooth.'em, and put the red stain 'pon 'em, why that wouldn't be onreasonable, you see, 'cause sich delical and slim fingers as woman's has, kin always manage them de..pects better than man's—but then, I'd dig the clay for you, my gal—I'd work it, ef I hadn't horse, I'd work it with my own legs—-I'd pile it up 'pon the board, and cut the wood to make the fire, and help you to burn it; and when all was done, I'd bend my own shoulders to the load, and you should follow me to Charleston, like a Lady, as you is. That's the way, my gal, that I'd treat wife of mine. But Ingin don't know much 'bout woman, and old Ingin don't care;—now, black Gempleman always has strong infections for the seck—he heart is tender—he eye is lub for look 'pon beauty—he hab soul for consider 'em in de right way, and when he sees 'em bright eye, ar smood, shiny skin, and white teet', and long arm, and slender wais', and glossy black hair, same like you's, ah, Caloya, he strengt' is melt away widin 'em, and he feels like not'ing only so much honey, lub and infections. He's all over infections, as I may say. Wha' you tink?"

Here the Driver paused, not so much from having nothing more to say, as from a lack of the necessary breath with which to say it. Knuckles heard every word, though it would be an error to assume that he understood one half. Still, the liquorish expression in the face of the negro sufficiently illustrated his meaning to satisfy the husband that the whole speech was pregnant with the most audacious kind of impertinence. The reflection upon his weight of years, and the exulting reference to his own youth and manhood, which Mingo so adroitly introduced, was, however, sufficiently intelligible and insulting to the Catawba, and he hesitated whether to draw the arrow to its head at once and requite this second Paris for his affront, even in the midst of it, or to await until farther wrong should yield him a more perfect justification for the deed. He reflected upon the danger of the attempt, and his resolution was already taken as to the mode and direction of his flight. But a morbid wish to involve Caloya in the same fate—a lingering desire to find a sanction in her weakness and guilt for all his own frequent injustice and brutality, determined him to await her answer, and see to what extremities the negro would be permitted to carry his presumption. Strange to say, the answer of the wife, which was such as must

have satisfied a husband that loved truly, gave him no gratification.

" Black man is too foolish !" said the woman with equal brevi
ty and scorn in reply to the long speech of the Driver.

" Don't say so, most lubly of all the Catawba gals—you don',
mean what you say for sartain. Look you—yer is as nice a
pullet as ever was roasted, and yer is some hard biled eggs, and
hoecake. I reckon that old fellow, your husband, aint brung in
your breckkus yet ; so you must be mighty hungry by this time,
and there's no better stay-stomach in the worl than hard biled
eggs. It's a mighty hard thing to work tell the sun stands atop
of your head, afore getting any thing to go 'pon : I guessed how
'twould be, and so I *brung* you these few catables."

He set down a small basket as he spoke, but the woman did
not seem to perceive it, and manifested no sort of disposition to
avail herself of his gift and invitation.

" What ! you wont take a bite ?"

" Enefisto **will** thank you when he come," was the answer,
coldly spoken, and the woman toiled more assiduously, while she
spoke, at her potteries.

" Enefisto !—oh, that's only an Ingin name for Knuckles, I
s'pose. But who care for him, Caloya ? Sure, you don't care
'bout an old fellow like that—fellow that makes you work and
gives you not eben dry hominey ? Prehaps, you're feard he'll
beat you ; but don't you feard—neber he kin lay heaby hand
'pon you, so long as Mingo is yer."

Could Mingo have seen the grin which appeared upon the
mouth of the Indian as he heard these words, and have seen the
deliberateness with which he thrice lifted the shaft and thrust its
point between the leaves so as to bear upon his heart, he might
have distrusted his own securities and strength, and have learned
to be more respectful in estimating the powers of his foe. But
the Indian seemed to content himself with being in a state of preparedness and in having possession of the entire field. He did
not shoot ; his worse feelings remained unsatisfied—he saw nothing
in the deportment of Caloya which could feed the morbid passion
which prevailed over all others in his breast, and he probably

forbore wreaking his malice upon the one victim, in hopes that by a little delay he might yet secure another.

"Black man is too foolish. Why he no go to his work? Catawba woman is do her work."

"And I will help you, my gal. It's mighty hard to do all by you self, so here goes. Lor', if I was your husband, Caloya, instead of that old fellow, Knuckles, you should be a lady—I'd neber let you touch a pot or a pan, and you should hab a frock all ob seersuck jist like this."

As the negro spoke, he threw off his hunting shirt, which he cast over a bush behind him, rolled up his shirt sleeves, display-ing his brawny and well made arms to the woman—perhaps the chief motive for his present gallant proceeding—and, advancing to the pile of clay in which Caloya was working, thrust his hands into the mass and began to knead with all the energy of a baker, stri-ving with his dough. The woman shrank back from her place, as she received this new accession of labour, and much to the an-noyance of Mingo, retired to a little distance, where she seemed to contemplate his movements in equal surprise and dissatisfac-tion. Meanwhile, a change had taken place in the mood and movements of Knuckles. The sight of the gaudy garment which Mingo had hung upon the myrtle bushes behind him, awakened the cupidity of the Catawba. For a time, a stronger passion than jealousy seized his mind, and he yearned to be the possessor of a shirt which he felt assured would be the envy of the tribe. It hung in his eyes like a fascination—he no longer saw Caloya—he no longer heeded the movements of the negro who had been meditating so great an injury to his honour and peace of mind; and, so long as the bright stripes of the seersucker kept waving before him, he forgot all his own deeply meditated purposes of vengeance. The temptation at last became irresistible. With the stealthy movement of his race, he rose quietly from the spot where he had been lurking, sank back in the depths of the woods behind him, and, utterly unheard, unobserved and unsuspected by either of the two in front, he succeeded in making a compass, still under cover, which brought him in the rear of the myrtles on which the coat was suspended. Meanwhile, Mingo, with his face to the kneading trough, and his back upon the endangered garment, was in the full stream of a new flood of eloquence, and the favourite Seersucker disappeared in the rapid grasp of the husband, while he was most earnest, though at a respectful distance, in an endeavour to deprive the Indian of a yet dearer possession. In this aim his arguments and entreaties were equally fond and impudent ; and with his arms buried to the elbows in the clay, and working the rigid mass as if life itself depended upon it, he was pouring forth a more unctuous harangue than ever, when, suddenly looking up to the spot where Caloya had retreated, his eye rested only upon the woods. The woman had disappeared from sight. He had been "wasting his sweetness on the desert air"— he had been talking to the wind only. Of this, at first, he was not so perfectly assured.

"Hello !" he exclaimed, " Whare you gone, Caloya ? Hello—hello ! Whoo—whoo—whoop !"

He waited in silence until he became convinced that his responses were those only of the echo.

"Can't be !" he exclaimed, " can't be, he gone and lef' me in de middle of my talking ! Caloya, Caloya,—Hello, gal ! hello —whay you day ? Whoo ! whoop !"

Utter silence followed the renewal of his summons. He stuck his fingers, coated as they were with clay, into his wiry shock of wool—a not unfrequent habit with the negro when in a quandary, —and, could the blushes of one of his colour have been seen, those of Mingo would have been found of a scarlet beyond all comparison as the conviction forced itself upon him, that he was laughed at and deserted.

"Cuss de woman !" he exclaimed, " wha make me lub em so. But he mus'nt tink for git 'way from me wid dis sort of acceedint. 'Speck he can't be too fur ; ef he day in dese woods wha' for keep me from fin' 'em. As for he husband, better he no meet me now. Ef he stan' in my way tree minutes, I'll tumble em sure as a stone."

Thus soliloquizing, he darted into the woods, traversing every opening and peeping behind every bush and tree for a goodly hour, but without success. Man and wife had disappeared with a success and secrecy equally inscrutable. Breathless and angry he emerged once more, and stood within the camp. His an-

ger put on the aspect of fury, and disappointment became desperation. He looked round for the dog, intending to renew the
flogging which he had administered on the first day of his acquaintance, and in bestowing which he had been so seasonably interrupted by the owner ; but the cur had departed also ; and no
signs remained of any intention on the part of the squatters to
resume their temporary lodging place, but the rude specimens of
clay manufacture, some two dozen pots and pans, which stood under
a rude shelter of twigs and bushes, immediately adjoining the wigwam. These, with foot and fist, Mingo demolished, trampling, with
the ingenious pains-taking of a wilful boy, the yet unhardened
vases out of all shape and character into the earth on which they
rested. Having thus vented his spleen and displayed a less noble nature than he usually pretended to, the driver proceeded to
resume his coat, in mood of mind as little satisfied with what he
had done in his anger as with the disappointment that had provoked it. But here a new wonder and vexation awaited him.
His fingers again recurred to his head, but no scratching of which
they were capable, could now keep him from the conviction that
there was " magic in the web of it." He looked and lingered,
but he was equally unsuccessful in the search after his hunting
shirt, as for his good humour. He retired from the ground in some
doubt whether it was altogether safe for him to return to a spot
in which proceedings of so mysterious a character had taken
place. All the events in connection with his new acquaintance
began to assume a startling and marvellous character in his
eyes ;—the lazy dog ;—the old husband of a wife so young and
lovely ! What could be more strange or unnatural ! But her
flight—her sudden disappearance, and that too at a time when he
was employing those charms of speech which heretofore had
never proved ineffectual ! Mingo jumped to the conclusion that
Knuckles was a Catawba wizard, and he determined to have
nothing more to do with him :—a determination which he maintained only until the recollection of Caloya's charms made him
resolve, at all hazards, to screen her from so ugly an enchanter.

CHAPTER IX.

But a little time had passed after Mingo had left the camp when Knuckles returned to it. He approached with stealthy pace, keeping himself under cover until he found that the enemy had departed. During the search which the Driver had made after himself and wife, he had been a quiet observer of all his movements. He fancied that the search was instituted for the recovery of the hunting shirt, and did not dream that his wife had left the ground as well as himself to the single possession of the visitor. When he returned and found her gone, his first impression was that she had departed with the negro. But a brief examination of their several footsteps, soon removed his suspicions and enabled him to pursue the route which the woman had taken on leaving the camp. He found her without difficulty, as she came forward, at his approach, from the copse in which she had concealed herself. He encountered her with the bitterest language of suspicion and denunciation. His jealousy had suffered no decrease in consequence of his failure to find cause for it ; but fattening from what it fed on—his own consciousness of unworthiness—the conviction that he did not deserve and could not please one, so far superior and so much younger than himself—vented itself in coarse charges and vindictive threats. With the patience of Griselda, the Catawba woman followed him in silence to the camp, where they soon found cause for new affliction in the discovery which they there made, of the manner in which the disappointed Driver had vented his fury upon their wares. The wrath of Knuckles increased at this discovery, though it did not, as it should have done, lead to any abatement of his jealous feeling towards his wife. Perhaps, on the contrary, it led to the farther proceeding of extremity, which he now meditated, and which he began to unfold to her ears. We forbear the unnecessary preliminaries in the conversation which followed between them, and which were given simply to a re-assertion, on his part, of old and groundless charges, and on hers of a simple and effortless denial of them.   Her final reply, spoken of course in her own language, to the reiterated accusation, was such as to show that even the exemplary patience which she had hitherto manifested was beginning to waver. There was something in it to sting the worthless old sinner, not with a feeling of remorse, but of shame and vexation.

"If Enefisto loves not the black man, wherefore does he take the meat which he brings, and the poison drink from his bottle ? If he loves not the black man, wherefore takes he the garment which wrapt his limbs ?   Caloya loves not the black man, and has eaten none of his meat, has drank none of his poison water, and has stolen none of his garments.   Let Enefisto cast the shirt over the myrtles, and now, now, let the woman go back to seek her people that camp on the waters of the Edisto.   Caloya looks not where the black man sits ; Caloya sees not where he stands, and hears not when he speaks.   Caloya hears only a snake's hissing in her ears.   Enefisto believes not the woman, and she cares not much to speak ;—but let him take up the hatchet and the bow, and she will follow where he leads.   Let her go to her people, where there is no black man.   She would not stay at the ' Red Gulley,' where the black man comes."

" But she would go to the Edisto where is Chickawa ?   Hah ! Caloya shall stay by the ' Red Gulley,' where is Enefisto—she shall not go to the Edisto where is Chickawa.   Enefisto sees ; Enefisto knows."

" Ah, and Caloya knows !   Caloya knows !   Enefisto sees Chickawa and the nigger Mingo every where.   But let Enefisto take up his hatchet and go from this place.   See," pointing to the broken pottery, " there is nothing to stay for.   The nigger will break the pans when she makes them."

" Enefisto will take up the hatchet,—he will drive it into the head of the nigger.   He will not go where Caloya may see Chickawa.   She shall stay by the ' Red Gulley,' and when Mingo, the nigger comes, she shall smile upon him.   She shall go into the wigwam.   Then will he go to her in the wigwam—Hah ?"

" What would Enefisto ?" demanded the squaw in some con
27

sternation at this seeming and very sudden change in the disposi
tion of her spouse.

"Mingo will say to Caloya, 'come, old man is gone hunting,
come. Am I not here for Caloya, come. I love Caloya, let
Caloya love Mingo, come !'"

"But Caloya hates Mingo, Caloya will spit upon the nigger!"
was the indignant exclamation.

"Oh, no, no !" was the almost musical and certainly wild reply of the husband, while a savage smile of scorn and suspicion
covered his features. "Caloya knows not what she says—she
means not what she says. Nigger is young man—Enefisto is old
man. Nigger hab good meat—Enefisto is old hunter, he cannot
see where the deer sleep, he cannot follow the deer in a long
chase, for his legs grow weary. Caloya loves young man who
can bring her 'nough venison and fine clothes, hah ? Let Caloya
go into the wigwam, and nigger will say 'come,' and Caloya will
come."

"Never !" was the indignant answer. "Caloya will never
come to the nigger—Caloya will never come to Chickawa. Let
Enefisto strike the hatchet into the head of Caloya, for his words
make her very wretched. It is better she should die."

"Caloya shall live to do the will of Enefisto. She shall go
where Mingo comes into the wigwam, and when he shall follow
her, she shall stay and look upon him face to face. Mingo is
young,—Caloya loves to look upon young man. When he shall
put his hand upon the shoulder of Caloya then shall Caloya put
her hand upon his. So shall it be—thus says Enefisto."

"Wherefore shall it be so ?"

"Thus says Enefisto. Will Caloya say no ?"

"Let Enefisto kill Caloya ere her hand rests upon the shoulder
of Mingo. The hatchet of Enefisto——"

"Shall sink into the head of the nigger, when his hand is upon
the shoulder of Caloya."

"Ha !"

"It is done. Does Caloya hear ?"

"She hears."

"Will she go into the wigwam when Mingo comes ?"

"She vill go."

" And when he follows her,—when he puts his hand upon her shoulder, and looks, Ha! ha! ha!—looks thus, thus, into her eyes"—his own assumed an expression, or he strove at that moment to make them assume an expression of the most wilful love, —an attempt in which he signally failed, for hate, scorn and jealousy predominating still, gave him a most ghastly aspect, from which the woman shrunk with horror—" when he looks thus into her eyes, then will Caloya put her hand upon the shoulder of Mingo and hold him fast till the hatchet of Enefisto goes deep into his head. Will Caloya do this,—Ha? Will Caloya look on him thus, and grasp him thus, until Enefisto shall strike him thus, thus, thus, till there shall be no more life in his forehead?"

A moment's pause ensued, ere the woman spoke.

" Let Enefisto give the hatchet to Caloya. Caloya will herself strike him in the head if he goes after her into the wigwam."

" No! Caloya shall not. Enefisto will strike. Caloya shall grasp him on the shoulder. Enefisto will see by this if Caloya loves not that the black man should seek her always in the wigwam of the chief. Is Caloya ready—will she do this thing?"

" Caloya is ready—she will do it."

" Ha! ha!—black man is foolish to come to the camp of Enefisto, and look on the woman of Enefisto. He shall die."

CHAPTER X.

MINGO GILLISON almost stumbled over his young master that morning, as he was returning home from his visit so full of strange and unwonted incidents. The latter was about to visit the camp of the squatters in compliance with his promise to that effect, when diverted from his intention by the intelligence which the negro gave him, that the Indians were gone from home. Somehow, it seemed to Mingo Gillison, that it was no part of his present policy that his master should see the intruders. A consciousness of guilt—a conviction that he had not been the faithful custodian of the interests given to his charge. and that, in some respects, they had suffered detriment at his hands, made him jealously apprehensive that the mere visit of his owner to the Red Gulley, would bring his defection to light.

"But where's your coat, Mingo?" was the natural question of Colonel Gillison, the moment after meeting him. Mingo was as ready as any other lover at a lie, and taking for granted that Jove would laugh at this, quite as generously as at a more dangerous perjury, he told a long cock-and-a-bull story about his having had it torn to such a degree in hunting cattle the evening before, as to put it beyond the power of recovery by the seamstress.

"A handsome coat, too, Mingo: I must give you another."

Mingo was gratified and expressed his acknowledgments quite as warmly as it was in his power to do under the feeling of shame and undesert which at that moment oppressed him His master did not fail to see that something had occurred to lessen the assurance of his driver, and diminish the emphasis and abridge the eloquence of his usual speech, but being of an inert disposition of mind, he was not curious enough to seek the solution of a circumstance which, though strange, was unimportant. They separated after a few inquiries on the part of the latter, touching various plantation topics, to all of which the answers of Mingo were uttered with a sufficient degree of readiness and boldness to make them satisfactory.   The master returned to the residence, while Mingo went off to the negro quarter to meditate how to circumvent Richard Knuckles, and win the smiles of his handsome but haughty wife.

It was probably two hours after the supper things had been removed, that the youthful proprietor of the estate of which Mingo held the highly important office in the duties of which we have seen him busy, was startled by the easy opening of the door of the apartment in which he sat, groping through the newspapers of the day, and, immediately after, by the soft tread of a female footstep, heedfully set down upon the floor.   He turned at the unusual interruption, for it may as well be stated passingly, that young Gillison had set out in life with notions of such inveterate bachelorship that his domestic establishment was not suffered to be invaded by any of the opposite sex in any capacity.   It is not improbable, that, later in life, his rigour in this respect, may have undergone some little relaxation, but as we are concerned with present events only, it will be no object with us either to speculate upon or to inquire into the future.   Sufficient for the day is the evil thereof.   Enough for us that his present regulations were such as we have here declared them, and had been laid down with so much emphasis in his household, on coming to his estate, that he turned upon the servant,—for such he assumed the intruder to be—with the determination to pour forth no stinted measure of anger upon the rash person who had shown herself so heedless of his commands.

The reader will be pleased to express no surprise, when we tell him that the nocturnal visitant of our young bachelor was no other than the Indian woman, Caloya.   She had threaded her way, after nightfall, through all the mazes of the plantation, and, undiscovered and unnoticed, even by the watch dog who lay beneath the porch, had penetrated into the mansion and into the presence of its master.   She had probably never been in the same neighbourhood before, but with that sagacity,—we might almost deem it an instinct—which distinguishes the North American Indian, probably, beyond all other people,—she had contrived to elude every habitation which lay between the " Red Gulley" and the dwelling.

house—to avoid contact with the negro houses of fifty slaves, and keep herself concealed from all observation, until that moment when she pleased to discover herself. The surprise of Gillison was natural enough. He rose, however, as soon as he was conscious that the intruder was a stranger, and perceiving her to be an Indian, he readily concluded that she must be one of the squatters at the "Red Gulley," of whom the eloquent Mingo had given him such emphatic warning. With that due regard for the sex which always distinguishes the true gentleman, even when the particular object which calls for it may be debased and inferior, Gillison motioned her to a chair, and, with a countenance expressing no other feelings than those of kindness and consideration, inquired into her wants and wishes. His language, to one of a tribe whom it is customary to regard as thieves and beggars, would have proved him to be something less hostile to the sex, than his household regulations would altogether seem to indicate.

Caloya advanced with firmness, and even dignity, into the apartment. Her deportment was equally respectful and unconstrained. Her face was full of sadness, however, and when she spoke, it might have been observed that her tones were rather more tremulous than usual. She declined the proffered seat, and proceeded to her business with the straightforward simplicity of one having a single purpose. She began by unfolding a small bundle which she carried beneath her arm, and in which, when unrolled and laid upon the table, Col. Gillison fancied he discovered a strong family likeness to that hunting shirt of his driver, of the fate of which he had received such melancholy intelligence a few hours before. But for the particularity of Mingo, in describing the rents and rips, the slits and slashes of his favourite garment, the youthful proprietor would have rashly jumped to the conclusion that this had been the same. His large confidence in the veracity of Mingo, left him rather unprepared for the narrative which followed. In this narrative, Caloya did not exhibit the greatest degree of tenderness towards the amorous driver. She freely and fully declared all the particulars of his forced intimacy with herself and husband from the beginning; and though, with instinctive feminine delicacy, she suppressed every decided overture which the impudent Mingo had made to herself *par amours*, still there was enough shown, to enable his master to see the daring game which his driver, had been playing. Nor, in this narrative, did the woman omit to inform him of the hams and eggs, the chickens and the corn, which had been brought by the devoted negro in tribute to her charms. Up to this point, the story had assumed none but a ludicrous aspect in the sight of the young planter. The petty appropriations of his property of which Mingo had been guilty, did not awaken any very great degree of indignation, and, with the levity of youth, he did not seem to regard in the serious light which it merited, the wanton pursuit and lascivious purposes of the driver. But as the woman quietly proceeded in her narrative, and described the violence which had destroyed her pottery, the countenance of the master darkened. This act seemed one of such determined malignity, that he inly determined to punish it severely. The next statement of Caloya led him to do more justice to virtue, and make a darker estimate yet of the doings of his driver. She did not tell him that her husband was jealous, but she unfolded the solemn requisition which he had last made of her to secure the arms of Mingo in her embrace, while he revenged himself for the insults to which he had been subjected with the sharp edge of the hatchet. The young planter started as he heard the statement. His eye was fixed intently and inquiringly upon the calm, resolute, and seemingly frozen features of the speaker. She ceased to speak, and the pause of a few seconds followed ere Gillison replied :

"But you and your husband surely mean not to murder the fellow, my good woman ? He has done wrong and I will have him punished ; but you must not think to use knife and hatchet upon him."

"When Enefisto says ' strike' to Caloya—Caloya will strike ! Caloya is the woman of Enefisto. Let not Mingo come into the wigwam of the Indian."

Gillison could not doubt her resolution as he heard the deliberate and subdued accents of her voice, and surveyed the composed features of her countenance. The determination to do the bidding of her husband was there expressed in language the least equivocal. His own countenance was troubled ; he had not resolved what course to pursue, and the woman, having fulfilled her mission, was about to depart. She had brought back the stolen coat, though, with the proper tenderness of a wife, she omitted to say that it had been stolen. According to her story Mingo had left it behind him on the myrtles. Her second object had been to save the driver from his fate, and no more effectual mode suggested itself to her mind than by revealing the whole truth to the master. This had been done and she had no further cause to stay. The young planter, after he had instituted a series of inquiries from which he ascertained what were the usual periods when Mingo visited the encampment, how he made his approaches, and in what manner the hovel was built, and where it lay, did not seek to delay her longer. His own knowledge of the "Red Gulley"—a knowledge obtained in boyhood—enabled him to form a very correct notion of all the circumstances of the place; and to determine upon the particulars of a plan which had risen in his mind, by which to save his driver from the danger which threatened him. This done, he begged her to await for a few moments his return, while he ascended to an upper chamber, from whence he brought and offered her a piece of bright calico, such as he well knew would be apt to provoke the admiration of an Indian woman; but she declined it, shaking her head mournfully as she did so, and moving off hurriedly as if to lose the temptation from her sight as quickly as possible. Gillison fancied there was quite as much of despondency as pride in her manner of refusing the gift. It seemed to say that she had no heart for such attractions now. Such indeed was the true exposition of her feelings. What pride could she have in gorgeous apparel, allied to one so brutal, so cruel, so worthless as her husband; and why should she care for such display, when, by his jealous policy, she was withdrawn from all connection with her people, in whose eyes alone she might desire to appear attractive. But the young planter was not to be refused. He would have forced the gift upon her, and when she suffered it to drop at her feet, he expressed himself in words of remonstrance, the tones of which were, perhaps, of more influence than the sense.

"Why not take the stuff, my good woman? You have well deserved it, and much more at my hands. If you do not take it, I will think you believe me to be as bad as Mingo."

She looked at him with some earnestness for a few seconds, then stooping, picked up the bundle, and immediately placed it beneath her arm.

" No, no!" she said, " white man is good.   Black man is bad. Does the master remember ?   Let not Mingo come into the wigwam of Enefisto."

Colonel Gillison promised that he would endeavour to prevent any further mischief, and, with a sad smile of gratitude upon her countenance, the woman retired from his presence as stealthily as she came.   He had enjoined her, if possible, to avoid being seen on leaving the settlement, and it was not hard for one of Catawba birth to obey so easy an injunction.   She succeeded in gaining the " Red Gulley" undiscovered, but there, to her consternation, who should she encounter, at the very first glance, but the impudent and formidable Mingo, sitting, cheek-by-jowl, with her jealous husband, each, seemingly, in a perfect mood of equal and christian amity.   It was a sight to gratify the credulous, but Caloya was not one of these.

CHAPTER XI.

MEANWHILE, the youthful master of the veteran Mingo, meditated in the silence of his hall, the mode by which to save that
amorous personage from the threatened consequences of his
impertinence.   Not that he felt any desire to screen the fellow
from chastisement.   Had he been told that husband and wife had
simply resolved to scourge him with many stripes, he would have
struck hands and cried "cheer" as loudly as any more indifferent
spectator.   But the vengeance of the Catawba Othello, promised
to be of a character far too extreme, and, the inferior moral sense
and sensibility of both Indian and negro considered, too greatly dis-
proportioned to the offence.   It was therefore necessary that what
he proposed to do should be done quickly ; and, taking his hat,
Colonel Gillison sallied forth to the negro quarter, in the centre
of which stood the superior habitation of the Driver.   His object
was simply to declare to the unfaithful servant that his evil
designs and deeds were discovered, as well by himself as by the
Catawba—to promise him the due consequences of his falsehood
to himself, and to warn him of what he had to fear, in the event
of his again obtruding upon the privacy of the squatters.   To
those who insist that the working classes in the South should enjoy
the good things of this world in as bountiful a measure as the
wealthy proprietors of the soil, it would be very shocking to see
that they lived poorly, in dwellings which, though rather better than
those of the Russian boor, are yet very mean in comparison with
those built by Stephen Girard, John Jacob Astor, and persons of that
calibre.   Nay, it would be monstrous painful to perceive that the
poor negroes are constantly subjected to the danger of ophthalmic
and other diseases, from the continued smokes in which they live,
the fruit of those liberal fires which they keep up at all seasons, and
which the more fortunate condition of the poor in the free States,
does not often compel them to endure at any.   It would not
greatly lessen the evil of this cruel destiny, to know that each

had his house to himself, exclusively; that he had his little garden plat around it, and that his cabbages, turnips, corn and potatoes, not to speak of his celery, his salad, &c., are, in half the number of cases, quite as fine as those which appear on his master's table. Then, his poultry-yard, and pig-pen—are they not there also?—but then, it must be confessed that his stock is not quite so large, as his owner's, and there, of course, the parallel must fail. He has one immunity, however, which is denied to the owner. The hawk, (to whose unhappy door most disasters of the poultry yard are referred,) seldom troubles his chickens—his hens lay more numerously than his master's, and the dogs always prefer to suck the eggs of a white rather than those of a black proprietor. These, it is confessed, are very curious facts, inscrutable, of course, to the uninitiated; and, in which the irreverent and sceptical alone refuse to perceive any legitimate cause of wonder. You may see in his hovel and about it, many little additaments which, among the poor of the South, are vulgarly considered comforts; with the poor of other countries, however, as they are seldom known to possess them, they are no doubt regarded as burthens, which it might be annoying to take care of and oppressive to endure. A negro slave not only has his own dwelling, but he keeps a plentiful fire within it for which he pays no taxes. That he lives upon the fat of the land you may readily believe, since he is proverbially much fatter himself than the people of any other class. He has his own grounds for cultivation, and, having a taste for field sports, he keeps his own dog for the chase—an animal always of very peculiar characteristics, some of which we shall endeavour one day to analyse and develope. He is as hardy and cheerful as he is fat, and, but for one thing, it might be concluded safely that his condition was very far before that of the North American Indian—his race is more prolific, and, by increasing rather than diminishing, multiply necessarily, and unhappily the great sinfulness of mankind. This, it is true, is sometimes urged as a proof of improving civilization, but then, every justly-minded person must agree with Miss Martineau, that it is dreadfully immoral. We suspect we have been digressing.

Col. Gillison soon reached the negro quarter, and tapping at the

door of the Driver's wigwam, was admitted, after a brief parley, by the legitimate spouse of that gallant.   Mingo had been married to Diana, by the Reverend Jonathan Buckthorn, a preacher of the Methodist persuasion, who rode a large circuit, and had travelled, with praiseworthy charity, all the way from Savannah River, in all weathers, and on a hard going nag, simply to unite this worthy couple in the holy bonds of wedlock.   **At** that time, both the parties were devout members of the Church, but they suffered from frequent lapses; and Mingo, having been engaged in sundry *liaisons*—which, however creditable to, and frequent among the French, Italian and English nobility, are highly censurable in a sla**ve** population, and a decisive proof of the demoralizing tendency of such an institution—was, at the formal complaint of the wife, "suspended" from the enjoyment of the Communion Table, and finally, on a continuance of this foreign and fashionable practice, fully expelled from all the privileges of the brotherhood.   Diana had been something of a termagant, but Mingo had succeeded in outstorming her.   For the first six months after marriage, the issue was consider d very doubtful; but a decisive battle took place at the close of that period, in which the vigorous woman was compelled to give in and Mingo remained undisputed master of the field.   But though overthrown and conquered, she was not quiescent; and her dissatisfaction at the result, showed itself in repeated struggles, which, however, were too convulsive and transient, to render necessary any very decided exercise of the husband's energies. She growled and grumbled still, without cessation, and though she did not dare to resent his frequent infidelities, she nevertheless pursued them with an avidity, and followed the movements of her treacherous lord with a jealous watchfulness, which proved that she did not the less keenly feel them.   Absolute fear alone made her restrain the fury which was yet boiling and burning in her soul.   When her master declared his desire to see Mingo, what was her answer ?   Not, certainly, that of a very dutiful or well satisfied spouse.

  " Mingo, mossa ?   Whay him dey ?   Ha ! mossa, you bes' **ax** ebbrv woman on de plantation 'fore you come to he own wife.   **I bin** marry to Mingo by Parson Buckthorn, and de Parson bin **make**

Mingo promis' for lub and 'bey me, but he forget all he promise tree day after we bin man and wife. He nebber bin lub 't all ; and as for 'bey,—lor' ha' massy 'pon me, mossa, I speak noting but de trute when I tell you,—he 'bey ebbry woman from yer to town 'fore he 'hey ne own dear wife. Der's not a woman, mossa, 'non de tree plantation, he aint lub more dan Di. Sometime he gone to Misser Jacks place—he hab wife dere ! Sometime he gone to Misser Gabeau—he hab wife dere ! Nex' time, he gone to Squir' Collins,—he hab wife dere ! Whay he no hab wife, mossa ? Who can tell ? He hab wife ebbry which whay, and now, he no *sacrify*, he gone—you aint gwine to bleeb me, mossa, I know you aint—he gone and look for wife at Indian camp, whay down by de ' Red Gulley.' De trute is, mossa, Mingo is a mos' powerful black rascal of a nigger as ebber lib on gentleman plantation."

It was fortunate for young Gillison that he knew something of the nature of a termagant wife, and could make allowances for the injustice of a jealous one. He would otherwise have been persuaded by what he heard that his driver was one of the most uncomely of all the crow family. Though yielding no very credulous faith to the complaints of Diana, he still found it impossible to refuse to hear them ; and all that he could do by dint of perseverance, was to diminish the long narratives upon which she was prepared to enter to prove her liege lord to be no better than ne should be. Having exhausted all his efforts and his patience in the attempt to arrive at some certain intelligence of the husband's " whereabouts," without being able to divert the stream of her volubility from the accustomed channels, he concluded by exclaiming—

" Well, d—n the fellow, let him take the consequences. He stands a chance of having his throat cut before twenty-four hours are over, and you will then be at liberty, Di., to get a husband who will be more faithful. Should Mingo not see me by ten o'clock to-morrow, he's a dead man. So, you had better stir your stumps, my good woman, and see after him, unless you are willing to be a widow before you have found out a better man for your husband. Find Mingo and send him to me to-night, or he's a dead man to-morrow."

" Le' 'em dead—who care ?   He d'zarb for dead.   I sure he
no care if Di bin dead twenty tousand time.   Le' 'em dead !"

Gillison left the hut and proceeded to other parts of the settlement where he thought it not improbable that the driver might be
found ; but a general ignorance was professed by all the negroes
with respect to the particular movements of that worthy ; and he
soon discovered that his search was fruitless.   He gave it up in
despair, trusting that he should be able to succeed better at an
hour seasonably early in the morning, yet half disposed, from
his full conviction of his roguery, to leave the fellow to his fate.

Strange to say, such was not the determination of the dissatisfied Diana.   Wronged and neglected as she had been, and was,
there was still a portion of the old liking left, which had first
persuaded her to yield her youthful affections to the keeping of
this reckless wooer ; and though she had avowed her willingness
to her young master, that the " powerful black rascal of a nigger"
should go to the dogs, and be dog's meat in twenty-four hours,
still, better feelings came back to her, after due reflection, to soften
her resolves.   Though not often blessed with his kind words and
pleasant looks, now-a-days, still, " she could not but remember
such things were, and were most precious to her."

Left to herself, she first began to repeat the numberless conju-
gal offences of which he had been guilty ; but the memory of
these offences did not return alone.   She remembered that these
offences brought with them an equal number of efforts at atonement on the part of the offender : and when she thought of his
vigorous frame, manly, dashing and graceful carriage, his gorgeous coat, his jauntily worn cap, his white teeth, and the insinuating smile of his voluminous lips, she could not endure the idea
of such a man being devoted to a fate so short and sudden as that
which her young master had predicted.   She had not been told, it is
true, from what quarter this terrible fate was to approach.   She
knew not under what aspect it would come, but the sincerity of her
master was evident in his looks, words, and general air of anxiety,
and she was convinced that there was truth in his assurance.   Per
haps, her own attachment for the faithless husband—disguised as
it was by her continual grumbling and discontent—was sufficiently
strong to bring about this conviction easily.   Diana determined
to save her husband, worthless and wicked as he was,—and pos-

sibly, some vague fancy may have filled her mind as she came to this resolution, that, gratitude alone, for so great a service, might effect a return of the false one to that allegiance which love had hitherto failed to secure. She left her dwelling to seek him within half an hour after the departure of her master. But the worst difficulty in her way was the first. She trembled with the passion of returning jealousy when she reflected that the most likely place to find him would be at the "Red Gulley" in instant communion with a hateful rival—a red Indian—a dingy squaw,— whose colour, neither white nor black, was of that sort, which, according to Diana in her jealous mood, neither gods nor men ought to endure. Her husband's admiration she naturally ascribed to Catawba witchcraft. She doubted—she hesitated—she almost re-resolved against the endeavour. Fortunately, however, her better feelings prevailed. She resolved to go forward—to save her husband—but, raising her extended hands and parted fingers, as she came to this determination, and gnashing her teeth with vindictive resolution as she spoke, she declared her equal resolve to compensate herself for so great a charity, by sinking her ten claws into the cheeks of any copper coloured damsel whom she should discover at the Red Gulley in suspicious propinquity with that gay deceiver whom she called her lord. Having thus, with due solemnity, registered her oath in Heaven— and she was not one under such circumstances to "lay perjury upon her soul"—she hurried away under the equal impulse of a desire to save Mingo, and to "capper-claw" Caloya. It was not long after, that young Gillison, who was more troubled about the fate of his driver than he was willing to acknowledge even to himself, came to a determination also to visit the "Red Gulley." A little quiet reflection, after he had reached home, led him to fear that he might not be in season to prevent mischief if he waited till the morning for Mingo's appearance ; and a sudden conjecture that, at that very moment, the audacious negro might be urging his objects in the wigwam of the squatters, made him fearful that even his instant interference would prove too late. As soon as this conjecture filled his mind, he seized his cap, and grasping his rifle, and calling his favourite dog, set forth with all possible speed towards the spot, destined to be memorable forever after in all local chronicles, in consequence of these events.

CHAPTER XII.

The horror and vexation of Caloya may be imagined, when, on returning from her visit to the master of the impudent Mingo, she discovered him, cheek-by-jowl, with her husband. The poor woman was miserable in the extreme from various causes. Resolved steadfastly and without scruple to do the will of her jealous spouse, she yet shrank from the idea of perpetrating the bloody deed which the latter contemplated, and which was so suitable to the fierce character of Indian vindictiveness. She was, in fact, a gentle, though a firm, simple, and unaffected woman, and had not this been the prevailing nature of her heart, the kindness with which Gillison had received, and the liberality with which he had treated her, would have been sufficient to make her reluctant to do any thing which might be injurious to his interests.

But, taught in the severe school of the barbarian those lessons which insist always upon the entire subordination of the woman, she had no idea of avoiding, still less of rebelling against, the authority which prescribed her laws. " To hear was to obey," and with a deep sigh she advanced to the wigwam, with a firm resolution to do as she had been commanded, though, with a prayer in her mind, not the less fervent because it remained unspoken by her lips, that the fearful necessity might pass away, and her husband be prevented, and she be spared, the commission of the threatened deed.

It was deemed fortunate by Caloya, that, observing the habitual caution of the Indian, she had kept within the cover of the woods until the moment when she came within sight of the wigwam. This caution enabled her still to keep from discovery, and " fetching a compass" in the covert so as to pass into the rear of the hut, she succeeded by pulling away some fragments of the bark which covered it, in entering its narrow precincts without having been perceived. With a stealthy footstep and a noiseless motion, she deposited her bundle of calicoes in a corner of the hut, and sink ing down beside it, strove to still even those heavings of her anxious bosom, which she fancied, in her fears, might become audible to the persons without.

To account for the return of **Mingo Gillison** to the spot where he had been guilty of so much impertinence, and had done so much mischief, is not a difficult matter. It will here be seen that he was a fellow whom too much authority had helped to madden —that he was afflicted with the disease of intense self-consequence, and that his passions, accordingly, were not always to be restrained by prudence or right reason. These qualities necessarily led to frequent errors of policy and constant repentings. He had not many moral misgivings, however, and his regrets were solely yielded to the evil results, in a merely human and temporary point of view, which followed his excesses of passion and frequent outbreaks of temper. He had not well gone from the " Red Gulley" after annihilating the pottery thereof, without feeling what a fool he had been. He readily conceived that his rashness would operate greatly, not only against his success with the woman, but against his future familiarity with the man. It was necessary that he should heal the breach with the latter if he hoped to win any favours from the former ; and, with this conviction, the rest of the day was devoted to a calm consideration of the *modus operandi* by which he might best succeed in this desire. A rough investigation of the moral nature of an Indian chief, led Mingo to the conclusion that the best defence of his conduct, and the happiest atonement which he could offer, would be one which was addressed to his appetites rather than to his understanding. Accordingly, towards nightfall, having secured an adequate supply of whiskey—that bane equally of negro and Indian—he prepared with some confidence, to re-appear before the parties whom he had so grievously offended. He had his doubts, it is true, of the sort of reception which he should meet ;—he was not altogether sure of the magical effect of the whiskey, in promoting christian charity, and leading the savage to forgiveness ; but none of the apprehensions of Mingo were of personal danger. He would have laughed to scorn a suggestion of harm at the hands of so infirm and insignificant a person as Richard Knuckles ; and looking upon his own stout limbs and manly frame, he would have found

28

in the survey, a sufficient assurance that Mingo Gillison was equally irresistible to man and wife. It was with a boldness of carriage, therefore, that corresponded adequately with the degree of confidence which he felt in his equal powers of persuasion, and the whiskey, rather than his personal prowess, that he appeared that night before the hovel of the squatters. He found Knuckles alone, and seated a little in-advance of his habitation. The Indian was sober from the necessity of the case. The policy of the negro had not lately allowed him liquor, and he had not himself any means for procuring it. He watched the approach of the enemy without arising from the turf, and without betraying in his look any of that hostility which was active in his bosom. His face, indeed, seemed even less grave than usual, and a slight smile upon his lips, in which it would have tasked a far more suspicious eye than that of Mingo to have discovered anything sinister, betrayed, seemingly, a greater portion of good humour than usually softened his rigid and coarse features. Mingo approached with a conciliating grin upon his visage, and with hands extended in amity. As the Indian did not rise to receive him, he squatted down upon his haunches on the turf opposite, and setting down the little jug which he brought between them, clapped the Indian on his shoulders with a hearty salutation, which was meant to convey to the other a pleasant assurance of his own singular condescension.

"Knuckles, my boy, how you does? You's bex with me, I reckons, but there's no needcessity for that. Say I did kick over the pots and mash the pans?—well! I can pay for 'em, can't I? When a man has got the coppers he's a right to kick; there's no use to stand in composition with a fellow that's got the coppers. He kin throw down and he kin pick up—he kin buy and he kin sell; he kin break and he kin men'; he kin gib and he kin tak'; he kin kill and he kin eat—dere's no'ting he can't do ef he hab money—he's mossa to all dem d—d despisable rackrobates, what's got no coppers. I once bin' ye'r a sarmint from Parson Buckthorn, and he tink on dis object jis' as you ye'r me tell you. He tex' is take from de forty-seben chapter—I 'speck it's de forty-seben—wh'ch say, 'what he gwine to profit a gempleman what's mak' de best crop in de world, if he loss he soul,'—which is de

same t'ing, Knuckles, you know, as ef I was to ax you, wha's
de difference ef Mingo Gillison kick over you' pans and pots, and
bre'k 'em all to smash, and ef he pick 'em, like he pick up eggs,
widout bre'k any, so long as he pay you wha' you ax for 'em.
You sell 'em, you git you money, wha' matter wha' I do wid 'em
arter dat? I bre'k 'em or I men' 'em, jis' de same t'ing to you.
'Spose I eat 'em, wha's de difference?   He stick in Mingo stomach, he no stick in your'n ; and all de time de coppers is making
purty jingle in you' pocket.   Well, my boy, I come to do de t'ing
now.   I bre'k you' pots, I 'tan ye'r to pay you for 'em.   But you
mus' be t'irsty, my old fellow, wid so much talking—tak' a drink
'fore we exceed to business.''

The Catawba needed no second invitation.   The flavour of the
potent beverage while the negro had been so unprofitably declaim-
ing, ascended to his nostrils with irresistible influence, in spite of
the stopper of corn cob which imperfectly secured it, and which,
among the negroes of the Southern plantations, makes a more common than seemly apology for a velvet cork.   The aroma of the
beverage soon reconciled Knuckles to the voice of his enemy, and
rendered those arguments irresistible, which no explanations of
Mingo could ever have rendered clear.   As he drank, he became
more and more reconciled to the philosophy of his comrade, and,
strengthened by his draughts, his own became equally explicit
and emphatic.

"Ha! Ha! Biskey good too much!" was the long drawn and
fervent exclamation which followed the withdrawal of the reluctant vessel from his lips.

"You may say dat wid you' own ugly mout', Dick, and tell no
lie nother," was the cool response.   "Any biskey is good 'nough,
but dat's what I calls powerful fine.   Dat' fourt' proof, gennywine, and 'trong like Sampson, de Philistian.   Der's no better in
all Jim Hollon's 'stablishment.   *We* gin a mighty great price for
it, so it ought to be good, ef ther's any justice done.   But don't
stan', Knuckles—ef you likes it, sup at it again.   It's not like
some women's I know—it gives you smack for smack, and holds
on as long as you let it.''

"Huh!—woman's is fool!" responded the savage with an air
of resentment which his protracted draught of the potent beverage

did not altogether dissipate. The reference to the sex reminded him of his wife, and when he looked upon the speaker he was also reminded of his presumptuous passions, and of the forward steps which he had taken for their gratification. But his anger did not move him to any imprudence so long as the power of reflection was left him. It was only as his familiarity with the bottle advanced that his jealous rage began to get the better of his reason and lead him into ebullitions, which, to a more acute or less conceited person than Mingo, would have certainly betrayed the proximity of that precipice in the near neighbourhood of which he stood. The savage grew gradually eloquent on the subject of woman's worthlessness, weakness, folly, &c.; and as the vocabulary of broken and imperfect English which he possessed was any thing but copious, his resort to the Catawba was natural and ready to give due expression to his resentment and suspicions.

"Huh! woman is fool—Ingin man spit 'pon woman—ehketee —boozamogettee!—d—n,—d—n,—damn! tree d—n for woman!—he make for cuss. Caloya Ganchacha!—he dog,—he wuss dan dog—romonda!—tree time dog! anaporee, toos-wa-nedah! Ingin man say to woman, go! fill you mout' wid grass,— woman is dog for cuss!"

The English portion of this blackguardism is amply sufficient to show the spirit of the speaker, without making necessary any translation of that part of the speech, which, in his own dialect, conceals matter far more atrocious. Enough was understood by Mingo, as well from the action and look of the Catawba, as from the vulgar English oath which he employed in connection with his wife's sex and name, to convince the negro that Caloya was an object rather of hate than of suspicion to her worthless husband. As this notion filled his sagacious cranium, new hopes and fancies followed it, and it was with some difficulty that he could suppress the eag r and precipitate utterance of a scheme, which grew out of this very grateful conjecture.

"You no lub woman, Knuckles,—eh?"

"Huh! woman is dog. Ingin man say to dog—go! and he go!—say to dog, come, and he come! Dog hunt for meat, woman's put meat in de pot! Woman is dog and dog is woman.

Nomonda-yaw-ee—d—n tree time—wassiree—woman is tree time d—n!"

"Well, Knuckles, old boy! take a drink! You don't seem to defections womans no how!"

"Heh?"—inquiringly.

"Prehaps you don't altogether know what I mean by defections? Well, I'll tell you. Defections means a sort of chicken-lub; as if you only had it now and then, and something leetler than common. It aint a pow'rful attack,—it don't take a body about de middle as I may say, and gib 'em an up and down h'ist. It's a sort of lub that lets you go off when you chooses, and come back when you wants to, and don't keep you berry long about it. That's to say, it's a sort of defections."

A monosyllable from the Indian, like the last, attested any thing but his mental illumination in consequence of the very elaborate metaphysical distinctions which Mingo had undertaken. But the latter was satisfied that Knuckles should have become wiser if he had not; and he proceeded, making short stages toward the point which he desired to attain.

"Well, now, Knuckles, if so be you don't affections womans, what makes you keeps her 'bout you? Ef she's only a dog in your sight, why don't you sen' her a-packing? Ingin man kin find somebody, I 'speck, to take care ob he dog for 'em."

"Heh? Dog—wha' dog?"

"Dat is to say—but take a drink, old fellow! Take a long pull—dat jug's got a long body, an' you may turn it upside down heap o' times 'fore you'll git all the life out of it. It gin my arm a smart tire, I kin tell you, to tote it all the way here! Dat is to say—but sup at it agin, Knuckles,—please de pigs, you don't know much about what's good, or you would'nt put it down, tell the red water begins to come into you' eyes."

"Aw—yaw—yaw! Biskey good too much!"

Was the exclamation, accompanied with a long drawn, hissing sound, of equal delight and difficulty, which issued spontaneously from the Indian's mouth, as he withdrew the jug from his lips. The negro looked at him with manifest satisfaction. His eyes were suffused with water, and exhibited a hideous stare of excitement and imbecility. A fixed glaze was overspreading them fast, revealing some of those fearful aspects which distinguish the last fleeting gleams of consciousness in the glassy gaze of the dying. Portions of the liquor which, in his feebleness he had failed to swallow, ran from the corners of his mouth ; and his fingers, which still clutched the handle of the jug, were contracted about it like the claws of a vulture in the spasms of a mortal agony. His head, as if the neck were utterly unsinewed, swung from side to side in his repeated efforts to raise it to the usual Indian erectness, and, failing in this attempt, his chin sunk at last and settled down heavily upon his breast. He was evidently in prime condition for making a bargain, and, apprehensive that he might have overdone the matter, and that the fellow might be too stupid even for the purposes of deception, Mingo hastened with due rapidity to make the proposition which he had conceived, and which was of a character with the audacity of his previous designs.

"Well, Knuckles, my frien', what's to hender us from a trade ? Ef so be you hates woman's and loves Biskey—ef woman's is a d—n dog, and biskey is de only ting dat you most defections in dis life,—den gib me you d—n dog, and I'll gib you 'nough and plenty of de ting you lub. You yerry me ?"

"Aw, yaw, yaw, yaw ! Biskey berry good !" A torrent of hiccoughs concluded the reply of the Indian, and for a brief space rendered the farther accents of the negro inaudible even to himself.

"To be sure,—da's trute ! Biskey is berry good, and da's wha' I'm sayin' to you, ef you'd only pay some detention. I'm a offering you, Knuckles—I'm offering to buy you dog from you. I'll gib you plenty biskey for you dog. Wha' you say, man ? eh ?"

"Aw, yaw ! Black man want Ingin dog !" The question was concluded by a faint attempt to whistle. Drunkenness had made the Catawba more literal than usual, and Mingo's apprehensions increased as he began to apprehend that he should fail entirely in reaching the understanding of his companion.

"Psho ! git out, Knuckles, I no want you' four-legged dog— it's you' two-legged dog I day arter. Enty you bin call you

woman a dog? Enty you bin say, dat you wife, Caloya, is d—n
dog?"

"Ya-ou! ramonda yau-ee, Caloya! woman is tree time d—n
log!"

"To be sure he is. Da's wha we bin say. Now, I want dog,
Knuckles; and you hab dog wha's jis suit me. You call him
Caloya—you dog! You sell me Caloya, I gie you one whole
barrel biskey for da same dog, Caloya."

"Hah!" was the sudden exclamation of the Indian, as this impudent but liberal offer reached his senses; but, whether in approbation or in anger, it was impossible, in the idiot inexpressive-
ness of his drunken glance, for the negro to determine. He
renewed his offer with certain additional inducements in the
shape of pipes and tobacco, and concluded with a glowing eulogy upon the quality of his "powerful, fine, gennywine, fourt'
proof," the best in Holland's establishment, and a disparaging reference to the small value of the dog that he was prepared to buy
with it. When he finished, the Indian evidently comprehended
him better, and laboured under considerable excitement. He
strove to speak, but his words were swallowed up in hiccoughs,
which had been increasing all the while. What were his sentiments, or in what mind he received the offer, the negro vainly strove,
by the most solicitous watchfulness, to ascertain; but he had too
completely overdosed his victim, and the power of speech seemed
entirely departed. This paralysis did not, however, extend entirely
to his limbs. He struggled to rise, and, by the aid of a hickory
twig which grew beside him, he succeeded in obtaining a doubtful equilibrium, which he did not, however, very long preserve.
His hand clutched at the knife within his belt, but whether the
movement was designed to vindicate his insulted honour, or was
simply spasmodic, and the result of his condition, could not be
said. Muttering incoherently at those intervals which his continual hiccoughing allowed, he wheeled about and rushed incon-
tinently towards the hovel, as if moved by some desperate design.
He probably knew nothing definitely at that moment, and had no
precise object. A vague and flickering memory of the instructions he had given to his wife, may have mingled in with his
thoughts in his drunken mood, and probably prompted him to the

call which he thrice loudly made upon her name. She did not answer, but, having heard in her place of concealment the offensive proposition which the negro had made her husband, she now crouched doubly closely and cautious, lest the latter, under this novel form of provocation, might be moved to vent his wrath upon her head. Perhaps, too, she fancied, that by remaining quiet, she might escape the necessity of contributing in any wise to the execution of the bloody plot in which his commands had engaged her. Whatever may have been her fear, or the purposes of the husband, Caloya remained silent. She moved not from the corner in which she lay, apprehensively waiting events, and resolved not to move or show herself unless her duty obviously compelled her.

Mingo, meanwhile, utterly blinded by his prodigious self-esteem, construed all the movements of the Catawba into favourable appearances in behalf of his desires; and when Knuckles entered the hovel calling upon his wife, he took it for granted that the summons had no other object than to deliver the precious commodity into his own hands. This conviction warmed his imagination to so great a degree, that he forgot all his prudence, and following Knuckles into the wigwam, he prepared to take possession of his prize, with that unctuous delight and devotedness which should convince her that she too had made an excellent bargain by the trade. But when he entered the hovel, he was encountered by the savage with uplifted hatchet.

"Hello, Knuckles, wha' you gwine to do wid you' hatchet? You wouldn't knock you bes' frien' 'pon de head, eh?"

"Nigger is d—n dog!" cried the savage, his hiccoughs sufficiently overcome by his rage to allow him a tolerable clear utterance at last. As he spoke the blow was given full at the head of the driver. Mingo threw up his left hand to ward off the stroke, but was only partially successful in doing so. The keen steel smote the hand, divided the tendon between the fore-finger and thumb, and fell with considerable force upon the forehead.

"Oh you d—n black red-skin, you kill mossa best nigger!" shrieked the driver, who fancied, in the first moment of his pain, that his accounts were finally closed with the world. The blood, streaming freely from the wound, though it lessened

the stunning effects of the blow, yet blinded his eyes and increas
ed his terrors.   He felt persuaded that no surgeon could do him
service now, and bitterly did he reproach himself for those amorous tendencies which had brought him to a fate so unexpected
and sudden.   It was the very moment when the exhortations of
the Rev. Jonathan Buckthorn would have found him in a blessed
state of susceptibility and saving grace.   The evil one had not
suffered so severe a rebuke in his present habitation for a very
long season.   But as the Reverend Jonathan was not nigh to take
advantage of the circumstance, and as the hapless Mingo felt the
continued though impotent struggle of his enemy at his feet, his
earthly passions resumed their sway, and, still believing that he
had not many hours to live, he determined to die game and have
his revenge in his last moments.   The Catawba had thrown his
whole remaining strength into the blow, and the impetus had carried him forward.   He fell upon his face, and vainly striving and
striking at the legs of his opponent, lay entirely at his mercy ;
his efforts betraying his equal feebleness and fury.   At first
Mingo doubted his ability to do anything.   Though still standing,
he was for some time incapable of perceiving in that circumstance
any strong reason for believing that he had any considerable portion of vitality left, and most certainly doubted his possession of
a sufficient degree of strength to take his enemy by the throat.
But with his rage came back his resolution, and with his resolution his vigour.

  " Ef I don't stop your kicking arter dis, you red sarpent,
my name's Blind Buzzard. Ef Mingo mus' dead, you shall
dead too, you d—n crooked, little, old, red rascal. I'll squeeze
you t'roat, tell you aint got breat' 'nough in you body to scar'
'way musquito from peeping down your gullet. Lor' ha' mas-
sey !—to 'tink Mingo mus' dead 'cause he git knock on de head
by a poor, little, shrinkle up Injun, dat he could eat up wid he
eyes and no make tree bite ob he carcass."

  This reflection increased the wrath of the negro, who prepared
with the most solemn deliberation to take the Indian's life by
strangling him.   With this design he let his knee drop upon the
body of the prostrate Knuckles, while his hand was extended in
order to secure an efficient grasp upon his throat.   But his move-

ments had been closely watched by the keen-eyed Caloya from the corner where she crouched, who, springing forward at the perilous moment, drew the hatchet from the hand of the sprawling and unconscious savage and took an attitude of threatening which effectually diverted the anger of the negro.   Surprised at her appearance, rather than alarmed at her hostility, he began to conjecture, in consequence of the returning passion which he felt, that his danger was not so great as he had at first fancied.   The sight of those charms which had led him into the danger, seemed to induce a pleasant forgetfulness of the hurts which had been the result of his rashness; and with that tenacity of purpose which distinguishes a veteran among the sex, the only thought of Mingo was the renewal of his practices of evil.   He thought no more of dying, and of the Reverend Jonathan Buckthorn, but with a voice duly softened to the gentler ears which he was preparing to address, he prefaced his overtures by a denunciation of the " dead-drunk dog what was a-lying at his foot."   A wretch, as he loudly declared, who was no more worthy of such a woman than he was worthy of life.

" But der's a man wha's ready to tak' you, my lubly one, and tak' care ob you, and treat you as you d'zarb. He's a gempleman—he's no slouch, nor no sneak. He's always dress in de bes'—he's always hab plenty for eat and plenty for drink—der's no scarcity where he hab de mismanagement; and nebber you'll hab needcessity for work, making mud pot and pan, ef he tak' you into his defections. I reckon, Caloya, you's want for know who is dat pusson I tell you 'bout. Who is dat gempleman wha's ready for do you so much benefactions? Well! look a' yer, Caloya, and I reckon you'll set eye on de very pusson in perticklar."

The woman gave him no answer, but still, with weapon uplifted, kept her place, and maintained a watch of the utmost steadfastness upon all his movements.

" Wha'! you won't say not'ing? Can't be you care someting for dis bag of feaders, wha's lie at my foot!"

With these words the irreverent negro stirred the body of Knuckles with his foot, and Caloya sprang upon him in the same instant, and with as determined a hand as ever her husband's had been, struck as truly, though less successfully, at the forehead of

her wooer.   This time, Mingo was rather too quick to suffer harm
from a feebler arm than his own.   His eye detected her design
the moment she moved, and he darted aside in season to avoid the
blow.   With equal swiftness he attempted to seize her in his arms
the instant after, but, eluding his grasp, she backed towards the
entrance of the wigwam, keeping her weapon uplifted, and evidently resolved to use it to the best advantage as soon as an opportunity offered.   Mingo was not to be baffled in this fashion—the
difficulties in the way of his pursuit seemed now reduced to a single issue—the husband was *hors de combat*, and the wife—she certainly held out only because she was still in his presence.   To
this moment, Mingo never doubted that his personal prowess and
pretensions had long since impressed Caloya with the most indulgent and accessible emotions.   He advanced, talking all the while
in the most persuasive accents, but without inducing any relaxation
of watchfulness or resolution on the part of the woman.   He was
prepared to rush upon, and wrest the hatchet from her hand—and
farther ideas of brutality were gathering in his mind—when he
was arrested by the presence of a new and annoying object which
suddenly showed itself at the entrance and over the shoulder of
the Indian woman.   This was no other than his lawful spouse,
Diana.

"Hello, Di! what de dibble you come for, eh?"

"I come for you, to be sure.   Wha' de dibble you is doing yer,
wid Injun woman?"

Surprised at the strange voice, and feeling herself somewhat
secure in the presence of a third person, Caloya ventured to look
round upon the new comer.   The sight of her comely features
was a signal of battle to the jealous wife, who, instantly, with a
fearful shriek, struck her talons into the cheeks of her innocent rival, and followed up the assault by dashing her head into her face.
The hatchet fell involuntary upon the assailant, but the latter had
too successfully closed in, to receive much injury from the blow,
which, however, descended upon her back, between the shoulders,
and made itself moderately felt.   Diana, more vigorous than the
Indian woman, bore her to the earth, and, doubtlessly, under her
ideas of provocation, would have torn her eyes from their sockets,
but for the prompt interposition of her husband, who, familiar with

the marital rights sanctioned by the old English law, prostrated her to the earth with a single blow of his fist. He might have followed up this violence to a far less justifiable extent, for the audacity which his wife had shown had shocked all his ideas of domestic propriety, but that he was interrupted before he could proceed further by a hand which grasped tightly his neckcloth from behind, and giving it a sudden twist, curtailed his powers of respiration to a most annoying degree. He turned furiously though with difficulty upon the new assailant, to encounter the severe eyes of his young master.

Here was an explosion! Never was an unfaithful steward more thoroughly confounded. But the native impudence of Mingo did not desert him. He had one of the fairest stories in the world to tell. He accounted for every thing in the most rational and innocent manner—but in vain. Young Gillison had the eye of a hawk when his suspicions were awakened, and he had already heard the testimony of the Indian woman, whom he could not doubt. Mingo was degraded from his trust, and a younger negro put over him. To compensate the Indian woman for the injuries which she received, was the first care of the planter as he came upon the ground. He felt for her with increased interest as she did not complain. He himself assisted her from the ground and conducted her into the wigwam. There, they found Knuckles almost entirely insensible. The liquor with which the negro had saturated him, was productive of effects far more powerful than he had contemplated. Fit had succeeded to fit, and paralysis was the consequence. When Gillison looked upon him, he saw that he was a dying man. By his orders, he was conveyed that night to the settlement, where he died the next day.

Caloya exhibited but little emotion, but she omitted no attention. She observed the decorum and performed all the duties of a wife. The young planter had already learned to esteem her, and when, the day after the funeral, she prepared to return to her people, who were upon the Edisto, he gave her many presents which she received thankfully, though with reluctance.

A year after, at the same season, the " Red Gulley" was occupied by the whole tribe, and the evening following their arrival, Col. Gillison, sitting within the hall of his family mansion, was surprised by the unexpected appearance of Caloya. She looked younger than before, comelier, and far more happy. She was followed by a tall and manly looking hunter, whom she introduced as her husband, and who proved to be the famous Chickawa, of whom poor old Knuckles had been so jealous. The grateful Caloya came to bring to the young planter a pair of moccasins and leggins, neatly made and fancifully decorated with beads, which, with her own hands, she had wrought for him. He received them with a sentiment of pleasure, more purely and more enduringly sweet than young men are often apt to feel ; and, esteeming her justly, there were few articles of ordinary value in his possession with which he would not sooner have parted, than the simple present of that Catawba woman.

LUCAS DE AYLLON.

A HISTORICAL NOUVELLETTE.*

CHAPTER I.

THE SNARE OF THE PIRATE.

SEBASTIAN CABOT is supposed to have been the first European voyager who ever laid eyes upon the low shores of Carolina. He sailed along the coast and looked at it, but did not attempt to land,—nor was such a proceeding necessary to his objects. His single look, according to the laws and morals of that day, in civilized Europe, conferred a sufficient right upon the nation by which he was employed, to all countries which he might discover, and to all people, worshipping at other than Christian altars, by whom they might be occupied. The supposed right, however, thus acquired by Cabot, was not then asserted by the English whom he

---

* The three chapters which constitute this narrative, originally formed part of a plan which I meditated of dealing with the early histories of the South, somewhat after the manner of Henry Neele, in his Romance of English History. Of course I did not mean to follow slavishly in the track pointed out by him, nor, indeed, would the peculiar and large difference between our respective materials, admit of much similarity of treatment. The reader must understand that the essential facts, as given in these sketches, are all historical, and that he is in *fact* engaged in the perusal of the real adventures of the Spanish voyager, enlivened only by the introduction of persons of whom history says nothing in detail—speaking vaguely, as is but too much her wont, of those whose deficient stature fails to inform or to influence her sympathies. It is the true purpose of fiction to supply her deficiencies, and to correct her judgments. It will be difficult for any chronicler to say, of what I have written, more than that he himself knows nothing about it. But his ignorance suggests no good reason why better information should not exist in my possession.

served. It was reserved for another voyager, who, with greater condescension, surveyed the coast and actually set foot upon it. This was Lucas Velasquez de Ayllon, whose adventures in Carolina we propose briefly to relate. Better for him that he had never seen it!—or, seeing it, if he had posted away from its shores for ever. They were the shores of destiny for him. But he was a bad man, and we may reasonably assume that the Just Providence had ordained that his crimes should there meet with that retribution which they were not likely to encounter any where else. Here, if he found paganism, he, at the same time, found hospitality ; and here, if he brought cunning, he encountered courage ! Fierce valour and generous hospitality were the natural virtues of the Southern Indians.

But we must retrace our steps for a brief period. Some preliminaries, drawn from the history of the times, are first necessary to be understood.—The feebleness of the natives of Hayti, as is well known, so far from making them objects of pity and indulgence in the sight of other Spanish conquerors, had the contrary effect of converting an otherwise brave soldiery into a reckless band of despots, as brutal in their performances as they were unwise in their tyrannies. The miserable Indians sunk under their domination. The blandness of their climate, its delicious fruits, the spontaneous gifts of nature, had rendered them too effeminate for labour and too spiritless for war. Their extermination was threatened ; and, as a remedial measure, the benevolent father, Las Casas,—whose humanity stands out conspicuously in contrast with the proverbial cruelty and ferocity of his countrymen,—suggested the policy of making captures of slaves, to take the places of the perishing Haytians, from the Caribbean Islands and from the coasts of Florida. The hardy savages of these regions, inured to war, and loving it for its very dangers and exercises, were better able to endure the severe tasks which were prescribed by the conquerors. This opened a new branch of business for these bold and reckless adventurers. Predatory incursions were made along the shores of the Gulf, and seldom without profit. In this way one race was made to supersede another, in the delicious country which seems destined never to rear a population suited to its characteristics. The stubborn and sullen Caribbean was made to bend his shoulders to the burden, but did not the less save the feeble Haytian from his doom. The fierce tribes of Apalachia took the place of the delicate limbed native of the Ozama ; and, in process of years, the whole southern coasts of North America became tributary, in some degree, to the novel and tyrannical policy which was yet suggested by a spirit of the most genuine benevolence.

The business of slave capture became somewhat more profitable than the fatiguing and protracted search after gold—a search much more full of delusions than of any thing substantial. It agreed better with the hardy valour of those wild adventurers. Many bold knights adopted this new vocation. Among these was one Lucas Velasquez de Ayllon, already mentioned as succeeding Cabot in his discovery of Carolina. He was a stern, cold man, brave enough for the uses to which valour was put in those days ; but having the narrow contracted soul of a miser, he was incapable of noble thoughts or generous feelings. The love of gold was the settled passion of his heart, as it was too much the passion of his countrymen. He soon distinguished himself by his forays, and was among the first to introduce his people to a knowledge of Carolina, where they subsequently made themselves notorious by their atrocities. Some time in the year 1520, he set forth, in two ships, on an expedition of this nature. He seems to have been already acquainted with the region. Wending north, he soon found himself in smooth water, and gliding along by numberless pleasant islands, that broke the billows of the sea, and formed frequent and safe harborages along the coasts of the country. Attracted by a spacious opening in the shores, he stood in for a prominent headland, to which he gave the name of Cape St. Helena ; a name which is now borne by the contiguous sound. The smoothness of the waters ; the placid and serene security of this lovely basin ; the rich green of the verdure which encountered the eyes of the adventurers on all sides, beguiled them onward ; and they were at length rejoiced at the sight, —more grateful to their desire than any other, as it promised them the spoils which they sought—of numerous groups of natives that thronged the lands-ends at their approach. They cast anchor

near the mouth of a river, which, deriving its name from the
Queen of the country, is called, to this day, the Combahee.

The natives were a race as unconscious of guile as they were
fearless of danger. They are represented to have been of very
noble stature ; graceful and strong of limb ; of bright, dark
flashing eyes, and of singularly advanced civilization, since they
wore cotton clothes of their own manufacture, and had even
made considerable progress in the arts of knitting, spinning and
veaving. They had draperies to their places of repose ; and
some of the more distinguished among their women and warriors,
wore thin and flowing fringes, by way of ornament, upon which
a free and tasteful disposition of pearls might occasionally be seen.
Like many other of the native tribes, they were governed by a
queen whose name has already been given. The name of the
country they called Chicora, or, more properly, Chiquola.

Unsuspecting as they were brave, the savages surrounded the
vessels in their boats, and many of them even swam off from
shore to meet them ; being quite as expert in the water as upon
the land. The wily Spaniard spared no arts to encourage and
increase this confidence. Toys and implements of a kind likely
to attract the eyes, and catch the affections, of an ignorant people, were studiously held up in sight ; and, by little and little,
they grew bold enough, at length, to clamber up the sides of the
ships, and make their appearance upon the decks. Still, with
all their arts, the number of those who came on board was small,
compared with those who remained aloof. It was observed by
the Spaniards that the persons who forbore to visit them were
evidently the persons of highest consequence. Those who came,
as constantly withdrew to make their report to others, who either
stayed on the land, or hovered in sight, but at a safe distance, in
their light canoes. De Ayllon shrewdly conjectured that if he
could tempt these more important persons to visit his vessels, the
great body of the savages would follow. His object was numbers ; and his grasping and calculating soul scanned the crowds
which were in sight, and thought of the immense space in his
hold, which it was his policy and wish to fill. To bring about
his object, he spared none of the customary modes of temptation.
Beads and bells were sparingly distributed to those who came.

and they were instructed by signs and sounds to depart, and
return with their companions. To a certain exten., this policy
had its effect, but the appetite of the Spaniard was not easily
glutted.

He noted, among the hundred canoes that darted about the
bay, one that was not only of larger size and better construction
than the rest, but which was fitted up with cotton stuffs and
fringes like some barge of state. He rightly conjectured that
this canoe contained the Cassique or sovereign of the country.
The canoe was dug from a single tree, and was more than forty
feet in length. It had a sort of canopy of cotton stuff near the
stern, beneath which sat several females, one of whom was of
majestic demeanour, and seemed to be an object of deference with
all the rest. It did not escape the eyes of the Spaniards that her
neck was hung with pearls, others were twined about her brows,
and gleamed out from the folds of her long glossy black hair,
which, streaming down her neck, was seen almost to mingle with
the chafing billows of the sound. The men in this vessel were
also most evidently of the better order. All of them were clad
in fringed cotton stuffs of a superior description to those worn by
the gathering multitude. Some of these stuffs were dyed of a
bright red and yellow, and plumes, similarly stained, were fastened in many instances to their brows, by narrow strips of coloured fringe, not unfrequently sprinkled artfully with seed pearl.

The eyes of De Ayllon gloated as he beheld this barge, from
which he did not once withdraw his glance. But, if he saw the
importance of securing this particular prize, he, at the same time,
felt the difficulty of such a performance. The Indians seemed
not unaware of the special value of this canoe. It was kept
aloof, while all the rest ventured boldly alongside the Spanish
vessels. A proper jealousy of strangers,—though it does not
seem that they had any suspicion of their particular object—restrained the savages. To this natural jealousy, that curiosity
which is equally natural to ignorance, was opposed. De Ayllon
was too sagacious to despair of the final success of this superior
passion. He redoubled his arts. His hawk's bells were made
to jingle from the ship's side ; tinsel, but bright crosses—the ho-
liest sign in the exercise of his religious faith—were hung in view,

abused as lures for the purposes of fraud and violence. No toy, which had ever yet been found potent in Indian traffic, was withheld from sight; and, by little and little, the unconscious arms of the Indian rowers impelled the destined bark nearer and nearer to the artful Spaniards. Still, the approach was slow. The strokes of the rowers were frequently suspended, as if in obedience to orders from their chiefs. A consultation was evidently going on among the inmates of the Indian vessels. Other canoes approached it from the shore. The barge of state was surrounded. It was obvious that the counsellors were averse to the unnecessary exposure of their sovereigns.

It was a moment of anxiety with De Ayllon. There were not twenty Indians remaining on his decks; at one time there had been an hundred. He beheld the hesitation, amounting to seeming apprehension. among the people in the canoes; and he now began to reproach himself with that cupidity, which, grasping at too much, had probably lost all. But so long as curiosity hesitates there is hope for cupidity. De Ayllon brought forth other lures: he preferred fraud to fighting.

" Look !" said a princely damsel in the canoe of state, as a cluster of bright mirrors shone burningly in the sunlight. " Look !" —and every eye followed her finger, and every feminine tongue in the vessel grew clamorous for an instant, in its own language, expressing the wonder which was felt at this surpassing display. Still, the canoe hung, suspended on its centre, motionless. The contest was undecided : a long, low discussion was carried on between a small and select number in the little vessel. De Ayllon saw that but from four to five persons engaged in this discussion. One of these, only, was a woman—the majestic but youthful woman, of whom we have already given a brief description. Three others were grave middle-aged men ; but the fourth was a tall, bright-eyed savage, who had scarcely reached the term of manhood, with a proud eager aspect, and a form equally combining strength and symmetry. He wore a coronet of eagle feathers, and from his place in the canoe, immediately next that of the queen, it was inferred correctly by the Spanish captain that he was her husband. He spoke earnestly, almost angrily ; pointed several times to the ships, whenever the objects of attrac-

tion were displayed; and, from his impatient manner, it was
very clear that the counsel to which he listened did not correspond with the desires which he felt. But the discussion was soon
ended. De Ayllon waved a bright scimitar above his head, and
the young chief in the canoe of state started to his feet, with an
unrestrainable impulse, and extended his hand for the gift. The
brave soul of the young warrior spoke out without control when
he beheld the true object of attraction. De Ayllon waved the
weapon encouragingly, and bowed his head, as if in compliance
with his demand. The young savage uttered a few words to his
people, and the paddles were again dipped in water; the bark
went forward, and, from the Spanish vessel, a rope was let down
to assist the visitors as soon as they were alongside.

The hand of the young chief had already grasped the rope,
when the fingers of Combahee, the queen, with an equal mixture
of majesty and grace, were laid upon his arm.

"Go not, Chiquola," she said, with a persuasive, entreating
glance of her deep, dark eyes. He shook off her hand impatiently, and, running up the sides of the vessel, was already safely
on the deck, before he perceived that she was preparing to follow
him. He turned upon her, and a brief expostulation seemed to
follow from his lips. It appeared as if the young savage was
only made conscious of his imprudence, by beholding hers. She
answered him with a firmness of manner, a dignity and sweetness
so happily blended, that the Spanish officers, who had, by this
time, gathered round them, looked on and listened with surprise.
The young chief, whom they learned to call by the name of Chiquola—which they soon understood was that of the country, also—
appeared dissatisfied, and renewed his expostulations, but with
the same effect. At length he waved his hand to the canoe, and,
speaking a few words, moved once more to the side of the ship at
which she had entered. The woman's eye brightened; she answered with a single word, and hurried in the same direction.
De Ayllon, fearing the loss of his victims, now thought it time to
interfere. The sword, which had won the eyes of the young
warrior at first, was again waved in his sight, while a mirror of the
largest size was held before the noble features of the Indian princess. The youth grasped the weapon, and laughed with a delighted

out brief chuckle as he looked on the glittering steel, and shook
it hurriedly in the air. He seemed to know the use of such an
instrument by instinct. In its contemplation, he forgot his own
suspicions and that of his people; and no more renewing his suggestions to depart, he spoke to Combahee only of the beauties and
the use of the new weapon which had been given to his hands.

The woman seemed altogether a superior person. There was
a stern mournfulness about her, which, while it commanded respect, did not impair the symmetry and sweetness of her very intelligent and pleasing features. She had the high forehead of our
race, without that accompanying protuberance of the cheek bones,
which distinguished hers. Her mouth was very small and sweet,
like that which is common to her people. Her eyes were large,
deeply set, and dark in the extreme, wearing that pensive earnestness of expression which seems to denote presentiment of many
pangs and sorrows. Her form, we have already said, was large
and majestical; yet the thick masses of her glossy black hair
streamed even to her heels. Superior to her companions, male
as well as female, the mirror which had been put into her hands
—a glance at which had awakened the most boisterous clamours
of delight among her female attendants, all of whom had followed
her into the Spanish vessel—was laid down, after a brief examination, with perfect indifference. Her countenance, though not
uninformed with curiosity, was full of a most expressive anxiety.
She certainly felt the wonder which the others showed, at the
manifold strange objects which met their eyes; but this feeling
was entertained in a more subdued degree, and did not display
itself in the usual language of surprise. She simply seemed to
follow the footsteps of Chiquola, without participating in his pleasures, or in that curiosity which made him traverse the ship in every
accessible quarter, from stem to stern, seeking all objects of novelty, and passing from one to the other with an appetite which
nothing seemed likely soon to satiate.

Meanwhile, the example set by their Queen, the Cassiques, the
Iawas, or Priests, and other headmen of the Nation, was soon followed by the common people; and De Ayllon had the satisfaction,
on exchanging signals with his consort, to find that both ships
were crowded with quite as many persons as they could possibly

carry. The vessel under his immediate command was scarcely manageable from the multitudes which thronged her decks, and impeded, in a great measure, all the operations of the crew. He devised a remedy for this evil, and, at the same time, a measure very well calculated to give complete effect to his plans. Refreshments were provided in the hold ; wines in abundance ; and the trooping savages were invited into that gloomy region, which a timely precaution had rendered more cheerful in appearance by the introduction of numerous lights. A similar arrangement conducted the more honourable guests into the cabin, and a free use of the intoxicating beverages, on the part of the great body of the Indians, soon rendered easy all the remaining labours of the wily Spaniard. The hatches were suddenly closed when the hold was most crowded, and two hundred of the unconscious and half stupid savages were thus entrapped for the slave market of the City of Columbus.

In the cabin the same transaction was marked by some distinguishing differences. The wily De Ayllon paid every attention to his guests. A natural homage was felt to be the due of royalty and rank, even among a race of savages ; and this sentiment was enforced by the obvious necessity of pursuing that course of conduct which would induce the confidence of persons who had already shown themselves so suspicious. De Ayllon, with his officers, himself attended Chiquola and the Queen. The former needed no persuasion. He freely seated himself on the cushions of the cabin, and drank of the proffered wines, till his eyes danced with delight, his blood tingled, and his speech, always free, became garrulity, to the great annoyance of Combahee. She had followed him with evident reluctance into the interior of the ves sel ; and now, seated with the rest, within the cabin, she watched the proceedings with a painful degree of interest and dissatisfaction, increasing momently as she beheld the increasing effect upon him of the wine which he had taken. She herself utterly declined the proffered liquor ; holding herself aloof with as much natural dignity as could have been displayed by the most polished princess of Europe. Her disquiet had made itself understood by her impatience of manner, and by frequent observations in her own language, to Chiquola. These, of course, could be understood only by themselves and their attendants. But the Spaniards were at no loss to divine the purport of her speech from her tones, the expression of her face, and the quick significant movements of her hands.

At length she succeeded in impressing her desires upon Chiquola, and he rose to depart. But the Spaniards had no intention to suffer this. The plot was now ready for execution. The signal had been made. The entrance to the cabin was closed, and a single bold and decisive movement was alone necessary to end the game. De Ayllon had taken care silently to introduce several stout soldiers into the cabin, and these, when Chiquola took a step forward, sprang upon him and his few male companions and bore them to the floor. Chiquola struggled with a manful courage, which, equally with their forests, was the inheritance of the American Indians; but the conflict was too unequal, and it did not remain doubtful very long. De Ayllon saw that he was secure, and turned, with an air of courteous constraint, to the spot where Combahee stood. He approached her with a smile upon his countenance and with extended arms; but she bestowed upon him a single glance; and, in a mute survey, took in the entire extent of her misfortune. The whole proceeding had been the work of an instant only. That she was taken by surprise, as well as Chiquola, was sufficiently clear; but her suspicions had never been wholly quieted, and the degree of surprise which she felt did not long deprive her of her energies. If her eye betrayed the startled apprehension of the fawn of her native forests, it equally expressed the fierce indignation which flames in that of their tameless eagle. She did not speak as De Ayllon approached; and when, smiling, he pointed to the condition of Chiquola, and with extended arms seemed to indicate to her the hopelessness of any effort at escape, she hissed at him, in reply, with the keen defiance of the angry coppersnake. He advanced —his hand was stretched forth towards her person—when she drew up her queenly form to its fullest height; and, with a single word hurriedly spoken to the still struggling Chiquola, she turned, and when De Ayllon looked only to receive her submission, plunged suddenly through the stern windows of the cabin, and buried herself in the deep waters of the sea.

CHAPTER II.

CHIQUOLA, THE CAPTIVE.

" **Now** mounts he the ocean wave, banished, forlorn,
  Like a limb from his country cast bleeding and torn."
                                                Campbell.

THE flight of Combahee, and her descent into the waters of the bay, were ominous of uproar. Instantly, the cry of rage arose from a thousand voices. The whole body of the people, as with a common instinct, seemed at once to comprehend the national calamity. A dozen canoes shot forth from every quarter, with the rapidity of arrows in their flight, to the rescue of the Queen. Like a bright mermaid, swimming at evening for her own green island, she now appeared, beating with familiar skill the swelling waters, and, with practised hands, throwing behind her their impelling billows. Her long, glossy, black hair was spread out upon the surface of the deep, like some veil of network meant to conceal from immodest glances the feminine form below. From the window of the cabin whence she disappeared, De Ayllon beheld her progress, and looked upon the scene with such admiration as was within the nature of a soul so mercenary. He saw the fearless courage of the man in all her movements, and never did Spaniard behold such exquisite artifice in swimming on the part of any of his race. She was already in safety. She had ascended, and taken her seat in one of the canoes, a dozen contending, in loyal rivalry, for the privilege of receiving her person.

Then rose the cry of war! Then sounded that fearful whoop of hate, and rage, and defiance, the very echoes of which have made many a faint heart tremble since that day. It was probably, on this occasion, that the European, for the first time, listened to this terrible cry of war and vengeance. At the signal, the canoes upon the bay scattered themselves to surround the ships;

the warriors along the shore loosened the fasts of the boats, and pushed off to join the conflict; while the hunter in the forests, stopped sudden in the eager chase, sped onward, with all the feeling of coercive duty, in the direction of those summoning sounds.

The fearless Combahee, with soul on fire, led the van. She stood erect in her canoe. Her form might be seen from every part of the bay. The hair still streamed, unbound and dripping, from her shoulders. In her left hand she grasped a bow such as would task the ability of the strong man in our day. Her right hand was extended, as if in denunciation towards that

> "—— fatal bark
> Built in the eclipse and rigged with curses dark,"

in which her husband and her people were held captive. Truly, hers was the form and the attitude for a high souled painter;— one, the master of the dramatic branches of his art. The flash- ing of her eye was a voice to her warriors;—the waving of her hand was a summons that the loyal and the brave heart sprang eager to obey! A shrill signal issued from her half parted lips, and the now numerous canoes scattered themselves on every side as if to surround the European enemy, or, at least, to make the assault on both vessels simultaneous.

The Spaniard beheld, as if by magic, the whole bay covered with boats. The light canoes were soon launched from the shore, and they shot forth from its thousand indentations as fast as the warriors poured down from the interior. Each of these warriors came armed with the bow, and a well filled quiver of arrows. These were formed from the long canes of the adjacent swamps; shafts equally tenacious and elastic, feathered with plumes from the eagle or the stork, and headed with triangular barbs of flint. broad but sharp, of which each Indian had always a plentiful supply. The vigour with which these arrows were impelled from the string was such, that, without the escaupil or cotton armour which the Spaniards generally wore, the shaft has been known to pass clean through the body of the victim. Thus armed and arranged, with numbers constantly increasing, the people of Combahee, gathering at her summons, darted boldly from the shore, and, taking up positions favourable to the attack, awaited only the signal to begin.

Meanwhile, the Spanish ships began to spread forth their broad wings for flight. Anticipating some such condition of things as the present, the wily De Ayllon had made his preparations for departure at the same time that he had planned the scheme for his successful treachery. The one movement was devised to follow immediately upon the footsteps of the other. His sails were loosened and flapping in the wind. To trim them for the breeze, which, though light, was yet favourable to his departure, was the work of a moment only ; and ere the word was given for the attack, on the part of the Indians, the huge fabrics of the Spaniards began to move slowly through the subject waters. Then followed the signal. First came a shaft from Combahee herself; wel aimed and launched with no mean vigour ; that, striking full on the bosom of De Ayllon, would have proved fatal but for the plate mail which was hidden beneath his coat of buff. A wild whoop succeeded, and the air was instantly clouded by the close flight of the Indian arrows. Nothing could have been more decided, more prompt and rapid, than this assault. The shaft had scarcely been dismissed from the string before another supplied its place ; and however superior might have been the armament of the Spanish captain, however unequal the conflict from the greater size of his vessels, and the bulwarks which necessarily gave a certain degree of protection, it was a moment of no inconsiderable anxiety to the kidnappers ! De Ayllon, though a base, was not a bloody-minded man. His object was spoil, not slaughter. Though his men had their firelocks in readiness, and a few pieces of cannon were already prepared and pointed, yet he hesitated to give the word, which should hurry into eternity so many ignorant fellow beings upon whom he had just inflicted so shameful an injury. He commanded his men to cover themselves behind the bulwarks, unless where the management of the ships required their unavoidable exposure, and, in such cases, the persons employed were provided with the cotton armour which had been usually found an adequate protection against arrows shot by the feeble hands of the Indians of the Lucayos.

But the vigorous savages of Combahee were a very different

race. They belonged to the great family of the Muscoghees; the parent stock, without question, of those indomitable tribes which, under the names of Yemassee, Stono, Muscoghee, Micka-sukee, and Seminole, have made themselves remembered and feared, through successive years of European experience, without having been entirely quelled or quieted to the present hour. It was soon found by De Ayllon that the escaupil was no protection against injury. It baffled the force of the shaft but could not blunt it, and one of the inferior officers, standing by the side of the commander, was pierced through his cotton gorget. The arrow penetrated his throat, and he fell, to all appearance, mortally wounded. The Indians beheld his fall. They saw the confusion that the event seemed to inspire, and their delight was manifested in a renewed shout of hostility, mingled with screams, which denoted, as clearly as language, the delight of savage triumph. Still, De Ayllon forbore to use the destructive weapons which he had in readiness. His soldiers murmured; but he answered them by pointing to the hold, and asking:

"Shall we cut our own throats in cutting theirs? I see not present enemies but future slaves in all these assailants."

It was not mercy but policy that dictated his forbearance. But it was necessary that something should be done in order to baffle and throw off the Indians. The breeze was too light and baffling, and the movements of the vessels too slow to avoid them. The light barks of the assailants, impelled by vigorous arms, in such smooth water, easily kept pace with the progress of the ships. Their cries of insult and hostility increased. Their arrows were shot, without cessation, at every point at which an enemy was supposed to harbour himself; and, under the circumstances, it was not possible always to take advantage of a cover in performing the necessary duties which accrued to the seamen of the ships. The Indians had not yet heard the sound of European cannon. De Ayllon resolved to intimidate them. A small piece, such as in that day was employed for the defence of castles, called a falconet, was elevated above the canoes, so that the shot, passing over the heads of their inmates, might take effect upon the woods along the shore. As the sudden and sullen roar of this unexpected thunder was heard, every Indian sunk upon his knees; every paddle was dropped motionless in the water; while the uplifted bow fell from the half-paralyzed hands of the war-rior, and he paused, uncertain of safety, but incapable of flight. The effect was great, but momentary only. To a truly brave people, there is nothing more transient than the influence of panic. When the Indian warriors looked up, they beheld one of their people still erect—unalarmed by the strange thunder—still look-ing the language,—still acting the part of defiance,—and, oh! shame to their manhood, this person was their Queen. Instead of fear, the expression upon her countenance was that of scorn. They took fire at the expression. Every heart gathered new warmth at the blaze shining from her eyes. Besides, they dis-covered that they were unharmed. The thunder was a mere sound. They had not seen the bolt. This discovery not only relieved their fears but heightened their audacity. Again they moved forward. Again the dart was clapt upon the string. Singing one chorus, the burden of which, in our language, would be equivalent to a summons to a feast of vultures, they again set their canoes in motion; and now, not as before, simply content to get within arrow distance, they boldly pressed forward upon the very course of the ships; behind, before, and on every side, sending their arrows through every opening, and distinguishing, by their formidable aim, every living object which came in sight. Their skill in the management of their canoes; in swimming; their great strength and agility, prompted them to a thousand acts of daring; and some were found bold enough to attempt, while leaping from their boats, beneath the very prow of the slowly ad-vancing vessels, to grasp the swinging ropes and thus elevate themselves to individual conflict with their enemies. These fail-ed, it is true, and sank into the waters; but such an event impli-ed no sort of risk to these fearless warriors. They were soon picked up by their comrades, only to renew, in this or in other forms, their gallant but unsuccessful efforts.

But these efforts might yet be successful. Ships in those days were not the monstrous palaces which they are in ours. An agile form, under favouring circumstances, might easily clamber up their sides; and such was the equal activity and daring of the savages, as to make it apparent to De Ayllon that it would need something more decisive than had yet been done, on his part, to shake himself free from their inveterate hostility. At a moment when their fury was redoubled and increased by the impunity which had attended their previous assaults,—when every bow was uplifted and every arrow pointed under the eye of their Queen, as if for a full application of all their strength, and skill and courage ;—her voice, now loud in frequent speech, inciting them to a last and crowning effort ; and she herself, erect in her bark as before, and within less than thirty yards of the Spanish vessel ;—at this moment, and to avert the storm of arrows which threatened his seamen who were then, perforce, busy with the rigging in consequence of a sudden change of wind ;—De Ayllon gave a signal to bring Chiquola from below. Struggling between two Spanish officers, his arms pinioned at the elbows, the young Cassique was dragged forward to the side of the vessel and presented to the eyes of his Queen and people, threatened with the edge of the very weapon which had beguiled him to the perfidious bark.

A hollow groan arose on every hand. The points of the uplifted arrows were dropped ; and, for the first time, the proud spirit passed out of the eyes of Combahee, and her head sunk forward, with an air of hopeless self-abandonment, upon her breast ! A deep silence followed, broken only by the voice of Chiquola. What he said, was, of course, not understood by his captors ; but they could not mistake the import of his action. Thrice, while he spoke to his people, did his hand, wresting to the utmost the cords upon his arms, smite his heart, imploring, as it were, the united arrows of his people to this conspicuous mark. But the Amazon had not courage for this. She was speechless ! Every eye was turned upon her, but there was no answering response in hers ; and the ships of the Spaniard proceeded on their way to the sea with a momently increasing rapidity. Still, though no longer assailing, the canoes followed close, and kept up the same relative distance between themselves and enemies, which had been observed before. Combahee now felt all her feebleness, and as the winds increased, and the waves of the bay feeling the more immediate influence of the ocean, rose into long heavy swells, the complete conviction of her whole calamity seemed to rush upon her soul. Chiquola had now been withdrawn from sight. His eager adjurations to his Queen and people, might, it was feared, prompt them to that Roman sort of sacrifice which the captive himself seemed to implore; and perceiving that the savages had suspended the assault, De Ayllon commanded his removal. But, with his disappearance, the courage of his Queen revived. Once more she gave the signal for attack in a discharge of arrows; and once more the captive was set before their eyes, with the naked sword above his head, *in terrorem*, as before. The same effect ensued. The arm of hostility hung suspended and paralyzed. The cry of anguish which the cruel spectacle extorted from the bosom of Combahee, was echoed by that of the multitude; and without a purpose or a hope, the canoes hovered around the course of the retreating ships, till the broad Atlantic, with all its mighty billows, received them.— The vigorous breath of the increasing wind, soon enabled them to shake off their hopeless pursuers. Ye still the devoted savages plied their unremitting paddles; the poor Queen straining her eyes along the waste, until, in the grey of twilight and of distance the vessels of the robbers were completely hidden from her sight.

Meanwhile, Chiquola was hurried back to the cabin, with his arms still pinioned. His feet were also fastened and a close watch was put upon him. It was a courtesy which the Spaniards considered due to his legitimacy that the cabin was made his place of imprisonment. With his withdrawal from the presence of his people, his voice, his eagerness and animation, all at once ceased. He sunk down on the cushion with the sullen, stolid indifference which distinguishes his people in all embarrassing situations. A rigid immobility settled upon his features; yet De Ayllon did not fail to perceive that when he or any of his officers approached the captive, his eyes gleamed upon them with the fury of his native panther;—gleamed bright, with irregular flashes, beneath his thick black eye-brows, which gloomed heavily over their arches with the collected energies of a wild and stubborn soul.

"He is dangerous," said De Ayllon, "be careful how you approach him."

But though avoided he was not neglected. De Ayllon himself

proffered him food ; not forgetting to tender him a draught of that potent beverage by which he had been partly overcome before. But the sense of wrong was uppermost, and completely subdued the feeling of appetite. He regarded the proffer of the Spaniard with a keen, but composed look of ineffable disdain ; never lifted his hand to receive the draught, and beheld it set down within his reach without indicating, by word or look, his consciousness of what had been done. Some hours had elapsed and the wine and food remained untouched. His captor still consoled himself with the idea that hunger would subdue his stubbornness ;—but when the morning came, and the noon of the next day, and the young savage still refused to eat or drink, the case became serious ; and the mercenary Spaniard began to apprehend that he should lose one of the most valuable of his captives. He approached the youth and by signs expostulated with him upon his rejection of the food ; but he received no satisfaction. The Indian remained inflexible, and but a single glance of his large, bright eye, re- quited De Ayllon for his selfish consideration. That look ex- pressed the hunger and thirst which in no other way did Chiquola deign to acknowledge; but that hunger and thirst were not for food but for blood ;—revenge, the atonement for his wrongs and shame. Never had the free limbs of Indian warrior known such an indignity—never could indignity have been conceived less en- durable. No words can describe, as no mind can imagine, the volume of tumultuous strife, and fiercer, maddening thoughts and feelings, boiling and burning in the brain and bosom of the gallant but inconsiderate youth ; — thoughts and feelings so strangely subdued, so completely hidden in those composed mus- cles,—only speaking through that dilating, but fixed, keen, invet- erate eye !

De Ayllon was perplexed. The remaining captives gave him little or no trouble. Plied with the liquors which had seduced them at first, they were very generally in that state of drunken- ness, when a certainty of continued supply reconciles the de- graded mind very readily to any condition. But with Chiquola the case was very different. Here, at least, was character—the pride of self-dependence ; the feeling of moral responsibility ; the ineradicable consciousness of that shame which prefers to feel itself and not to be blinded. De Ayllon had known the savage nature only under its feebler and meaner aspects. The timid islanders of the Lucayos—the spiritless and simple natives of Hayti—were of quite another class. The Indian of the North American continent, whatever his vices or his weaknesses, was yet a man. He was more. He was a conqueror—accustomed to conquer! It was his boast that where he came he stood; where he stood he remained; and where he remained, he was the only man! The people whom he found were women. He made them and kept them so.—

> " Severe the school that made them bear
> The ills of life without a tear;
> And stern the doctrine that denied
> The sachem fame, the warrior pride,
> Who, urged by nature's wants, confess'd
> The need that hunger'd in his breast:—
> Or, when beneath his foeman's knife,
> Who utter'd recreant prayer for life;—
> Or, in the chase, whose strength was spent,
> Or, in the fight, whose knee was bent;
> Or, when with tale of coming fight,
> Who sought his allies' camp by night,
> And, ere the missives well were told,
> Complain'd of hunger, wet and cold!—
> A woman, if in strife, his foe,
> Could give, yet not receive, a blow;—
> Or if, undextrously and dull,
>   His hand and knife should fail to win
> The dripping warm scalp from the skull
>   To trim his yellow mocasin!"

Such was the character of his race, and Chiquola was no recreant. Such was his character. He had no complaint. He looked no emotions. The marble could not have seemed less corrigible; and, but for that occasional flashing from his dark eye, whenever any of his captors drew near to the spot where he sat, none would have fancied that in his bosom lurked a single feeling of hostility or discontent. Still he ate not and drank not. It was obvious to the Spaniard that he had adopted the stern resolution to forbear all sustenance, and thus defeat the malice of his enemies. He had no fear of death, and he could not endure bonds

That he would maintain that resolution to the last, none could doubt who watched his sullen immobility—who noted the fact, that he spoke nothing, neither in the language of entreaty nor complaint. He was resolved on suicide! It is an error to suppose, as has been asserted, that the Indians never commit suicide. The crime is a very common one among them in periods of great national calamity. The Cherokee warrior frequently destroyed himself when the small pox had disfigured his visage : for, it must be remembered, that an Indian warrior is, of all human beings, one of the vainest, on the score of his personal appearance. He unites, as they are usually found united even in the highest states of civilization, the strange extremes of ferocity and frivolity.

De Ayllon counselled with his officers as to what should be done with their captive. He would certainly die on their hands. Balthazar de Morla, his lieutenant—a stern fierce savage himself —proposed that they should kill him, as a way of shortening their trouble, and dismissing all farther cares upon the project.

" He is but one," said he, " and though you may call him King or Cassique, he will sell for no more than any one of his own tribe in the markets of Isabella. At worst, it will only be a loss to him, for the fellow is resolved to die. He will bring you nothing, unless for the skin of his carcase, and that is not a large one."

A young officer of more humanity, Jaques Carazon, offered different counsel. He recommended that the poor Indian be taken on deck. The confinement in the cabin he thought had sickened him. The fresh air, and the sight of the sky and sea, might work a change and provoke in him a love of life. Reasoning from the European nature, such advice would most probably have realized the desired effect; and De Ayllon was struck with it.

" Let it be done," he said; and Chiquola was accordingly brought up from below, and placed on the quarter deck in a pleasant and elevated situation. At first, the effect promised to be such as the young officer had suggested. There was a sudden looking up, in all the features of the captive. His eyes were no longer cast down ; and a smile seemed to pass over the lips

30

which, of late, had been so rigidly compressed. He looked long, and with a keen expression of interest at the sky above, and the long stretch of water before and around him. But there was one object of most interest, upon which his eyes fastened with a seeming satisfaction. This was the land. The low sandy shores and island slips that skirt the Georgia coast, then known under the general name of Florida, lay on the right. The gentleness of the breeze, and smoothness of the water, enabled the ships, which were of light burthen, to pursue a course along with the land, at a small distance, varying from five to ten miles. Long and earnestly did the captive gaze upon this, to him, Elysian tract. There dwelt tribes, he well knew, which were kindred to his people. From any one of the thousand specks of shore which caught his eye, he could easily find his way back to his queen and country! What thoughts of bliss and wo, at the same moment, did these two images suggest to his struggling and agonized spirit. Suddenly, he caught the eyes of the Spanish Captain gazing upon him, with a fixed, inquiring glance ; and his own eyes were instantly averted from those objects which he alone desired to see. It would seem as if he fancied that the Spaniard was able to look into his soul. His form grew more erect beneath the scrutiny of his captor, and his countenance once more put on its former expression of immobility.

De Ayllon approached, followed by a boy bringing fresh food and wine, which were once more placed within his reach. By signs, the Spaniard encouraged him to eat. The Indian returned him not the slightest glance of recognition. His eye alone spoke, and its language was still that of hate and defiance. De Ayllon left him, and commanded that none should approach or seem to observe him. He conjectured that his stubbornness derived something of its stimulus from the consciousness that eyes of strange curiosity were fixed upon him, and that Nature would assert her claims if this artificial feeling were suffered to subside without farther provocation.

But when three hours more had elapsad, and the food still remained untouched, De Ayllon was in despair. He approached Chiquola, attended by the fierce Balthazar de Morla.

" Why do you not eat, savage !" exclaimed this person, shaking his hand threateningly at the Indian, and glancing upon him with the eyes of one, only waiting and anxious for the signal to strike and slay. If the captive failed to understand the language of the Spaniard, that of his looks and action was in no wise unequivocal. Chiquola gave him glance for glance. His eye lighted up with those angry fires which it shed when going into battle ; and it was sufficiently clear to both observers, that nothing more was needed than the freedom of hand and foot to have brought the unarmed but unbending savage, into the death grapple with his insulting enemy. The unsubdued tiger-like expression of the warrior, was rather increased than subdued by famine ; and even De Ayllon recoiled from a look which made him momentarily forgetful of the cords which fastened the limbs and rendered impotent the anger of his captive. He reproved Balthazar for his violence, and commanded him to retire. Then, speaking gently, he endeavoured to soothe the irritated Indian, by kind tones and persuasive action. He pointed to the food, and, by signs, endeavoured to convey to his mind the idea of the painful death which must follow his wilful abstinence much longer. For a few moments Chiquola gave no heed to these suggestions, but looking round once more to the strip of shore which lay upon his right, a sudden change passed over his features. He turned to De Ayllon, and muttering a few words in his own language, nodded his head, while his fingers pointed to the ligatures around his elbows and ancles. The action clearly denoted a willingness to take his food, provided his limbs were set free. De Ayllon proceeded to consult with his officers upon this suggestion. The elder, Balthazar de Morla, opposed the indulgence.

"He will attack you the moment he is free."

"But," replied the younger officer, by whose counsel he had already been brought upon the deck—"but of what avail would be his attack ? We are armed, and he is weaponless. We are many, and he is but one. It only needs that we should be watchful, and keep in readiness."

"Well!" said Balthazar, with a sneer, "I trust that you will be permitted the privilege of undoing his bonds ; for if ever savage had the devil in his eye, this savage has."

"I will do it," replied the young man, calmly, without seeming to heed the sneer. "I do not fear the savage, even if he should grapple with me. But I scarcely think it possible that he would attempt such a measure. He has evidently too much sense for that."

"Desperate men have no sense!" said the other; but the counsels of the younger officer prevailed with De Ayllon, and he was commissioned to undo the bonds of the captive. At the same time every precaution was taken, that the prisoner, when set free, should do the young man no hurt. Several soldiers were stationed at hand, to interpose in the event of danger, and De Ayllon and Balthazar, both with drawn swords, stood beside Jaques Carazon as he bent down on one knee to perform the duty of supposed danger which had been assigned him. But their apprehensions of assault proved groundless. Whether it was that Chiquola really entertained no design of mischief, or that he was restrained by prudence, on seeing the formidable preparations which had been made to baffle and punish any such attempt, he remained perfectly quiescent, and, even after his limbs had been freed, showed no disposition to use them.

"Eat!" said De Ayllon, pointing to the food. The captive looked at him in silence, but the food remained untouched.

"His pride keeps him from it," said De Ayllon. "He will not eat so long as we are looking on him. Let us withdraw to some little distance and watch him."

His orders were obeyed. The soldiers were despatched to another quarter of the vessel, though still commanded to remain under arms. De Ayllon with his two officers then withdrew, concealing themselves in different situations where they might observe all the movements of the captive. For a time, this arrangement promised to be as little productive of fruits as the previous ones. Chiquola remained immovable, and the food untouched. But, after a while, when he perceived that none was immediately near, his crouching form might be seen in motion, but so slightly, so slily, that it was scarcely perceptible to those who watched him. His head revolved slowly, and his neck turned, without any corresponding movement of his limbs, until he was able to take in all objects, which he might possibly see, on almost every part of the deck. The man at the helm, the sailor on the yard, while beholding him, scarcely saw the cat-like movement of his eyes. These, when he had concluded his unobtrusive examination of the vessel, were turned upon the shore, with the expression of an eager joy. His heart spoke out its feelings in the flashing of his dilating and kindled eyes. He was free. That was the feeling of his soul! That was the feeling which found utterance in his glance. The degrading cords were no longer on the limbs of the warrior, and was not his home almost beneath his eyes? He started to his feet erect. He looked around him; spurned the food and the wine cup from his path, and shrieking the war whoop of his tribe, with a single rush and bound, he plunged over the sides of the vessel into those blue waters which dye, with the complexion of the Gulf, the less beautiful waves of the Atlantic.

This movement, so unexpected by the captors, was quite too sudden for them to prevent. De Ayllon hurried to the side of his vessel as soon as he distinguished the proceeding. He beheld, with mingled feelings of admiration and disappointment, where the bold savage was buffeting the billows in the vain hope of reaching the distant shores. A boat was instantly let down into the sea, manned with the ablest seamen of the ship. It was very clear that Chiquola could neither make the land, nor contend very long with the powerful waters of the deep. This would have been a task beyond the powers of the strongest man, and the most skilful swimmer, and the brave captive had been without food more than twenty-four hours. Still he could be seen, striving vigorously in a course straight as an arrow for the shore; rising from billow to billow; now submerged, still ascending, and apparently without any diminution of the vigour with which he began his toils.

The rowers, meanwhile, plied their oars, with becoming energy The Indian, though a practiced swimmer, began, at length, to show signs of exhaustion. He was seen from the ship, and with the aid of a glass, was observed to be struggling feebly. The boat was gaining rapidly upon him. He might be saved. It needed only that he should will it so. Would he but turn and employ his remaining strength in striving for the boat, instead of wasting it in an idle effort for those shores which he could never more hope to see!

"He turns!" cried De Ayllon. "He will yet be saved

The boat will reach him soon. A few strokes more, and they are up with him !"

" He turns, indeed," said Carazon, " but it is to wave his hand in defiance."

" They reach him—they are up with him !" exclaimed the former.

" Ay !" answered the latter, " but he sinks—he has gone down."

" No! they have taken him into the boat !"

" You mistake, sir, do you not see where he rises ? almost a ship's length on the right of the boat. There spoke the savage soul. He will not be saved !"

This was true. Chiquola preferred death to bondage. The boat changed its course with that of the swimmer. Once more it neared him. Once more the hope of De Ayllon was excited as he beheld the scene from the ship; and once more the voice of his lieutenant cried discouragingly—

" He has gone down, and for ever. He will not suffer us to save him."

This time he spoke truly. The captive had disappeared. The boat, returning now, alone appeared above the waters, and De Ayllon turned away from the scene, wondering much at the indomitable spirit and fearless courage of the savage, but thinking much more seriously of the large number of pesos which this transaction had cost him. It was destined to cost him more, but of this hereafter.

CHAPTER III.

COMBAHEE ; OR, THE LAST VOYAGE OF LUCAS DE AYLLON.

" —— Bind him, I say ;
Make every artery and sinew crack ;
The slave that makes him give the loudest shriek,
Shall have ten thousand drachmas !   Wretch ! I'll force thee
To curse the Pow'r thou worship'st."
                    Massinger.—The Virgin Martyr.

BUT the losses of De Ayllon were not to end with the death of his noble captive, the unfortunate Chiquola.   We are told by the historian, that " one of his vessels foundered before he reached his port, and captors and captives were swallowed up in the sea together.   His own vessel survived, but many of his captives sickened and died ; and he himself was reserved for the time, only to suffer a more terrible form of punishment.   Though he had lost more than half of the ill-gotten fruits of his expedition, the profits which remained were still such as to encourage him to a renewal of his enterprise.   To this he devoted his whole fortune, and, with three large vessels and many hundred men, he once more descended upon the coast of Carolina."*

Meanwhile, the dreary destiny of Combahee was to live alone. We have heard so much of the inflexibility of the Indian character, that we are apt to forget that these people are human ; having, though perhaps in a small degree, and in less activity, the same vital passions, the same susceptibilities—the hopes, the fears, the loves and the hates, which establish the humanity of the whites. They are colder and more sterile,—more characterized by individuality and self-esteem than any more social people ; and these characteristics are the natural and inevitable results of their habits of wandering.   But to suppose that the Indian is " a man without a tear," is to indulge in a notion equally removed from

* History of South Carolina, page 11.

poetry and truth. At all events, such an opinion is, to say the least of it, a gross exaggeration of the fact.

Combahee, the Queen of Chiquola, had many tears. She was a young wife ;—the crime of De Ayllon had made her a young widow. Of the particular fate of her husband she knew nothing; and, in the absence of any certain knowledge, she naturally feared the worst. The imagination, once excited by fear, is the darkest painter of the terrible that nature has ever known. Still, the desolate woman did not feel herself utterly hopeless. Daily she manned her little bark, and was paddled along the shores of the sea, in a vain search after that which could never more be found. At other times she sat upon, or wandered along, the head-lands, in a lonely and silent watch over those vast, dark, dashing waters of the Atlantic, little dreaming that they had already long since swallowed up her chief. Wan and wretched, the sustenance which she took was simply adequate to the purposes of life. Never did city maiden more stubbornly deplore the lost object of her affections than did this single-hearted woman. But her prayers and watch were equally unavailing. Vainly did she skirt the shores in her canoe by day ;—vainly did she build her fires, as a beacon, to guide him on his home return by night. His people had already given him up for ever ; but love is more hopeful of the object which it loves. She did not yet despair. Still she wept, but still she watched ; and when she ceased to weep, it was only at moments when the diligence of her watch made her forgetful of her tears.

The season was becoming late. The fresh and invigorating breezes of September began to warn the tribes of the necessity of seeking the shelter of the woods. The maize was already gathered and bruised for the stocks of winter. The fruits of summer had been dried, and the roots were packed away. The chiefs regarded the condition of mind under which their Queen laboured with increasing anxiety. She sat apart upon the highest hill that loomed out from the shore, along the deep. She sat beneath the loftiest palmetto. A streamer of fringed cotton was hung from its top as a signal to the wanderer, should he once more be permitted to behold the land, apprizing him where the disconsolate widow kept her watch. The tribes looked on from a distance un-

willing to disturb those sorrows, which, under oi dinary circumstances, they consider sacred. The veneration which they felt
for their Queen increased this feeling. Yet so unremitting had
been her self-abandonment—so devoted and unchangeable her
daily employments, that some partial fears began to be entertained lest her reason might suffer. She had few words now for
her best counsellors. These few words, it is true, were always
to the purpose, yet they were spoken with impatience, amounting
to severity. The once gentle and benignant woman had grown
stern. There was a stony inflexibility about her glance which
distressed the observer, and her cheeks had become lean and thin,
and her frame feeble and languid, in singular contrast with that
intense spiritual light which flashed, whenever she was addressed,
from her large black eyes.

Something must be done! such was the unanimous opinion of
the chiefs. Nay, two things were to be done. She was to be cured
of this affection; and it was necessary that she should choose
one, from among her " beloved men,"—one, who should take the
place of Chiquola. They came to her, at length, with this object.
Combahee was even then sitting upon the headland of St. Helena.
She looked out with straining eyes upon the sea. She had seen
a speck. They spoke to her, but she motioned them to be silent,
while she pointed to the object. It disappeared, like a thousand
others. It was some porpoise, or possibly some wandering gram-
pus, sending up his *jets d'eau* in an unfamiliar ocean. Long
she looked, but profitlessly. The object of her sudden hope had
already disappeared. She turned to the chiefs. They prostrated
themselves before her. Then, the venerable father, Kiawah,—
an old man who had witnessed the departure of an hundred and
twenty summers,—rose, and seating himself before her, addressed
her after the following fashion:

" Does the daughter of the great Ocketee, look into the grave
of the warrior that he may come forth because she looks?"

" He sleeps, father, for Combahee. He has gone forth to hunt
the deer in the blue land of Maneyto."

" Good! he has gone. Is the sea a hunting land for the
brave Chiquola? Is he not also gone to the blue land of
spirits?"

" Know'st thou ?   Who has told Kiawah, the old father ?   Has it come to him in a dream ?"

" Chiquola has come to him."

" Ah !"

" He is a hunter for Maneyto.   He stands first among the hunters in the blue forests of Maneyto.   The smile of the Great Spirit beckons him to the chase.   He eats of honey in the golden tents of the Great Spirit."

" He has said ?   Thou hast seen ?"

" Even so !   Shall Kiawah say to Combahee the thing which is not ?   Chiquola is dead !"

The woman put her hand upon her heart with an expression of sudden pain.   But she recovered herself with a little effort.

" It is true what Kiawah has said.   I feel it here.   But Chiquola will come to Combahee ?"

" Yea !   He will come.   Let my daughter go to the fountain and bathe thrice before night in its waters.   She will bid them prepare the feast of flesh.   A young deer shall be slain by the hunters.   Its meat shall be dressed, of that shall she eat, while the maidens sing the song of victory, and dance the dance of rejoicing around her.   For there shall be victory and rejoicing. Three days shall my daughter do this ; and the night of the third day shall Chiquola come to her when she sleeps.   She shall hear his voice, she shall do his bidding, and there shall be blessings. Once more shall Combahee smile among her people."

He was obeyed religiously.   Indeed, his was a religious authority.   Kiawah was a famous priest and prophet among the tribes of the sea coast of Carolina—in their language an Iawa,— a man renowned for his supernatural powers.   A human policy may be seen in the counsels of the old man ; but by the Indians it was regarded as coming from a superior source.   For three days did Combahee perform her lustrations, as required, and partake plentifully of the feast which had been prepared.   The third night, a canopy of green bushes was reared for her by the sea side around the palmetto where she had been accustomed to watch, and from which her cotton streamer was still flying.   Thither she repaired as the yellow moon was rising above the sea.   It rose, bright and round, and hung above her tent, looking down with eyes of sad, sweet brilliance, like some hueless diamond, about to weep, through the green leaves, and into the yet unclosed eyes of the disconsolate widow. The great ocean all the while kept up a mournful chiding and lament along the shores. It was long before Combahee could sleep. She vainly strove to shut her eyes. She could not well do so, because of her expectation, and because of that chiding sea, and those sad eyes of the moon, big, wide, down staring upon her. At length she ceased to behold the moon and to hear the ocean; but, in place of these, towards the rising of the morning star, she heard the voice of Chiquola, and beheld the young warrior to whom her virgin heart had been given. He was habited in loose flowing robes of blue, a bunch of feathers, most like a golden sunbeam, was on his brow, bound there by a circle of little stars. He carried a bow of bended silver, and his arrows looked like darts of summer lightning. Truly, in the eyes of the young widow, Chiquola looked like a very god himself. He spoke to her in a language that was most like a song. It was a music such as the heart hears when it first loves and when hope is the companion of its affections. Never was music in the ears of Combahee so sweet.

"Why sits the woman that I love beside the cold ocean? Why does she watch the black waters for Chiquola? Chiquola is not there."

The breathing of the woman was suspended with delight. She could not speak. She could only hear.

"Arise, my beloved, and look up at Chiquola."

"Chiquola is with the Great Spirit. Chiquola is happy in the blue forests of Maneyto;" at length she found strength for utterance.

"No! Chiquola is cold. There must be fire to warm Chiquola, for he perished beneath the sea. His limbs are full of water. He would dry himself. Maneyto smiles, around him are the blue forests, he chases the brown deer, till the setting of the sun; but his limbs are cold. Combahee will build him a fire of the bones of his enemies, that the limbs of Chiquola may be made warm against the winter."

The voice ceased, the bright image was gone. In vain was it that the woman, gathering courage in his absence, implored him to return   She saw him no more, and in his place the red eye of the warrior star of morning was looking steadfastly upon her.

But where were the enemies of Chiquola ?   The tribes were all at peace.   The war-paths upon which Chiquola had gone had been very few, and the calumet had been smoked in token of peace and amity among them all.   Of whose bones then should the fire be made which was to warm the limbs of the departed warrior ?   This was a question to afflict the wisest heads of the nation, and upon this difficulty they met, in daily council, from the moment that the revelation of Chiquola was made known by his widow.   She, meanwhile, turned not once from her watch along the waters where he had disappeared !   For what did she now gaze ?   Chiquola was no longer there !   Ah !   the fierce spirit of the Indian woman had another thought.   It was from that quarter that the pale warriors came by when he was borne into captivity.   Perhaps, she had no fancy that they would again return.   It was an instinct rather than a thought, which made her look out upon the waters and dream at moments that she had glimpses of their large white-winged canoes.

Meanwhile, the Iawas and chief men sat in council, and the difficulty about the bones of which the fire was to be made, continued as great as ever.   As a respite from this difficulty they debated at intervals another and scarcely less serious question :

" Is it good for Combahee to be alone ?"

This question was decided in the negative by an unanimous vote.   It was observed, though no argument seemed necessary, that all the younger and more handsome chiefs made long speeches in advocacy of the marriage of their Queen.   It was also observed that, immediately after the breaking up of the council, each darted off to his separate wigwam, and put on his newest mocasins, brightest leggins, his yellowest hunting shirt, and his most gorgeous belt of shells.   Each disposed his plumes after the fashion of his own taste, and adjusted, with newer care, the quiver at his back ; and each strove, when the opportunity offered, to leap, dance. run, climb, and shoot, in the presence of the lovely and potent woman.

Once more the venerable Iawa presented himself before the Queen.

"The cabin of my daughter has but one voice. There must be another. What sings the Coonee Latee? (mocking-bird.) He says, 'though the nest be withered and broken, are there not sticks and leaves; shall I not build another? Though the mate-wing be gone to other woods, shall no other voice take up the strain which I am singing, and barter with me in the music which is love?' Daughter, the beloved men have been in council; and they say, the nest must be repaired with newer leaves; and the sad bird must sing lonely no longer. Are there not other birds? Lo! behold them, my daughter, where they run and bound, and sing and dance. Choose from these, my daughter,—choose the noblest, that the noble blood of Ocketee may not perish for ever."

"Ah!"—she said impatiently—"but have the beloved men found the enemies of Chiquola? Do they say, here are the bones?"

"The Great Spirit has sent no light to the cabin of council."

"Enough! when the beloved men shall find the bones which were the enemies of Chiquola, then will the Coonee Latee take a mate-wing to her cabin. It is not meet that Combanee should build the fire for another hunter before she has dried the water from the limbs of Chiquola!"

"The Great Spirit will smile on their search. Meanwhile, let Combahee choose one from among our youth, that he may be honoured by the tribe."

"Does my father say this to the poor heart of Combahee?"

"It is good."

"Take this," she said, "to Edelano, the tall brother of Chiquola. He is most like the chief. Bid him wear it on his breast. Make him a chief among our people. He is the choice of Combahee."

She took from her neck as she spoke, a small plate of rudely beaten native gold, upon which the hands of some native artist, had, with a pointed flint or shell, scratched uncouth presentments of the native deer, the eagle, and other objects of their frequent observation.

"Give it him—to Edelano!"—she added; "but let him not come to Combahee till the beloved men shall have said—these

are the bones of the enemies of Chiquola. Make of these the
fires which shall warm him."

There was something so reasonable in what was said by the
mourning Queen, that the patriarch was silenced. To a certain
extent he had failed of his object. That was to direct her mind
from the contemplation of her loss by the substitution of another
in his place—the philosophy of those days and people, not unlike
that of our own, leading people to imagine that the most judicious
and successful method for consoling a widow is by making her a
wife again as soon as possible. Combahee had yielded as far as
could be required of her; yet still they were scarcely nearer to
the object of their desire: for where were the bones of Chiquola's
enemies to be found?—He who had no enemies! He, with
whom all the tribes were at peace? And those whom he had
slain,—where were their bodies to be found? They had long
been hidden by their friends in the forests where no enemy might
trace out their places of repose. As for the Spaniards—the white
men—of these the Indian sages did not think. They had come
from the clouds, perhaps,—but certainly, they were not supposed
to have belonged to any portion of the solid world to which they
were accustomed. As they knew not where to seek for the "pale
faces," these were not the subjects of their expectation.

The only person to whom the proceedings, so far, had produced
any results, was the young warrior, Edelano. He became a
chief in compliance with the wish of Combahee, and, regarded as
her betrothed, was at once admitted into the hall of council, and
took his place as one of the heads and fathers of the tribe. His
pleasant duty was to minister to the wants and wishes of his
spouse, to provide the deer, to protect her cabin, to watch her
steps—subject to the single and annoying qualification, that he
was not to present himself conspicuously to her eyes. But how
could youthful lover—one so brave and ardent as Edelano—submit to such interdict? It would have been a hard task to one far
less brave, and young, and ardent, than Edelano. With him it
was next to impossible. For a time he bore his exclusion manfully. Set apart by betrothal, he no longer found converse or
association with the young women of the tribe; and his soul was
accordingly taken up with the one image of his Queen and future

spouse. He hung about her steps like a shadow, but she beheld him not. He darted along the beach when she was gazing forth upon the big, black ocean, but he failed to win her glance. He sang, while hidden in the forest, as she wandered through its glooms, the wildest and sweetest songs of Indian love and fancy; but her ear did not seem to note any interruption of that sacred silence which she sought. Never was sweeter or tenderer venison placed by the young maidens before her, than that which Edelano furnished; the Queen ate little and did not seem to note its obvious superiority. The devoted young chief was in despair. He knew not what to do. Unnoticed, if not utterly unseen by day, he hung around her tent by night. Here, gliding by like a midnight spectre, or crouching beneath some neighbouring oak or myrtle, he mused for hours, catching with delighted spirit every sound, however slight, which might come to his ears from within; and occasionally renewing his fond song of devoted attachment, in the hope that, amidst the silence of every other voice, his own might be better heard. But the soughing of the sad winds and the chafing of the waters against the sandy shores, as they reminded the mourner of her loss, were enough to satisfy her vacant senses, and still no token reached the unwearied lover that his devotion had awakened the attention of the object to whom it was paid.

Every day added to his sadness and his toils; until the effect began to be as clearly visible on his person as on hers; and the gravity of the sages became increased, and they renewed the inquiry, more and more frequently together, " Where can the bones of Chiquola's enemies be found?"

The answer to this question was about to be received from an unexpected quarter. The sun was revolving slowly and certainly while the affairs of the tribe seemed at a stand. The period when he should cross the line was approaching, and the usual storms of the equinox were soon to be apprehended. Of these annual periods of storm and terror, the aborigines, through long experience, were quite as well aware as a more book-wise people. To fly to the shelter of the forests was the policy of the Indians at such periods. We have already seen that they had been for some time ready for departure. But Combahee gave no hee

to their suggestions. A superstitious instinct made them willing
to believe that the Great Spirit would interfere in his own good
time; and, at the proper juncture, bestow the necessary light for
their guidance. Though anxious, therefore, they did not press
their meditations upon those of their princess. They deferred,
with religious veneration, to her griefs. But their anxiety was
not lessened as the month of September advanced—as the days
became capricious,—as the winds murmured more and more
mournfully along the sandy shores, and as the waters of the sea
grew more blue, and put on their whiter crests of foam. The
clouds grew banked in solid columns, like the gathering wings of
an invading army, on the edges of the southern and southeastern
horizon. Sharp, shrill, whistling gusts, raised a warning anthem
through the forests, which sounded like the wild hymn of the advancing storm. The green leaves had suddenly become yellow as in
the progress of the night, and the earth was already strewn with
their fallen honours. The sun himself was growing dim as with
sudden age. All around, in sky, sea and land, the presentments
were obvious of a natural but startling change. If the anxieties
of the people were increased, what were those of Edelano? Heedless of the threatening aspects around her, the sad-hearted Combahee, whose heaviest storm was in her own bosom, still wilfully
maintained her precarious lodge beneath the palmetto, on the
bleak head-land which looked out most loftily upon the sea. The
wind strewed the leaves of her forest tent upon her as she slept,
but she was conscious of no disturbance; and its melancholy
voice, along with that of the ocean, seemed to her to increase in
interest and sweetness as they increased in vigour. She heeded
not that the moon was absent from the night. She saw not that
black clouds had risen in her place, and looked down with visage
full of terror and of frowning. It did not move her fears that the
palmetto under which she lay, groaned within its tough coat of
bark, as it bent to and fro beneath the increasing pressure of the
winds. She was still thinking of the wet, cold form of the brave
Chiquola.

The gloom thickened. It was the eve of the 23d of September.
All day the winds had been rising. The ocean poured in upon
he shores. There was little light that day. All was fog, dense

fog, and a driving vapour, that only was not rain. The watchful
Edelano added to the boughs around the lodge of the Queen.
The chief men approached her with counsel to persuade her to
withdraw to the cover of the stunted thickets, so that she might be
secure. But her resolution seemed to have grown more firm, and
duly to increase in proportion to their entreaties. She had an
answer, which, as it appealed to their superstitions, was conclusive
to silence them.

"I have seen him. But last night he came to me. His brow
was bound about with a cloud, such as goes round the moon.
From his eye shot arrows of burning fire, like those of the storm.
He smiled upon me, and bade me smile. 'Soon shalt thou warm
me, Combahee, with the blazing bones of mine enemies. Be of
good cheer—watch well that ye behold them where they lie. Thou
shalt see them soon.' Thus spoke the chief. He whispers to my
heart even now. Dost thou not hear him, Kiawah? He says
soon—it will be soon!"

Such an assurance was reason good why she should continue
her desolate and dangerous watch. The generous determination
of the tribe induced them to share it with her. But this they did
not suffer her to see. Each reared his temporary lodge in the
most sheltered contiguous places, under his favourite clump of
trees. Where the growth was stunted, and the thicket dense, little groups of women and children were made to harbour in situations of comparative security. But the warriors and brave men
of the tribe advanced along the shores to positions of such shelter
as they could find, but sufficiently nigh to their Queen to give her
the necessary assistance in moments of sudden peril. The more
devoted Edelano, presuming upon the prospective tie which was
to give him future privileges, quietly laid himself down behind the
isolated lodge of the princess, with a delight at being so near to
her, that made him almost forgetful of the dangers of her exposed
situation.

He was not allowed to forget them, however! The storm increased with the progress of the night. Never had such an
equinoctial gale been witnessed, since the memory of Kiawah.
The billows roared as if with the agony of so many wild monsters
under the scourge of some imperious demon. The big trees of

the forest groaned, and bent, and bowed, and were snapped off, or torn up by the roots; while the seas, surcharged with the waters of the Gulf, rushed in upon the land and threatened to overwhelm and swallow it. The waves rose to the brow of the headland, and small streams came flashing around the lodge of Combahee. Her roof-tree bent and cracked, but, secure in its lowliness, it still stood; but the boughs were separated and whirled away, and, at the perilous moment, the gallant Edelano, who had forborne, through a natural timidity, to come forward until the last instant, now darted in, and with a big but fast beating heart, clasped the woman of his worship to his arms and bore her, as if she had been a child, to the stunted thickets which gave a shelter to the rest. But, even while they fled—amidst all the storm—a sudden sound reached the ears of the Queen, which seemed to awaken in her a new soul of energy. A dull, booming noise, sullen, slow rolling, sluggish,—something like that of thunder. rolled to their ears, as if it came from off the seas. No thunder had fallen from the skies in the whole of the previous tempest. No lightning had illuminated to increase the gloom. "What is that sound," said the heart of Combahee, filled with its superstitious instincts, "but the thunder of the pale-faces—the sudden thunder which bellows from the sides of their big-winged canoes?"

With this conviction in her mind, it was no longer possible for Edelano to detain her. Again and again did that thunder reach their ears, slowly booming along the black precipices of the ocean. The warriors and chiefs peered along the shores, with straining eyes, seeking to discover the hidden objects; and among these, with dishevelled hair, quivering lips, eyes which dilated with the wildest fires of an excited, an inspired soul, the form of Combahee was conspicuous. Now they saw the sudden flash—now they heard the mournful roar of the minute gun—and then all was silent.

"Look closely, Kiawah—look closely, Edelano; for what said the ghost of Chiquola?—' watch well! Soon shall ye see where the bones of my enemies lie.'—And who were the enemies of Chiquola? Who but the pale-faces? It is their thunder that we hear—the thunder of their big canoes. Hark, ye hear it now, —and hear ye no cries as of men that drown and struggle?

Hark! Hark! There shall be bones for the fire ere the day opens upon us."

And thus they watched for two hours, which seemed ages, running along the shores, waving their torches, straining the impatient sight, and calling to one another through the gloom. The spirit of the bravest warrior quailed when he beheld the fearless movements of Combahee, down to the very edges of the ocean gulf, defying the mounting waves, that dashed their feathery jets of foam, twenty feet above them in the air. The daylight came at last, but with it no relaxation of the storm. With its light what a picture of terror presented itself to the eyes of the warriors—what a picture of terror—what a prospect of retribution! There came, head on shore, a noble vessel, still struggling, still striving, but predestined to destruction. Her sails were flying in shreds, her principal masts were gone, her movement was like that of a drunken man—reeling to and fro—the very mockery of those winds and waters, which, at other periods, seem only to have toiled to bear her and to do her bidding. Two hundred screaming wretches clung to her sides, and clamoured for mercy to the waves and shores. Heaven flung back the accents, and their screams now were those of defiance and desperation. Combahee heard their cries, detected their despair, distinguished their pale faces. Her eyes gleamed with the intelligence of the furies. Still beautiful, her wan, thin face,—wan and thin through long and weary watching, exposure and want of food—looked like the loveliness of some fallen angel. A spirit of beauty in the highest degree—a morning star in brightness and brilliance,—but marked by the passions of demoniac desolation, and the livid light of some avenging hate. Her meagre arms were extended, and waved, as if in doom to the onward rushing vessel.

"Said I not," she cried to her people,—"Said I not that there should be bones for the fire, which should warm the limbs of Chiquola?—See! these are they. They come. The warrior shall be no longer cold in the blue forests of the good Maneyto."

While one ship rushed headlong among the breakers, another was seen, bearing away, at a distance, under bare poles. These were the only surviving vessels of the armament of Lucas de Ayllon. All but these had gone down in the storm, and that which was now rushing to its doom bore the ill-fated De Ayllon himself. The historian remarks—(see History of South Carolina, p. 11,) —"As if the retributive Providence had been watchful of the place, no less than of the hour of justice, it so happened that, at the mouth of the very river where his crime had been committed, he was destined to meet his doom." The Indian traditions go far-ther. They say, that the form of Chiquola was beheld by Com-bahee, standing upon the prow of the vessel, guiding it to the place set apart by the fates for the final consummation of that des-tiny which they had allotted to the perfidious Spaniards. We will not contend for the tradition ; but the coincidence between the place of crime and that of retribution, was surely singular enough to impress, not merely upon the savage, but also upon the civilized mind, the idea of an overruling and watchful justice. The breakers seized upon the doomed ship, as the blood-hounds seize upon and rend the expiring carcass of the stricken deer. The voice of Combahee was heard above the cries of the drown-ing men. She bade her people hasten with their arrows, their clubs, their weapons of whatever kind, and follow her to the beach. She herself bore a bow in her hand, with a well filled quiver at her back ; and as the vessel stranded, as the winds and waves rent its planks and timbers asunder, and billows bore the struggling and drowning wretches to the shore, the arrows of Combahee were despatched in rapid execution. Victim after victim sunk, stricken, among the waters, with a death of which he had had no fear. The warriors strode, waist deep, into the sea, and dealt with their stone hatchets upon the victims. These, when despatched, were drawn ashore, and the less daring were employed to heap them up, in a vast and bloody mound, for the sacrifice of fire.

The keen eyes of Combahee distinguished the face of the per-fidious De Ayllon among the struggling Spaniards. His richer dress had already drawn upon him the eyes of an hundred war-riors, who only waited with their arrows until the inevitable bil-lows should bear him within their reach.

"Spare *him !*" cried the widow of Chiquola. They under-stood her meaning at a glance, and a simultaneous shout attested their approbation of her resolve.

"The arrows of fire!" was the cry. The arrows of reed
and flint were expended upon the humble wretches from the
wreck. The miserable De Ayllon little fancied the secret of this
forbearance. He grasped a spar which assisted his progress, and
encouraged in the hope of life, as he found himself spared by the
shafts which were slaying all around him, he was whirled onward by the breakers to the shore. The knife touched *him* not
—the arrow forbore *his* bosom, but all beside perished. Two
hundred spirits were dismissed to eternal judgment, in that bloody
hour of storm and retribution, by the hand of violence. Senseless amidst the dash of the breakers,—unconscious of present or
future danger, Lucas De Ayllon came within the grasp of the
fierce warriors, who rushed impatient for their prisoner neck deep
into the sea. They bore him to the land. They used all the
most obvious means for his restoration, and had the satisfaction to
perceive that he at length opened his eyes. When sufficiently
recovered to become aware of what had been done for him, and
rushing to the natural conclusion that it had all been done in
kindness, he smiled upon his captors, and, addressing them in his
own language, endeavoured still further, by signs and sounds, to
conciliate their favour.

"Enough!" said the inflexible Combahee, turning away from
the criminal with an expression of strong disgust—

"Enough! wherefore should we linger? Are not the limbs
of Chiquola still cold and wet? The bones of his enemies are
here—let the young men build the sacrifice. The hand of Combahee will light the fire arrow!"

A dozen warriors now seized upon the form of De Ayllon.
Even had he not been enfeebled by exhaustion, his struggles
would have been unavailing. Equally unavailing were his
prayers and promises. The Indians turned with loathing from
his base supplications, and requited his entreaties and tears with
taunts, and buffetings, and scorn! They bore him, under the instructions of Combahee, to that palmetto, looking out upon the
sea, beneath which, for so many weary months, she had maintained her lonely watch. The storm had torn her lodge to atoms,
but the tree was unhurt. They bound him to the shaft with
withes of grape vines, of which the neighbouring woods had their

abundance.   Parcels of light-wood were heaped about nim,
while, interspersed with other bundles of the resinous pine, were
piled the bodies of his slain companions.   The only living man,
he was the centre of a pile composed of two hundred, whose fate
he was now prepared to envy.   A dreadful mound, it rose conspicuous, like a beacon, upon the head-land of St. Helena ; he,
the centre, with his head alone free, and his eyes compelled to survey all the terrible preparations which were making for his doom.
Layers of human carcasses, followed by layers of the most in-
flammable wood and brush, environed him with a wall from which,
even had he not been bound to the tree, he could never have effected his own extrication.   He saw them pile the successive layers, sparing the while no moment which he could give to expostulation, entreaty, tears, prayers, and promises.   But the work-
men with steady industry pursued their task.   The pile rose,—
the human pyramid was at last complete !

Combahee drew nigh with a blazing torch in her hand.   She
looked the image of some avenging angel.   She gave but a single glance upon the face of the criminal.   That face was one of
an agony which no art could hope to picture.   Hers was inflexible as stone, though it bore the aspect of hate, and loathing, and
revenge !   She applied the torch amid the increased cries of the
victim, and as the flame shot up, with a dense black smoke to
heaven, she turned away to the sea, and prostrated herself beside
its billows.   The shouts of the warriors who surrounded the
blazing pile attested their delight ; but, though an hundred throats
sent up their united clamours, the one piercing shriek of the burning man was superior, and rose above all other sounds.   At length
it ceased ! all ceased !   The sacrifice was ended.   The perfidy
of the Spaniard was avenged.

The sudden hush declared the truth to the Queen.   She started to her feet.   She exclaimed :—

" Thou art now blessed, Chiquola !   Thou art no longer cold
in the blue forests of Maneyto.   The bones of thy enemies have
warmed thee.   I see thee spring gladly upon the chase ;—thine
eye is bright above the hills ;—thy voice rings cheerfully along
the woods of heaven.   The heart of Combahee is very glad that
thou art warm and happy."

A voice at her side addressed her. The venerable Kiawah, and the young Edelano were there.

"Now, thou hast done well, my daughter!" said the patriarch. "Chiquola is warm and happy in heaven. Let the lodge of Combahee be also warm in the coming winter."

"Ah! but there is nothing to make it warm here!" she replied, putting her hand upon her heart.

"The bird will have its mate, and build its nest, and sing a new song over its young."

"Combahee has no more song."

"The young chief will bring song into her lodge. Edelano will build a bright fire upon the hearth of Combahee. Daughter! the chiefs ask, 'Is the race of Ocketee to perish?'"

"Combahee is ready," answered the Queen, patiently, giving her hand to Edelano. But, even as she spoke, the muscles of her mouth began to quiver. A sudden groan escaped her, and, staggering forward, she would have fallen but for the supporting arms of the young chief. They bore her to the shade beneath a tree. They poured some of their primitive specifics into her mouth, and she revived sufficiently to bid the Patriarch unite her with Edelano in compliance with the will of the nation. But the ceremony was scarcely over, before a second and third attack shook her frame with death-like spasms. They were, indeed, the spasms of death—of a complete paralysis of mind and body. Both had been too severely tried, and the day of bridal was also that of death. Edelano was now the beloved chief of the nation, but the nation was without its Queen. The last exciting scene, following hard upon that long and lonely widow-watch which she had kept, had suddenly stopped the currents of life within her heart, as its currents of hope and happiness had been cut off before. True to Chiquola while *he* lived, to the last moment of *her* life she was true. The voice of Edelano had called her his wife, out her ears had not heard his speech, and her voice had not replied. Her hand had been put within his, but no other lips had left a kiss where those of Chiquola had been. They buried her in a lovely but lonely grove beside the Ashepoo. There, the Coonee-Latee first repairs to sing in the opening of spring, and the small blue violet peeps out from her grave as if in homage to her courage and devotion. There the dove flies for safety when the fowler pursues, and the doe finds a quiet shelter when the beagles pant on the opposite side of the stream. The partridge hides her young under the long grass which waves luxuriantly above the spot, and the eagle and hawk look down. watching from the tree-tops in vain. The spirit of the beautiful Princess presides over the place as some protecting Divinity, and even the white man, though confident in a loftier and nobler faith, still finds something in the spot which renders it mysterious, and makes him an involuntary worshipper! Ah! there are deities which are common to all human kind, whatever be the faith which they maintain. Love is of this sort, and truth, and .devotion; and of these the desolate Combahee had a Christian share, though the last deed of her life be not justified by the doctrine of Christian retribution. Yet, look not, traveller, as in thy bark thou sailest beside the lovely headlands of Saint Helena, at the pile of human sacrifice which thou seest consuming there. Look at the frail lodge beneath the Palmetto, or wander off to the dark groves beside the ,Ashepoo and think of the fidelity of **that** widowed heart.

> " She died for him she loved—her greatest pride,
> That, as for him she lived, for him she died:
> Make her young grave,
> Sweet fancies, where the pleasant branches **lave**
> **Their drooping tassels** in some murmuring wave!"